A PLUME BC

RESURRECTING HOME

A. AMERICAN is the national bestselling author of the Survivalist series. He has been involved in prepping and survival communities since the early 1990s. An avid outdoorsman, he has spent considerable time learning edible and medicinal plants and their uses as well as primitive survival skills. He currently resides in Florida with his wife of more than twenty years and their three daughters. He is the author of *Going Home, Surviving Home, Escaping Home,* and *Forsaking Home.*

Also by A. American

Going Home
Surviving Home
Escaping Home
Forsaking Home

RESURRECTING HOME

A Novel

Book 5 of the Survivalist Series

A. American

A PLUME BOOK

PLUME
Published by the Penguin Group
Penguin Group (USA) LLC
375 Hudson Street
New York, New York 10014

USA | Canada | UK | Ireland | Australia | New Zealand | India | South Africa | China
penguin.com
A Penguin Random House Company

First published by Plume, a member of Penguin Group (USA) LLC, 2014

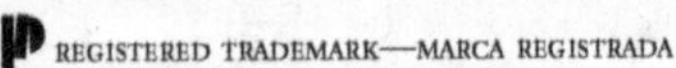

REGISTERED TRADEMARK—MARCA REGISTRADA

LIBRARY OF CONGRESS CATALOGING-IN-PUBLICATION DATA

American, A. (Angery)
Resurrecting home : a novel / A. American.
pages ; cm. — (The survivalist series ; Book 5)
ISBN 978-0-14-751532-2 (softcover)
1. Survivalism—Fiction. 2. Wildfires—Fiction. I. Title.
PS3601.M467R47 2014
813'.6—dc23 2014038066

Printed in the United States of America

Set in Bembo Std
Designed by Leonard Telesca

This is a work of fiction. Names, characters, places, and incidents either are the product of the author's imagination or are used fictitiously, and any resemblance to actual persons, living or dead, businesses, companies, events, or locales is entirely coincidental.

Here we are again. A lot has happened since Forsaking Home. *This book is dedicated to you, the reader. If not for the incredible feedback, encouragement, and enthusiasm you guys provide, I wouldn't be where I am today. Thank you. Additionally,* Resurrecting Home *is dedicated to my dad, who retired this year, finally. Congrats, Old Dude, and I look forward to a lot more time together. Lastly, I want to offer a dedication to Mrs. Roach—not her real name, but she and many others know who she is. She beat breast cancer this year and is on the road to recovery. Our prayers are with you. We have a battle cry for her that I offer to anyone dealing with any form of the disease: fuck cancer!*

RESURRECTING HOME

Chapter 1

Being home felt good, even if it wasn't *our* home, per se. The house next to Danny and Bobbie was as good as we were going to get, considering our own home was trashed. The guy who owned this house had left it during the mortgage crisis, lucky for us. We tried to make the best of a less-than-perfect situation, and so far, so good. Mel and the girls took it all in stride, which I was thankful for. Little Bit hardly commented on the change in location, and Lee Ann and Taylor didn't grumble, a teenager's way of saying they were okay with it. Just being back in the old neighborhood provided a sense of normalcy and familiarity we hadn't had in months. For that, I was grateful. Our little community had grown so much in the past few weeks, with the arrival of Fred and Jess, who were slowly getting settled. Now that there were plenty of bodies willing to help with the cleanup, progress in the neighborhood was moving along nicely. Everyone pitched in without being asked. We'd been at it for a couple of days now and things were really starting to come together, particularly in our house.

Danny's house was another story entirely. He and Bobbie always kept an orderly home, unlike mine, where everything had a place, and that place just happened to be wherever I laid something down. Seeing their home in such a condition was hard on them. They never said much about it, but I knew otherwise. I could tell from some of Danny's exasperated looks and Bobbie's sighs that the never-ending cleanup of the house was getting to them. Given that, I tasked everyone to pitching in one summer day. It was a hot day—the days were getting hotter and hotter as summer began to stretch out into longer days—but everyone took it in stride. I was in charge of dragging out what was left of their shattered lives and dumping it in the truck.

Turning the wheelbarrow up, I dumped another load into the bed of the little red truck—the same one Reggie had acquired from the kid. We'll never know for sure if he had anything to do with Reggie's niece or not: both of them are dead now.

Thad had gotten the little rig running and backed it up against Danny's back porch as we cleaned. Watching the dust settle, I thought about Reggie and how we discovered the truck. It seemed so long ago that I'd walked to the dry bed of Baptist Lake and found those bodies, or what was left of them. I can still see Reggie's face when he said he had to "take her to her momma."

Now the truck was being used around the neighborhood, albeit sparingly, as gas was a premium worth more than gold. As I worked, I could hear the voices of my friends as they helped clean out the trash from the inside of Danny and Bobbie's place. We had been at it for a couple of days, sorting out what was worth saving and what was beyond salvage, and hauling the latter out. The truck made life easier, but we still had to figure out what to do with all the debris. The trash man certainly wasn't coming on Thursday and there was no way to get to the dump, so we had to divide the haul into what could be burned and what couldn't. If it wouldn't, we hauled it off to a pit on the back of Danny's property.

A hand landed on my shoulder. "Break time's over."

I looked over to see Thad standing beside me. "Yes, sir, boss!" I said with a smile and wheeled the barrow back into the house. Thad smiled and shook his head as he followed me inside.

It was quite a scene inside. Mel, Taylor, and Lee Ann were going through the kitchen, putting broken dishes and various electric kitchen appliances in stacks along with the silverware and cooking utensils that were scattered all over it. Bobbie was kneeling down on the floor, wiping her forehead with the back of an oversized work glove. Danny pushed a shovel into the pile in front her, and she used her hands to push more into it and it was dumped into the bin.

When we began the cleanup, the floor was littered with everything from broken dishes and furniture to general dirt and grime. The house had been thoroughly trashed, searched from top to bottom. Whoever had gone through the house had ransacked every drawer, closet, and cabinet. In most cases the contents were tossed onto the floor, then walked over repeatedly. The worst was the malicious destruction of furniture and other household items. It made me mad to think about someone coming into another person's home simply for the sake of destruction.

"What'd you guys decide to do about this sofa?" Jeff asked, lounging on the torn and slashed settee.

"Take it out—we'll burn it," Danny said.

"If we put a sheet over it, we could still use it," Bobbie said.

Danny shook his head. "I don't know, it's pretty torn up."

"What else are we going to sit on?"

Danny shrugged. "I guess you're right. Let's keep it, at least till we find something better."

Jeff jumped up. "All right, so the sofa stays, but I gotta say, man, this recliner has seen better days. Let's toss it. Thad, wanna grab the other end of this chair?" he said as he made his way toward Danny's beloved recliner.

With a smile I looked at Danny. "Should we observe a moment of silence?"

"I can't watch. Just get it out of here."

Thad laughed as he and Jeff hefted up the chair and waddled toward the door. With most of the floor now swept clean, I grabbed a bucket and filled it at the sink, marveling at having running water again. Using a crusty mop that was lying in the kitchen I began to mop the floor, starting at the front door.

"I don't want any footprints on my clean floor!" I shouted as I swept the sopping mop back and forth.

"So should we use the back door, then?" a voice asked from behind me.

I turned to see Jess and Fred on the porch. "Hey! How's it going in your new place? Getting settled in?"

"We're getting there. Fred wants a favor," Jess said.

Fred asked with pleading eyes, "Can you take me to the camp, please? I want to go see Aric."

"Uh, sure, just let us finish up here and we can take a ride over there. Are you going to stay there or come back?"

Fred nodded her head. "Oh, I'm coming back. Hopefully Aric can too."

"All right, then, just give us a bit to wrap this up here and we'll head out."

"Thanks so much. I really appreciate it, Morgan," Fred said with a smile.

Thad and Jeff were on the back porch, having unceremoniously dumped Danny's chair in the truck. I glanced over to see Thad hugging Jess. It brought a smile to my face, remembering when we all first met.

"Careful, Jess, how do you know you can trust that guy?" I shouted, still swinging the mop back and forth.

She turned her head and stuck her tongue out at me, which made me grin.

Fred was looking around the living room. "Wow, you guys have really made a lot of progress in here."

Bobbie had gotten to scrubbing the floors on her hands and knees. She looked around the house. "You should've seen it before all this happened. It was spotless. Danny and I worked so hard to get it in shape. It'll never be the same again."

"Hey, at least you've still got your house," Mel said, examining a blender sitting on the counter. "Besides, we all know that you and Danny will have this place spic and span in no time. Y'all are like Martha Stewart."

Danny looked up slyly. "Except for the insider-trading-and-going-to-prison part," he said, getting a laugh from me and Thad.

Fred chuckled. "Whatever I can do to help, I'd be happy to. Mel, how's your place working out?"

"I like our new house, Fred!" Little Bit said brightly.

"Me too, my room's bigger. You should come over and see it soon," Lee Ann said. In the past few weeks, the older girls had been getting along with Jess and Fred. Lee Ann's mood had improved considerably since they had become part of her community. It was nice to see her connecting to girls closer to her age.

"Oh, I think it's a little early for visitors, but soon enough, you and Jess should come through. We are neighbors now, after all. Speaking of neighbors . . . have you guys seen Brandy and Tyler today?" Mel asked.

"Yeah, we saw them on our way over here. They're doing the same thing you guys are—cleaning up," Jess replied.

Little Bit jumped. "I want to go play with Edie! Mom, can I go?"

Mel chuckled. "Go ahead, you can go play."

Little Bit leapt up in the air, pumping her fist, and took off at a run for the gate. Jess and Fred laughed at the sight of her little legs running.

Fred was shaking her head. "Where does all that energy come from when they're so young?"

Bobbie looked up from her scrubbing. "I want to know where it goes as you get older."

Thad laughed. "If you figure that one out be sure and let me know."

We worked for another hour or so. The extra hands helped to move the process along more quickly. With all the damaged furniture and trash removed, the place looked a lot better—almost back to normal. Danny looked around the living room, nodding to himself approvingly. Bobbie was still hard at work scrubbing the counters, a frustrated look on her face. It would take a little longer for her to feel at home.

Seeing how things were coming together, I figured it would be a good time to run to the camp. Sarge's plan to take the camp without a fight worked out, almost. He'd been wounded by Aric in a terrible mistake that he'd paid for in return. With the Guard now in control of the camp I wondered about the fate of the DHS troops now under their control. It seemed to me unlikely that they could keep them locked up for too long. Having to feed and care for them as well as the possibility of an uprising made for a very touchy situation. It was an issue I hoped Sheffield and Livingston were working on.

"Danny, you want to go up to the camp with me?" I asked.

He looked around again. "Nah, I'm going to stay here, there's still a lot to do." I could see him doing a mental checklist of everything that needed to be done.

"I'll go with you," Thad volunteered.

"Right on, brother," I said. "Let's head out of here in five," I said, nodding to Jess and Fred.

"How long will you guys be gone?" Mel asked.

"Not long, we're just going to check on Aric, maybe bring him back here if he's up to it."

"Which one is Aric, again?" Mel asked.

"He's the DHS guy that helped Jess and Fred get out. He was trying to bust them out of the jail when Sarge and the boys showed up. I guess Fred's got a thing for him."

Bobbie pursed her lips. "Just what we need, someone else to feed."

I looked at her and smiled. "We'll be fine—we know how to make do. But speaking of food, how are we doing on it? How much do we have left?"

"Not much," Mel said. A worried look crossed her face. "Morgan, I know you want to help people out, but the more people we bring in here, the less food for everyone else. You gotta remember that."

I sighed. "When I get back, we'll do an inventory of everything and see where we are."

"That won't take long," Bobbie said sarcastically.

I smiled sweetly at both of them. "Ladies, we'll be sure to have everything covered. You ready to go, Thad?"

He nodded and picked up his shotty from the table, heading toward the door. I kissed Mel on the cheek and followed him out, cutting through the fence to my place. Rolling toward the gate, Thad said, "Mel and Bobbie are right. We're going to have to do something about food."

I nodded in agreement. "We need to try and get a garden started here with what seeds we have left. It's a shame we planted some already at the river," I said.

"They won't go to waste, at least. Sarge and the guys will take care of them."

"I know they will, but that doesn't help us much right now. We gotta think of some alternate means."

Thad snorted. "Alternate means. Story of my life." I punched him on the shoulder. "We'll get that garden going ASAP. There's only so much to hunt. Plus, I think the cold weather is pretty much over," Thad said.

I nodded. "It'll take some time, but it's worth it. In the meantime, we use what we have. And we've got the pigs and chickens. There's fish in Danny's pond, but they won't last forever if we press it too hard."

"You still ain't answered my question: What are we going to do?"

I looked at him. "I guess we're going to have to get used to being hungry," I said with a halfhearted laugh. "Seriously, though, it's going to be tough. It's going to take a lot of work to keep everyone fed."

"I think we're up to the challenge."

As we rolled to a stop at the end of the road, Fred and Jess climbed in, chatting excitedly. I looked back at Fred, then over at Thad and smiled. Fred had made a decent attempt at cleaning up her face and brushing her hair. She looked excited, like a schoolgirl.

It was a short ride to the camp, mostly spent brainstorming with Thad over food supplies. When we reached the gate, Fred bounced up and down in her seat, but Jess appeared more reserved, a serious look in her eyes. I knew the camp had painful memories for both of them, but I was happy that Fred got to have a little moment of happiness.

The Guardsmen at the gate waved us through, and I could immediately see that the camp had a different feel now. It was more relaxed, but there was still an air of tension over the place. I don't know if I could ever shake that feeling, knowing what had gone down here. I could tell by Jess's face that she couldn't either.

As we drove around, we took in the sights. There were still work crews scattered around, though their numbers were smaller and there was no armed guard standing over them. It looked as though an inventory of sorts was going on, with substantial piles of crates and boxes piled around being counted.

A side-by-side ATV stopped beside us as we rode through the camp. Ian sat back with a foot up on the roll bar, grinning like a shit-eating dog. Jamie was beside him, her head rocked back. I stopped beside them. "What's up, Gomer?" I asked.

Ian grinned. "Not taxes. Hard dicks will always be up, though."

Jamie slapped him lightly on the head. "Shut up, Ian."

Thad and I both laughed. "You two are still up to your antics, I see. What's going on around here? You guys doing an inventory?" Thad asked.

Ian nodded. "Yeah, trying to see what's here. These federal boys have a load of shit piled up."

Jamie pushed her sunglasses up onto her forehead. "It's a pain in the ass." She looked in the back of the truck and waved. "Hey, Fred, Jess."

I looked back at one of the nearby tents, a cordon of boxes stacked in front of it like a tunnel. Looking back at Ian I asked, "Find anything interesting yet?"

Ian waved a dismissive hand. "A ton of shit. Interesting to see what the DHS had been stockpiling."

"Speaking of the Feds, what's happening with them?" Thad asked.

Ian stretched. "We're keeping them corralled for now. I don't know what they're going to do with them, though. No orders have come down yet—same old game, hurry up and wait."

"How have the civilians been, any trouble from them?" Thad asked.

Ian shook his head. "Not really. They seem a little unsure of things. They'd grown accustomed to being told what to do, so they're having a hard time dealing with the level of freedom they have now."

"I can see that being a bit of a shock. Have any of them left?"

"Yeah, some have, several actually. Honestly I thought there would be more, though. I've talked to a bunch of them. The ones that are still here all pretty much say the same thing:

Where are we going to go? The ones that left were ones that were grabbed up, a lot of prepper types and real hardheads."

I laughed. "I can relate to them."

Thad looked at me. "Yeah, you damn sure are hardheaded."

Ian laughed. "I could just see you two in here. But that's why we've rounded these guys up: it just isn't right what they were doing."

"You can't keep them here forever," I said.

"No, the captain is working on something. We think a couple of the Feds have blended into the crowd, trying to hide."

"Why in the world would the people here allow that? I mean, they weren't exactly nice to the folks in the camp. You'd think they'd get ratted out quick," Thad said.

Ian looked off toward some of the tents. "You'd think, but we've learned there are some folks here who liked the idea of being under federal control. Hell, some of them even managed to join the Feds while it was still under their control, till we showed up anyway."

"Why in the hell would they want to do that?" I asked, shaking my head.

"They got better food and more freedom that way. And some of them just wanted to boss folks around," Ian replied.

Thad grunted. "If you can't beat 'em, join 'em."

"Something like that. What are you guys doing here?"

I jerked my head toward the girls. They were chatting with Jamie, who had climbed off the ATV and was speaking with animated gestures at the window.

Ian nodded. "Let me guess—Aric?"

Thad laughed. "You know it."

"Where is he?" I asked.

"He's over in the mess hall, where Kay works."

"How's he doing?"

"He's mobile, up and moving around. That arm will be in a sling for quite some time, though. Ole Ted did a number on him."

"He's lucky to be alive considering who he shot to start with." I laughed.

Fred patted my seat eagerly, clearly finished with her conversation. "Hell yeah, he's lucky to be alive. Now can we go see him?"

Ian laughed. "Better get a move on. And, hey, come by brass alley before you guys leave. Sarge and Mike are over there."

As I started the truck up, Thad asked, "How is the old man?"

Jamie was back at the ATV, holding on to the roll bar and looking over the top. "Grumpy!" she yelled.

Ian laughed. "Yeah, he's limping around. He fashioned himself a real nice cane out of cypress."

"It's a walking stick. Believe me, you *don't* want to call it a cane," Jamie said.

I laughed and looked at Thad, who clearly had the same idea that I did. "Rock, paper, scissors?"

Thad smiled and held up a fist. On three I had paper, Thad had scissors. "Looks like you're calling it a cane," Thad said, grinning ear to ear.

Ian shook his head. "We warned you"—he pointed at me—"remember that."

I dropped the truck into gear and we made our way toward the mess hall, following signs that identified the route. In the rearview mirror I could see Fred's face as she craned her neck to see up the road. We pulled up in front of the mess tent, and Fred was out before we even stopped. Jess was close behind her.

Thad looked over and smiled. "Think she's in a hurry?"

I laughed as we got out and went inside. The dining hall was empty but we could hear voices in the back, behind the swinging doors. Thad got a mischievous look on his face and slapped his palms into the doors, throwing them open with a bang. There was a yelp as I came through behind him. Kay was holding her chest, eyes wide.

"Dammit, Thad, you scared the hell out of us!" Jess shouted, then started to laugh. She was quickly joined by Fred, Aric, and Kay, who was trying to catch her breath.

Thad held his hands out. "What'd I do?"

I stepped around him. "Told him not to do it."

Thad shook his head. "Thanks, buddy." I winked in reply.

"How's the shoulder?" I asked Aric.

He looked down at the sling supporting his arm. "It is, 'bout all I can say for it."

"Don't listen to him, it's healing real well. I change the dressing every day," Kay said.

"It's going to take a long time to get it back up to speed. It'll probably never be the same again," Aric added.

"Once you get out of here, I'll take care of it," Fred said with a warm smile. He smiled back at her. It was clear that there was mutual affection.

Kay looked at her. "You're not taking him, are you?"

Fred looked at Aric and shifted back from foot to foot. "Well, that's actually why I came here. Do you wanna go back to Morgan's neighborhood with us, Aric?"

Before Aric could reply, the back door to the kitchen

opened. Jess and Fred both let out a gasp and started to run. "I forgot to tell you girls!" Kay shouted.

Jess slammed into Mary, almost knocking her over, and wrapped her up in a tight embrace. Fred came up behind them and wrapped her arms around them both.

"You're crushing me," Mary choked out.

Jess let go. "Sorry, sorry, I'm just so happy to see you! How are you?" she said, wiping tears from her face.

"I'm okay, getting better," Mary answered with a smile. "It's good to see you girls."

"We were so worried about you. You were, like, in shock or something. We didn't know what was wrong with you," Fred said. Jess shot her a look.

A pained expression flashed across Mary's face. "I'm better now, getting better every day." Mary smiled and looked at Kay. "Thanks to Kay—she's really kind."

Kay gave her a dismissive wave. "I haven't done nothing."

"Mary, you should come with us, get out of this place," Fred said.

"Yeah, come with us. We're staying in Morgan's neighborhood. It's safe there. You need to come with us," Jess added.

Oh shit, just what we need. The girls will just love this: adding even more people to the group.

Mary looked over at me and Thad. "So you're the famous Morgan?"

I smiled. "Don't know about famous—infamous, maybe."

"I've heard a lot about you"—Mary looked at Jess—"she talked about you all the time. Jess said you saved her."

"Don't know about that, she just wouldn't take no for an answer so I was forced to listen to her yammering for days and days."

Jess looked over and said, "Hey!" which got a laugh out of Thad.

Mary looked at Thad. "And you must be Thad."

Thad's grin quickly vanished. "Uh, yes, ma'am."

Mary smiled. "I've heard a lot about you too."

Now I was laughing as Thad was clearly flushed and getting a little embarrassed. Looking at him I said, "All lies, I'm sure."

Mary walked up and offered her hand to me. "It's nice to finally meet you."

I shook her hand gently and replied, "Likewise."

Stepping over to Thad she again offered her hand. "And you, nice to meet you. Jess talked about you two so much it's almost as if I already know you."

Thad took her hand and with a nod of his head said, "Pleasure."

Mary held his gaze a moment, making Thad even more uncomfortable before releasing his hand.

"Mary, are you coming?" Jess asked.

Mary looked at Kay, then back to Jess. "I want to, I'd love to go with you, but I'm afraid." Mary paused, her eyes drifting to the canvas wall of the kitchen tent. "As bad as it is here, at least I know what it is, and with the army controlling the camp now, I feel safer. I just wish those people in the black uniforms were gone."

"That may or may not happen, Mary," I said gently. "We talked to a few of our buddies in the know, and there's not a plan for what to do with them yet. But you're welcome to come with us. There's plenty of room," I said. Knowing what she'd been through there was no way I would refuse to allow her to join Jess and Fred.

"Yeah, we'll all be together again, like old times," Fred said.

Mary's eyes dropped. "I don't much care for the old days."

"Oh, I didn't mean that—" Fred was saying before Kay cut her off, putting a hand on her arm.

"She knows."

"You'll be safe there, Mary. There's a lot of people, and it's really nice," Jess said. "We even have *running water.*"

"Are you sure there's room for more people?" Aric asked.

"Plenty of room, Aric. You and Mary both are welcome, and so is Kay," I said.

"We've got plenty of space, but there's lots of work to do to get the houses into shape. It's not exactly relaxing, but we're doing all right," Thad added.

"Well, I wouldn't be much help," Aric said, looking at his wounded shoulder.

"That's all right, we have to man the barricade at the end of the street. Your eyes still work, and I'd wager you could wield a pistol all right," I said.

Aric nodded. "Oh yeah, I can handle a pistol, no problem."

"Then you can help out. And when the shoulder is ready we have plenty of physical therapy for it," Thad said with a smile.

Out of the corner of my eye I caught Mary looking at him, a smile on her face.

"What about food? You said there are a lot people there already. Is there going to be enough food for everyone?" Aric asked.

"Food's always an issue and always will be, but we get by," Thad said.

Aric looked at Kay. "Hmm. You still staying here, Kay?"

She nodded. "I'm still needed here"—she patted his good shoulder—"but you go ahead and go. I'll be fine."

"You're definitely welcome to stay, Aric. But in the meantime, while you guys sort this out, I'm going to go find the old man," I said.

Thad clapped his hands. "I'm going too. I gotta be there for this conversation."

Giving Thad a sour look, I said, "We'll be back."

We decided to walk to the command post, or brass alley, as Ian called it. As we walked, we surveyed the camp. Guardsmen and refugees alike were moving freely about. Even though I had only been here once before I could see a change in some of the residents. Put simply, they looked more at ease than they had under the control of the DHS.

We passed two tents where people were hanging around—some lying on their bunks, others sitting on various improvised seats outside. Other tents were empty though obviously lived in, the inhabitants off on some sort of task. At one of them, we saw Perez and a couple of other Guardsmen along with a number of people sorting boxes and crates. He smiled at our approach.

"Hey, Morgan, Thad, what's up?"

"Hey, Perez, how's tricks?" I asked.

His smile faded as he took a quick glance over his shoulder. "Keep an eye on things," he told one of the soldiers.

A stern-faced young man in ACU digital camo nodded and turned back to the people. Perez jerked his head and started to walk.

"What's going on here?" Thad asked.

Perez shook his head. "We're trying to get a handle on

what sort of supply situation this place is in, but people are stealing them faster than we can count them."

"That why you guys are standing over them?"

"It's not like we're making them work—most of them volunteer. But we're finding out quickly that a lot of them do 'cause they wanna see what we have. Some of 'em got sticky fingers, is all I'm sayin'."

I looked back at the work group. "Can't say I blame them. I mean, they were essentially prisoners for a long time."

"True, but they aren't anymore. They've got the freedom to do what they want, go where they want. We're giving them some supplies, but rationing them out. But you can tell some people don't want to play fair. The captain is already talking about banishing some of them from the camp."

"That bad already?" Thad asked.

"Don't get me wrong, it's not like everyone here is out for grabs, but there are cliques here and a couple of them are vying for power."

I turned back to face the trail we'd walked down and jutted my chin. "Like that tent by the entrance with those guys sitting around out front?"

Perez nodded. "Yeah, that's one of them."

Looking back at Perez, I said, "You guys better put the kibosh on that with the quickness."

He nodded. "We're hoping to. We've started by cutting rations for groups like that one. They're taking more than their fair share. I mean, when it comes down it, if you're healthy and strong, you shouldn't be here. They should be out taking care of themselves."

I snorted. "It's harder than you think, my friend."

"Don't get me wrong, I know it's hard, but there ain't no more free lunch. The gravy train has been derailed."

Thad chuckled. "That's an understatement."

I thought about what it would mean to be part of this camp, to be liberated from it and then find yourself being booted out the door.

"It isn't going to matter much longer anyway," Perez quipped, still looking at the group lazing in front of the tent.

"Why's that?" Thad asked.

"This was a detention facility. Now it's not, and it's not going to be a refugee camp. Sheffield got word from higher-ups that we're not in the refugee business. He doesn't like it, but he was told we won't be resupplied, that there simply isn't enough to support camps like this."

"There were others?" I asked.

Perez nodded. "Still are in some places. DOD is making an effort at taking them down but we don't have the usual resources at our disposal, which is part of the reason they want these people to get back to taking care of themselves."

"It's not easy, you know. We're barely getting by and we're more prepared than most," I said.

Perez nodded. "But you are getting by, that's the point. Your little community was actually mentioned in the discussions, the fact that you guys are making a go of it. If you can do it, so can everyone else."

"I understand that, but a lot of people simply don't have the knowledge. Hell, any one of us alone would be up shit creek, but with everyone working together we do all right," I said.

"It's a harder way of living, for sure. Takes a lot of work," Thad offered.

"We know it isn't going to be easy on these folks. The brass up the command chain are trying to find the FEMA stockpiles. They haven't given any of it out yet. If we can find it and organize transport we're going to try and hand it out."

"FEMA isn't working to help?" Thad asked.

Perez's face contorted. "Shit no, all that talk about stockpiles in case of emergency was just that. The marines found a couple of them up in Virginia somewhere and started giving it out, but it got ugly. That's the other part of the problem—everyone is in so much need that whenever something is available they act like animals. Remember seeing video from any third-world country when food was being handed out, the crowds and chaos? That's what it gets like. We're pretty much in a third-world state ourselves now."

Thad looked out across the camp. "These people act like that?"

"No, they're pretty calm for the most part, but they also know when and where their next meal is coming from. Most of them are happy we're here. We don't intimidate them like the DHS did, and they are basically free. Some have already left, but there are others who just want someone to take care of them."

With a small laugh I said, "Yeah, there always seems to be plenty of them."

"Always will be," Perez replied.

"We're going to find Sarge," I said. "See ya, Perez."

He nodded and walked back over to his detail.

As Thad and I walked back up the trail, I thought about what Perez had told us. I could understand what Perez was saying—this situation was too big for any government to deal with on an individual level. Sure, it'd be nice to stay in a comfy little camp where someone else provided everything for you, but that just wasn't a manageable reality. The new reality was much, much harder than what we were all used to, but in some ways, it was almost better, because we appreciated it more. Plus, we didn't have to worry about other things anymore: work, taxes, traffic. Honestly, though, that was little compensation for the added difficulty of daily life. I'd happily pay my taxes if things would return to normal.

Thad and I found Sarge sitting in a chair in the sugar sand in front of the office connex, his foot up on a crate and his cane lying across his lap. Mike was lying on his back on a stack of crates beside him, his boonie hat covering his face.

"Hey, fellers, what brings you two around?" Sarge called out as we approached. Mike sat up, pulling his hat on straight.

I waved at Mike and gave Sarge a pat on the shoulder. "The girls wanted to come by. Fred wanted to see Aric."

Sarge nodded. "Figured that wouldn't take long," he said, stabbing the cypress cane into the sand.

Thad nudged me with an elbow. I laughed to myself and looked at the piece of wood. Sarge had done a lot of work to it: the top was a nearly perfect round ball with three fingerlike points coming up around it from the staff, as if a claw were holding it.

"Nice cane. You make it?" I asked.

Mike stifled a laugh. Sarge smiled and stood up.

"I did, check it out." He took a couple of steps using the cane to support his weight. When he passed in front of me he planted it on the top of my toes, then leaned on it.

"Ow, dammit, that hurts like hell!" I shouted, but he didn't let up.

Looking me in the eye, he asked, "You like my walking stick?"

"Yes, yes, for fuck's sake get that thing off my toes!"

By now Thad and Mike both were roaring with laughter. Sarge snatched the *walking stick* off my poor foot and returned to his chair. I wiggled my toes. They hurt like hell.

"You're one mean ole bastard, you know that?" I said, shaking my foot.

Sarge smiled broadly. "You ain't the first to say it and you won't be the last, my boy."

I looked at Mike. "How're your toes?"

He shook his head, rubbing his elbow. "Didn't get my toes, but he almost broke my elbow when he whacked it with that damn stick."

Thad laughed and I looked at him. "It could have just as easily been you. Keep that in mind."

He grinned and held his fingers up like a pair of scissors. I slapped at his hand and laughed again. Looking back at Sarge, I asked, "Why are you here anyway? Aren't you supposed to be out at the river recovering?"

Sarge jutted a finger over his shoulder. "The captain in there called me up. He wanted me to come over to figure out what to do with all them DHS boys. Can't keep 'em here much longer. He got word from up the chain that we've got to move 'em."

"Good point. They must be getting restless. They starting to be trouble?" I asked.

"They tried to revolt once, and figured out pretty quick that was a bad idea," Mike said.

"What happened?" Thad asked.

Mike looked off toward the north side of the camp. "I think they're still digging graves over there."

"No shit, how many were killed?" I asked.

"Just the really stupid ones," Sarge replied.

"Three killed, couple others wounded," Mike said.

"Perez said some of the refugees are giving you trouble too?" Thad said.

"A little, they're just feeling their oats is all. They settle down pretty quick, though," Sarge replied.

"Hey, not to change the subject, but how's our garden doing?" I asked.

Sarge actually seemed to brighten up. "Doing real good. The squash is coming up pretty good and okra is already about this high." He held a hand about eighteen inches from the ground. "We're working on it, keeping it weeded an' all."

Mike sat back up with a shot. "*We?* Hell!" He pointed at Sarge. "That old shit ain't pulled the first weed! Me an' Ted are doing all the damn work!"

Sarge raised the walking stick and thumped it into the sand. "As it should be."

Thad smiled. "You know, Sarge, with that stick and the way you're sitting in the chair, you got a regal look about you."

Sarge smiled. "It's good to be king."

Mike threw a small piece of wood he pried from a crate at Thad. "Thad, you suck any harder, your damn eyes'll cross!" Thad laughed uproariously.

Pointing at Mike I said, "If he's the king, guess that makes you the jester."

Sarge and Thad started to laugh, though Mike didn't appear to see the humor. "All of you can go to hell," he said, giving us the finger.

"Lighten up, Mikey. And, hey, where's that box you had earlier?" Sarge asked.

Mike hopped down from the crates and opened a cardboard

box. He removed a can from it and tossed it to Sarge. Sarge turned the can around in his hands, looked at the label, and held it out to Thad.

"Here, Thad, take that back with you guys."

Thad looked at the can inquisitively. "Seeds?"

Sure enough it was a can of nitrogen-packed garden seeds. A wave of relief washed over me. "Where'd you get these?" I asked.

Sarge waved his hand over his head. "The DHS had all kinds of shit here! Them preppers would love to get their hands on this joint."

"You know you aren't going to grow a damn thing here," I said, sweeping my arm to gesture around the camp. "It's just sand."

Sarge nodded. "I know, that's why we haven't planted any of it yet. We're talking about planting the entire area around the cabins but we ain't decided yet. Gotta coordinate with Sheffield and the boys about what they want to do with the supplies."

"So what's the plan with the DHS guys?" I asked.

"We're going to move them out to Frostproof. It's a bigger camp and is also under our control now. A Guard unit out of Haines City is there."

"I've seen that place. Looks like a prison," Thad said.

"Remember back in the day, how everyone saying it was a FEMA prison? Bet they never thought it would be used for their own people," I said.

"How do you guys plan to house and feed them all? I mean, there's no food, no running water . . ." Thad said.

"We're letting the boys at Frostproof work that out," Sarge said flatly. "Ain't my business, besides, they probably won't be there long. The plan as of now is to get them all over to MacDill in Tampa."

"What are they going to do over there?" I asked.

"We can't house them forever. Some will probably be released, and the hard-core ones will kept locked up. They've got the manpower and facilities there to handle them."

"I take it from that that the military is on our side in this?" I asked.

Sarge nodded. "For the most part, at least the ones that matter. A few small units went over to the other side, but they didn't manage to take much in the way of hardware. The real question is NORAD. No one's talked to them yet as far as I know."

Thad's eyebrows went up. "Isn't that where they control all the nukes from?"

Sarge nodded. "Yep."

It was a sobering thought to consider that with all the shit going on, we didn't know who was in control of the nuclear arsenal.

"You're just full of good news, aren't you?" I asked. Sarge replied with a grin.

Thad nodded and held the can out. "These for us to keep?"

"What the hell you think I gave 'em to you for?" Sarge barked. "Take that case with you, there's plenty here."

"Damn, thanks," I said, looking over the other five cans in the box. It was kind of like Christmas morning, with tomatoes, corn, green beans, yellow squash, spinach, and kidney beans each in a sealed can.

"Yeah, thanks, Sarge. We'll get these in the ground pretty quick. Not going to help much right now, but if we can make it a couple months, it sure will," Thad said.

I nodded. "It'll be a nice little project for us to work on." We stood there for a few more minutes, shooting the shit, filling in Mike and Sarge about what we had done in our neighborhood. After promises for them to come over, I looked over at Thad. "You ready?" I asked, then looked at Sarge. "Time for us to get back. Take care of yourself."

Sarge waved a hand at me. "Y'all take care."

"See you later, Mike," Thad said. Mike nodded and waved at him. We headed back for the truck to see the girls. Aric and Kay were all standing around the truck.

"Y'all ready?" Thad asked.

Jess nodded. "Yep, just waiting on you guys."

Aric nodded. "Yeah, I'm ready to get the *hell* out of here. And thanks again for taking me in." He was holding Fred's hand and she smiled at him, stars in her eyes.

"Are you sure that you're going to be all right, Kay?" Jess asked. Concern was etched across her face. I knew how much she and Fred cared for her.

Kay smiled brightly. "Oh, I'll be fine. Don't worry about me. But you have to come back and visit."

Jess wrapped her up in a hug. "Don't worry about that, we will."

Aric looked at Kay. "If you need anything just let me know." He looked at me. "You guys have a radio, right?"

I nodded. "Sarge knows how to get in touch with us."

Aric gave Kay a hug. She patted his back. "You go be happy now."

He smiled and kissed her cheek. "I will, but you need to be happy too."

Jess looked at Mary. "Well?"

Mary hesitated a moment, then looked at me and Thad. "If I won't be a burden . . ." she said, her voice trailing off.

"No burden at all, we'd be glad to have you," Thad replied.

Mary smiled. "Then I'll come. It's got to be better than this place."

Once everyone was loaded up, I started to drive out, taking a route that took us past the command complex. Sarge raised his walking stick in salute to us as we passed, and I tooted the horn at him. Out on the road I drove down the center line, slowly weaving back and forth across both lanes. In the backseat Aric had his face out the window as the wind blew past him. It was clear that he was happy to be outside of the camp. Mary, Fred, and Jess chatted one another up as I drove. Looking at them in the rearview mirror I couldn't help but smile. Our little community was growing in leaps and bounds. I just hoped we could sustain it.

"I'll drop you guys off at your place so Aric can stow his stuff," I said, looking at Fred in the mirror. She nodded as I turned at the intersection of their small road. While it was going to be a little crowded, Mary was going to stay there as well. She was in no condition to stay alone, and besides, Fred and Jess were really excited to have her back as well.

"What the hell is that?" Aric asked as we made the turn.

Thad looked out the window. "It's a set of stocks."

"That's what I thought. What the hell are they for?"

"Just what you think they're used for. Don't worry, we've only used them a couple of times," I replied.

In the mirror I saw Aric give Fred a "WTF?" look. She shrugged. Even though Aric was a good guy, as part of the DHS, he had been sheltered from some of the worst of what was happening. Though his reaction annoyed me, I let it go. I knew he'd be an asset, bum arm and all, and plus, if Jess vouched for him, I figured he had to be trustworthy.

After dropping them all off, we went back to Danny's house, which had become the central meeting place for our burgeoning little community. Thad carried the box of seeds to the back porch, where everyone was sitting. Naturally, it got everyone's attention.

"What's that?" Danny asked.

"Please let it be mac 'n' cheese, please let it be mac 'n' cheese," Taylor said, crossing her fingers.

Thad set the box on the floor and opened it, lifting one of the cans. "Seeds."

Danny practically jumped up. "Really?"

He tossed him the can. "Yeah, Sarge gave them to us."

"That's great, how many are there?" Danny asked looking the can over.

"Six of them. Should be enough to start a pretty good garden," I said.

"What kind?" Mel asked as she got up.

Danny started pulling out the cans. "Tomatoes, spinach, corn, green beans, kidney beans, and squash."

"Fried squash sounds good," Danny said, patting his stomach.

"That's good, because we're going to need it," Bobbie added.

I looked at her. "What do we have left, food-wise?"

"Some beans and rice. A little freeze-dried veggies, but with the number of people here it isn't going to last long."

"Define *not long*," Thad said.

Bobbie looked at Mel. "A week, ten days maybe," Mel said.

"Oh shit! That bad?" I said. My mind started racing. I didn't even tell them that we had invited two more into our neighborhood.

Mel cupped her face with her hands, clearly stressed. "What are we going to do?"

"How long do you think before the seeds produce anything?" Brandy asked. She seemed apologetic, almost, and she shot Tyler a look that seemed to say *I knew we shouldn't have come here.*

"It'll be a month, month and a half before we get anything out of the seeds," Thad said.

Now Brandy's face showed fear. "What are we going to do?"

Tyler smiled. "We'll do all right. It's not like we had a lot of food at the campground, you know, we had to work for it every day. Nothing's really changed."

I was thinking about all this and made a suggestion. "I think we need to search every house here again, thoroughly, and check out the few we haven't been into yet. We need to bring back anything that could be of use that we might've ignored before. Seeds, oil, salt, spices, that type of stuff. We can't be picky. Whatever we can use to stretch our supply."

"Canning jars too. We need to keep an eye out for them," Thad said.

"Right. Bring any of those we find back as well," I said.

"Sounds like we have a lot to do, then. Might as well start today. Maybe we should divide into two teams, one to get the garden plot ready and another to search the houses," Danny said. "I'll start on the garden. We need to get everything into the ground as quick as possible."

"If it's all right with everyone, I'll help Danny," Thad said.

"We can search houses," Tyler said.

Mel looked at Brandy. "If you'll watch the kids, we'll check the houses."

"Okay, I feel like I should be helping, though," Brandy said timidly.

Mel laughed. "Like watching them isn't work."

Brandy smiled. "I guess you're right."

"Cool, we've got a good little team here." I looked at Mel, Bobbie, and Tyler. "Let's take the truck and get Fred, Mary, and Jess. We'll work a street at a time."

"What about us?" Lee Ann asked.

"You two are coming too. We need all the help we can get."

Chapter 2

I stopped at the girls' place to let them know what was going on. Fred and Jess said they would be part of the searching team, while Mary asked if she could help with the kids, saying she had a soft spot for children. It seemed like that might be good for her to do, considering the transition she had been through, so I pointed her in the right direction. With Fred and Jess loaded up we drove down to the end of the road to begin the hunt.

It was strange being back in this area. Everywhere I looked there was a memory of what happened before we left for the cabins. The wrecked Hummer from the day we were raided by the DHS from the camp was still sitting just inside the woods. At the intersection of the main road was the spot Reggie was killed. It got me in a brief funk, but I couldn't dwell on it—we had to keep on moving.

It was a long afternoon of searching. We went house to house, checking each one very thoroughly. Every closet was opened, every drawer was rummaged through, every outbuilding was searched. Most of the houses had already been scavenged—that was obvious enough to tell in many cases, particularly when the front door was kicked open. In these houses, there was generally little, if anything, of worth.

Going through the houses gave us an idea of what the

people who abandoned them had gone through. Some of the houses emitted a horrible stench, just an ungodly smell. In a couple it turned out to be the bathrooms, the toilets having been used without water, to excess. Others had mold growing in them. In all of them, though, it was the bedrooms that really caught my attention. Soiled linens on the beds, filthy clothes strewn about the floors. It was as if the people just quit, gave up.

While not every house was a wreck, even the cleaner ones showed some of the same signs of wear. The one thing that each house had in common, regardless of its condition, was a trash pile. Sometimes they were set far from the house, but in one particular case, the pile was outside a kitchen window. I had to laugh at the thought of simply tossing the trash out the window. Mel would go crazy if I even attempted to do that.

After going through about ten houses, we had little to show: a half-used bottle of vinegar, a can of peas, some cans of pepper—there always seemed to be pepper. With each house, spirits were flagging. After what seemed like several hours, we came across one house that we hadn't noticed before. It was set back off the road, somewhat obscured by trees, and it didn't look like anyone had tried breaking into it yet.

"Everything around back is secure," Tyler reported.

"I can't believe no one's been in here yet," Mel said.

"I wonder what's in there?" Fred asked. A lively discussion ensued. Suddenly the house was transformed into the ship from Swiss Family Robinson, containing everything we'd need. If only we could get to it.

"Why hasn't anyone gotten in? I mean, the windows aren't even broken," Tyler said.

"Looks like someone beat the shit out of this one," I said, knocking on one of the windows. It was covered in scratches and strike marks and had obviously taken quite a bit of abuse at some point.

"What are they, bulletproof?" Aric asked, examining them up close.

I ran my hand over it. "Doubt it, probably has a security film on it."

"What's that?" Bobbie asked.

"It's like a supersecure tint. You put it on the same way."

"If it's just tint, shouldn't you be able to break it?"

"I read some stuff on it once. They claim it would take a fire axe ten minutes to get through it. And it's expensive. This window here probably cost close to a grand to cover."

"A grand? They were trying to protect something in there, then," Tyler said.

"How are we going to get in?" Taylor asked, hopping from foot to foot.

"Let me take a look around," I said.

I walked around the house, checking all the doors. Tapping on a door off the garage, I realized it was a solid metal commercial-grade door with a dead bolt. On the rear of the house was a set of French doors. These too turned out to be metal, and from the shattered plastic frames lying on the ground, someone had tried to break in there too. The only other door was the front door, made of a really nice solid wood. It was also sturdy, showing signs where someone had unsuccessfully tried breaking it with an axe.

"Well?" Mel asked.

"I have an idea. Let me run back to the house real quick."

I hopped in the truck and went back to our house and dragged my pack out. Digging around in it, I found what I was looking for and headed back.

Mel looked at me as I got out of the truck, her eyes scanning my person. "Thought you were going to get something?"

I held up a small black case. "I did."

"What's that?" Aric asked.

With a smile I said, "Lock picks."

Aric smiled. "Ah, that's so cool! You think you can pick it?"

Mel rolled her eyes, smiling. "Men and their toys."

I started around the corner of the house to the garage, everyone following me curiously.

"I gotta see this," Jess said.

I selected a tension wrench and rake from the kit and inserted the wrench in the lock, then went to work with the rake. After a few minutes with the rake it was obvious it wasn't going to be that easy, so I pulled a single pick out.

"What's wrong? You can't get it?" Jess asked.

Without looking back, I answered, "Some locks are harder to pick than others. Some you can get by raking, what I was just doing, and some you have to pick individually."

"What do you mean individually?" Aric asked.

"Inside the lock are pins," I said. "This one has five. You've got to pick them one at a time till the lock opens."

Everyone watched in silence as I worked on the lock. After another couple minutes, I felt the tension on the wrench give. Looking over my shoulder, I smiled and rotated the lock open.

"You got it!" Mel shouted, clapping her hands.

"That's so cool!" Jess said.

"Dad, that is the coolest thing I've ever seen," Taylor

said. Lee Ann was grinning from ear to ear and nodding in agreement.

"Man I would never have thought of that, to have lock picks," Aric said.

"Yeah, me neither," Tyler added.

"Let's go see what's inside," Bobbie said excitedly.

"Yeah, that's what I want to know too," Fred said.

Only a wedge of light shone through the open door, casting strange shadows around the cavernous room. I flipped on my flashlight, the bright white LED lighting up the room.

"Looks like someone left in a hurry," I said.

The floor of the garage was covered in stuff, save for a rectangle of barren concrete on the far side. I stepped in, followed immediately by Tyler, then Aric. Mel and Bobbie stood at the door looking in, but Fred brushed past them, saying, "Finders, keepers." They quickly followed her, with Jess bringing up the rear.

"Shine the light over here," Aric said.

I aimed it to where he was trying to release the garage door. Tyler helped him raise the door, filling the room in the bright light of day.

"Hey, this door's open," Mel said, standing at the door to the house.

"Hang on, don't go in just yet. Let's make sure this place is actually empty," I said moving for the door. I looked back over my shoulder. "Who's got a gun?"

There were shared looks around the garage, then one by one their eyes returned to me. "You mean none of you have a gun?" I asked, shaking my head.

"Oops," Bobbie said.

I looked at Fred, and she and Jess simply shrugged. Aric glanced at his sling-supported arm, as if to say *I couldn't shoot if I tried.* Tyler looked at me sheepishly and said, "I have no excuse, none at all." I couldn't help but laugh.

"Seriously, though, in the future, everyone should be armed when you leave your house." I drew my pistol and nodded over to Tyler. "Come back me up anyway."

Tyler took a flashlight from Bobbie and came up behind me as I stepped through the door. Passing through a laundry room into the kitchen, I scanned the area, which was clear. We moved into the dining room and through the rest of the house and found it to be disheveled but unoccupied. The last room we searched was the master bedroom. When I shone my light into the closet, a massive safe appeared.

"Holy shit, look at the size of that thing," Tyler blurted out.

"Yeah, it's a big 'un," I replied, looking it over.

Tyler stepped up to it and tried the handle. "Damn, it's locked."

"Wouldn't be much good if it wasn't," I replied with a laugh.

Running a hand over it, he said, "I know, just really makes me wonder what's in here."

"Might be silver and gold, but we can't eat that."

"Yeah, guess you're right," he said, stepping back.

"You guys all right?" Bobbie shouted.

"Yeah, it's clear, come on in," I called back as I headed down the hall toward the kitchen. The cabinets were already being flung open and searched by the time I got there.

"No, no, no, don't do that!" Mel shouted as I walked into the doorway.

Everyone in the kitchen turned to whom she was yelling

at. Aric stood frozen in front of the fridge, his fingers wrapped around the handle.

"We don't want to know what's in there," Bobbie said.

Aric quickly released it. "Oh yeah, guess not. Habit—or used to be a habit, I guess."

"That could've been a disaster. But, hey, look at what we've found, Morg," Mel said.

I went to the counter where all the loot was being piled. Picking up a can of corn, I said, "Not bad, crew. This will last us a couple of days, maybe three."

"What do you mean, two or three days?" Jess asked, crouched from the floor. She triumphantly held up two cans of soup. "Look at all this stuff! I mean, there's got to be fifteen cans of soup here, and that's just the soup."

"How many people are here now?" I asked.

I could see her trying to count everyone in her head. To save her the trouble I answered my own question. "Seventeen. There's seventeen people in our little community now."

Jess set the can back down, glancing at the pile of cans and other foodstuffs with a defeated look in her eyes.

"I can go back to the camp. I don't need to stay here," Aric said, shifting his weight from foot to foot.

I looked at him. "Dude, it's not that, we're happy to have you." Looking back at everyone, I said, "Don't get me wrong, this will help, but we should probably keep these as our emergency stock."

"If this isn't an emergency to you, I'd hate to see what is," Fred said.

Laughing, I replied, "Fred, this is just the new normal."

She shrugged. "Guess you got me there."

Tyler came into the kitchen holding an armload of stuff,

dumping it on the opposite counter. "Look at all this stuff!" He looked like a kid in a candy shop as he laid out an assortment of guns, knives, flashlights, and other pieces of gear. Picking up a Ruger 10/22, he murmured to himself, "This one is really nice."

Bobbie rolled her eyes. "What did you say before, Mel? Men and their toys."

The food was loaded into plastic grocery bags that Lee Ann had pulled out from under the sink. Grabbing a few, I carried them out to the truck. As I entered the garage, I took a minute to look around. Whoever lived here was very organized. The wall over a store-bought workbench was covered in pegboard, each tool neatly outlined in black. Boxes of empty beer bottles were stacked neatly in one corner next to a large keg. I made a mental note about these items, in case we needed them in the future. Despite how organized everything was, it was clear that whoever was here had left in a hurry. There was an open suitcase lying on the floor, some clothes hanging out of it. There probably wasn't enough room in the car for it and so it was ditched at the last minute, but they dug something out before leaving. I could almost picture the chaos of the scene. I wondered—did they flee because of a threat of physical harm? Was someone sick? Did they have kids? For the first time in a while, I was reminded of how inhumane our situation was. Just because we had been able to get by didn't mean that we were safe by any means. I shuddered at the thought but was quickly snapped back to reality by everyone coming out to fill the truck with bags of supplies.

I drove back the short ride to Danny's house in silence. Even though everyone was chatting excitedly about their haul, I had a pit in my stomach the whole time. The scene had spooked me out and reminded me that even though we had been dealing with some troubles, we had barely seen the worst of it. What we'd found was helpful, but it really wouldn't make that big a difference in the end. We were going to have to come up with a real plan, and real damn soon.

When we pulled up, the guys were sitting on the porch, the new communal gathering place. I could see the garden spot all tilled, dark coffee-colored loam in a perfect rectangle. The color of the earth was striking, as most of the ground in this area is sand, granules of whitish-gray lifelessness. But there, just behind the chicken coop, was this beautiful patch of dark brown earth. It looked like it would grow golf balls.

"Man, that plot looks awesome," I said.

"It'll be even better when we're done with it," Thad replied, grinning.

"It better, it was a lot of work," Jeff added.

I looked over at him with eyebrows raised. "I wondered where the hell you were."

"I stayed behind. There were more than enough of you guys and getting that damn garden turned was a hell of a job."

"Look at all the stuff we found!" Jess sang out, coming through the screen door. Everyone filed in and dropped their bags on the floor.

Thad was sitting on the edge of the big chase, knees akimbo, when a bag landed between his feet.

"Damn!" he said, then looked up and smiled.

"Wow, all this has been out there in these houses all this time?" Jeff asked.

"This is all from one house, actually," Mel said.

Thad and Danny looked at her and in unison asked, "What?"

"Dad had to pick the lock to get in," Taylor said.

"Yeah, it was pretty damn secure. Got some serious doors on it and I think the windows have security film on them. It looked like a lot of people had tried to break in, but no one had the tools. We hit the other houses, but most of those had already been searched. That one was a nice surprise," I said.

Jeff reached out and looked in Tyler's bag. "Hey, this is some nice shit!" he exclaimed, then quickly looked up at Mel. "Sorry, I mean stuff. But look at this flashlight." He pulled a Streamlight out of the bag and clicked the switch. It didn't seem to work, and he pointed it toward his face and switched it on again. "Damn, that's bright!" he shouted.

"I hope you don't test guns like that," I said, getting a belly laugh out of Thad.

Jeff returned a goofy grin. We went about inventorying the booty from our search. Since Mel and Bobbie did all of the cooking, with the other gals pitching in, they decided to take charge and sort the bags, discussing what they could do with the various cans and cartons. Aric sat in a rocking chair, looking a little green around the gills.

"What's up, dude?" I asked him. "Looks like you're gonna puke any second now."

"I'm in a lot of pain right now." He grimaced.

"You don't have any painkillers?" Fred asked.

"From the camp? No, nothing strong."

Fred looked worried. "Is there anything we can do for him?"

For some reason everyone looked at me. Surprised, I said, "What?"

"You're the one around here who knows about plants and stuff," Danny said.

"I don't know of anything around here right now that would make much difference to him."

Immediately after saying that I remembered something. "Well . . . hang on, I'll be right back," I jumped up and headed back to my place. I was getting in shape from all this running back and forth these days, I had to admit. I jogged into the house and found my pack in the bedroom. Digging through it, I found what I was looking for, muttering, "Aha!"

Coming through the screen door, I tossed the small package to Aric. Picking it up, he looked at it. "What's this?"

Sitting on a stool, I smiled and said, "Weed."

Everyone on the porch looked at it, then at me, with wide eyes. Taylor was the first to ask, "Dad? Where'd you get that?"

"I took it off . . ." Realizing what I was about to say I thought for a moment. "I found it in a stash on my way home. Had more but used it to distract a bunch of hippies in the woods on my way in."

Jeff took it from Aric. "Dude, you been holding out on us?"

"It's not for you or anyone else as a hobby," I said flatly.

"I don't smoke weed, Morgan," Aric said.

"It'll help with the pain. It's not like you're going to sit around all day sucking on a hookah. We'll still be putting you to work," I said with a chuckle.

Aric took the bag back from Jeff and eyed it suspiciously. "Will it really help?"

Jeff smiled broadly. "Oh yeah, it'll help. You'll still hurt but it will change your perspective on it."

"Aric, just try it. If it doesn't help or you don't like it then don't do more, but you won't know unless you try," Fred said.

"Dad, isn't that illegal?" Lee Ann asked.

"Sweetie, it used to be, but right now . . . rules don't really apply," Mel answered. Lee Ann frowned, and Taylor shrugged, both clearly shocked that their dad even *knew* what it was.

"How am I going to smoke it? Not like I could roll it, even if I had papers . . ." Aric said, trailing off.

Jeff jumped up. "Hang on!" He took off at a run and disappeared. In a couple of minutes he was on his way back, a big dumb grin on his face. Coming back up on the porch he opened his clenched fist to reveal a small brass pipe.

"Why am I not surprised," I said, shaking my head.

Putting on his best attempt at looking innocent, he said, "Whatever do you mean?"

"All right girls, let's go," Mel said as she stood up.

"Yeah, let's figure out something for dinner," Bobbie said.

"We'll help too," Jess said as she and Fred both picked up bags and followed them inside.

"I'll go get Brandy and the kids," Tyler said.

In a matter of moments it was just Aric, Danny, Thad, Jeff, and me on the porch. Jeff whistled and looked around. "So you gonna smoke this or what?"

Aric looked uneasy. "I guess so."

"Let me load this thing. You only got one arm right now," Jeff said.

"Let me guess—you're going to light it for him too," Thad said.

Jeff looked up with a smile. "What are friends for?"

"I'll leave you two to it. I wanna go see the garden," I said.

Thad and Danny followed me out. It was looking good, but I wanted to make sure we were doing everything to maximize its potential. "What else can we do to get it ready?"

"We need manure. We have a pile of it from the pigs over

at our place, plus I'm going to look around. Looks like a lot of folks had horses and other livestock. I'm going to collect any I can find and turn it in as well,"Thad said.

"I know where most of the large animals were around here. I'll help you," Danny said.

We milled around talking about our plans for the garden. It was going to be hard to keep it going, especially without insecticide or fertilizer. While Danny and Thad were talking seed saving, I went into the chicken coop and found four eggs. Not much in the grand scheme of things, but in our current situation, every little bit counted.

"We need to have a serious discussion about food with everyone," I said as we looked over the plot.

"We probably should, but what is there to talk about? There isn't much we can do about it," Danny replied.

"Gonna be some hungry days ahead,"Thad added.

Scratching my head I replied, "All very true, but I think we need to have a serious discussion about it, not to mention we need to get more organized. We need a work schedule of sorts, who's doing what when."

"Seems to me everything is getting done,"Thad said.

"Yeah, but there's always a discussion about it, and with how many people we have now, I think we need to have an established schedule for things like guard duty, cooking, hunting, that sort of thing."

"You've got a point. It would make things a little easier if everyone knew when they were supposed to be doing something," Danny said.

"That's what I was thinking. If we do it right, then everyone will know when they are supposed to be working on something and when they have time to themselves."

"That makes sense. Just be sure and keep the couples together—you know, off at the same time and all,"Thad said.

"Good idea. Danny, you're way more organized than I am, can you make it up?" I asked.

"Sure, let's go over this with everyone after dinner and make a list of what all needs done and I'll set it up. I've got a wipe board, I'll write it out on that and hang it on the front porch."

We talked for a little while longer. Already I was feeling more at ease, knowing we'd be getting organized in this way. As the sun touched the horizon, the sound of laughter drifted on the cool breeze. Looking over toward the house I saw Little Bit, Edie, and Jace running toward us, laughing and screaming.

"Ain't that a sight,"Thad said.

As they ran by, Danny grabbed Little Bit and swung her up over his back. She squealed with delight. In a matter of moments we each had one of the little ones by their hands, swinging them in circles. Soon the yard was filled with the raucous sounds of youthful excitement. Letting the kids glide in for a slow landing, the three of us staggered around like winos with bad feet, to a chorus of "Do it again, do it again!"

"That's it for me, guys, I'm spent,"Thad said.

Danny and I concurred, so the kids ran off. Looking over at the porch, I spotted Aric, looking mellow, like he was a part of the chair he sat in. Fred was laughing at him and he was smiling a sloppy grin.

"We need more tables and chairs," Bobbie yelled out to Danny, standing in the open door to the house.

She was right—even now, the house was full of people and there were more on the porch. If we were going to have communal meals, then it would make sense to have enough seating for everyone.

"We can get some from the abandoned houses," Mel suggested, walking out past Bobbie.

"Yeah, we'll round some up tomorrow," Danny said.

"All of this cleaning and planning has got me beat. What's for supper?" Thad said, patting his belly.

"A little of this and a little of that," Mel said with a grin.

Thad's brow narrowed.

"Don't worry, you'll like it," Jess said with a laugh. "There's something special for you."

Now Thad looked really concerned. "What'cha mean?"

"Well, we're having beef stew," Jess said with a smile. Thad's face turned into one enormous smile. Jess continued, "But you're not." She gave a very coy smile, batting her eyebrows at him.

Before Thad could say anything I burst out laughing, which got Jess laughing. Thad gave me a shove that nearly knocked me over. As for everyone else on the porch, they had no idea why it was so funny and were looking at us as though we'd gone mad.

Mel cocked her head to the side, hands on her hips. "Okay, what's the story?"

"Oh, they think they're funny, Miss Mel. Let them tell you," Thad said.

I was still laughing and couldn't get it out, but thankfully Jess had managed to get herself under control.

"When we were walking home we were going to have beef stew for dinner one night, and when Thad asked what we were having I told him but said there wasn't enough for him. Let's just say he did not react well."

The explanation didn't seem to do it for them. "Guess you had to be there," Jess added.

We had dinner together with people scattered everywhere, some at the table, some at the bar, others on the back porch. There were even people sitting on the deck on the floor. It was noisy with so many people, so many different conversations going on at once, but it was a good time. We'd spent so long with so few of us that it was nice to be around other people. Other people you could trust, not having to worry about whether or not they were going to try and rob you blind or worse.

After everyone was done with their meal I stood up. "Hey, guys, we need to have a discussion."

"Uh-oh, this doesn't sound good," Jeff said as he pushed his plate away.

"It's nothing like that, we just need to go over a schedule. There's a lot that needs done around here and we need get it organized so everyone knows what they are supposed to be doing and when."

"That makes sense," Mel said.

"So let's go over the things we need to be doing. Guard duty is the first thing."

"We need to have at least two people down there at all times. Their relief should know when they are supposed to be there and make sure they get there on time," Thad said.

"Everyone here is capable of pulling guard duty," I said, then noticed Brandy giving Tyler a nervous look.

Tyler looked at her, then back to me. "Morgan, Brandy isn't very good with a gun. Can we keep her off that job? She can work on something else to make up for it."

"I'm scared of guns, just don't like them," Brandy added.

"Not a problem, there's plenty more to do," I said.

Tyler nodded. "Thanks. If need be I'll pull extra duty down there to make up for it."

I shook my head. "That's not necessary. There's plenty of people."

"Next thing is the cooking," Danny said.

Bobbie held up her hand. "No offense to you guys, but we'll handle the cooking."

"I can help with that every day. I don't mind a bit," Brandy offered.

"I can do both, wherever I'm needed," Mel said.

"Me too," Bobbie added.

"Well, if you ladies want to do the cooking, we'll try and make sure you guys have early shifts at the barricade then," I said.

Jeff raised a hand. "I want third shift out there. I like it at night."

We discussed the details of the schedule for another hour or so, going over the other items that needed done daily, such as hunting and, most important of all, the distribution of water. Since Danny's and my houses were the only ones with running water, we would use the tank on the trailer to haul water to the other houses and fill buckets or barrels or whatever we could find so they could use the toilets and have drinking water.

When it came to the hunting, Taylor raised a hand. "Can we hunt?"

"Of course you can," I replied.

"Can I hunt too? I want to hunt. I have my Cricket," Little Bit pled.

I smiled. "Yes, you can hunt too, just don't go alone." I

looked at Lee Ann and Taylor. "At least one of you two needs to be with her."

The girls nodded. Taylor in particular looked excited about the prospect.

Jess held up a hand. "I have a question." I nodded at her and she continued, "What about showers, since we're talking about water? Your houses have running water—is there a way we could schedule it so everyone could get a shower once or twice a week? I'm tired of washing in a bucket."

"Me too!" Fred concurred.

I looked at Danny and he nodded. "I don't see why not. We just have to space them out so we don't draw too heavily on the system, and they won't be hot showers."

"Fine by me. I'd just like to able to wash thoroughly," Fred said.

"Me too, that sounds wonderful," Brandy added.

After our discussion was done, everyone volunteered to clean up. Bobbie was very particular about her kitchen—hell, her whole house. She was like a drill sergeant in the way she dictated orders. Nonetheless, we all pitched in to get the job done quickly. As everyone was preparing to leave, I pulled Danny off to the side.

"I think tomorrow I'm going to move the bulk of the solar setup over here. I mean, if we're going to do all the cooking and having our meals over here it only makes sense, plus the added running of the pump for showers."

Danny nodded. "Yeah, looking like this is becoming the center of our little community."

"That's what I was thinking—make your place kind of our command post. It's the biggest house around and everyone already kind of thinks of it that way."

"Whatever you want to do, I'm in."

Aric and Fred were moving toward the door. "Hey, Aric, did it help the pain?" I asked.

He nodded, seeming a little more "with it" now. "Actually it did, and a lot better than the painkillers I had."

"They should have legalized it a long time ago, shame there's only a little," Jeff added.

"Well, it's for *medicinal* purposes," I said with a chuckle.

Mel sidled up next to me. "I'm tired. Let's go home."

I nodded. "Come on, Little Bit, time to go," I called.

She protested for a minute but quickly gave up—she was tired too. Her sisters were already on the front porch. Everyone said their good nights and headed off toward their homes. We cut through the hole I'd made in the fence.

"Where've you two been all night?" I asked Lee Ann. "I barely saw you and Taylor at dinner."

"We were hanging out with Jess. She's really cool."

"Good, how's she doing?" I asked.

"She's good, I guess. She's fun to be around."

As we crossed the yard, the three dogs came trotting up. Looking at Meathead, I asked, "Where the hell have *you* three been?"

Mel laughed. "Like he's going to answer."

"I haven't seen them since we got home."

She scratched Drake's head. "They look healthy enough and seem to be happy."

The dogs were bounding around, making Little Bit laugh. The three girls started to run the last stretch to the house with the dogs in hot pursuit. Going inside we quickly got everyone settled down and Mel and I went to bed. It was still cool in the evening, and with the windows open, it was really nice.

Mel curled up in the blankets. "It feels so good in here."

"I know, shame it isn't going to last forever."

"Ugh, I know, it's going to get so hot soon. What are we going to do?"

"Change the sheets, often."

She rolled over and looked at me. "What?"

I laughed. "'Cause we're going to sweat like pigs at night. Remember that camping trip to North Carolina? The one up on Wilson Creek where it was a hundred degrees but it felt like a hundred and ten?"

"*Craaaap,* that was miserable. I really hope it isn't that bad."

I swatted her on the ass. "Don't worry, it won't be."

"Good."

"It'll be worse."

She kicked me in the back of my leg. "I hate you right now."

I stifled another laugh. "Don't worry, it gets worse."

She laughed. "Good night, babe, love you."

"Love you too."

Chapter 3

The next couple of weeks went by quickly. We were developing a pretty sound routine. The garden plot had been finished, thanks to the manure that we had collected. *That* was a process. Our expedition had revealed the outcome of many of the livestock that once inhabited our neighborhood. On our first expedition, Lee Ann, Tyler, Jeff, Danny, and I found a horse carcass, picked clean to the bone.

"Who would eat horse?" Tyler asked.

I looked at him. "If the Lone Ranger showed up about now I'd shoot Silver right out from under his ass."

Danny and Jeff laughed, but Lee Ann didn't see the humor. She stared down at the bones of the animal. "I used to feed him apples and carrots. He was always at the fence when I would go out for a walk. He was a nice horse." The sight of the remains of the old gelding had an obvious impact on her. I could feel the sadness wrapping around her.

Putting my arm around her, I said, "I'm sorry, kiddo. These people must have been very hungry to resort to this."

"I know, but it's still sad."

Once word got back to the rest of the group it was the subject du jour for the rest of the day and would have been at dinnertime till Brandy squashed it, not wanting her kids to hear it. No one argued, as by then everything that could be said about it had been. But food and sources of it were never-ending topics of conversation.

During this pleasant spell there'd been two trips out to the camp and one to the river. Trips to the camp were mainly so Aric and the girls could check up on Kay and Danny and I could see what we could scrounge. The trip to the river was a nice day. We hung out with Sarge, who was getting around a lot better now, fishing and combing the riverbanks for food. The fishing had been good. Using the gillnet we caught an impressive number of mullet, so much so that we left the guys with enough for several days. The rest would be smoked at Thad's place. The garden plot looked great, with squash plants already impressively large and plump green tomatoes hanging on the plants. Sarge took impressive care of the garden, vicariously of course, considering the main efforts were put forth by Mike, Ted, and Doc.

The weather had been very nice during this period, with many warm days and cool nights. After nearly two weeks in the ground, the seeds had sprouted and were growing very nicely. The cans had contained a good assortment of seeds, and if things went right in a few weeks we'd have fresh vegetables from the garden. The real problem was the *now*. Things were getting desperate around the hood. With great effort we'd managed to stretch out what we had, and the bounty we'd found in the house had certainly helped things go this long. But as the old saying goes, *all good things must come to an end*, and we were now at the end. Fortunately, though, we had seen it coming and taken action. Hunting had become an industry as of late, which helped ease our troubles. Since setting up the schedule, there were one or two people hunting every day. While not always successful it did manage to keep us in some meat, and on the days there was a surplus Thad put his smoker to use.

In an attempt to manage our resources, we divided the area up into sections so as to not clean the game from any one area. My girls became very proficient in snare sets. They took to it like a job, and it became our primary source of steady meat. Using small sets of simple loop snares, they caught rabbits in profusion. Limb rats were also taken in this manner or with a .22. This is where Little Bit really thrived: she became an expert marksman with her small rifle. She learned the habits of the animals and how to hunt them, how to circle a tree or have one of her sisters do it to force the rat around so she could get a shot. Her trophy was the tail, which she cut herself and tied to the fence to dry. There was now a very impressive string of tails suspended on the fence between Danny's and our house.

Up to this point, we were essentially hunting every day for that day's food. While it was a system that was working, it wasn't a very comfortable way to live. It was going to take a concerted effort at a serious hunt to try and bag a couple of deer. It was odd that there were still so many around—I could see them moving at night with my NVGs.

With spring now in full swing, every day there were more plants to eat. While many of them weren't as palatable as crisp young spinach, a source of greens was a source of greens. We didn't want to fall into the trap of malnutrition. I spent as much time as possible collecting edible plants. While most anyone could hunt, you really had to know what you were looking for when it came to plants. Modern society has a near phobia about wild edibles, but with a good eye, it's possible to enjoy nature's bounty without harm.

Aric showed an interest in the collection of plants; he was always looking for ways he could contribute and started following me on my outings. With Aric came Fred, of course, then Jess joined in. I spent a considerable amount of time showing them what to collect and how it was used. They quickly became expert foragers and soon there was more available in the way of wild edibles.

We kept the kitchen supplied with the likes of lamb's-quarters, chickweed, wood and sheep sorrel, dandelions, thistles, evening primrose, and my personal favorite, kudzu. It was my favorite not because it was any sort of culinary delight but because it was plentiful and very easy to collect. It took considerable effort to convince everyone that it was safe to eat. Once the conversion was made, though, it was hard for me to keep up with the demand.

Without a doubt the favorite use of the kudzu was kudzu chips. The house we had raided had yielded us a couple gallons of peanut oil. Using this, Mel and Bobbie would fry the leaves, dropping them in one at a time and frying until they were crisp. We still had plenty of salt—it takes a long time to eat five gallons of it—and so they would lightly salt the crisp leaves. They were much like store-bought chips and soon were the most popular snack we had—not that we had many options.

The real work came one afternoon when I decided to dig up some of the kudzu roots. Kudzu roots can go as deep as ten feet and achieve impressive size, but the reward is worth the effort in the production of a fine starch. Starting at the base of a vine, I started digging. Four feet later I found the root. It was nearly eighteen inches long and as big around as a coffee can. The thing probably weighed five pounds or better. Enlarging the hole, I found several more, by the end of the day I had filled a wheelbarrow.

These roots were peeled, sliced up, and laid out on screens to dry. They took a couple of days to completely dry out in the sun. Once they were dry, they needed to be pounded into powder. This presented a problem, as we didn't have the proper container for it, but Thad, Jeff, Danny, and Tyler worked with me to make a tub for the job. First we cut a three-foot section from the trunk of a large downed oak tree. It was so heavy we couldn't move it, so we worked it in place. After splitting the log down the center along its length, Danny used the saw to begin gouging out the center of it. Once he'd done what he could with the saw, we used the limbs from the tree and built a fire inside the hollow. By raking the coals around inside, we controlled where and how much was burned. It took most of a day and lots of shit-talking to get done. We had a lot of fun, though, which really took the work out of it.

We worked in the midst of the fallen tree, branches and small limbs everywhere. We collected them as needed and dropped them into the fire. I kept a close eye on it as it burned, using a stick to push the coals around. Danny stepped up and dropped a handful of small twigs in. I laughed at him. "Don't throw your back out or anything."

Jeff dropped an enormous piece of wood into the fire. Using the stick I flipped it out. "Dude, we want to hollow it, not burn through it."

With his hands on his hips, he replied, "Bitch, bitch, bitch. Make up your mind."

Thad started laughing. "Don't make me separate you, kids."

"Pfft, like you could," I shot back.

Thad straightened up and glared at me. I swung around

with the stick I'd been using to move the coals, its tip a glowing ember leaving a trail of smoke as it moved. "Git back, I'll burn the shit outta you!" I shouted in my best hillbilly drawl.

Thad started laughing. "I'll stick it where the sun don't shine."

"Damn!" Jeff shouted, rubbing his backside. "Would that hurt or what?"

"Yeah, like a hot poker in the ass!" I shouted over my shoulder.

The rest of the day went about the same, plenty of carrying on and trash-talking. But the work went smoothly. There were no big discussions, no arguments over who was doing what—it simply got done.

Looking at the finished product, Thad said, "That is pretty cool. I never would have thought of it."

Tyler looked over at me. "Yeah, where'd you learn this kind of stuff?"

"Research. I used to read a lot."

"We're glad you did, Teach," Danny said as he wiped sawdust from his pants.

"Now we have to make another piece: the pestle to pound everything out with," I said.

Thad leaned into the tangle of what was once the canopy of the old tree. Coming out with the end of a limb about eight inches in diameter, he asked, "Will this work?"

I nodded and grabbed it. Together we pulled it out and Danny used the saw to cut it off about five feet long. I picked it up and put it over my shoulder while the guys grabbed the tub. We carried everything over to Danny's shop. It'd be easier to work on the pestle there. Using hand saws, rasps, and some sandpaper, we shaped the pestle. At the lower end it was nearly its full girth, with only the bark removed. Going up the handle was about two inches in diameter. The face of the lower end was rounded slightly and smoothed with sandpaper, then hardened in a small fire Danny quickly built for the task. While we were making the pestle, Tyler and Jeff sanded the interior of the tub, getting nearly all of the charred wood off. When they were done, it was as smooth as glass.

Thad picked up the pestle, grasping the top two-handed, and pounded it into the tub. "Think the tub can handle it?"

I nodded. "I think so—the bottom is nearly four inches thick. Let the weight of the pestle do the work."

"Cool." Thad smiled. "Let's pound some roots!"

The dried root was piled into the tub, and I started pounding. It was "for real, no shit" work, and after a couple of minutes, I held my hands up. "My arms are killing—time for someone else to do some work."

We took turns, making it into a competition of sorts. There were plenty of comments and quips thrown in for motivation, again, taking out the sting of the job.

Jeff was working the pestle like a jackhammer when Jess, Lee Ann, and Taylor walked up. Sweat fell from his face in steady drips.

"What are you guys doing?" Jess asked.

"Processing these roots," I said.

"I pounded 'em into dust!" Jeff said triumphantly.

Jess looked at him with a small smile on her face. "I see that."

Jeff smiled and went to raise his arm, to make a muscle. "Yeah, check these out." But he'd put so much effort into the task that he couldn't raise his arm. "Ow, ow," he said.

Jess started to laugh, as well as the rest of us. He was doing his best to impress her, but it wasn't quite working out.

"You need someone to rub them for you?" Jess asked with a sly smile.

Jeff grinned and nodded in reply. Jess batted her eyes at him. "I'm sure Thad will do it for you. He's got strong hands." Her reply caused everyone to bust out laughing—everyone except for Jeff, that is.

Thad looked up from his work. "You want me to massage them chicken wings?"

Irritated, Jeff rotated his shoulders. "I don't need no massage. I need a drink of water." With that he walked off.

Taylor was covering her mouth. "That was funny."

"You shouldn't be so mean to him, Jess," I said, chuckling.

"He's a big boy, he can take it," Jess replied.

Danny reached into the tub and scooped up a handful of the powder. It was full of fibers from the root. "How are we going to get the fiber out?"

"We need some sort of a sieve or something," Thad said.

Looking at Danny, I asked, "You have one in the kitchen?"

He shook his head. "No, it was broken." Then he looked up. "What about the classifiers?"

"You still have them?"

He nodded and stood up, heading for the shop.

"What's a classifier?" Thad asked.

"Danny and me used to go up into the Carolinas and pan for gold. Classifiers fit in a bucket and have different-sized mesh in them, to sort out rocks and stuff." I examined the mound of powder in the bottom of the tub. "They'll work great."

Danny came back with the classifiers and a bucket. Setting

one in the top of the bucket, he nestled it with a slightly larger mesh into it and started to drop handfuls of the powdered root in. Thad knelt down beside him and started bouncing the screens, and the starch quickly began to filter through, leaving the coarse fiber behind.

"This works pretty good," Thad said.

"Can we help?" Lee Ann asked.

"You want to do it?" I asked.

"Yeah, you guys did the hard part—let us do this," Jess said.

Danny and Thad stepped back and let the girls in. They quickly went to work using the same basic technique.

"Thanks for the help, girls," Danny said.

Taylor looked up and smiled in reply.

"What I want to know," Thad said, "is did you guys ever find any gold up there?"

"We did, actually. Nothing big—dust, really, but it was fun."

Thad was looking at the bucket. "That's cool."

"Wish we had some of that gold dust now. It may have a real use soon," Danny said.

I shrugged. "I don't know. Who are we going to buy from? There's no one around."

Thad slapped his hands together, knocking the dust off. "That's true. Ain't nuthin' to buy."

Danny looked back at the girls sifting the starch. "What are we going to do with that stuff?"

I looked at Thad. "How about some chicken-fried steak tonight?"

"I need a meat mallet. We could cube some venison up, then I guess we can dust it with that and fry it up?" Thad asked.

I nodded. "Yeah, let's give it a try."

"I've got a tenderizer," Danny said.

"Go get it, and tell the ladies we'll make supper tonight," Thad said with a smile.

With a laugh Danny replied, "I'm sure they won't complain."

The dogs came trotting through the yard, as if on a mission. I watched them head out the gate and start down the road. "Where in the hell are they going?"

Thad looked over and shrugged. "Who knows, why don't you ask 'em?" He laughed at his own little joke.

"I think I'll follow them. They look like they've got something they're checking out."

"Be careful," Danny said. Thad nodded his agreement.

Tyler offered to go with me. "I could use a walk."

I nodded. "Let me run and get my gear."

After grabbing my carbine, I went out to the road and called to the dogs. They stopped and looked back, ears erect. Seeing me walking toward them, they turned and waited. As we passed Tyler's house, he ran in real quick. This time he came out with a pistol strapped to his side and his Ranch Rifle over his shoulder.

I nodded at the dogs. "Let's follow them and see where they're going. They're gone a lot and don't eat much, so they've got to be getting it from someplace."

"Cool, let's go."

As we started walking toward the dogs, they turned and resumed their travel, indifferent to our approach. At the end of the street they turned left.

"They sure look like they know exactly where they're going," Tyler said.

"Yeah, I'm curious to see what they've found."

Tyler kicked a rock down the road. "Hey, man, thanks for bringing us over here. It's been really great. Brandy's really happy having the other women around."

"No problem, man. It's great having your kids around for Little Bit too, and not to mention you've been a big help."

"Sure thing. A little work is a fair trade to be able to sleep soundly at night and have some food to eat."

"Yep. Having more people around makes the workload a little easier to manage."

"Yeah but it's more mouths to feed," Tyler said, sounding a bit guilty.

"Dude, don't sweat it. Brandy does her part too. You guys aren't an uneven burden or anything."

Tyler looked over and smiled. "Thanks, man, that's really good to hear. Brandy's kind of worried you guys are going to ask us to leave—you know, food being so scarce and all."

"Would never dream of it."

The dogs hit the intersection with Highway 19 and turned left, trotting in the the middle of the road. I shook my head. "Hope these mutts don't go far."

"Me too."

Just as Tyler replied, the dogs made a right onto a small dirt drive. We had to pick up our pace a bit to catch up to them. Just like the dogs, we walked down the center line of the highway. It was an odd feeling, the old mores of modern life still firmly in place.

Tyler gave voice to my thoughts. "Wonder how long it will take before it no longer feels weird to walk down the middle of the road."

I looked at him and laughed. "I was just thinking the same thing. It's funny, isn't it?" I said as I looked back, fully expecting to see a car zipping down the road toward us.

"It is kind of cool, though. Feels like we're breaking the rules or something."

"All things considered, I'd rather this road be full of cars."

"That's true. I can dig that, man."

The drive they turned onto had a few small houses on it, all sheltered under a hammock of oaks. It was actually a nice area, though it was obvious all the houses were abandoned.

"I don't think anyone is here," Tyler said.

"I was going to agree, but look here—tracks," I said, pointing at a smallish set of footprints in the roadbed.

"Let's follow them," Tyler replied with a smile.

The footprints lead to a small house typical of early Florida: wood frame, lapboard siding, with a porch. The yard was enclosed in a fence, the gate shut. The barking of the dogs took away any uncertainty as to where they had run off to. We edged closer.

"Sounds like they're playing," I said.

"Sounds like more than just those three too."

We stopped at the gate. The front door was open behind a screen door. Barely thirty feet of neatly cut St. Augustine grass separated us from the porch.

I cupped my hand to my mouth and called out, "Hello, the house!" Silence.

After a moment I called again.

"I don't think anyone's in there," Tyler said.

He was immediately proven wrong when a woman's voice came through the screen. "I heard you the first time." The voice had a hint of an Appalachian twang, but her tone wasn't unpleasant. Through the screen door, I could make out a small figure standing there. She looked all of five foot nothing.

"Hi there. I'm Morgan, this is Tyler."

"That's close enough, Morgan and Tyler." To emphasize her point, the door opened a couple of inches and the barrel of a shotgun came out.

"Sorry, we didn't mean to scare you," I said. "We were just looking for our dogs."

"You two just wait where you are till Batman gets back. He should be here shortly."

Tyler looked at me and whispered, "Batman? Who's Batman? This chick's lost her marbles."

A burly man in a white T-shirt and cut-off jeans came around the corner of the house. He wore a nice leather holster hung low in a western fashion with a very large revolver tucked in it. I nodded toward him. "I guess he is."

"Batman, you out there?" she called out.

"I'm here, Gena." He glared at us and walked toward the gate. As he did the screen door behind him opened, and the petite woman stepped out. She wore a broad-brimmed straw hat, a pair of overalls cut off into shorts, and a T-shirt. The shotgun she held looked nearly as big as she was.

Batman stopped a little short and looked at us. "I can't spare any food, boys, sorry."

"Oh no, sir, we're not looking for food." I nodded at the dogs, now lying in the grass. "I was just curious where our dogs were getting off to every day, so we followed them here."

He looked down. "These three yours?"

"Yes, sir—well, two of them are really mine, that black lab just kind of fell in with them."

"I love dogs. They been coming around here for a while now. We feed 'em a little," the woman said.

I stuck out my hand toward Batman. "I'm Morgan, this is Tyler. We live just down the road from you guys."

He stepped forward and shook it. "I'm Dylan."

Tyler stepped up to shake hands as well. "I thought you were Batman."

Dylan smiled. "That's just her nickname for me, don't ask."

Gena stepped up. "I'm Gena." Jutting her thumb toward Dylan, she said, "I'm his doomsday bitch." She said it with a smile, looking genuinely happy. She proffered the shotgun to Dylan. "Honey, take this, it's heavy."

He took the gun and looked at her. "You all right, you feeling bad?"

"No, I'm fine, just can't carry that thing too long."

Dylan looked back at us. "Gena has MS."

"Oh, I'm sorry. We're not trying to get into your business," I said.

"Oh, it's fine, don't worry about that. He just worries about me," Gena said. What she said next really surprised us. "You want to come in? We're about to have supper."

"Oh, uh, that's really nice, but we couldn't impose ourselves on you. Besides, there'll be supper waiting for us back at home," I said.

"Thank you, though. You don't see that sort of hospitality nowadays," Tyler added.

"It's no bother. You're welcome," Gena said.

"If you won't have supper, how about a mead?" Dylan asked.

Tyler looked at him questioningly. "What's mead?"

"It's the bestest stuff on earth! Honey wine. I make it myself," Gena said, proudly.

"I'd love one," I said.

Tyler held up his social finger. "Yes, please."

Dylan opened the gate. "Come on up to the porch."

We followed them up to the house, where several chairs were arranged on the porch. Dylan told us to have a seat and disappeared inside. Gena sat down as well, the effort apparent on her face.

I unslung my carbine and leaned it against the house, then looked at Gena. "Sorry about the hardware."

She gave me a dismissive wave. "Don't worry about it. Just the way things are now."

Dylan emerged from the house with several large brown bottles in tow. He handed Tyler and me each one. Dylan took a seat and opened his, taking a long pull. I opened mine and took a drink. It was like a shock to my taste buds, so flavorful and unlike anything I had had before.

"Wow, what's in this?" I asked.

"This one has strawberry in it. Good, ain't it?" Dylan said with a grin.

Tyler sniffed the bottle suspiciously, then took a timid sip. He swished the brew around in his mouth, a broad smile spreading across his face. "That's . . . amazing. Wow. I feel alive again! Woo!" We all chuckled at his enthusiasm.

Examining the bottle, I asked, "Are you still brewing?"

"Oh yeah. We've got several hives, so honey isn't an issue," Dylan said.

"Where are you getting the yeast?"

"It took a little experimentation, but we're allowing natural yeast to do the job now. It makes the process longer, but it works." Dylan picked at the label on the bottle. "These were bottled before things went to shit, though."

I raised the bottle in a salute. "Whatever you're doing, it's working. Really good," I said, then took another long drink.

I was surprised when Gena produced a small silver case and took out what looked like a home-rolled cigarette from it and lit it. The smell, though, instantly told me it wasn't tobacco. Gena caught me looking at her and grinned. "It's for the MS, it's the only thing I have. Doesn't take the pain away but puts my mind in a place where I can deal with it."

"It does have its uses. We recently had to use some for one of our people with a bad wound. Don't have any painkillers or anything, and he said it helped. It was just dumb luck that I had it," I said.

"You need more?" she asked.

I was taken aback. "Uh, well, actually, we could use some for him. I'm not into it and we don't use it recreationally, but I think it's good to have on hand. What could we trade you for some?"

"I don't know, y'all seem like decent people. You don't have to trade. I'll give you some if it will help someone."

"I appreciate it, okay. But fair's fair. I'll think of something to bring over here for you."

"Sounds like a deal," Dylan said, then he stood up. "Follow me around back."

Taking our bottles, we followed him around the corner of the house, Gena bringing up the rear. The small house hid a very nice greenhouse behind it.

"Wow, that's nice," Tyler said.

"Oh yeah, I love my greenhouse," Gena said.

When we stepped through the door the temperature rose immediately, along with the humidity. Inside was a tropical paradise with lush green hanging from the ceiling and climbing up from the ground. A seemingly infinite variety of vegetables and fruits were growing in several raised beds. On one end was a thick, unruly stand of marijuana plants.

"Holy crap, look at all this," I said. Tyler echoed my sentiment with a low whistle.

"You don't have a garden?" Dylan asked.

"We just got it in recently, so it's going to be a while before we see anything from it," Tyler said.

"If you need some, we can spare it," Gena said.

Again, I was dumbfounded. Not only were they showing us the store, but they were offering to give it away. I couldn't imagine letting someone, anyone, in on what we may or may not have. It made me realize just how this situation had challenged our typical rules of courtesy and civility.

"Okay, we will take you up on this offer, but I insist that we trade for it. I mean, food is tough to come by now. You've got to need something," I said.

Gena thought for a moment, then looked at Dylan. "Can you think of anything?"

He shrugged then asked, "Got any salt?"

"Yes!" I practically shouted, causing Tyler to choke on his mead and startling Dylan and Gena."Sorry, but that is one thing we *do* have. How about a pound of salt," then thinking, ahead I added, "and some fresh pork?"

"Fresh pig meat and salt? Hell yeah!" Dylan said.

"We don't get much meat. We stay close to home here, trying not to be seen," Gena said.

"I tell you what, how about we keep you in meat for some of your harvest?" I said.

"I'm in, for damn sure. We can certainly keep you in veggies," Dylan said.

"Well, you can't keep us in veggies. We've actually got a pretty big group with several kids and a bunch of adults—we would probably run you dry. But anything will help and fresh fruits and veggies will be more than welcome. Do you like liver?"

"Oh yeah, liver and onions is terrific," Gena said.

"I tell you what, we're going to run home and come back with some things to trade. We may have some other folks with us, if that's okay."

"Fine by me," Gena said.

"I have to ask you guys . . . not trying to be a smart-ass, but why are you showing us all this? I mean, it's dangerous to be so open these days," I said.

"You guys seem all right. You came to the gate with your rifles slung over your shoulder, so it's not like we caught you sneaking around the yard. Plus you won't take anything without a trade, so that says a lot about your character."

I smiled. "I think you're nuts, but I like you. We'll be back in a bit," I said and set the bottle on a small bench.

"Take it for the road, just bring it back. Not so easy to find bottles at the moment," Dylan said with a wink.

Chapter 4

"When are the buses supposed to arrive?" Sheffield asked Livingston.

Livingston looked at his watch. "They said around one or two, barring any delays. I expect to see them in the next hour or so."

"And where's that old man and his band of misfits? He should have been here already."

Livingston laughed. "I think he travels to the beat of a different drum."

"Yeah, you got that right. *Different* isn't even the word."

"I'm just glad he's on our side. Could you imagine dealing with that sumbitch if he was after you?"

"There's a scary thought," Sheffield said, shaking his head.

"What's a scary thought?" Sarge asked as he stepped into Sheffield's office. Sheffield had taken over Tabor's old haunt after relieving him of command of the camp.

"Speak of the devil," Livingston said as he reached out to shake Sarge's hand.

Sheffield looked at his watch. "If you can't get here on time, get here when you can."

Sarge shook Livingston's hand. "You seem to forget, Captain, that I am retired, and time in retirement is a relative thing. Besides, the show ain't started yet."

"You bring your crew with you?" Livingston asked.

Sarge nodded as a means of response. "Yeah, they're outside. Mikey's out there trying to get into Jamie's pants."

Livingston sat in one of the chairs occupying the ancillary side of the desk. "Good luck with that," he said with a snort.

Sarge lowered himself into the other chair. "Ah, gives the boy something to do."

"How's the hip?" Sheffield asked from across the desk.

Sarge patted his side. "It's getting better every day. I figure another week and it'll be back to normal."

"That's some good news."

"Them DHS boys know they're going on a road trip today?" Sarge asked.

"We've tried to keep it quiet, but we'll see soon enough," Livingston said.

"I'll be glad to be rid of them, personally," Sheffield said.

"I bet, where are they going?" Sarge asked.

"Frostproof. There's a larger camp there, actually set up as a detention facility. Command wants them there," Livingston replied.

A petite brunette stuck her head in the door. "Main gate just called, said the buses are pulling up now."

"Thanks, Corporal," Sheffield responded. Looking at Sarge, he said, "Let's get the show on the road. I'm ready to be rid of these bastards."

"Ain't that the truth!" Livingston shouted. "Also, gentlemen, we need to talk. I got orders today to close the camp," Sheffield said.

Sarge's hairy eyebrows seemed to climb up his forehead. "Really? I didn't think they'd have the stones to do it."

"I questioned their reasoning, but they made it clear: we are not in the refugee business. We're to close the camp after the DHS boys are out of here."

"We've already started demobilization," Livingston said.

"Good. Close the camp, put them on the road. It ain't your job to take care of 'em. Your goal was to liberate, and you did," Sarge said matter-of-factly.

"I asked where they thought they would go. I told them we can't just put them out on the road," Sheffield said.

"How the hell are you going to take care of them? You got supplies coming in?" Sarge waved his arm, sweeping the camp. "Desperate times call for desperate measures. Cut off support—you need to look out for your own. Hell, we're living off that river ourselves. You guys aren't feeding us."

"I just don't know if we can do that," Sheffield said, shaking his head. "I don't know what these people would do without our support, not to mention we already have a bunch of civilians we're taking care of: all the family members of our guys."

"Shit, it's not your prerogative! Besides, you've got orders. You have to take care of the families of your men—if you didn't, you wouldn't have any troops. These people will be fine. Look at Morgan and his bunch. They're getting by. Sure, they aren't living the high life, but they aren't here begging at the door either. Times are tough, times are hard, kick their asses out of the yard." Sarge smiled at his little rhyme.

Sheffield was shaking his head. "You really are a mean ole bastard, aren't you? You got any compassion for people?"

"Sure I do, plenty of it for people who help themselves. But I can't spare a shit for those who won't. That's what was wrong with our society before things went to hell. Too many people thinking they were entitled or owed something just for being born. The only thing each of them is owed is the chance to try." Sarge stood up. "Hell, this was probably the best thing to happen to this country. If we come out of it on the other side, we'll be better for it. The playing field's been leveled. Everyone pretty much went back to square one."

"Not everyone was set back to zero. Your buddy Morgan and his friends got all sorts of stuff most people don't have. He didn't have to start from scratch."

"Because he planned ahead. And you really have no idea the kind of shit he went through just trying to get home to his family. When he showed up at my place he was nearly dead. But he ain't sat around on his ass crying poor mouth. He's out there making a go of it. Everyone over there is. Hell, they've got quite the little community going on now."

"He's right, Captain. Plus, we've got orders," Livingston said.

"So you want to put everyone out? You're taking his side?" Sheffield asked.

"I'm not taking sides, it's just a simple fact. Our obligation is to maintain our force and provide security. I don't think we should be responsible to take care of everyone. Hell, half these people around here don't want to lift a finger now. The DHS made them work, so they did, but now that we're here and not pushing them around at gunpoint, they aren't so keen on helping themselves or helping us help them."

"Did they give you any reason for closing the camp?" Sarge asked.

"Their reasoning was pretty simple: they can't provide enough supplies to us to support a few hundred refugees.

The colonel said now everyone is essentially a refugee, so people are just going to have to take care of themselves. I don't agree with it, but that's what I got."

"So where are you guys going?" Sarge asked.

"Back to the armory. They want us back there as soon as we can manage," Sheffield replied.

Sarge stared at the floor, nodding, thinking it over. "So I assume they have some sort of plan for you guys."

"Yes, they do, but I don't know yet what it is. I was just told to get moved and stand by."

"I can hardly wait to hear what it is," Livingston said sarcastically.

"Well, for what it's worth, I agree with them. These folks need to take care of themselves—you can't do it for them," Sarge replied.

"What do you think these people are going to do? Where do you think they're going to go? Some of them are from as far away as Gainesville. How are they going to get back?" Sheffield asked.

"Again, not our fucking problem. They'll have to figure it out. If it makes you feel better, load 'em up with some supplies—food, water, and the like. Then it's up to them, not us."

Sheffield's face flashed with anger. "We'll worry about this later. Right now we've got a job to do, so let's get to it."

The three men left the office to find Ted, Doc, Mike, and Jamie hanging out around the Hummer out front. Sarge and crew got in theirs while Sheffield, Livingston, and Jamie got in the other. Mike followed Jamie as she drove through the camp.

"This should be fun," Ted said, riding in the back with his elbow propped on the open window.

"I just hope it goes smooth," Mike replied.

"It'll be all right. If they start any shit, putting a couple of them in the dirt should take care of it," Sarge added.

The Hummers stopped in front of a couple of tents ringed by Guardsmen. Four buses sat off the main road into the camp, doors open, with their drivers and security milling around. There were also two Hummers, one in the lead and one at the rear of the column. Both of these had belt-fed weapons mounted to their turrets.

Sheffield stepped out of the Hummer and looked around. Seeing Ian, he called him over. As Ian approached, Sheffield asked, "Everyone ready?"

Ian nodded. "Sure thing, boss. We've broken them up into four groups. The guys at the bus will cuff them up with flex cuffs as they get on."

Sheffield nodded. "Do they know what's going on yet?"

"They know something is up, just not sure what."

"You pass the rules of engagement along?" Livingston asked.

"Everyone's clear."

"What's the ROE?" Sarge asked as he came up to the group.

Sheffield looked at him. "No shooting unless absolutely necessary. That applies to you guys too," he pointed at Mike, Ted, and Doc.

"No worries, boss man," Mike said with a grin. Doc held up his hands in mock surrender.

"All right, Ian, get the first bus up here and let's get 'em loaded," Livingston said.

Ian nodded and turned to face the buses. Whistling, he waved an arm at the lead bus. The bus quickly began to move up toward the tents where the DHS personnel were being guarded.

"I'm going to sit here and enjoy the show," Sarge said as he leaned back against the hood of Sheffield's Hummer.

Jamie followed Ian to the tent where Perez and several Guardsmen stood at the entry.

"All right, Perez, let's get the first group out," Ian said.

Perez nodded and opened the door, telling one of the soldiers inside to bring out the first group. The soldiers outside formed a loose cordon to the door of the bus. Soon the DHS folks were walking out, looking unsure of what was going on. The lead agent asked the obvious question, "Where are we going?"

"Don't worry about it, just head for the bus," Perez said.

"This is bullshit! Where are we going? What's going on?"

Soon they were all shouting questions. Sarge was grinning as he watched the proceedings. The old man looked over at Ted. "Teddy, go get them bastards moving."

Ted and Mike quickly started to move toward the action. "Roger that, boss."

"What are you doing?" Livingston asked.

"LT, this shit is going to take forever if we don't get them moving. They just need to know you guys are serious."

"We said no shooting," Sheffield said, pointing at the knots of civilians that were still gathering to watch the proceedings. "We can't risk a firefight with all these people around here."

"Don't worry, Captain, they aren't going to shoot anyone. Yet."

Sheffield and Livingston both looked back to the bus, unsure of what was about to happen.

As Ted approached he heard one of the DHS agents. "We

aren't going anywhere until we know what's going on. Where are you taking us?"

Ted stepped through the soldiers. "Shut up and get on the bus! It's the only time I'm going to say it."

The agent looked at Ted. "Or wha—" He was cut off by the pop of Mike's Taser. The agent immediately went rigid and fell backward. None of his fellows bothered to catch him—they actually stepped aside, allowing him to hit the ground.

"Anyone else want to know what's going on?" Ted asked.

The suddenness of the action startled the other agents in line, their only reply the silent shaking of their heads.

Ted pointed to the stricken agent. "Get him on his feet and on that bus." Ted looked at Mike. "Leave those in him until he's cuffed up."

Mike looked at the man he'd just tased. "Let's go, Princess."

Without any further complaint, the agent moved to the bus, where the security personnel secured his hands behind his back with the flex cuffs. The others were all likewise secured and the bus was quickly loaded. It pulled forward to allow the next in line to pull up and the process was started again with the next bus.

Sarge was laughing to himself. "Told you boys. He didn't shoot anyone."

Neither Sheffield nor Livingston replied, they simply watched as the next two buses were loaded without any further incident. The fourth bus pulled up and the process was started for the final time. This one would carry the officers and any deemed troublemakers. Early on they had been segregated to keep them from instigating any trouble with the rank and file agents.

Charles Tabor was the first to come out. He looked around,

scanning the crowd. When his eyes landed on Sarge, Sheffield, and Livingston, he was incensed. Sarge tipped his hat sarcastically as Tabor waited to be cuffed up, his trusty sidekick Ed right behind him.

Next up was Singer. When she came out, Jamie patiently waited for her opportunity to make eye contact. As usual Singer had that same miserable look on her face, as though she perpetually smelled shit. Jamie shook her head. *What a miserable bitch*, she thought. Singer squinted against the intense afternoon light. When they locked eyes, a slight smile cut Jamie's face as she winked at her. Singer's sneer morphed into a snarl of sorts, which only brought Jamie more pleasure.

As these priority prisoners were being led toward the bus, Calvin and Shane walked up to where Sarge was reclining against the front of a Hummer.

"How's it going, there, Linus?" Calvin asked.

"Fair ta middlin', how's the ribs?"

"Getting better. Would be a lot better if I were at home, though."

Sarge stood up. "I was going to ask why you're still here—I thought you'd be long gone by now."

Calvin nodded toward Sheffield, then replied, "They told us we were free to leave, but it's a long walk, and in my current condition, it's just not possible."

"Plus we don't have any weapons. Ours were confiscated when we came in here, and now they've gotten mixed in from when they did the inventory a few weeks ago," Shane added.

Sheffield let out a long sigh, exasperated. "I'm sorry. I told you guys I don't have the manpower right now to go checking for your specific hardware. Like I said, as soon as we get rid of these guys, I'll see what I can do."

As they were talking a group of four civilians moved toward the front of the bus. Livingston saw them and called out, "Jamie, get them out of there."

Jamie approached them, pointing her weapon in their general direction. "Move away from here, now, please," she said in a stern voice.

The four men looked at one another and began backing away. Jamie turned her attention back to the last group to be loaded. When the first of the group was about to be cuffed, Tabor shouted, "Now!"

The group suddenly erupted, each of them grabbing the nearest Guardsmen and trying to take their weapons. Jamie quickly moved into the fray, striking one man in the face with the butt of her M4. She was tackled from the side, going down hard. Out of the corner of her eye she could see that sneer and the red hair.

At the same moment the four civilians who had been ordered away from the bus broke into a sprint, running toward the brawl now taking place. Sarge stood passively, analyzing what was going on. He saw the four men running toward the melee. Calmly drawing his .45, he fired an offhand shot at the lead man, striking him in the abdomen. The man crumpled on the ground, his comrade who was trailing behind him, falling on top of him. The other two paused for a moment, the shot catching them off guard. Looking around they saw Sarge, pistol leveled at them. Hesitating for a moment they looked at each other, and then turned and took off at a run, leaving the other two behind.

Shane and Calvin were stunned by the suddenness of what was going on. At the bark of Sarge's pistol, Shane looked over to the two men on the ground, one obviously wounded, the other getting to his feet. "Son of a bitch!" Shane shouted.

Sarge looked at him. "What?"

Pointing to the man getting up, Shane shrieked, "He's one of them!"

It was Niigata, unmistakably, even though he was wearing civilian clothes. Shane's face twisted with hatred at the sight of his torturer. Sprinting up to him, Shane went to deliver a kick. It was a clumsy effort, which Niigata caught, raising Shane's leg over his head and delivering an open-palm strike to Shane's groin. Shane let out a groan and fell to the side. Taking advantage of the hit, Niigata started to rise to his feet. But before he could stand upright another shot rang out and the dirt between his feet erupted. Niigata looked down, then up to see Sarge holding a leveled pistol at him. While confident of his skills, he knew there was no way he would outrun a bullet. Niigata surrendered, raising his hands and lowering himself to a kneeling position.

The sound of the shots caused alarm, increasing the intensity of the fighting. Jamie was now on her back with Singer on top of her. Tabor and Ed had one soldier on the ground, trying desperately to strip his weapon. Mike and Ted leapt into the fray, making their way toward that scuffle. Ted shot Ed in the neck with his Taser, dropping him to the ground. Coming in at a run, Mike kicked Tabor in the face, a crushing blow that threw him onto his back, unconscious.

Singer was delivering a fusillade of closed-fist hammer blows to Jamie's face. Jamie was trying to fend them off but darkness was closing in around her. She couldn't get her weapon up because Singer was sitting on it. As a last resort she reached for the knife attached to her body armor. It had been a gift from her dad, a nice Bark River Recon. Many a deer and hog had been skinned with it. As she drew the knife there was a sudden pause in the assault. Jamie didn't know that Ian and stepped in and grabbed Singer by the hair, wrenching her head back. Seizing the opportunity, Jamie thrust the blade as hard as she could with her right hand into Singer's ribs.

Singer let out a yelp, looking down at Jamie with wide eyes. Jaime pulled the blade out and thrust it into her ribs again. Singer was pulled off by Ian as Jamie lay there trying to catch her breath. Her face was on fire and she could taste the blood running down the back of her throat from what she was certain was a broken nose. She coughed and a splatter of blood covered her chin.

Ian rolled Singer over and quickly cuffed her. Once secure he dropped down beside Jamie, cradling her head. Then he saw the knife and the blood.

"You're going to be all right," Ian reassured her, then called out, "Doc!"

She didn't reply to say she wasn't hurt—even the effort of breathing hurt. Doc was quickly at her side, checking her over. Seeing the knife on the ground, he started looking for wounds, but only found fresh blood.

"Jamie, have you been stabbed? Are you cut?" he asked as he undid her armor.

Rolling her head to the side she spat a slug of blood into the sand. In a garbled voice she replied, "It's not me, it's her. I stuck that bitch."

Doc stepped over to Singer and rolled her over, but it was obvious she was dead. Doc left her and returned to Jamie who was now trying to sit up. He started wiping the blood from her face, but Jamie pushed his hands away. "I'm fine, Doc, let me just sit up."

"You think you're fine, let's get you up."

While Doc worked on Jamie, the rest of the prisoners were being secured, the fight having been quickly put down. Tabor and Ed were lying facedown in the sand, side by side. Mike and Ted jerked them to their feet. Sarge led them at gunpoint to the door of the bus. As Tabor approached the door, he asked with a heavy voice, "Where are we going?" His upper lip was split in two just right of center, which gave him a grotesque look.

"When the bus stops you'll know," Sarge replied with a smile.

"What do you people think you're doing? What do you think you're going to accomplish?"

"You had these people living like prisoners. You should be ashamed of yourselves, acting as if you were higher than God. I guess if you think you're the solution to cleaning up this mess we're in, then maybe the government isn't the answer to everything. What'd you guys think you were going to do, lock everyone up? You can't cage the entire country."

"This ain't over yet. I'll be seeing you again," Tabor spat.

Sarge smiled. "Every boy needs a dream, and I hate to squash dreams, but I'll make an exception for you. This is over, Sport, and somehow I don't think we'll ever see each other again." Tabor glared back in response. Sarge looked at Ian. "This one here needs some cuffs."

After Tabor was cuffed and led on the bus, two Guardsmen brought Niigata over. As Ian was cuffing Niigata, Sarge looked at him. "So what's *your* story? What'd you think *you* were going to accomplish?"

With great effort Shane managed to walk over to the bus, and instead answered Sarge's question. "He's their interrogator. And he's a piece of shit too."

Sarge looked at him. "Well then, looks like you're getting on the bus too."

"Nothing more than an inconvenience," Niigata replied, then looked at Shane. "I'm sure everything will work out, one way or another."

Shane spat into Niigata's face, he smiled. "And here I thought you and I were friends."

"You're lucky I don't kill you," Shane replied.

"I'm sure it wouldn't be that easy."

Sarge raised his pistol and put it against Niigata's temple. "Wanna bet?"

Niigata glanced sideways but said nothing.

"Lower the pistol, this is done!" Sheffield ordered.

Sarge raised the muzzle. "Guess we'll have to wait and see."

"So it would seem," Niigata replied.

"Get them on the bus," Sheffield ordered.

Once the bus was loaded, Sheffield walked up to the officer in charge of the security detail. "Thanks for taking them off my hands."

"Oh, you're welcome. Now I've got to deal with them. They should feel at home once we get them there," he replied with a smile.

Sheffield smiled. "Better you than me. How many of them are there in Frostproof?"

"Oh, there's a ton. They've been consolidating from all the camps. Originally, they were holding them at MacDill, but now that we've taken over the camp in Frostproof, they're shipping them all there. It's one of those FEMA camps that everyone used to say didn't exist. You know, I used to hear about those things, and I was one of the people always saying it was all bullshit"—he shook his head—"but I can assure you it's all true."

"What's the plan for them?" Sheffield asked.

"Shit, like I'd know. You're a captain and you're asking me?"

Sheffield laughed. "Guess you've got a point. Thanks for taking care of this situation. And thanks for the supplies you brought."

"Well, I was told to tell you there won't be any more."

"I appreciate it anyway, thanks."

The officer stepped up on the side of the Hummer. Giving a loud whistle, he twirled his hand in the air to signal the convoy to pull out. Everyone watched as the buses and Hummers drove toward the gate.

"Damn. I'm glad they're gone. That was a shit show," Livingston said, giving voice to what everyone else was thinking.

"We're going to take Jamie to the clinic to check her out," Doc said as Ian helped her get in a Hummer.

"She all right?" Sheffield asked.

"Yeah, she just took a bit of a beatin'," Doc replied.

Sheffield looked over at Singer's body. "Who shot her?"

"No one. Jamie stuck a blade in her."

"I know I heard a shot," Sheffield replied.

"I shot one of them 'civilians' that was rushing in to help them," Sarge said.

"What? What civilians?" Livingston asked.

"Remember them ones that was getting close to the bus, you told them to back up?" Livingston nodded. "When the fight started they tried to rush in, so I put a round into one of them. You didn't even see them, did you?" Sarge replied.

Sheffield looked around. "Where's the body, the guy you shot?"

"One of his buddies helped carry him off," Sarge replied.

Sheffield turned to Livingston. "Get a detail together to find them."

Livingston nodded. "Hey, Perez! Get some guys and find the civilian who's been shot."

Perez nodded and waved at a couple of the Guardsmen. Mike and Ted walked past Sarge, telling him they were going to the clinic to check on Jamie.

Sheffield turned to face Sarge. Jabbing his finger at him, he shouted, "I told you no shooting!"

"Did you even see those guys coming in? Why didn't you know one of them was DHS? He was hiding here right in the midst of you people and you had no idea," Sarge shot back.

"A gun isn't the answer to every problem."

"Quite to the contrary, Captain, it's been my experience that pulling a trigger usually takes care of the problem, permanently."

Sheffield shook his head in disgust.

"With the threat gone, what's your plan for shutting everything down?" Sarge asked, trying to change the topic.

"I've got orders to move back to the armory, so that's what we're going to do," Sheffield replied.

"What about for releasing the civilians? What's your plan for them?"

Sheffield looked at the camp. "We'll do it in waves. You know my feelings on the issue. Try to be as humane as possible. I don't think now is the time for us to be abandoning people.

If there ever was a time for us to be assisting the citizens of this country, it's now."

"If it were like Katrina, isolated in scope, then I would agree. But this is the entire country. It's everyone, and the full might of the combined branches of all services couldn't make a dent in this," Sarge replied.

"I hate to say it, Cap, but he's right," Livingston added.

"It just feels to me like we're running out on people," Sheffield replied tiredly.

"Then take comfort in the fact that it's not your decision," Livingston said.

Sheffield looked at him. "And live with the fact that I'm essentially throwing people out to their deaths? It just doesn't seem right to me. I don't want that on my conscience."

"Captain, be realistic. How long do you think you can take care of them if you try? How long can you feed them and your people? What if more people arrive and want to come in? You're looking at a headache of management at the least, a full-blown crisis or mutiny if it continues. And those civilians before . . . You think they were aligned with DHS? Better to shut it down," Sarge said.

Sheffield shifted on his feet. "The decision has been made. We're heading back into town."

"That'd be a good idea. Get you closer to the community, offer protection. There's a lot of badness coming our way soon," Sarge added.

Sheffield raised his eyebrows. "What do you mean?"

"Where you from, Cap'n?" Sarge drawled.

"I'm from upstate New York, been down here for a couple of years. Why?"

"Then you probably haven't been able to experience the

best of our hurricane season, my friend. Another couple of months it's going to kick off, maybe we'll get lucky, maybe we'll get hit. Hell, in oh-four they played a game of piñata with us."

"The last thing we need is a damn hurricane," Sheffield said, scratching his head. Even over the time period Sarge had known him, the captain looked like he had aged years. "We wouldn't even have any warning, would we?" he said, sounding exhausted.

"Not sure what kind of satellite resources the boys upstairs at MacDill have. They may be able to give us a warning, but I wouldn't count on it."

Sheffield paced around. "You bring up some good points. I need to talk to Livingston about how this will all play out. We need to weigh out the needs of who is here versus the needs of the community. I don't want to just abandon these folks. I want to give them as much of a chance as we can."

Sarge leaned back and put his hands behind his head. "I didn't say it would be easy, but you gotta watch out for your own hide, just take it from me."

As they were finishing up their chat, Livingston pulled up in front of the Hummer with Kay in tow. She looked up at Sarge. "Well, hi, Linus. Nice to see you again."

The old man smiled. "Good to see you too, Miss Kay."

She smiled and looked at Sheffield. "Captain, what can I do for you?"

"First, some good news: the boys from the Frostproof camp came with some supplies. I want you to look it over and give me an idea of what it will do for us, how long it will last."

"Well, how many people do we have here now that the DHS are gone?" Kay asked.

Sheffield looked at Livingston. "Last count was two hundred and seventeen civilians, but some leave every day, it seems, plus our people. We're currently just shy of a hundred including dependents."

Kay looked at the stack of boxes. They had various labels on them: MOUNTAIN HOUSE, THRIVE, and several others. All contained cans of various freeze-dried foods.

Kay squinted and let out a long exhale. "Even with this, we're really going to be stretching it. There's just so many mouths to feed," Kay said. "I'm trying to do my best. I've already cut back to two meals a day, but I don't know how long we can hold out with what's on hand plus this. We might get two weeks if we're feeding everyone." She paused and timidly asked, "What's the government doing with this stuff? It looks civilian."

"The DHS went on a spending spree a couple years ago, stocking up on freeze-dried food and ammo," Sarge replied. "It was all over the place. I followed a lot of alternative news, but it got so bad it actually made it into the mainstream media, though they didn't do much with it."

"Oh, I never heard about that. Why would they do that, though?" Kay asked.

Sarge held his arms out and spun around. "Look around, what do you think?"

Surprised, Kay asked, "You think they knew this was coming?"

"Knew? Hell, I think they were in on it."

Sheffield stared at the boxes, then rubbed his temples. Two weeks? This was so much more than he had bargained for. He was fine with taking care of his unit. He could depend on them, and for the most part they took orders and pitched in.

But these civilians were a different story. There were just so many of them, and many offered little effort in the maintenance of their own lives. It made for a heavy burden.

Sheffield rubbed his chin. "LT, join me in my office."

Sheffield fell into the chair behind the desk and let out a long breath. Livingston took a seat across from him. "What's on your mind?"

"I don't know how to do this. I mean, how do we tell these people?"

"I guess we just tell them like it is. They've got to move on. Tell them that right now we're just not in a position to support them."

"Why did they send us in here to do this? What was the point of taking over the camp just to leave it?" Sheffield asked.

Livingston laughed. "For the same reason we'd take cities in Iraq only to leave them. Remember, *military intelligence* is an oxymoron."

"I wish MacDill would give me more info. If I knew what was going on it would really help."

"All we can do is act on the orders we have, like it or not."

"Get all the squad leaders in here so we can brief them. They need to know what's going on," Sheffield said.

Livingston nodded and left the office. Seeing him leave, Sarge stuck his head in the door. "What's the plan, Captain?"

Sheffield rubbed his face. This was really wearing on him. "We're going to brief the squad leaders, give them time to get their people up to speed, then I'll address the camp."

Sarge nodded. "Good deal. I know you don't like it, but the sooner we deal with this the better."

Sheffield nodded. "Let's go over to the conference room. They should start showing up pretty quick."

Once all the NCOs were accounted for, Sheffield stood up. "All right, listen up. Some things have changed and you guys need to be aware of them. We're now in regular contact with command at MacDill in Tampa." This wasn't news to many of the assembled—the rumor mill was fast and efficient. "We've been ordered to close the camp. We're relocating back to the armory, and before you ask, no, I don't know why. In a little while, after you've had time to inform your people, I'll address the camp and let the refugees know we're leaving."

"Why'd we even bother with this, then?" Perez asked.

"Because we had orders. Now we have new ones. I don't make them up and I don't know any more than I've just told you. We were ordered back to the armory and are to await further orders."

A staff sergeant in the back of the room called out, "What are we supposed to do with all these people?"

"As much as I hate to say this, it's not our problem." The statement stirred those assembled, and they began talking among themselves, Sheffield raised his voice and continued, "MacDill is of the opinion that these folks are in the same position as everyone else. Nowadays, everyone is essentially a refugee, and we are no longer in the refugee business. I don't like it any more than you do, but we have orders and we will carry them out." Sheffield paused, and there were no comments. "I'll give you thirty minutes to let your people know before I address the refugees. Get to it."

The squad leaders quickly got to their feet and left the room. Sheffield looked over at Sarge, and the old man nodded his approval.

"All right, LT, call them together for an address. We're going to start putting them out. Let's go through the gear we have and see how we can equip them. I don't want to send them out with nothing."

"What about weapons? You know they're going to ask," Livingston asked.

Sheffield looked at him. "Okay, but only what we retained from when the DHS did their sweeps of the civilians. No military-grade hardware. And do something with that body," he added, referring to Singer's corpse.

"Roger that, boss," Livingston replied and headed off to make an announcement to the camp.

"Have you sent anyone out to the armory yet, to check on it?" Sarge asked.

"No, we only got the orders this morning, but we need to. As soon as this address is over we'll get a patrol down there."

"You look like shit, Jamie." Ian said with a smile. Doc had moved her back to the barracks and was examining her more closely there.

Jamie turned her head. Her left eye was nearly swollen shut and her lip was likewise inflated. She did indeed look like shit.

"Go to hell, Ian," she said through gritted teeth.

Doc checked her ears and eyes, trying to raise the lid of the left eye to check her pupils. While it looked bad, Doc pronounced that she wasn't in any immediate danger.

"You'll be sore and sport some trophies for a couple of weeks, but you'll be all right. Just take it slow for a while. I'll talk to the captain and tell him to go easy on you." Jamie gave him a smile of thanks. She wasn't one to lie around and not pull her weight, but she knew she needed a little time to recover.

Mike and Ted walked in. Ted gripped her shoulder. "How you doing, kid?" She simply nodded in response.

Mike stepped up beside her and made a show of looking her over. "You know, I think you're a little young for plastic surgery."

Jamie swatted him with the back of her hand.

"Get some rest. We'll watch out for you," Mike said, giving her hand a squeeze. To his surprise she squeezed back, holding it just a moment longer.

Ted's radio crackled and Sarge's voice filled the air. *"Teddy, you and Mike meet me over at the command bunker."*

"Roger that," he replied, then looked at Mike. "Let's go."

Mike looked at Jamie. "I'll check on you later."

Mike and Ted walked out to the Hummer, they got in, and before Ted started it up he looked at Mike. Mike looked over. "What?"

"You finally making a little headway with her?"

Mike rolled his eyes. "Shut up and drive."

As Ted pressed the starter he smiled and began to sing, "Jamie and Mike sitting in a tree, *K-I-S-S-I-N-G*!"

Mike looked at him. "What are you, four?" Ted let out an uproarious laugh and floored the truck, tossing a spray of sand into the air.

At the command bunker they got out and found Sarge. "What's up, boss?"

Sarge pointed at Sheffield. "Captain here's about to make an announcement that some of these folks aren't going to like. I want you to go to the armory and get out some of the less-lethal goodies in case they get out of hand."

Ted nodded as he and Mike started walking toward the bunker that contained all the things that go bang. A Guardsman was standing watch in front of it. He smiled and nodded as they approached. "You guys my relief?"

"Sorry, man, we're not. We just need some stuff."

"Damn," he replied as he opened the padlock on the door.

Inside the two guys hung tear-gas grenades on their body armor and filled their pockets with more. Mike grabbed a shotgun from a ready rack and looked around for the less-lethal shells. Finding them he loaded the Remington 870 and opened the dump pouch on his belt and emptied several boxes of shells into it. Ted took another shotgun and did the same.

"See anything else we need?" Ted asked.

"Nah, I think this will do it," Mike replied.

As they emerged from the bunker the guard asked, "What's with that stuff? What's going on?"

"They're about to make an announcement, telling the folks here they ain't got to go home but they can't stay here anymore," Mike said.

"No shit. I was just told but didn't believe it. Guess it's legit."

"Looks like it. Keep an eye on this place. Some of them might get some bright ideas. I'll have another one or two sent over here to back you up," Ted replied.

"Great. And tell them to bring some water too. I'm dyin' out here."

Ted nodded and he and Mike headed back to the command bunker. As they walked, the PA system in the camp announced itself with a high-pitched squeal. Livingston's voice quickly followed, telling the refugees in the camp to assemble for an address from the camp commander.

"Hey, what's going on?" a man asked Ted.

"I don't know. Guess we'll all find out," Ted replied.

"Hey, when's lunch going to be served today? There wasn't any breakfast," a woman said.

"Don't know about that one either."

"This is bullshit," a third added. Mike and Ted shrugged in response.

Once out of earshot, Mike said, "Oh boy, this is going to be interesting."

"Ya think?"

Back at the command bunker, Ted approached Sheffield. "Hey, Cap, there's only one guard on the armory. It might be a good idea to send a couple more over there in case these folks get any ideas."

Sheffield told Ian to take care of it. Ian nodded and walked off to find a couple of volunteers.

"Looks like they're gathering up, Captain. You ready?" Sarge asked.

Sheffield nodded, a hint of nervousness on his face.

"Just tell them like it is, remember that. You've got orders to close the camp. They've got to start taking care of themselves like the rest of the country is. It is what it is."

Sheffield stood up straighter, like he got a shot of confidence. "Exactly. They're not the only ones. We're all refugees now."

"Times, they are a-changin'."

Sheffield let out a long breath and headed out to face the assembled crowd. Mike and Ted took up positions flanking the captain on either side. Livingston handed Sheffield a mic as the crowd continued to build. Scanning the crowd as the last of the civilians trickled in, Sheffield began.

"Thank you for giving me your time. As I hope most of you know, I am Captain Sheffield of the Florida National Guard. I am truly troubled by what I am about to tell you."

He paused for a moment to gauge the crowd, noting the sideways whispers and furtive glances to one another. "We are no longer in a position to provide for you. We have been ordered by the upper levels of our command to close the camp. We are currently inventorying the supplies of the camp and will provide you as much as we can."

Suddenly the nervous crowd became animated, seemingly vibrating with action as people moved about, talking to one another. From the crowd a man's voice shouted the question, "What does that mean to us?"

Sheffield took a deep breath. "It means you're going to have to leave."

The crowd erupted in shouts and cries. The reaction of the adults scared several of the children in the assembly and soon they were crying, adding to the commotion.

"I know this is a scary thing. Believe me, we understand. But there is not enough food here and there simply isn't anything we can scavenge from the surrounding area. If you stay here, you'll simply starve."

A man burst forth from the crowd and raised an accusatory finger at Sheffield. "Why did you do this? Why are you here if you can't take care of us? At least the DHS fed us!" There were shouts of agreement from the crowd, as well as accusations.

"You just want to keep the food for yourselves!" a woman shouted from the crowd.

"You said you were here to protect us! What are we supposed to do?" a woman cried out, her voice cracking.

"We didn't ask for you to *save* us!" a man shouted in a sneer. "Now you're going to kill us all!"

In an attempt to keep things from getting worse, Sheffield offered them support. "Look, we're not going to just send you down the road. We'll provide you with equipment, what food we can, and some weapons so you can defend yourselves."

For some in the crowd, hearing *weapons* got their attention. "Weapons, what sort of weapons?" a man called out.

"We have a collection of confiscated weapons that we'll hand out, with as much ammo as there is for them," Sheffield replied.

"Hell, if you'll give me a gun, I'll leave now!"

"I say we just stay here. They can't make us leave!" another shouted.

"Screw that, let's just take what we want and get out of here!" a man shouted.

"This isn't going to deteriorate into a riot. You're not going to loot this camp. We will organize the distribution of supplies, and weapons will be distributed at the gate on your way out. Anyone who tries to take anything will be dealt with accordingly. The fact is we can no longer stay here. The camp is closing. My people are pulling out as well," Sheffield announced.

"If you're leaving, then why can't we stay? Take your shit and go, we'll stay here!" a burly man shouted, then added, "Who's with me?"

The crowd erupted in shouts and applause. Sheffield looked at Sarge questioningly, and Sarge simply shrugged his shoulders.

Turning back to the crowd, Sheffield asked, "How do you intend to provide for yourselves? We have brought in water, and the food supply here will last two weeks, tops. How will you survive out here?"

"Don't worry about us, just get out! Leave us the tents and other equipment you offered and let us sort it out," the man shouted back.

Sheffield turned to Livingston, putting his hand over the mic. "What do you think?"

He shrugged. "We need to organize some things for those who want to go, but as for the rest . . . it's their death wish."

Sheffield turned back to the crowd. "I'll consult with my staff about you staying here. If we agree to it, we'll leave you as much as we can in the way of supplies, but you've got to understand there isn't anything around here for you in terms of food."

"Let us worry about that," the man at the front of the crowd replied, venom in his voice.

Sheffield motioned for the man to step forward. Pulling him off to the side, he said, "I'll work with you on this transition. Get whoever wants to stay together and decide who's in charge. I'll deal with one or two of you, but I'm not going to have hundreds of people shouting demands at me." The man nodded his approval. "But that means I will also hold whoever is selected accountable for the actions of the people here." The man nodded again, and Sheffield stuck out his hand. "What's your name?"

"Neil Baker," the man said as he shook Sheffield's hand.

"All right, Neil, I'll get with you later today. Where do you live?"

"Tent thirty-seven. Ask anyone around and they'll know where to find me."

Sheffield nodded. "I'll find you later to discuss the transition."

Neil nodded and walked back to the crowd, which parted as if he were Moses and they were the sea. Sarge walked up beside Sheffield. "You better keep an eye on that one, Captain."

Without looking over, Sheffield replied, "I told him whoever they select to represent their interests is accountable for the actions of the people here in the camp until we leave."

"I've got a feeling this isn't going to be as easy as you think."

Sheffield looked over. "What else can I do? If they want to stay, who am I to make them leave?" He paused and looked at the departing crowd. "They just don't understand what they're getting into."

"Some lessons have to be learned the hard way."

Livingston snorted. "They're about to get a hell of an education."

"Amen, LT. Now let's get a patrol headed toward the armory. I need to get more details about its condition ASAP."

Chapter 5

Tyler and I made the trip back to the house as fast as we could, practically jogging. As was now the custom, everyone was at Danny's place as it was getting on to suppertime. I told them about meeting Gena and Dylan, and the trade I was about to make. Danny in particular was impressed. "Mead? Why you holdin' out on us, brother?"

"I just got it, can't a man have a drink? Sheesh."

We passed the bottles of mead around. It was a big hit—everyone was commenting on the unique flavors.

"Can I try some, Dad?" Taylor asked.

Mel swatted at her. "Just because there's no laws here right now, doesn't mean you're allowed to be drinking in my household."

Jess was taking a sip from one of the bottles. Mary was watching her closely. Lowering the bottle, Jess wiped a small trickle running down her chin. She held the bottle out. "Want some?"

Mary smiled. "You know I don't drink."

Fred grabbed the bottle and took a long tug and stuck it in Mary's lap. "Girl, right now *you* could use a drink, trust me."

Mary looked at the bottle for a moment before taking a timid sip. As she did, Fred reached over and lifted the bottom of the bottle. Mary's eyes grew wide as the honey-flavored liquor flowed into her mouth. Fred and Jess started to laugh as Mary's cheeks were swollen, like a chipmunk hoarding nuts. After a couple of swallows she held the bottle out and looked at it. "That's really good!" she finally said and turned it up to take another. When she lowered the bottle, Fred took it from her.

"Careful, it'll sneak up on you," she said, then took another drink herself and passed it Jeff.

Jeff smiled. "Let me show you how to do this." He turned the bottle up like a professional drinker.

Thad rolled his eyes and grabbed the bottle, wrenching it from Jeff's hand, spilling a little down his shirt. "You ain't the only one needs a drink around here," he said with a smile before taking a drink himself.

As I filled a baggie with kudzu flour, I talked about the beautiful greenhouse that Gena kept with all the fruits and veggies growing in it. Thad was really interested in the greenhouse and said he wanted to go back with me. Brandy volunteered to cook in his place, and Mel and Bobbie jumped in to offer assistance as well.

Mary raised a hand. "I'd like to help too."

Mel smiled. "The more the merrier, come on." The ladies disappeared into the kitchen.

As I moved around the kitchen, gathering what we needed to trade, I asked Aric how he was feeling.

"Useless," he replied.

"How's the shoulder?"

"It's all right, I just feel like a mooch not doing anything," Aric replied, staring at the floor.

"Don't sweat it, man. You're still healing. There'll be plenty for you to do when you're back up to speed," Danny said. I nodded, and patted him on the back. "You'll be back in fighting shape in no time."

As the women sorted out dinner, I knew it was time to make our exit.

"You ready, Thad?"

"Yeah, I got the liver. Did you get the salt?"

"I did. And, hey, do me a favor and grab them some of the mullet too."

Thad took a plastic shopping bag and put a few handfuls of the smoked fish in it. Once that was done, we went and climbed on the ATVs to make the trip as fast as possible. Gena and Dylan were still sitting on the front porch when we returned. I introduced Thad to the couple.

"Good to meet you," Dylan said.

"An' you an' the missus too," Thad replied.

"Morgan, we were talking while you were gone. A few weeks ago, we heard a lot of shooting, out that way," she said, pointing her arm toward the direction of our neighborhood. "Was that you guys?" Gena asked.

"'Bout a month and a half ago? Yep, that was probably us," I replied.

"Well, glad to see you guys made it through," Dylan said.

"We were getting visits from some local goons the DHS were using. When we fended them off, the Feds decided we weren't getting the hint and paid us a visit personally."

"How have you guys managed to stay hidden so long?" Thad asked.

"Oh, we haven't been totally hidden. We've had our share of visitors," Gena answered.

"What'd you do when they arrived?" I asked.

"Oh, I've got the answer for most folks. Got this big-ass

sword in the house. It's a cheap piece of junk but looks badass," Dylan said.

"You scared them off with a sword?" Thad asked, eyebrows raised.

"Yeah, if he was running at you naked with a big-ass sword, wouldn't you run?" Gena asked, trying not to laugh.

I thought about it for a minute, then a smile started to spread across my face. "Yeah, guess I would."

"People are scared of two things: crazy people and naked people. Add them together and it scares the shit out of folks. Plus, if they think you're nuts, they think you ain't got nothing," Dylan said. Thad and I both busted out laughing.

"I guess so," I replied, "but how did you avoid the Feds?"

"Oh, they sent one of their mailmen around once," Dylan said with a grin.

"What happened?" Thad asked.

"Batman buried him under the compost pile. He tried to tell us we had to move and that we were going to be taken to different places. Batman told him that wasn't going to happen and he told us, with some colorful language, that we would go where we were told. That didn't sit well with Batman," Gena answered.

"Sit well? Pissed me right off. I got the feeling that if he made it back to wherever he was going we'd have trouble. He didn't make it back to wherever," Dylan said.

Gena asked me, "Did you guys ever run into any, wanting you to register or some such thing?"

"Nope, and guessin' on the outcome, he came here first." My answer got a laugh out of Dylan and Gena.

"What about you, Thad? You ever see one?" Dylan asked.

"Yeah, I encountered one. Fed him to the hogs."

Dylan smiled. "Hogs gotta eat too."

"That they do. And speaking of food, we brought you some smoked mullet too," Thad said, holding the bag. It was clear he wanted to change the subject, not wanting to further discuss the painful memories of that day.

"Oh, that's great! I'll make a dip out of it," Gena said as she took the bag.

I held up the flour. "Brought you some kudzu flour too. You can use it to dust the liver before you cook it, or to thicken stews, that sort of thing."

Dylan took the bag. "Did you say kudzu flour?" he asked looking suspiciously into the bag.

"Oh yeah, you can eat all parts of it except for the little tubers that grow aboveground," I replied.

With a look of surprise on his face, he said, "No shit? I didn't know that!" I went on to tell them about making chips out of the tender leaves and how the flowers were also edible. Once we'd made our exchange, Dylan went into the house and returned with several large sacks, stuffed full.

"Oh wow," Thad said as he took them. "That's a lot of groceries."

"Don't worry, we got plenty, I also put some honeycomb in there for the little ones. You didn't say how many there were, but it should be plenty," Gena said.

Thad looked up, his eyes wide. "Ooh, I like me some honeycomb," he said, rubbing his hands together.

Gena squinted an eye, and, pointing at him, she replied, "Now, those honeycombs are for them little ones, Thad."

A big grin spread across his face. "Yes, ma'am. Maybe next time."

"That's better." Turning back to me she pulled a small vial out of her pocket. "Here's the medicine."

We thanked them for everything, making plans to drop in on each other. Gena said she didn't like to leave the house, but maybe Dylan could come by for a visit. I told them we would bring meat over whenever we had it and how much I appreciated the trade. In my mind, we certainly got the better end of the deal. They assured us they were very happy with the trade. Having not had any meat in a while, they were really looking forward to the liver.

"It's going to be dark soon. We'll see you guys later," I said, and they agreed.

Thad and I waved as we fired up the ATVs. As we pulled out onto the road, we both stopped instantly. A large group of people were walking down the road, like a herd of cows. They took up both lanes as they approached.

"We won't make it to the turnoff before they do," Thad said.

I was nodding my head. "I was thinking the same thing. I damn sure don't want them to see us turn off there."

"I don't think they've seen us yet."

"They sure don't act like it. Let's just head that direction. We'll go past our road and turn into the woods, come in the back way," I said.

Thad adjusted the shotgun in his lap. "All right"—he looked over at my rifle—"that thing ready?"

I checked the safety. "Yeah, but I sure hope it doesn't come to that. There's a hell of a lot more of them than there are of us."

Thad was correct that they didn't see us initially, because it was obvious when they did. The men in the group ran to the front, with the women and a handful of kids behind them.

"They see us now," I said.

"Yeah, they do. Let's just keep moving."

The group had stopped almost in front of our road. We approached them slowly, trying not to look intimidating. I was now really regretting the slight buzz the liquor had given me. As we drew near, several of the men shouldered their weapons. While not pointed directly at us, the message was clear. We stopped fifty or so feet from them, I raised one of my hands. "We don't mean no harm."

The men looked at one another and to the side of the road, they were clearly nervous. One of them finally spoke up, "We're just passing through!"

"So are we," Thad replied.

Another of the group stepped forward. "How is it you got gas for them four-wheelers?"

"All we have is what's in them. When they run dry they'll sit where they stop," I replied. Just a little lie.

"Well, what's so important that you would use the last of your gas for it?"

Thad looked at me. He was holding the bag of veggies on his lap, and it gave me an idea. "We went to the market in town for a little trading."

The men exchanged words that we couldn't hear, then the one questioning us spoke again. "Where's this market?"

"It's in Eustis," I said, jabbing a thumb over my shoulder to the south.

"What'd you trade for?"

Thad answered before I could. "I don't think that much matters."

The man pointed behind him. "We got hungry young 'uns here. We need food."

"We can relate, so do we," Thad replied.

The man looked around. "Where y'all stay at?"

"That doesn't matter either," I said.

"I reckon it does, you want past us. There's more of us than there is of you, and if you want by you'll have to give us the food you've got." One of the women came forward and pulled on his sleeve. She said something to him and he pushed her away.

"We can't do that either. We don't have much and we have families too," Thad replied evenly.

"All I'm asking for is some food." He hesitated for a moment, then his demeanor changed: he became very animated and gripped his rifle in front of him and started shouting, "Or we can just take your food and your wheelers!"

Thad muttered, "Oh shit."

"Yeah, that's what I was thinking," I replied.

Our lack of immediate reply seemed to annoy him even more. "Well! What's it going to be!"

"Look, we don't want any trouble, we already told you that. You go your way and we'll go ours. When you get to Eustis you can trade for food there," I replied.

"Trade! What the hell you think we got to trade! You ain't getting past me till you give it up!"

"This ain't working," Thad whispered.

"I know, let's try it a different way," I whispered back, then stood up on the footrests. "No, plain and simple. No."

The words seemed to stun the man as though he were physically struck by them. He looked at the men to his side, then back at us. Just as he was about to speak I quickly raised my carbine and started to shout at the top of my lungs in a maniacal tone, "There may be more of you than there are of us, but garun-damn-tee you one thing, you will be the first to die! Bullets don't discriminate, and them young 'uns behind you will probably be hit by the rounds that pass through your worthless ass! Someone will be burying your kids tonight!"

The men with him took a step back, looking at one another uncertainly. The man I was addressing stood there as if turning the statement over in his mind. The woman who had tugged on his sleeve earlier now ran forward and pulled at him, obviously pleading with him. His eyes stayed fixed on me with an expression I couldn't quite make out.

I wanted this resolved—we weren't getting anywhere standing in the middle of the road. "What's it going to be?" I shouted. "There's only two things stopping you right now: fear and common sense, and somehow I don't think you got much in the way of sense, common or otherwise!"

One of the other men with him held up a hand. "Look, mister, we don't want no trouble, he's just wore out." He swept his hand at the crowd behind him. "We all are."

"Then be on your way. We'll pull off the road here and let you pass, like I originally said."

The man nodded and Thad and I pulled off the road, turning so we were facing it. The group started to move, making their way to the far side of the paved strip.

"I can't believe that worked," Thad whispered.

I gave a little laugh while keeping my eyes on the group. "Tell me about it. Guess what ole Dylan said about crazy people was right."

I heard Thad snort and chanced a quick glance at him. Even though he had a hand up over his face I could still see his grin. "What?" I asked.

Trying to stifle his laughter, he replied, "I'm just glad you didn't get nekkid."

Despite the tension of the moment it was all I could do not to start laughing. I would have been okay too if Thad hadn't looked at me from between his fingers. I could see tears on his cheeks. I could only imagine what these people thought of us as they came closer, Thad with his face in hands, me grinning like some kind of water-headed moron. But seeing the look on the face of the man who'd challenged us took all the funny out of the moment and I was instantly back into reality. He was staring—no, glaring at me as he passed. I casually shifted the muzzle of the carbine so it was lying on the handlebars, the message clear.

The other men in the group offered little more than furtive glances as they passed. The women did look in our direction, one actually offering a small nod, which I returned. Once they passed we waited for them to get some distance, making sure they didn't turn off on Gena and Dylan's road. When we were comfortable with the distance between us we started up the ATVs and headed down the road, taking the trail through the woods. Thad slowed nearly to a stop. I did as well.

"What?" I asked.

"That was a big group. Why was a group that big on the move?"

"I don't know, but I get what you mean. Something's pushing them."

Thad sat there for a moment, then looked at me, his face almost solemn, and said, "Nekkid," before bursting out in laughter. It caused me to crack up too, and we rode the rest of the way to the house laughing so hard the tears made it hard to see. As we slowly moved down the last stretch of dirt road to Danny's house Thad looked over with a sobered look on his face. "You wanna tell everyone about this?"

I nodded. "I think we should. We should have had someone at the barricade too. We can't leave it unmanned anymore. I hope Danny has that schedule ready."

We arrived at twilight, bags of produce in hand. Mel was out on the porch, chatting with Jess and Fred as we pulled in.

"Where on earth have you guys been? I thought that was going to be a short trip. We've been ready to make dinner for an hour."

"Yeah," said Jess. "I'm about ready to eat my hand."

I looked at Thad. "Sorry, ladies, but we had some . . . technical difficulties. I'll explain later," I said. "Now can you help us with our loot?"

It was an incredible haul of garden goodness, with everything from tomatoes and potatoes to carrots and some squash. One bag was completely full of potatoes, enough to make a couple of meals for everyone.

"Can we have mashed potatoes, please, please, please?" Little Bit said, jumping up and down. The other kids got excited too.

I laughed at the sight of their eager faces. Grinning, I mussed her hair. "You bet, kiddo." After the incident, seeing her smiling face was the best feeling in the world.

"Hey, we gotta save some for stew!" Lee Ann called from the other side of the kitchen, where she was unloading some carrots.

"Oh, I can already see it—a nice stew, with some carrots,

potatoes, some of that deer meat," Thad said, rubbing his stomach.

"Stop talking about food," Taylor groaned. "I'm *starving*."

Mary was leaning on the bar and looked at Taylor. "Girl, let me tell you, you don't know what hungry is."

I rolled my eyes. "Teenagers." That got a laugh out of everyone, except for Taylor, that is.

Mel held up the jar with the comb in it.

"What's this?"

"Gena put that in for the kids, a little sweet for them," Thad answered.

The word *sweet* got their attention and they quickly came running to look at the comb.

"Can we please have some now?" Edie asked.

Mel put the jar on a windowsill. "After you eat your dinner."

Because we were held up, we all pitched in for dinner, and I have to say, it was fantastic. We made steamed squash and a Dutch oven full of fried potatoes and onions to go along with the venison. Having some fresh food had a big impact on everyone's mood. The talk was lively with lots of laughter. It was an incredible evening, probably one of the best since the lights went out. After we ate, the adults sat around on the back porch passing the last bottle of mead around. Having gone for so long without alcohol, it provided a really nice buzz.

Little Bit, Edie, and Jace came running out onto the porch. "Mom, can we have the honeycomb now?" Little Bit asked.

"Sure, let me get it," Mel said as she stood up and headed for the kitchen.

The kids were jumping up and down in excitement. When she returned, Mel took a long piece of comb from the jar and broke it into three pieces, handing one to each of the kids. Little Bit immediately stuck hers in her mouth, while Jace and Edie looked at it uncertainly.

"Go ahead, honey. Take a bite. It's really good," Brandy encouraged. "They've never seen honeycomb before," she added.

"I remember my granny always had the jar of honey with the comb, always had to have the comb," Tyler said with a smile.

Jace held the comb to his nose and smelled it, then cautiously licked at the waxy glob. As he sucked on his tongue a smile began to spread across his face, and suddenly he thrust the whole piece into his mouth. He was still smiling as the honey began to run out of the corners of his mouth. Seeing her brother's reaction, Edie took a timid bite of hers, and just as with Jace, a broad smile spread across her face. The kids ran back into the house, quieter this time with mouthfuls of honeycomb.

"Hey, what about us? We're kids too," Taylor asked.

"Really? I'll remember that next time you ask to try this," I said, holding up the bottle of mead.

Mel smiled and took out a second piece, breaking it in half and giving the older girls each a piece. They were enjoying theirs when the little ones reappeared wanting more. When Mel and Brandy said no, they descended on the older girls, trying to beg a bite off them.

Taylor held the comb aloft, keeping it out of reach of the swirling mass of kids at her feet. "No, you had yours, this is mine," she said, laughing as the kids tried to climb her like a tree.

It was fun to watch the kids being kids, laughing and playing. Laughter was a precious commodity these days. As the evening wound down, Brandy and Tyler cleaned up the kitchen. Bobbie was learning to let folks help her, so she was sitting in a chair on the porch while they went about the job. After everyone was done, I cleared my throat.

"Not to be a little black rain cloud or anything, but"—I paused for a moment to make sure I had everyone's attention—"we ran across some people on the road when we were on our way back." That certainly got their attention.

"What happened?" Danny asked.

"It was a big pack of people. They wanted food," Thad replied.

"How many of them were there?" Jess asked.

"Thirteen," Thad replied. "I counted them when they passed us."

"That's a group nearly as big as ours," Fred said.

"Did they have kids?" Brandy asked. I nodded.

"That's sad, seeing hungry children," Mary said.

"It's sadder when they're your children," Mel added. Mary gave her a "you're right" look.

"What happened?" Jeff asked.

"There was quite the lively discussion, but nothing more. We're just lucky it worked out the way it did," I replied.

Thad looked at me. "Yeah, you have quite the way with words."

"Were they armed?" Danny asked.

"Oh yeah, they were armed, but once I explained that if they took what they wanted, they would pay for it in blood, they lost the motivation to push the issue," I replied.

"Yeah, it was something like that," Thad added.

"Which brings me to the issue," I said, then looked at Danny. "You got that schedule ready yet?"

He nodded and went into the bedroom off the kitchen, returning with the wipe board. "I was going to hang it in the morning."

"Now's as good a time as any to go over it. Everyone take a look. If you have any questions now's the time to ask them."

Danny set the board on the counter, propping it against a post at the end of it. Everyone moved up to look it over, discussing the various jobs, commenting on who was with who and when. Overall it was very well received, and no one complained about any of the tasks or assignments.

"This isn't set in stone. If you need or want a change just let me know," Danny said.

"Any questions about it?" I asked.

Jess looked around. "Looks pretty simple. There's work to be done and it looks like it's divided up evenly."

"With that in mind, Thad, looks like you and Tyler are on the barricade," I said.

"I'm ready when you are," Thad said, looking at Tyler.

"Looks like me and Aric will relieve you guys later," Jeff said, then looked at Aric. "You good with that?"

Aric nodded. "Yeah, I can still shoot."

"Let me walk Mel and the girls home. I'll grab the NVGs and meet you on the road. We need to have them there at night," I said.

Mel and I walked out onto the porch as everyone got ready to leave.

Jess came out. "Morgan, I need a favor," she said.

"Sure, Jess, what is it?"

"I need a gun. I don't have one."

Seeing the opportunity to mess with her I smiled. "What happened to the last one I gave you?"

She gave me a look of frustration. "You know what happened."

"Come on over to the house. I have one I can give you."

"Thanks."

It was a large group leaving Danny and Bobbie's place, as Thad, Jeff, Jess, Fred, and Aric were all walking with us. Jeff gave Little Bit a piggyback ride. The evening was warm, the air incredibly still. There wasn't even a whisper of a breeze. For some reason, watching this moment really struck me—despite everything going on in the world, we were damn lucky. All the people in our lives now were good people. Was it just dumb luck, or was there more to it? Whatever the reason, I was thankful. It was easier to go through this with the support of likeminded friends.

As we came to our house and were about to split ways, I called out to Aric, "Hey, man. Catch."

He turned and I tossed him a small jar of the "medicine." He caught and looked at it. "Thanks, this'll help me sleep. That's all I want it for, to sleep. I'm getting better during the day."

"Whatever works for you, brother, just don't use it recreationally. We need it for medicinal purposes."

"Thanks, Morgan," Fred said as she held on to Aric's good arm. They looked like two lovebirds, another really heartwarming thing to watch blossoming in spite of the circumstances.

I told Jess to wait there for a minute and ran inside the house. I took out the .45 I'd taken off the man I found dead in his recliner. It was a nice Colt and would certainly do the job for her. Taking the pistol, a spare mag, and a box of Blazer ammo, I went back outside.

"Here, take this. It's a little like the other one I gave you except this is a .45. It works basically the same. Later this week I'll show you how to take it apart."

Jess took the pistol and looked it over quickly. She dropped the mag and stuck it in her pocket then pulled the slide back and looked into the chamber. Letting the slide close, she reinserted the mag and racked the slide, looking at it uncertainly.

"How do you put the hammer down?"

I took a few minutes to explain the safeties on the weapon and how it functioned. Once she understood there was no hammer drop and that it wasn't double-action, she said she was comfortable. She decided to keep the hammer down, for safety, understanding she would have to manually cock the weapon before firing it. I tried to explain to her that it was actually safer to have it cocked and locked but I just couldn't get it through her head.

She looked up and smiled. "Thanks, Morgan, I appreciate it. It's the second time you've given me a gun."

I smiled and nodded. Mel was standing beside me. With a smile she replied, "Just don't shoot him with this one."

Jess smiled and covered her face with her free hand. Shaking her head, she replied, "I won't, promise."

I laughed. "Damn, I hope so!"

"Good night, Mel, Morgan," Jess said, and headed off for her house.

As Mel and I went inside I jabbed her. "That was mean—funny, but mean."

"Pfft, whatever, you're just mad I said it before you did."

The girls quickly got ready for bed, each grabbing a quick drink of cold water before settling down for the night. Since moving half of the solar setup to Danny's house there wasn't enough power at my place to run the big fridge, but we did have the DC one, which was very efficient.

The house felt stuffy and warm. The thought of the heat heading our way depressed me. The summer would be miserable without AC. The only relief we would get would be from the summer storms, which of course would bring their own share of issues. Thinking about the summer storms made me think about rain and how long it'd been since it last rained. We were out on the creek the last time, I recalled, so it'd been a while. That explained the dust everywhere.

Using only the sheet to cover us, Mel and I turned in and both were quickly asleep. That was another new reality—being tired. In the Before, I would stay up late, until the wee hours of the morning, regularly, just because. Even then, when I went to bed I would lie awake, having a hard time getting to sleep. But it was different now. Unless I was on watch, I would go to bed around nine or ten and sleep soundly until the light from the sun woke me up. I guess this was how it was supposed to be. Maybe this situation was forcing us into a more natural rhythm.

Given that I could now sleep like a rock, I was surprised when I woke up in darkness, an uneasy feeling enveloping me. I lay there for a moment trying to figure out what had woken me up. It was deathly quiet. I sneezed once, and then again. Taking a sniff of the air, I could clearly smell smoke. Jumping up, I grabbed my flashlight and rifle and went to the porch, not bothering to put any pants on. I smiled when I thought of Thad, *nekkid*.

Outside the smell of smoke was much, much stronger. The air sat heavy and motionless, not a leaf or a pine needle stirred. Walking out into the yard I scanned what I could of the horizon but couldn't tell where the smoke was coming from, which was worrisome. How big was this fire? Where was it? More important, where was it heading? This last question was most troublesome.

I couldn't go back to sleep. When I got back inside, I got dressed and checked the time: 3:37 a.m. I decided to stay up and see the sun rise. Maybe the dawn would reveal where the fire was. It was killing me not to have the answer. Heck, even the dogs seemed worried. The three of them stayed on the porch with me, pacing back and forth. Drake sat staring to the north, issuing a low whine. Maybe he could sense where the fire was, I thought to myself.

Mulling this over, thoughts of my dad's days fighting wild fires for the state popped into my head. Before he retired a couple of years ago he more often than not worked on prescribed burns—wildfires were less of an issue through their use. He had taken some pictures of one of the fires he was on and showed them to me. I remember the equipment in those pictures. It was interesting to see them set the fire: what started out as a trickle of flame coming from a metal can soon turned into a huge inferno. *What was that thing called?* I tried to remember. *Something torch—duh, drip torch, that's it.*

I remember asking him then how they controlled what burned where. He said they could steer a fire where they wanted it to go using the wind and back burns, setting fires along the perimeter to use up the fuel before the fire reached it. The more I thought about what he'd told me, the more I thought it might turn out to be some very valuable information, though I hoped it wouldn't.

As night began to transition to day, I walked out into the

yard and scanned the sky. It revealed little. There was no visible column of smoke, no ash falling from the sky. Maybe it was far away or maybe upper-level winds were simply pushing the smoke away. With anxiety building, I went inside and sat down at the radio.

"Stump Knocker, you out there?"

After a pause there was a reply. *"Go for Stump Knocker."*

"Mike? That you?"

"Yeah, what's up, Morgan?"

"You guys see any fire out there on the river? Smoke or anything?"

"We're not at the river, we're at the camp, and yeah, we can smell the smoke but can't see it."

"I don't see it either, just smell it, but I'm worried."

"We are too."

"I'm going to take a ride up that way in a bit, see what I can find out."

"Come on up, we'll be here, but don't take too long. We're pulling out of here soon."

I looked at the mic. "Really? Why?" That would explain the group, I thought to myself.

"Orders."

"All right, I'll see you guys in a bit."

I laid the mic down and went back outside. The sun was higher now, but it revealed nothing new, other than it looked like it was going to be a hot day. As I sat on the porch the dogs suddenly bolted off into the yard, tails erect. Meathead barked once and I stood up and stepped off into the yard.

"I still say that dog is racist," Thad said, big smile on his face as he walked up.

I smiled. "He's just a good judge of character is all."

Thad looked around for a moment. "Wonder where this fire is."

"Don't know, I just talked to Mike. They're at the camp, and they don't see anything there but they can smell it too."

"I sure would like to know where it is. The idea of a fire right now scares me," Thad said, squinting into the rising sun as he spoke.

Knowing what had happened to his family, I could only imagine how he felt about fire. "I'm going to ride up to the camp in a bit. Wanna go?"

Thad nodded. "Yeah, when are you gonna leave?"

"In a few minutes. I'm going to go over and see if Danny wants to go too."

"Sure, let me get my stuff. I'll be back in a few." As Thad walked back home, I headed over to Danny's place.

Danny was sitting on the front porch when I walked up. "Something's burning," he said by way of greeting.

"You don't have to tell me, brother. I've been up since three thirty. I'm going to take a ride up to the camp to see what I can make out. You wanna go?"

"Yep, let me get my boots on."

"Just come over to the house. I'm going to let Mel know we're leaving," I said as I headed back toward the house.

Mel was still in bed when I got back. Sitting on the edge of the bed, I told her about the smoke, which alarmed her.

"Do you think it's close?" she asked. Fear shone in her eyes.

"I can't tell, but that's why we're going to check it out. Mike's down at the camp, he said they could smell it but couldn't see it."

She nodded, taking in the details. "How long are you going to be gone?"

"I don't know, depends on what we find."

She sat up. "Oh no, I can smell it now. I hope it isn't coming this way," she said, jumping out of bed and nervously pacing, pausing to look out a window.

"Me too, babe, me too. I'll be back as soon as I can. We won't let you guys get hurt."

Giving her a kiss, I gathered up my gear, grabbing my pistol and vest on the way out the door. Thad was leaning on the hood of the Suburban when I got there, Danny busy securing his vest.

"Let's get this show on the road," I said as I climbed in.

Pulling out onto Highway 19, I turned north and pressed down on the gas. As we passed the Pittman Center, I glanced at the Forestry Service facility sitting off the road behind the Ocala National Forest welcome center. A lot of equipment used for firefighting would be stored there.

"On the way back it might be worth a look around there," I said, pointing out the window.

"You think there's anything left there?" Danny asked.

"Only one way to find out," I replied.

As we passed the turn off to Grasshopper Lake, I noticed a dark look overtaking Thad's face. He stared off into the woods as we drove. I know what we found out there really bothered him. My own memory was haunted by the sight of that body. I wished for him we hadn't found it. To distract him from his thoughts I told Thad about my dad and firefighting.

He slowly turned his attention to me. "He teach you anything?"

"All I know is what he told me through some conversations, but hey, I did stay in a Holiday Inn Express once," I replied with a grin.

Thad smiled and stretched his arms out on the back of the seat. "Oh hell, we're all right, then."

"Yeah, we're saved," Danny said.

The three of us were stopped in conversation by what we saw. Up ahead, far ahead, the horizon was a black menacing mass that stretched high into the sky, where a gray cloud spread out like a malignant mushroom.

"Holy shit, would you look at that," I said.

"Oh my God," Danny said.

Thad leaned forward to look through the windshield. "Damn, that's bad."

"Look how high it goes," I said, pointing.

"That's a massive fire. Damn, that's a big fire," Thad said, slowly shaking his head.

"This is going to be bad. Shit. Shit. Shit. What the hell are we going to do?" Danny said.

"I don't know, but it looks far away. Might be up near Palatka. Maybe it won't make it down here," I said, knowing that was a long shot.

"We need to be ready, though, just in case. Let's definitely stop at the Forestry facility and see if there's anything there on the way back," Danny said.

At the camp the guys at the gate waved as we pulled in. I drove quickly through to the command post.

"Something's up here," Thad said, looking around.

Danny was looking around. "Probably getting ready to evacuate the camp."

"Maybe," Thad replied.

"I forgot. Mike said they were pulling out of the camp, had orders from someone," I said.

"Orders? Because of the fire?" Thad asked.

"I don't think so. He didn't say it was because of the fire, just said they had orders."

Ted and Mike were sitting in front of the bunker as we pulled up.

"Hey, guys, what up an' shit?" Mike said as we climbed out.

"Trying to avoid this inferno. What's going on around here? Y'all buggin' out?" Thad asked, watching a group of civilians in an animated discussion.

"We are, but they aren't. Or at least, some of them aren't," Ted said, gesturing to one of the groups. "Trying to pick their new leader now."

"What, are you guys running out on them?" I asked.

"Nope, they want to stay. We told them we were closing the camp and some of them protested. The Guard is pulling back to the armory in Eustis."

"No shit, why?" Danny asked.

"They can't feed 'em anymore. The gravy train has jumped the tracks, and they got orders to move out," another voice announced. Sarge appeared, standing in the door of the bunker.

"What are all of these people going to do?"

"We told them we would give them what supplies we could, told 'em to hit the road, but they want to stay here, said they'll figure it out for themselves."

"We came across a group last night on the road by our place. It was a pretty big one too. They were walking toward Eustis," I said.

Sarge nodded his head. "That fire's prolly got 'em on the move. I bet you see even more."

"I hope not. They weren't too friendly," Thad said.

"Things get ugly?" Sarge asked.

"No, just words, but it could have. It was a little shaky for a few minutes," I said.

"Well, these people are in for the same," Sarge replied.

Thad pointed north. "Have they seen that smoke? They know what a fire like that will do to this place?"

"I guess they do, but it's on them now. Soon as the patrol gets back from the armory, we're going to start bugging out."

"Why are you guys pulling out?" Danny asked.

"Sheffield got orders to, told him to go to the armory and await further orders."

"I can't believe they're just going to abandon these people," Danny replied.

"It's a hard truth to face, but what the command in MacDill said is everyone is a refugee and we aren't in the refugee business. Sad but true," Sarge replied.

"So you guys are in contact with MacDill now? Get any news from them?" I asked.

"I haven't talked to them, Sheffield has. I don't know more than I told you."

"It's good to hear MacDill is still up and running, though. Maybe there's a little hope there," Thad said.

"Not for any of us, from the sound of it," Danny said.

"You guys are doing all right. You've got it together over there," Sarge added.

"We do, but it's a lot of work, ain't easy," I replied.

"Life's hard," Sarge said with a smile.

Calvin and Shane walked up as Sarge was talking. I greeted Calvin and asked him his opinion on the situation. "What about you guys? You staying here? I thought you'd be long gone by now."

"We've been wanting to go home since those DHS bastards were stopped, but my injuries were healing and that captain said he can't spare us a ride home," Calvin said.

"He's a lot better now, though," Shane added, and smiled at his dad.

"Your camp up near Lake Kerr?" I asked. Calvin nodded.

I looked at Danny and Thad. "You guys want to take a ride up that way? We can see get a better idea of where the fire is."

"I'm in," Danny said quickly.

"Me too," Thad added.

"You guys going to give 'em a ride home?" Sarge asked.

I nodded. He looked at Ted. "Get us a Hummer ready, we'll go with them." Ted nodded and he and Mike left to get a truck ready. "Hey, Sarge, can I get some fuel for this thing?" I asked, patting the hood of the Suburban.

"Sure, pull around to the tanks and fill it up. I'll ride with you."

We got back into the truck and I drove back to the motor pool. Sarge got out and had the guard on duty unlock the pump. He handed me the hose while Thad raised the hood and connected the wires to the pump to the battery. Fuel was quickly flowing into the old truck.

"How much is left in this tank?" Sarge asked the guard.

He took a clipboard out of a box on the side of the pump. After doing a little quick math he replied, "Six hundred gallons or so."

Sarge nodded, clearly thinking about all the trucks they were going to have to move to the armory. After filling the

Suburban, we drove back around to the bunker. Ted and Mike were there with a Hummer ready to go with us. Calvin and Shane would ride with us, and Sarge and the guys would take the Hummer. As we were sorting all this out, Jamie and Doc walked up.

I did a double take, surprised at her appearance. "Holy shit, Jamie, what the hell happened to you?"

"I fell," she replied.

"How many times?" Thad asked, a disturbed look on his face.

"We had an incident with the DHS when we were loading them up," Doc said, "but Jamie got the better of the deal. They had to bury the other gal."

Jamie looked a bit smug. "*Anywaaay,*" she said, drawing out the syllables. "What's up?"

"We're taking a ride up the road to check on the fire," Mike replied. "Gotta figure out the best way to avoid being burned to a crisp an' all."

"Let me get my stuff. I'm going too."

Doc started to protest, saying she should stay behind and rest more, but the look she shot him this time had plenty to say so he relented. Holding his hands up, he said, "Guess I'm coming too."

Jamie quickly returned with her gear and we all loaded up. Driving through the camp toward the gate, we could clearly see the billowing cloud of smoke rising up into the sky. Calvin let out a low whistle. "It's like looking straight into hell."

"It is nasty-looking. Calvin, if your place is over by the lake, it's right in the path of that mess. What are you guys going to do?" I asked.

"We'll figure that out when we get there. I just want to get home."

"Yeah, I'm worried about Mom," Shane added.

"Not nearly as much as she is about us," Calvin said.

Once we got out to the road, we headed north, moving fast. We quickly crossed over Highway 40, the smoke now even more menacing. Approaching the take out on Juniper Run, we noticed the parking lot that was crowded with people, all milling about. They were gathered in knots talking and gesturing toward the wall of smoke.

The parking lot and the surrounding woods were crowded with tents and makeshift shelters, several small fires were burning, and a great number of kids were running around playing.

"Hey, Morgan, pull in there," Shane said.

I slowed and flipped on the blinker so the guys behind me would know we were turning in. Naturally our sudden appearance garnered considerable attention. Many of those gathered suddenly bolted for the woods. At first I didn't understand why, but then I caught a glimpse of the Hummer in the rearview mirror as I turned. Mike was in the turret manning the SAW.

There were a number of wagons scattered about. It seemed every sort of cart was used to transport one's belongings, with shopping carts, garden carts, little red wagons, and even baby strollers pressed into service to haul all that one possessed. The faces of many of those scattered around the parking lot displayed the anxiety of this new terror facing them. While for the most part the kids seemed oblivious to it, the very young among them, toddlers and infants, seemed to sense the stress from their mothers. A number of them were wailing, seemingly ignored by their mothers, who could offer little to soothe them.

While some of the group ran, most stayed where they stood, obviously clutching weapons and eyeing us with suspicion. We pulled to a stop, and Calvin and Shane jumped out and walked toward a group of men. We all stayed back as there were certainly more of them than there were of us. In the turret, Mike was alert. Ted had pulled the Hummer up on my side. Looking up, I could see Mike.

We were forty-odd feet from Calvin and the men he was talking to. Being out of earshot, I asked Mike, "See anything hinky from up there?"

"Naw, not yet."

As he replied, a very loud engine suddenly started. The source of the sound revealed itself when a familiar-looking old green truck pulled out from a paved path.

As soon as Thad saw the truck his eyes lit up with rage. "That's them sumbitches from the woods that day." Hearing Thad, Doc, Jamie, and Ted got out of the Hummer, offering him formidable backup.

He didn't need to elaborate. We all knew what he was talking about. It was the green truck from Grasshopper Lake, the day we found the body hanging in the tree. Thad quickly stepped out, his eyes locked on the cab of the truck. It stopped as the driver spoke to one of the people gathered in the parking lot. They were looking at the Hummer and at Mike in the turret. My eyes moved between Thad and the truck. Looking at the truck, I saw the passenger when he noticed Thad. He quickly grabbed the driver by the shirt and tugged, pointing at Thad.

Thad started walking toward the truck, his shotgun at his

side. Seeing him start moving, I called, "Mike, Mike!" pointing at Thad. Mike looked down and followed my arm out. He quickly swung the turret and his SAW around to cover Thad. Jamie and the guys were right behind him. The truck started to move, slowly at first, but Thad was quickly closing in on it. The driver suddenly floored the old truck, causing the antique engine to belch a huge cloud of blue smoke. As they hit the exit onto the road, the passenger looked back and flipped Thad off. He stopped walking and watched the truck as it sped away.

"Who the hell was what?" Mike called down.

I got out of the Suburban, opened the door of the Hummer, and stepped up on the ledge of the door. "We came across those guys the day we found that body hanging in the trees."

Mike looked back at Thad, then back at me. "You think they did it?"

"Did what?" Sarge asked.

"I'm not sure." Pointing at Thad, I added, "But he damn sure is." Then, looking at Sarge, I added, "Hung that guy we found in the woods a while back."

Sarge looked over at Thad, and after a moment he said, "Oh yeah, that—we'll have to fix that."

After a moment Thad came back to the trucks. "You all right, man?" I asked.

I was surprised how he looked. The last time he saw these guys he looked really messed up, but this time he looked like the old Thad. It's almost like the encounter gave him a jolt of energy. "Oh yeah, I'll get 'em one of these days," he said as he leaned back on the Hummer. Jamie and the guys stayed just off to the side, forming a bit of a perimeter.

Calvin and Shane returned to the trucks. I asked if any of their people were part of the group.

"No, but we know many of them. They all thought we were dead," Calvin replied.

"Well, let's get you home so they'll know you're not. Why are there so many people here?" Danny said.

Calvin looked back for a moment. "Most of them are fleeing the fire, said it's burning up toward Palatka. A bunch of these folks have walked for a couple of days to get here."

"They think the river will stop the fire," Shane added.

"That little creek won't amount to a speed bump to that fire. If they were smart they'd get back on the road and fast," Sarge replied.

"That's what we told them, but a lot of them are tired. Plus they're scared, don't know which way to go. No one knows exactly where it is, where it's going," Shane said.

"Sitting here damn sure isn't helping them any at all," Sarge replied.

We got back in the trucks and headed back down the road. As we crossed the bridge over the run I looked down. Many people were in the water with fishing poles, or walking the shallows along the banks looking for food. A number of kids were playing at the water's edge, their mothers standing on the bank looking north at the ever-increasing mass of gray and black in the sky, their trepidation obvious. The opposite side of the river was also crowded with camps, smoke hanging in the canopy of the trees.

As I drove I thought about those souls down there on the river, about how this fire was compounding an already dire situation for them, for us. With all that's happened to our world, the plunge back to a lifestyle a hundred or so years distant, mother nature didn't care, and we were still at her mercy. The thought of having to grab what you could and flee in the face of an advancing inferno was terrifying.

Coming into Salt Springs, Calvin told me to hang a left onto Salt Springs Highway. After another couple of miles he directed me onto a small dirt drive. Stopping at a closed gate, Calvin got out and disappeared into the woods. After a few moments he reappeared and unlocked the padlock on the gate, opening it so we could pull through.

Back in the truck, he told me to follow the road but go slowly. He and Shane both were leaning out of the windows intently watching the woods on either side of the road. The dirt track wound through scrub oaks and pines mixed with palmettos. The edge of the road was lined with puffy green lichen, and dead leaves and pine needles littered the two-track.

Eventually the woods broke out into a clearing, live and scrub oaks creating a canopy over the area. Under the cover of the trees were a number of small houses. It reminded me a lot of the place we dropped Jess off. Calvin told me to stop and for us to stay in the truck. He and Shane both got out and started looking around, checking the small houses, which all appeared to be locked.

"I think they've left," I heard Calvin say.

"No, they haven't," Shane said, pointing at a tall oak with a large spreading canopy.

Calvin looked over to where Shane was pointing. Danny and I did as well. Shane was pointing at a birdhouse mounted to the trunk.

"Looks like it, but where are they?"

Curious about the significance of the birdhouse, I asked Calvin about it. "Hey, what's with the birdhouse?"

"It's one of our signals. If for any reason we had to bug out, the house would be turned upside down." He smiled. "Who's going to pay attention to a birdhouse?"

"Wow, I guess that works," I said, more to myself than to him.

Calvin looked around, then cupped a hand to his mouth. "Lori! Daniel! Anybody!"

After a moment a reply came out of the woods. "Calvin?"

Calvin spun around. "Yeah, it's me! Where are you guys?"

A woman's voice erupted from the woods, accompanied by the sounds of crashing brush. "Calvin?! Is Shane with you?"

Both men moved in the direction of the sound, and soon a woman appeared. Shane and Calvin embraced her, and she burst into tears. Several other people, armed people, emerged from different points of the tree line surrounding the small compound.

As the group gathered around their returning members I saw a familiar face and called out, "Hey, Daniel!"

Hearing me, he walked over. I offered my hand as he approached. As we shook hands I said, "Hey, man, good to see you're all right."

"We're better now that these guys are back. Where'd you find them?"

"They were taken to the DHS camp." I pointed to Sarge and Ted and added, "These guys took the camp over and we finally managed to get 'em home." I then introduced everyone to Daniel, and a quick round of handshakes went around.

Daniel shook Sarge's hand. "Thanks for getting them out. I was with them the day we were ambushed."

"I know, I saw you," Sarge replied.

Confused, Daniel asked, "You saw?"

"We were there for the ambush. Most of it, anyway," I said.

"I didn't know, I thought you guys went the other way after our little meeting. Don't blame you for not getting involved. It was ugly."

"We wanted to, but it would have been suicide," I said.

"No worries, you guys got him back just in time. With this fire so close, it looks like we're going to have to move now," Daniel said.

Sarge asked, "Do you know where the fire is?"

"It's only a couple miles north of Salt Springs now, and it's moving fast." As he spoke he looked up, causing the rest of us to do the same. The smoke was now heavier and ash had begun to slowly drift down.

"Looks that way," I said, holding my hand out as a piece of delicate white ash drifted into my palm.

"Where are you guys going to go?" Danny asked.

"We've got another place at the lake over there," he said, pointing north. "It's a last resort, though. We're going to watch the fire and see if goes around the west side of the lake. If it does, we're heading out. If it sticks to the east side, we'll try and wait it out."

"Don't wait too long. As fast as this thing is moving, it's going to be damn dangerous to wait," Sarge said.

Daniel nodded. "Yeah, but everything we have is here. Leaving here means a hard life."

"Well, brother, I can relate. I think we all can. I hope for the best for you," I said.

He looked around the group. "What about you guys, you going to try and stick it out or are you going to move out of the way?"

Danny looked at me. Now that we knew how close it was,

we were going to have to come up with a game plan. "Well, now that we know where it is, we're staying put. Hopefully it will burn itself out first," Danny said.

Daniel looked at Sarge. "What about the camp?"

"That camp don't stand a chance. We're pulling back to Eustis, to the Guard armory there. Some civilians want to stay, can't say I agree," Sarge replied.

"Smart move for you, dumbass move for them," Daniel said, agreeing.

Calvin and Shane walked over, Calvin's wife between them holding their hands.

"Thanks for getting us back, we really appreciate it," Calvin said.

I smiled. "No worries. Sorry it took so long."

The woman, her cheeks still wet from tears, added, "I can't thank you enough. I thought I'd lost them both. It was terrible not knowing where they were."

Calvin smiled and looked at his wife. "It's all right now, honey, we're back."

We spent another few minutes saying good-bye to everyone, telling them if they needed anything to look us up. I gave him directions to our place, offering his group a place if they needed it. He thanked me but said they had a plan. Shaking his hand, I said, "Hope we see you again someday."

Calvin smiled. "Me too."

After Daniel opened the gate for us I stopped for a moment to shake his hand again and wish him luck. He did the same and watched as we drove away. At the intersection with Highway 19, I stopped and looked north again. The smoke, if possible, seemed thicker now and ash fell like light snow. It completely covered our view of the horizon to the north and east, like an enormous cancer on the blue sky.

We made the trip back to the camp quickly. At the road to the main gate I pulled off the side of the road just past it. Ted pulled the Hummer into the drive and stopped and we all got out.

"What are you guys going to do? You don't normally stay here. You gonna stick it out on the creek or what?" Thad asked.

Sarge rubbed the stubble on his chin. "Don't know yet. The way that looks it could get ugly down in them woods."

"Why don't you guys come up to our place?" Thad said.

"I'm for that," Mike said from the turret.

"Me too," Ted added. "I could use one of Mel's home-cooked meals."

"How do you think your place is going to fare with this fire?" Sarge asked.

"Tough to say. We're going to hit the Forestry Service facility and see if there is any of the firefighting gear left, just to be safe," I said.

"You know how to fight fires?" Mike asked.

"I know some theory, that's about it," I replied.

"Before joining the army I spent a couple of summers after high school working wildfires out west. I can help you a little," Mike said.

"And when were you going to share this information?" I asked, shaking my head.

"I just did," Mike replied with a smile.

"I'm a volunteer for Lake County, or I was," Jamie said.

"Anyone else a closet firefighter?" I asked, looking at everyone.

"I have an idea for something too," Danny said.

We all looked at him. "Do tell," Thad said.

Danny looked at Thad. "Over behind your place there are a couple of those big poly tanks in the cages. I thought we could take those and put them on my trailer. Then, using my generator and the irrigation pump from Morgan's place, we plumb it all up and have a fire trailer of sorts."

"Holy crap, that's a hell of an idea," I said.

Thad smiled broadly. "Where you been hidin' all them smarts?"

Danny laughed and I said, "And here we thought you were just another pretty face."

"Hey, I thought I was the pretty face," Jamie said, trying to smile, which didn't come off well.

Mike looked at her and grimaced. "Eeesh, don't smile. Just don't."

Jamie kicked sand at him. "Screw yourself, Mike."

"Ahh, but it's not as fun to screw myself," he replied. "Care to join?" he asked, with a wink.

If looks could kill, the one Jamie gave him in return would have turned him into cinders. Mike laughed even harder until Sarge reached over and slapped him on the bottom of his chin, forcing his mouth closed with a pop.

"Ow, dammit, bit my tongue," Mike shouted.

"Serves you right," Jamie said with a smirk.

"This is fun and all, but it looks like we've got work to do," I said.

Sarge nodded. "Us too. We need to get to it. I wish you luck, Morgan."

"We're going to need it," Danny replied.

Chapter 6

Perez drove the Hummer down the center line of the road, passing through Altoona. Ian was up in the turret, scanning the road with a SAW. There were two other Guardsmen, one riding shotgun and one in the back. They were being followed by another Hummer with four Guardsmen in it. As they made their way through Altoona, conditions worsened considerably. Ash was now falling on them as a nightmarish snow, the sunlight filtering through it. This gave everything an odd appearance, like it was being viewed through a sepia filter. For the first time, the world did look apocalyptic.

Coming into Umatilla, they noticed several people out in the parking lots of the Kangaroo Store and the McDonald's. They were gathered in groups and all looking to the north and at the growing malignancy in the sky. At the sight of the two approaching Hummers, many of them scattered, peering out from behind corners or around trees as the trucks passed.

"I've got bodies," Ian said into the headset radio attached to his helmet.

"Roger that, I see them," the Guardsmen in the turret of the second Hummer said.

Sheffield, Livingston, and Sarge were listening to the radio back in the CP. Hearing the call about bodies, Sheffield raised his eyebrows and looked at Sarge. Sarge shrugged and looked back at him. "Nothing to worry about yet."

"Let's hit the drive-through and get a burger," Ian joked.

"You can walk in if you want," Perez replied.

They were through the small town quickly. On the stretch between Umatilla and Eustis, just before the Three Lakes area, they passed a subdivision of well-tended older houses and a liquor store. Ian scanned the store. Its parking lot was covered in trash: scraps of cardboard and empty cans and bottles.

"Imagine that, a looted liquor store," Perez said.

Ian looked over at the metal gates that once covered the windows, now pried open and hanging in their frames. "One of the essentials of survival."

Coming into Eustis, Highway 19 was four lanes divided by a grass median. As the trucks rolled across Highway 42, a small two-lane road running east–west, Ian had a bird's-eye view of the Publix grocery store on the west side and the Winn-Dixie sitting across the divided highway from it on the east. All of the windows of both stores were shattered, and the Winn-Dixie had been partially burned. Just like at the liquor store, the parking lots of these two were completely littered with trash and debris, burned cars, and piles of shopping carts, but unlike the other, there were many, many people milling about.

"We've got lots of people ahead," Perez shouted into his mic.

"Look at 'em all!" Ian shouted back.

"It's like a Mad Max movie," the gunner from the other Hummer added.

"Let's hope there's no Thunderdome," Ian replied.

Several of them were standing around fires or a few tattered makeshift shelters. Again, the appearance of the two

Hummers drew the attention of many of these people. Unlike those in Umatilla who hid from the trucks, some of these people actually began to run toward them. And some of these people had weapons.

Seeing the armed people reacting to the sight of the trucks, Ian swiveled the turret around to face them and quickly shouted into the radio, "Gun!"

The other gunner quickly replied, "Got 'em!"

"I've got the left!" Ian called.

The reply from the other gunner was terse. "I'm on the right."

Of those running, some were waving and nearly all were shouting. Ian stuck his head down into the cab of the truck. "Step on it, Perez!"

Perez gunned the truck, and the driver of the other Hummer did likewise. A group came toward them. It wasn't clear what they were doing—maybe they wanted help, maybe they had violent intentions. However, there were several armed men who appeared particularly agitated, and Ian and Perez didn't want to take any chances.

One man was waving a bolt-action rifle over his head, as you would to get someone's attention. His face was flushed red behind an enormous beard. Ian watched him intently, anticipating his next action. Realizing the trucks weren't going to stop, the man gripped the rifle, holding it in a low ready manner. He shouted at the Hummer, his words drowned out by the screaming diesel engine. In a final act of desperation, he raised the rifle to his shoulder.

The red holographic sight of Ian's gun stayed centered on the man as best he could as they bounced down the uneven road. As soon as the man raised the rifle, Ian lifted the muzzle slightly and squeezed off a short burst. With the 725 rounds per minute the weapon was capable of, the brief trigger pull spit 11 rounds over the man's head. The loud rapid staccato report and the crack of the passing bullets stunned the man, causing him to fall backward.

The sudden outburst of gunfire caused those running toward them to either dive face-first into the dirt or flee in any and every direction. For just a brief moment, Ian was taken back to his days in Iraq. It was the same type of scene: a crowd gathered, then would quickly disperse with a short burst.

"You clear back there?" Ian called into the radio.

"Yeah, looks like they lost interest."

"Good, let's get the hell out of Dodge," Ian muttered to himself.

With Lake Eustis on one side and Trout Lake on the other, the highway bottlenecked right before it entered Eustis. The bottleneck was the perfect place for a roadblock, and someone indeed had taken advantage of it. Using several cars and various other objects, the small canal that connected the two lakes was essentially blocked.

"Roadblock!" Ian shouted as he ducked behind the armor plates of the turret.

"No shit!" Perez shouted back.

Ahead both of them could see bodies moving around behind the barricade, taking cover. Perez jerked the wheel onto a side road and gunned the engine, cutting across two lanes of pavement. As they crashed through some trees, a few choice words were thrown around by Ian. He paralleled the canal, coming out on North Shore and following the lake up to Bates Avenue. The trailing Hummer followed the maneuver. Taking Bates to the intersection of Bay, Perez made a quick right and started the final stretch to the armory. As they approached the armory, Ian called the other Hummer and told them to hang a left on Woodward to check the other side of the facility to make sure no one was camped out back there.

"Meet us at the gate to the yard," Ian instructed.

"Roger that."

Perez drove slowly past the building while Ian and the other Guardsmen in the front seat scanned the area.

"You guys see anything over there?" Ian asked.

"The fence has been cut back there, but that's about all that's visible," the gunner replied.

"All right, let's go check it out. You stay here and cover us." The gunner nodded as everyone else dismounted.

They began their search by walking the exterior of both buildings. They found several obvious places where people tried to gain entry, though from the looks of it, none of their attempts were successful. When they originally left the armory to struggle in the woods of the Ocala Forest, any gear that couldn't be taken was moved inside. Very little was left outside, but some things couldn't be moved, like fuel tanks and other stationary equipment.

Perez walked over to the fuel tanks and stepped up on the scaffold beside them. The cap to one of the tanks was hanging by its chain, and Perez looked into it.

"Anything in there?" Ian asked.

Perez started pulling a string, eventually revealing a small plastic cup. "Looks like they got nearly the last drops out," he replied, dropping the cup on the ground.

They moved back toward the motor pool, weapons always at the ready. Beside the bays for repairing the vehicles was a metal carport once used to store new and used motor oil. Ian kicked the drums as he passed, and they rang with a hollow echo. "Damn, they even took the used motor oil."

"Yeah, looks like people were camped here for a while," Perez replied, pushing a pile of cans around with the toe of his boot.

"What's that smell?" Ian asked, looking around.

"Smells like a clogged toilet."

Ian moved around behind the large building. "Oh damn, found it."

"Let me guess, the latrine?"

"Yeah, they didn't even dig a hole, just shit on the ground. That'll have to be cleaned up. You up for the job?" Ian joked. Perez grunted as a means of response.

They moved to check the bay doors on the front of the building. "Looks like they tried like hell to get in," Perez said, rubbing a thumb in a deep gouge in the heavy metal door.

"Yeah, and let's make sure they didn't," Ian replied, reaching into his pocket and fishing out a key.

Perez shouldered his carbine, prepared for whatever was behind the door. Ian quickly opened the door, jerking it open. Perez rushed in with the other Guardsmen right behind him as Ian brought up the rear.

The building was as they left it, their movement through the work bays disturbing the fine layer of dust that covered every surface. It drifted up into the air, defining the laser-like beams of light coming in through the high windows. With confirmation that the building was secure, they moved on to the main structure.

"All right, let's go inside," Ian said. Perez and the other guys nodded. Ian keyed his radio to let Sheffield know what they were about to do. "We're going in."

"Roger that."

He unlocked the door and jerked it open, and they quickly moved through the door in a stack. Inside they entered into the assembly hall. The windows over the hall area allowed enough light in to see that the room was empty, and they swiftly cleared it and moved to check the administration areas. It was immediately obvious that this one was empty as well.

"Looks like it's been left alone," Perez said.

Before anyone could reply, a call came over the radio. "We've got company!"

"Where?" Ian asked.

"I see some people on Eustis Street. You better check Bay."

"Perez, take Nick and check the front of the building. You guys come with me," Ian said as he turned and headed for the lot.

As they came around the corner, Ian could see four or five people outside the fence on Eustis Street. Three women and a boy held on to the fence and were talking to the gunner in the turret. Ian came up to the Hummer, keeping his weapon pointed in their direction, though not directly at them.

"What's up?" Ian asked as he took cover behind the open driver's door.

"They think we're here to help," the gunner replied.

"Sorry ladies, we're just an advance unit. We're not here to help right now," Ian called out.

"Please, we just need some help. Why isn't anyone helping us?" one of the women called out.

"ATVs heading this way," Perez called over the radio.

"Maybe they don't know where we are. Keep an eye on them," Ian replied.

Perez watched as the two ATVs came down Bay Street,

two men on each machine. The Guardsmen with him tapped him on the shoulder, pointing across the street from the armory to a group of three people lazing about under an oak tree. Perez figured word must be traveling that they were in the area. The four men on the ATVs saw them and stopped, it was obvious they were asking them questions, then Perez saw one of the three people point at the armory.

"They're coming. Wonder who the hell they are, running around on those machines," Perez called.

"Looks like we're about to find out," Ian replied.

Ian told one of the other Guardsmen to get up into the turret of his Hummer and man the SAW. Both gunners complied and rotated their turrets to face the sound of the approaching vehicles. The two ATVs pulled up to the gate and stopped, four men quickly hopping off.

Ian called out, "What do you want?"

"Hey, are you guys moving into this place? Are you coming back?"

"Maybe."

The four men shared glances around. "Well, I'm the sheriff. If you guys are coming back then that puts you under my jurisdiction."

"You're not the sheriff of Lake County," one of the Guardsmen replied.

"No, I'm the sheriff of Eustis," the man replied.

"The what?" Ian asked.

"The sheriff of Eustis. Things are going back to how they used to be."

Ian looked back at the group of women at the fence. "He the sheriff?"

The man claiming to be the sheriff looked over at them.

His glance obviously unsettled them, and they shrank back from the fence.

"Uh, yeah, he's the sheriff," one of them replied.

Ian glanced back at the man and noted the look on his face, looking at the women. Then he asked, "What makes you the sheriff?"

"Someone had to do it. Someone had to step in and try to make this place safer. So me and my boys did."

"You got any experience in law enforcement?" Ian asked.

He shrugged. "Well, no, but all you need is common sense. It ain't hard to tell right from wrong."

"So you just decided to *make yourself* sheriff?" Ian asked.

He obviously caught the mocking tone. "Damn right I did. And I heard the address by the Feds. They said the National Guard was supposed to put themselves under the jurisdiction of the local authorities. That's me."

Ian laughed. "Uh, lawfully elected authorities maybe, not just some dude who's decided to make himself sheriff."

"Well, I am the sheriff," the man said, his eyes narrowing.

Ian laughed. "I'm done with you," he said, turning his back on the men.

The sheriff was incredulous. He looked at his men. "You believe these idiots? Who the hell do they think they are?"

One of the men replied, almost in a whisper, "The guys with the machine guns."

The sheriff sneered at him. "Yeah, well, when they come back we'll be here."

"We tried that once, we couldn't get in," another of the men replied.

"Yeah, well, we will this time," the sheriff spat back.

While they spoke Perez had returned to the trucks and

everyone loaded up. The trucks were started up and maneuvered to go back out the gate. Pulling up to the gate, Ian swung the SAW around, pointing it at the four men. "Move!" he shouted. The four men backed up from the gate a short distance, and the trucks pulled through. Outside the gate Ian ordered them to back farther away. They needed to secure the gate.

"Back up!" Ian shouted.

Begrudgingly the four men started to back away. Ian watched them intently as they were all armed. The sheriff shifted the grip on the AK he carried. Ian caught the slight movement and shouted at him, "Don't even fucking think about it! I'll cut you fuckers in half!"

The other three moved their hands to keep them in plain view. The sheriff, however, simply glared back. One of the other guys hopped out and secured the gate then quickly got back in. Once back Ian told Perez to take off. The two trucks moved out quickly, heading the wrong way down Bay Street.

At the barricade they didn't detour this time, driving straight to it. There were still men there and he ordered them to push a car out of the way that acted as a gate in the center. The men hesitated for a moment. Ian stood up in the web seat of the turret and pointed at them. "Move that fucking car now or I'll open up!"

Two of the men quickly began moving the car out of the way. As they did, the gunner in the rear Hummer called over the radio, "*They're closing in on us.*" Ian looked back and could see the two ATVs closing quickly. Looking forward to make sure the car was nearly out of the way, Perez stomped on the gas and the Hummer started to roll. Seeing the big truck coming the two men strained against the car, pushing it from the rear. As the Hummer closed in they had to dive out of the way, and the right front corner of the bumper caught the car and slammed it into the ones in front of it.

Now through the barricade the trucks sped up, putting distance between them and it. Ian looked back and could see the sheriff standing in front of it, hands on his hips, watching as the distance between them increased.

"He's going to be a problem," Perez shouted over his shoulder.

Ian ducked his head down through the turret. "That's what he thinks, but he has no idea of the shit storm heading his way."

Heading back toward the camp, they were staring directly into the smoke—it covered the entire horizon before them. The rising smoke now had a mix of colors in it: white, black, yellow, and what almost looked like green.

"Holy Mary, Mother of God," Perez nearly whispered. "Look at it, that fire is massive."

The Guardsman beside him looked over. "It looks like the entire world is burning."

"We need to get the hell out of that forest, fast."

Perez could hear Ian on the radio relaying the situation at the armory back to the brass at the camp. It was just noise in his ears, though, as he was totally engrossed in the sight before him. There were more people now on the road, all of whom were looking to the north.

"Where are you now?" Sheffield asked over the radio.

"We're passing the orange juice plant in Umatilla," Ian replied.

"Find a place to pull off and wait. We've already got the first convoy of trucks heading out."

Perez pulled the Hummer into the grassy median. Ian

thought about what was going on. "Captain, we're probably going to have to deal with a self-proclaimed sheriff on the way back."

"A what?"

"Some guy claims to be sheriff of Eustis, said we were supposed to be under his control."

After a long pause Sheffield's voice came back over the radio. *"Stump Knocker will talk to him when he gets there, see what he's about."*

Ian smiled, thinking of the old man. That poor bastard in Eustis had no idea the trouble headed his way. Ian turned in his turret and called out to the other gunner, "Keep an eye out, we're going to wait here."

He gave a thumbs-up in reply. Across the street was an old gas station sitting beside a small shopping plaza. Even in the Before, the plaza was essentially defunct, but now it looked even more depressing and empty than ever. Despite that, a group of kids were playing in the parking lot. Ian smiled and waved at them and then ducked down into the truck. Dragging a box of MREs over, he started pulling the meals out and opening them. He was looking for the candies that were inevitably in every meal. Once he had several packs of M&M's and Skittles, he grabbed his carbine and got out.

"Hey!" he shouted at the kids, waving them over. They came running over in a stampede.

He started handing out small handfuls of candies to the kids. It soon turned into a mob scene, with the bigger kids pushing the smaller ones out of the way. Seeing one particular face for the second time, he said, "You've had yours, beat it." The kid's shoulders slumped and Ian pushed through the crowd to the smaller ones in the back, making sure they got their share.

"Are you soldiers?" a little girl in a filthy dress asked. She smiled and he could see the plaque crusted on her teeth.

"Hell no. My parents are married. I'm a marine," Ian replied with a big smile, not at all considering the audience he delivered the joke to.

"What are you doing?"

"Waiting for some of my friends."

One of the bigger kids, a boy, said, "My dad says you guys are a bunch of cowards."

Ian made a show of looking at himself. "Does it look to you like I'm afraid of anything?"

"Not to me! You look scary!" the little girl shouted.

"Do you have any more candy?" a boy of about five or six asked shyly.

Ian held up his hands. "Nope, it's all gone."

"I'm still hungry," another little one said.

Ian was a tough guy, but hearing their little pleas got to him. After a tour in Iraq and two in Afghanistan, it was always kids he really felt for. They hadn't asked to be born into these wars, they had no control over which religious sect their family was part of, and inevitably they were always caught in the middle. He'd arranged with his mom to send toys over—soccer balls were popular—and she'd done a drive once and sent him over two dozen. He remembered the days when he'd give them out, a few at a time in each village. The smiles on their faces when they received something as simple as a ball was amazing. It gave them the chance to be kids again, even if just for a little while, and that was worth it. Back then, he had become popular with the kids and many knew him on sight.

Ian went back to the Hummer and took the case of meals out, setting it on the hood of the truck. He started taking the meals apart and pulling the individual foil packages out and opening them. The smaller, sickly looking kids got the main entrées. The bigger, healthier ones ended up with side dishes. There weren't enough spoons to go around, but it didn't deter any of the kids. If they didn't get a spoon they simply used their dirty fingers to scoop the food into their mouths.

After ensuring each kid had something to eat, Ian sat back and watched them. Every one of them took what they were offered without complaint, a bit of a novelty with modern children.

Once whatever was in the package was consumed, the kids would lick the inside, leaving no trace whatsoever of the original contents. When they finished the kids simply dropped the remnants of the pouch where they stood. At first this bothered him, but with the amount of trash already around, it made little difference. These kids no longer knew a world where trash was expected to be placed into a container only to magically disappear. To them the world was one large trash can.

Invigorated with the nourishment, the kids started running around screaming and shouting. Some were wrestling, as kids will do, while some version of tag seemed to be going on with the majority. As an afterthought he started tossing them the packs of gum each MRE contained as well, and soon all of them were smacking their gum as they ran and played.

Perez stepped out of the truck. "Here they come!"

Ian looked up the road to see a line of trucks and Hummers approaching. The column pulled up and stopped in the road beside him. Ian walked out to the lead Hummer that held Sarge, Ted, Mike, and Doc.

"You guys ready to have some fun?" Ian asked.

Sarge smiled. "Ah, this ain't going to be nothing."

"I just can't wait for that ole boy to tell you that you'll be working for *him*," Ian said with a laugh.

"Oh, this is going to be rich," Mike said from the turret.

"We ain't getting anywhere standing here chewing our cud. Let's get this goat rope on the road," Sarge said.

Ian slapped the top of the Hummer and quickly returned to his truck, climbing back up into the turret. With so many trucks there, the kids stood with mouths open in awe, many waving at the Guardsmen. Some of the Guardsmen were tossing out items to them: bottles of water, whole MREs, and whatever else they could come up with. Seeing the kids in such bad shape clearly had affected them.

Ian's two Hummers took the lead of the column as they pulled back out onto the road.

"The roadblock is just up ahead. How do you want to handle it?" Ian called.

"What's blocking the road?" Sarge asked.

"Some cars—they've got one they roll out of the way like a gate."

"Just head for that car. If they don't want to move it, we will. We need clear access to the armory."

"Roger that."

Perez lined the truck up with the gate car as they approached. Just as previously they could see the men behind the barricade peeking out from behind it, Ian kept his eyes on them as they drew near. Stopping short of it, he called out, "Move that car!"

One of them men on the other side stuck his head up. "The sheriff told us not to let anyone through!"

"What's going on up there?" Sarge asked over the radio.

"They don't want to open it."

"*Whatever truck has the Mark 19 on it, pull up to the front.*"

After a couple of minutes a Hummer pulled up beside Ian, then Sarge walked up with Ted and Doc in tow. He looked up at Ian. "Cover us, I'm going up there to have a talk with 'em."

Ian nodded and shouldered the weapon as Sarge and the guys walked toward the line of cars blocking the road. Behind them the men on the other side shared glances, unsure of what was going on. Stopping twenty or so feet away, Sarge called out, "Which one of you booger-eaters in charge here?"

"The sheriff isn't here right now," came the reply.

"That's not what I asked, I asked which one of you idjits was in charge here."

One man rose up behind the cars. "I guess I am."

"What's your name?" Sarge asked.

"Mitch," the man called back.

"Well, Mitch, you need to move that car out of the way or we will. If we do it, you won't be here to see it."

"Like I said, the sheriff said not to let anyone through."

"Mitch, you seem to be missing the point here. I'm not asking you, I'm telling you." Sarge turned and pointed at the Mark 19. "You see that thing up there?"

Mitch looked over at the weapon mounted to the top of the truck, then back at Sarge.

"You know what it is?" Sarge asked. Mitch shook his head. "It's a Mark 19 forty-millimeter grenade launcher that can rain three hundred and twenty-five of those nasty little bastards down on you in a minute. Now, if you don't move that car out of the way"—Sarge pointed to the gunner behind the weapon—"he will."

The men behind the barricade once again shared furtive glances. After a quick whispered exchange the car began to roll back.

"Smart man, Mitch!" Sarge shouted.

Perez pulled through the barricade and off the side of the road, covering it from the rear. Ted ran back and brought their truck up, picking up Sarge and Doc. As they pulled through the barricade, Sarge motioned for Ted to stop and waved Mitch over. "Now, we're going to be coming back out in a bit. Over the next few days we'll be making several more trips. We won't have to have this discussion again, will we?"

"I'm just doing what I'm told. I'll tell the sheriff."

"Well, tell him to come see me."

"Who are you?"

"Just tell him to ask for Sarge." Mitch nodded and Sarge waved Ted on.

The short drive to the armory occurred without incident and all the trucks were soon inside the fenced yard behind the facility. Along with the mountain of supplies, the trucks carried a contingent of twenty Guardsmen who would be left behind to provide security. Everyone got busy quickly to get the trucks unloaded while Sarge went in to check out the hall, telling Ted to call the camp and let them know they had arrived.

After looking the facility over, Sarge came out and found Ian. "Why don't you and Perez stay here, keep your truck too. Take control of this place and start getting things set up."

Ian nodded. "Sure thing. We've got to fix a cut in the fence back there. We'll get that done and get some security established."

"Good deal. You've got enough food and water for a few days, but take it easy on it just in case."

"Will do."

"All right, let's get this circus back on the road," Sarge shouted.

After a little jockeying of trucks, they were all lined up in front of the armory. The activity was once again drawing a crowd of onlookers, though they kept their distance. Sarge walked the line of trucks, making sure everyone was ready. He still used the cane but was relying on it less and less every day. Shouts from the rear of the column got his attention, and, turning around, he saw a couple of ATVs stopped at the rear. Word quickly spread down the column that a man claiming to be the sheriff was back there. Sarge walked back down the line to where a group of Guardsmen were covering the men.

Sarge walked straight to the men. "What can I do for you fellers?"

"I'm Sheriff Parker," a big man replied.

"Well I'm King George," Sarge replied, getting a perplexed look from the man. "If we're making shit up, why not be king?" Sarge added.

The man's eyes narrowed. "I'm not making nothing up. I am the sheriff of Eustis."

Sarge crossed his arms. "Were you elected?"

"Well, no, someone had to step up, so I did. We've made the town safer. It was rough around here for a while."

"That's good, good you're working to make the town safer. Back to my original question, what can I do for you?"

"Are you guys moving into the armory to stay?" the sheriff asked.

"We are. There's a lot more coming too."

Parker looked around. "Are you bringing in supplies for the town?"

Sarge shook his head. "Not right now. We'll be able to support ourselves, won't need anything from the folks here. But right now we can't offer them any help either."

Parker licked his lips. "How many men are you bringing in?"

Sarge smiled and rocked on his heels, not answering the question. Parker waited a moment for a response then asked, "Where've you been?"

"We had to deal with some federal boys. Now that that's taken care of, we're coming back."

Parker kind of nodded his head. "Oh, okay. I was telling one of the guys that was here earlier that I heard a broadcast from the government that the National Guard was supposed to put themselves under control of the local authorities." He paused for a moment, then continued, uncertainty clearly present in his voice, "And since I'm the sheriff, that makes me the local authority."

Sarge rocked back on his heels again and spit into the dust at his feet. "Well, Sheriff, it's like this: we're not going to be under your authority. We're under the authority of the Department of Defense, and that's not going to change. But I'll tell you what, you take care of your town and we won't get in your way"—Sarge pointed at him—"so long as you're doing the right thing. I catch you fucking up and you'll be dealt with."

Parker shook his head. "Oh no, I mean, we're just working

for the town, trying to keep things safe and take care of everyone."

Sarge nodded. "That's good, you just keep doing that. The CO of this place is Captain Sheffield. Once these guys are all moved in, he'll probably want to talk to you. Just give 'em some time to get settled in."

"You're not in charge here?"

"Naw, not me." Sarge smiled. "I don't have the people skills for that sort of thing."

"So I need to talk to the captain, then?" Parker said.

"You can talk to him—he'll probably want to—but don't expect anything different from him than I told you. You fellas have a good day. We gotta get on the road." Sarge squinted at Parker. "We have to make several more trips this way. I know we won't have any more trouble at your roadblock, will we," Sarge said, the last being a statement, not a question.

"I'll let my deputies know to allow you through," Parker replied.

Sarge nodded and waved as he headed back down the line of trucks. As he climbed up into the Hummer, Ted looked at him. "Well?"

Sarge shook his head and clicked his tongue. "I don't know, hard to get a read on the fella. He may just be trying to help the town out. But his grand idea that he's going to take over this unit is fucking nuts."

"He shouldn't be too much of a problem," Ted replied as he put the Hummer in gear and started down the road. "You set him straight, Sarge."

Word was spreading of the convoy's presence and on the trip back more people were out on the side of the road. From his perch in the turret, Mike watched the people as they passed, looking like something from an old film reel of World War Two, the countless scenes of refugees lining the sides of the road as military vehicles passed. It was a profound image to Mike. During his multiple tours of service in the Middle East, the throngs of people lining the side of the road never bothered him, but here, in the country of his birth, the effect was different. A deep sense of sadness filled him as he watched these poor people in their filthy clothes, some of the children displaying the classic signs of malnutrition. The bloated bellies really brought it home.

While Mike never was a religious man, though in his youth he'd attended Sunday School and Bible studies, a line of scripture came to him from the book of Samuel: *how the mighty have fallen*. He thought of all those months, years spent trying to defend this same nation from those that craved this very result. *What a waste,* he thought. Quickly he realized he was in a daze, not paying attention to the road about him, his hands hanging limply from the weapon. *It is what it is. Deal with it,* he thought and focused his attention to the task at hand. The convoy made it back to camp without incident and the loading of the trucks was begun again.

Chapter 7

Back at the neighborhood, we spotted my girls as we drove in. Taylor, Lee Ann, and Little Bit were out hunting.

"Any luck?" I asked as we pulled up.

"Not yet. The squirrels are getting smarter," Taylor said.

Lee Ann was looking north. "Dad, is that fire going to come here?"

"I don't know, baby, it might. We've got to get ready for it just in case."

"Fire scares me," Taylor said.

"Don't be afraid yet," I said with a smile. "You guys want a ride home?"

"No, we'll walk so we can look for squirrels," Taylor replied.

"All right. When I get home I'll lay the camo out. It'll help you blend in and then maybe they'll come out. Just take care of it," I said.

"Okay, we will. Love you, Dad!" Taylor shouted, her sisters quickly echoing her affection.

Danny leaned forward. "Hey, what about me?"

Little Bit smiled. "We love you too!"

"And Thad!" Lee Ann said, catching me by surprise.

Thad leaned out the window. "Love you girls too. Thanks, Miss Lee Ann."

"Yeah, Thad too—we love you too, Thad!" Little Bit shouted.

Thad smiled warmly. "I love you girls. Good luck," he said, waving at them.

As we drove away I looked at Thad in the rearview mirror. "Well, guess you're part of the family now."

Thad smiled again. "It feels good." It touched me to see that Thad could be happy, despite what tragedy he had experienced. He truly had the warmest smile of any person I'd ever met, and I was glad my family got to count him as one of their own.

Pulling up to Danny's, we went to the shed to look for sledgehammers, because on our quick stop at the Forestry Center, it was clear we were going to need a lot more manpower. Danny had two, so we loaded them up along with some pry bars, bolt cutters, and a hacksaw.

"You guys mind if I stay here? I want to work on the trailer," Danny said.

"Fine by me. We'll get Jeff or Tyler to go with us," I said.

"That's a good idea—having them tanks on the trailer might come in right handy," Thad said.

"Let's go see if there's anything for lunch and talk to the womenfolk real quick," I said.

Coming through the door, a wonderful aroma greeted us. "Damn!" Thad shouted. "What is that smell?"

The house was full—nearly everyone was there. Walking out on the back porch I saw Edie and Jace out at the pond wading in the shallow water.

"We're making a stew, thanks to all of our veggies," Brandy replied with a smile.

The kerosene stove was set up on the picnic table on the

back porch, a large kettle sitting on it. I lifted the lid on the pot. The smell was incredible. "Damn, this smells good," I said, inhaling the wonderful aroma again.

"Where is the fire? Is it going to make it here? There's ash everywhere now," Bobbie said.

"It's north of Salt Springs, but it's moving fast," Danny said.

"Moving this way?" Mel asked.

I nodded. "It's moving south for sure. There's just no way to tell where it's going right now."

"What are we going to do? Do we need to leave now?" Brandy asked.

"I don't think we need to leave, hon, we need to wait and see," Tyler reassured her.

"Well, I, for one, don't want to get trapped by some giant-ass fire. I say if we're going to have to leave I'd rather do it sooner than later," Jeff added.

"Is there anything we can do about it?" Fred asked.

"We don't know yet. They're about to head back out to the Forestry Service place up at Pittman to see if we can get some firefighting equipment," Danny said.

Then, my mind changed gears. I looked around the room, scanning who was here, and asked, "Hey, who's on duty at the barricade?"

Everyone looked around, but no one replied. I started for the front door and just as I reached for the knob, it burst open. Taylor stumbled in breathing heavily. "There's . . . there's people down at our house."

My head snapped around. "What?" I asked, looking toward our house.

Pointing, she said, "No, our old house. There's a bunch of people down there."

The house was suddenly filled with activity as everyone went for a weapon. "How many?" Danny asked as he pulled the sling of his carbine over his head.

"I don't know, there looked like a lot."

"Where are your sisters?" Mel asked, her voice tight.

"They're coming. I just ran as fast as I could."

The other two made it to the house and came stumbling in as well. Little Bit was crying, obviously scared by the sight of the strangers. She went straight to Mel, who immediately bent down and gave her a hug. "Shh, shh, it's going to be all right."

"You okay?" I asked Lee Ann as she tried to catch her breath.

She nodded and asked, "What do they want?"

"We don't know, but we're about to find out.

"Let's load up in the Suburban," I said as I went out the door.

All the guys followed me out and everyone loaded up. Jeff and Tyler dropped the rear gate and sat on it. Pulling out of the gate, we could see an old truck sitting in the road down near my old place. As we got closer, I could see it was an old grove truck, a common enough sight on the roads when oranges were in season. However, all that remained of this truck was the frame, a sheet steel bed, and the engine. The steering wheel seemed to sprout from the old relic, and a bucket was the only seat for the driver.

The people obviously saw us coming and soon there was a group of eight gathering around the truck, all armed. Thad and Danny both had their doors open before the truck stopped, and Jeff and Tyler were already on the ground when I got out.

The group stood around their truck with a collective look of defiance on their faces. They certainly had us outnumbered, but we had them outgunned. They carried a collection of arms, all of the hunting variety. I took in the scene, noticing that on the bed of the truck were a number of kids, all with dirty faces and dead eyes. This group was giving me a creepy vibe, like old-dude-in-a-van-level creepy. Thad was first to speak. "What are you doing here?"

An older man who appeared to be in his sixties stepped toward us. He had a shaggy gray beard and was wearing a cowboy hat that'd seen better days. "We're looking for a place to stay. The fire pushed us out of ours."

"I'm sorry to hear that," Thad replied, looking in the direction of the encroaching smoke, "but there's nowhere here for you to stay."

The old man pointed at my house. "Why not, this 'un's empty."

I stepped up beside Thad. "That's my house. I own it. I'm sorry you lost your place, but you can't stay here."

One of the younger men stepped around the old man. "Why not? We need a place and this isn't being used. If it's yours, why aren't you living there?"

"Doesn't matter why. I said no. I'm sorry for your hardship, but you folks need to be on your way," I replied.

"That's fine, then. We'll just take one of the other empty houses here," the old man said.

"That's not going to happen either. This is our neighborhood—you just be on your way," Thad said.

"You can't make us leave. Who do you think you are to tell us to leave? How about you leave," one of the younger men spat back.

"Look, there are plenty of abandoned places around. Lots of folks are gone. Just keep looking and you'll find one. There's no reason to make a big deal out of this. We're already here and there aren't enough resources around here as it is. There's no water source you can use and we're already hunting what game there is and it isn't much," Danny said, using a reasonable tone.

"Where you gettin' water?" the old man asked.

"Doesn't matter, just keep going a little farther toward Altoona and you'll find plenty of places. In Umatilla there's a bunch of empty houses and two big lakes for water."

The old man waved an arm toward the truck, where I noticed a group of young children, huddled together. "We need a place for these young 'uns. They need a safe place, that's all we're looking for."

Danny nodded. "I can appreciate that, but the next town is just another couple of miles up the road."

"I don't much take to being told what to do," the old man said as he rubbed his beard.

"We're not telling you what to do, just what you can't do here," I said.

The young man pointed at me. "You're a smart-ass."

Danny whispered to me, "Chill out . . . they'll go."

"One way or another," I shot back.

"How many people you got here?" the old man asked.

"Enough," Thad replied.

Pointing at my truck, he asked, "You got any fuel to trade?"

"That's one thing we really don't have," I said.

"Yeah, gettin' pretty scarce now." The old man dug at his beard again and looked around. "I reckon we can go on down the road." He smiled. "There's plenty of places no one owns."

The young man looked at him. "You going to let them run us off? We got as much right to be here as they do"—he paused and looked at us—"and there's more of us than there is of them."

"Now, now, Billy, this ain't the time for that."

Before I could say anything, Thad said, "And there won't be a time for it. It ain't worth it."

The old man looked back at him. "You reckon?"

"No, I know," Thad replied.

"Billy, I think we'll go on down the road and find us a place with better neighbors."

"Good luck to you," Thad said as they began to load up in the truck.

The young man with the attitude sat on the open bed giving us the stink eye until they pulled out onto the road and disappeared from view.

"Damn, I thought it was about to go to shit," Tyler said, letting out a long breath.

"I have a feeling this ain't over," Jeff said.

"Who the hell was supposed to be on duty down here? We can't let this kind of crap happen. We were lucky this time," I said.

"And there can't be a second time," Danny added.

"We really need to keep our eyes open. With the fire and the camp being released, I have a feeling we'll be seeing a lot more of this."

"Everyone needs to be armed at all times now too," Thad said.

"How are we going to do all this? We need to go to the Forestry place and see if there's anything there, we have these gabions to finish filling so we have some sort of ballistic protection, and we have to keep watch here," Danny said, shaking his head.

"We've got eight more people down the road, just remember that. Everyone's just going to have to pitch in more. We'll get Jess, Fred, and the girls to work on filling the gabbions. Tyler and Jeff can take the first watch while we go see if we can get into the building. Just modify the board to show who's where, doing what," I said.

When we got back to the house, Mel was on the couch with Little Bit, who was still upset. To our relief they both had weapons on them. I reminded them to keep them close at all times now.

"Whoever was supposed to be on duty down there right now and isn't, just allowed a truckload of people to drive right in here. We can't have this happen again. I know we just started this whole work schedule thing, but it's imperative that you know where you're supposed to be and be there without anyone telling you. We've got to work together here, all of us."

Aric was sitting at the bar in the kitchen. "Sorry, Morgan. Me and Fred were supposed to be down there. It's my fault. Tyler had come down here to get me because we hadn't shown up, then you guys came in and started talking about the fire. It won't happen again."

"No one's perfect, and we're all going to screw up. Let's just take a lesson from this. Don't let it happen again."

I sat on the couch beside Little Bit and ran my hand through her hair. "You all right, kiddo?"

She'd stopped crying but stayed tight to Mel, nodding to my question.

"Don't worry, sweetie, no one's going to hurt you."

"When will you be back?" she asked.

"An hour or two—we won't be gone long. Tyler and Jeff

are at the end of the road, they're keeping an eye on things." I gave Mel a quick kiss on the forehead. "We'll be back."

It was a short drive to the Pittman Center, but it gave us a prime view of the looming disaster. As I slowed to turn into the compound, Danny pointed up the road. "Would you look at that," he said with a low whistle.

Up the road, we could see what looked like at least fifty people walking south.

"The next few days are going to be damn difficult," I said. "This fire is adding a whole new element to the shit storm that is our situation."

"You can say that again," Thad agreed.

We got out and unloaded the tools, feeling even more pressure to get inside, and quickly.

I grabbed a hammer and stepped up to the wall. "You guys are going to think I'm nuts, but . . ." I tapped the block wall a couple feet from the door.

"That sounds solid, probably poured," Danny said.

Stepping back and taking up a swinging stance, I replied, "Only one way to find out," and swung the hammer with as much force as I could muster. The hammer struck with a dull thud. We all leaned in to inspect the damage.

"Well, you knocked the paint off," Thad said, chuckling.

"Hardy-har-har," I replied.

"Step back, let me show you how to swing this jack," Thad said as he gripped the handle.

Thad brought the hammer in hard, slamming it into the block. This time some small pieces fell from the impact. Thad stepped back and smiled. "Now, *that's* how you swing a hammer."

"Okay, but the block is soft. When you get to the concrete it's going to be a different story," Danny said.

Thad and I took up positions on either side and took turns striking the wall one after another. The cinder block gave way quickly. However, Danny was right about the concrete. It wasn't nearly as forgiving.

"This is going to take some time," I said, wiping sweat from my forehead.

"Sure is, but I think we can do it," Thad said.

Danny took the hammer from my hand. "Let me take a swing at it."

We stepped back and Danny went to work. After he took a few swings, a round-robin of sorts commenced, with each of us taking a turn working on it. We were concentrating on one block, trying to get it knocked all the way down. It took nearly an hour, but we finally broke through. It wasn't a big hole, but it was large enough to shine a light through and see if this was simply an exercise in frustration. Kneeling down I pulled my flashlight out and clicked it on, shining it at the hole.

"Anything in there?" Thad asked.

I stood up and handed him the flashlight. "Take a look for yourself."

Thad knelt down. "Damn! Look at all that stuff."

"What's in there?" Danny asked.

"Pumps, hoses, drip torches, Pulaskis, brush axes. I see some gas cans—maybe there's fuel," Thad replied.

"You see the chainsaws?" I asked.

Thad's head bobbed around the hole. "Yeah, there's a lot in here." He stood up and handed me the light back. "We need to get in there. This could be the key to stopping this fire."

"You know how long it's going to take to make a hole big enough to get through there?" Danny asked, clearly exasperated from all of our efforts.

I fished around in the pocket of my vest that held my small survival kit. "Maybe we don't have to," I said.

"Prepper Morgan strikes again," Thad said. "What do you have in mind?"

Removing a small signal mirror and duct tape wrapped around a pencil stub, I went out under the trees and found a stick. Using the tape I secured the mirror to the stick and knelt down with the flashlight again. Poking the stick through the hole, I shined the light onto it and moved the mirror around until I found what I was looking for.

"If we can find a piece of wire we may be able to catch the doorknob. It's the handle type. Maybe we can hook it and open it."

"Anything is worth a try right now," Danny said. "Let me see if I can find some wire."

"I'll work on making this hole a little bigger, give you more room to work," Thad said as he hefted the sledge again.

Danny and I went out behind the building to see what we could find, splitting up in different directions.

Along the perimeter of the property, a large pine tree had fallen and taken some of the fence down with it. I climbed up on the massive trunk—it was a huge long-leaf pine and was as big around as a fifty-five-gallon drum. As I straddled it, something caught my eye—tension wire from the top of the downed fence. There was a section about five or six feet long lying tangled in the tree.

"Hey, Danny, go get that hacksaw!" I shouted.

He trotted off toward the truck and came running back with the saw. "What do you got?"

I'd freed most of the wire and held the loose end up. "I think this will work."

"Woo boy! Now that's what I'm talking about. Hold it while I cut it."

With the wire in hand, we returned to Thad, who'd made considerable progress on the hole. It was now about the size of a five-gallon bucket. We fashioned a loop in the end of the wire and fed it through the hole. Danny knelt down and tried to hold the mirror while I worked the wire, but it just wasn't happening.

"Dammit! I don't think I can get it," I said, standing up.

Danny took the wire. "Let me try something." He put the wire through the hole and stuck his right arm though, then his head. "Hand me your light," he said, sticking his left hand in the air.

I handed him the light. Pulling his head out, he stuck the light in his mouth then poked his head back in. We could hear the wire scraping the door, then the floor, then the door again. I looked over at Thad and muttered, "I don't think we're going to get it." Thad nodded his head, agreeing.

The scraping stopped, then Danny's muffled shout, "Foo et."

"What?" Thad asked.

"Foo et, foo et!"

"I think he's saying pull it," I said. The only problem was the knob on our side was gone. Thinking quickly, Thad pulled out his knife and stuck it between the frame and door and pried the door open. Danny wriggled out of the hole and let out a loud breath.

Thad stepped in as light poured into the small storage room. "Look at all this," he said. "We've struck a gold mine."

"We sure have. Now let's hope it's the type of gold mine that can stop a fire," I said.

"What are we going to take?" Danny asked.

Thad and I looked at one another and replied in unison, "All of it." We busted out laughing.

We went to work on bringing everything out. It was an impressive amount of gear: two-inch gas-powered pumps, miles of hose and nozzles, drip torches, bunker gear, four full five-gallon DOT gas cans, three blue DOT cans full of mixed fuel for the drip torches, and probably my favorite part of our haul, flare guns.

By the time we got everything loaded it was coming on to dark, so we hustled to get back. I realized that while we worked, the people we saw on the road may have walked past, which made me nervous. I didn't want our group to encounter more characters like the ones we had met earlier this afternoon.

As we got closer to the house, we could see a large group farther south of our development. I exhaled a breath of relief that they had walked by, and hoped that would be the last large group for a while—though, obviously, with the fire looming, that possibility seemed dim.

Rolling up to the barricade, I stopped. "'Sup, ladies?" I asked with a smile.

"Whatever, Haywood," Jeff replied.

Thad leaned over. "That group give you guys any trouble?"

Tyler shook his head. "Nah, one of them came up and talked to us for a minute asking about water. Other than that, though, they didn't ask for anything. Said they're running from the fire and told us we should get moving too."

"That's good. See why we're doing this now, why we have to keep someone here at all times?" I asked. Jeff and Tyler nodded. "As for the fire, let's see what we can do about that too."

"What'd you get?" Jeff asked.

Thad stuck his big head in my face again, jutting a thumb over his shoulder. "Take a look for yourself."

Jeff and Tyler checked out the rear of the truck. "Look at all that stuff!" Tyler exclaimed.

"Yeah, we got a little bit," Danny replied, grinning.

Pointing to the gabions, I asked, "How'd the girls do?"

"They got one of them filled, it was rough though. They were pretty beat by the time they finished, but they wanted to complete one of them," Tyler said.

"Well, we'll have to get back to them tomorrow," I replied and waved out the window as we drove off.

Back at Danny's we decided to leave the gear in the truck, as we were all starving. The stew from hours ago was calling my name.

Jess, Fred, and Aric got up from the table they were sitting at. "Here, you guys sit and eat," Aric said.

The three of us sat down and Mel brought bowls over to us. It was hard to tell exactly what was in the stew, but it was good. Hell, anything would be good at that moment. Blowing on a hot spoonful, I said, "Hey, good job on getting that basket filled."

"Oh my God, Dad, that was so hard," Taylor said.

"I bet." I smiled, taking a bite.

"You have no idea, Dad. My hands have blisters," Lee Ann said, looking at her palms.

I laughed. "More than you know, kiddo. When you guys were really little I did more than my fair share of ditch digging." I held out one of my hands. "Don't worry, those blisters will turn into calluses soon enough."

"Eew, I don't want calluses!" Lee Ann shouted.

"Yeah, that's rough work. I think it would be better to do it in the morning or late afternoon. The middle of the day is brutal," Aric said.

Danny looked up and smiled. "Well, it's only going to get worse."

"Speaking of getting worse, it's getting hard to breathe out here!" Brandy said.

"Yeah, there's so much smoke in the air," Lee Ann added.

"What were you guys able to find?" Mel asked. I detailed what we had brought back, and though impressed, I could see doubt in her eyes. "Is that even going to help?"

I laughed. "Let me just put it this way: even before things went south they'd have had a hell of time putting this one out."

"Well, shit! What are we going to do?" Mel asked. You could tell that she was stressed simply from the fact that she cursed.

"Well, that's what we need to figure out."

"I don't know crap about firefighting, anyone else?" Aric asked.

"A little, theory mostly, but Mike, one of Sarge's guys, said he fought wildfires for a couple of summers after high school," I said.

"I figured we could set the trailer up with those tanks and use the pumps we found. Essentially, use it as a fire truck," Danny said.

"Those striker pumps will help, but they'll be about as effective as pissing into Hell trying to fight the blaze. They'll be used for hot spots or if ash sets other smaller fires around here."

"Then what the heck are we going to do? We're going to have to leave again," Bobbie said, panic in her voice.

Lee Ann moaned. "Aww, I don't want to leave again."

Taylor looked at me with wide eyes. "Dad, are we really going to have to go? Is there anything we can do?"

"The only thing I can think of is to set another fire," I said between bites.

Everyone looked at me like I was crazy. "What? Are you nuts?" Aric asked.

"It's called a back burn. We'll wait until it gets closer and then light a fire in front of it. If all goes as planned, that fire will burn toward the other one and use up all the fuel. When the two meet, the blaze should stop moving in that direction."

"What's to keep it from moving this way?" Mel asked.

"Well, what I'm thinking is to start the fire at 485, the road to Alexander Springs. The road will be a barricade this way, and the fire we'll light will be small so it's not likely to jump the road. On the east hopefully the run will be a barricade there, and it'll just burn down into a pocket with no way out."

Danny was nodding. "That's a good idea. With the trailer we can use it for any place it does jump."

"Do we have enough people for this?" Thad asked.

I shook my head. "No, but Mike has some knowledge as well as Jamie. I think we can get their help."

"Will that really work? The back fire?" Mary asked.

"It's our only shot. Well, that or run," I said.

"I'm not running unless I have to. I'm done running," Danny replied.

"Tomorrow we'll get a hold of Sarge and see what he thinks. Right now, though, we need to get Jeff and Tyler off the barricade," I said, standing up from the table. "You guys have worked pretty hard today," I said to Jess and Fred, and then looked at my girls. "You too. Guess it's me and you, Danny."

"You guys go for four hours or so and then my shift starts," Thad said. "And I'm with . . . ." He trailed off as he ran his finger down the list. "Aric."

"You feel up to it?" Fred asked Aric.

He nodded. "We just need to change the bandages. I'll be good."

Fred looked over at me. "Morgan, I hate to bring up another problem, but we're almost out of the bandages Doc gave us. Do you have anything we can use?"

Chewing on a mouthful, I thought about it for a moment, then Thad stepped in and answered, "Reuse what you have. Boil the old ones and let them dry, then reuse them."

Fred wrinkled her nose. "That's kind of gross."

"You got a better idea?" I asked.

"I've heard you can use maxi pads as dressings?" Aric said, getting a laugh out of Lee Ann and Taylor.

I snickered. "Have you seen the number of women around here? We need all of those we can get."

"All right, boiling and Betadine it is," Fred said.

"How's the wound looking, anyway?" Thad asked.

"Doc told us what infection would look like, and I don't think there is any. It's not red around the edges or anything," Aric replied.

"Good, let's hope it stays that way."

Looking at Danny I said, "Let me get my NVGs and we'll head down the road."

Mel stood up. "All right, girls, time to go." She went to the screen door and called out, "Ashley! It's time to go!"

"Aww, come on, can't we stay longer?"

"They'll be here tomorrow! Let's go."

Reluctantly she came trotting up the hill, Jace and Edie hot on her heels. I thanked the ladies for dinner and we left. Walking back to the house, Mel was holding my hand. Little Bit had the other.

"Daddy, is that fire going to burn our house down?" Little Bit asked.

"I hope not, baby. We're going to try and stop it."

"I hope we can. I like it here. I don't want to leave again," she replied.

"Me too, monkey. Me too."

As the older girls ran in the house shouting something about playing Scrabble, I went in and found the NVGs. Grabbing a canteen, I filled it from the Berkey and stuck it in a pouch on the back of the vest.

"How long are you going to be gone?" Mel asked.

"Few hours. I'll just be at the end of the road, though."

"I know, I just don't like it when you're not here at night."

I wrapped my arms around her. "Me too, can't sleep unless you're around nowadays."

She smiled and gave me a kiss. "Love you."

"Love you too. I'll be back in a bit," I said and walked back over to Danny's.

We took two of the four-wheelers and rode down to the barricade. The smoke was getting heavier, as was the ash, falling like light snow. Jeff and Tyler were happy to see us, and even happier to see the food we brought.

"See anything?" Danny asked.

"A few people came by. They looked pitiful. Remember the people we used to see walking the road, you know, in the beginning?" Jeff asked.

I nodded. "Worse than that."

"A group came by earlier with a wagon that only had three

wheels. I felt so bad for them. Just a look of utter defeat on their faces," Tyler said.

"I can understand. Think about it: they've made it this far, and probably had some sort of life reestablished, and now it's all going to be burned up," Danny said.

"I hope that doesn't happen to us," Jeff said. "I've grown to really like it here."

I smiled. "Yeah, we're like mold: we'll grow on ya."

Jeff laughed. "You're an idiot."

They got on the four-wheelers and headed down the road. Danny and I went out to the barricade and leaned on the top log.

"Like déjà vu," Danny said.

"Yeah, the more things change, the more they seem to stay the same."

We watched as the sun began to drop for the horizon. The smoke acted as a filter and gave it a strange, ominous look, like a large red ball kissing the horizon. As soon as the sun dipped from view, the skeeters emerged with a vengeance.

"Holy shit, these things are thick," I said, slapping the back of my neck.

"This'll help," Danny said with a grin. He pulled a can of OFF! out of his vest, and my eyes just about rolled out of my head.

"Oh, thank the Lord. How much of that do you have?"

"Couple of cans, not much," Danny replied as he began spraying his arms.

With the sun finally down I walked out into the road and looked north. Just above the horizon, the fire seemed to flicker and dance, changing colors as it did. Danny walked out and we stood there in silence for a moment.

"Man, that looks like it could burn the entire world," Danny said.

"I guess it'll stop about Key West," I said with a snort.

"You really think the back fire plan will work?"

"In theory. That's all I can say."

"I hope your theory proves right."

"Me too, man. Hey, look at the bright side. Hurricane season's going to start soon. That'll put the fire out for sure."

Danny laughed. "Oh yeah, that makes it better."

We stood in the road for a long time watching the glow. As it got darker the sinister glow got brighter, extending as far to both sides as we could see. I pictured a map of Florida in my mind, trying to think of what was out there. If it went too far to the west it could potentially hit Ocala. All the pastureland surrounding it on the west side might slow it, and the city was pretty spread out and would probably be spared. But there were countless little towns scattered all over the forest that would surely be burned to the ground.

Between us and the blaze was nothing but forest at this point. This thing looked like it was hundreds of square miles. If we managed to stop it from burning through here, to turn it with the back burn, the fire would burn all the way down to the St. Johns and destroy countless more lives. As awful as it sounded, though, I knew I couldn't worry about those lives. I just wanted to protect the ones here. If it didn't jump the river, it would burn itself out, and if it did, Deland would be the next to go—and we wouldn't be too far behind.

Thinking about the cities that would be affected, DeBary popped into my head. Mom and Dad lived there. Their place was down on the river—the other side, thankfully. I had no idea if they were still there, or even still alive for that matter. I wished I could go find out, but the trip by truck would probably be impossible. I could make it via the St. Johns, going down the Alexander Run to where it dumped into the big backward-flowing river, but that would take days and I had no idea what the river was like. Surely there were a lot of people roaming it. I just had to put faith in the fact that they were surviving just as we were. And if I knew my parents, they were probably even better off than I was. My dad was a tough guy, even more prepared than me. The thought brought a smile to face. I could just see him in his kayak out on the river fishing. He loved to fish and even being forced to do it out of need would never dampen his enthusiasm for the sport.

Danny wandered back over to the barricade and I followed him. It was full-on dark now, the skeeters testing the limits of the OFF! I climbed up on the barricade and sat on the top log. Danny came up beside me and we sat there in the silence. Even though it had been months now, the silence of this new era always struck me. The night was so quiet—the days were too, for that matter—but after the sun went down it took on another level. With no man-made sound, the world was a very quiet place.

From time to time I would take the NVGs out and scan the road. Toward the end of our shift, we heard some shouts. Both of us dropped off the log and jogged out into the road. The shouts were far off to the north, and while we couldn't make out the words, it sounded angry. A single gunshot rang out, followed by the piercing scream of a woman. The shouting stopped, but the wails of the woman continued.

"Somebody's having a bad day," Danny said.

"Sounds like it," I said as I looked through the NVGs.

"See anything?"

"No, there's what might be a small fire, but it's way up there."

We walked across the road and sat in the grass. Using the goggles I looked up at the stars. The smoke in the air blocked out a number of them, but there was still an amazing variety to see. Looking at the Big Dipper, movement caught my eye. It looked like a star was slowly moving across the sky.

"I see a satellite," I said.

"No shit, where?" Danny asked, grabbing for my goggles.

I handed them over. "Over there. Look at the end of the Big Dipper."

Danny held them up and searched the sky for a moment. "I see it. Hauling ass, isn't it?"

"Yeah, wonder what kind it is."

"I wonder who it belongs to," Danny quipped. He scanned the sky again for a bit. "Remember that night we saw the space station?"

"Yeah, wonder if it's still up there?"

"If it is, I feel for the poor bastards who are on it."

"Man, that would suck. Run out of O2 or maybe food and water," I said, shaking my head.

"I guess they have an escape pod or something."

"Yeah, coming down in the middle of the ocean would sure suck, though."

Danny grunted. "Be better than being stuck in space."

I laughed. "Got a point there."

Danny dropped the goggles, looking down the road. "People."

I leaned forward to look down the road. "Where?"

"Walking right down the middle of the road," he replied, handing me the goggles.

Sure enough there was a couple walking down the road. They didn't appear to have much with them, no wagon or cart, as was the norm with passing refugees. I couldn't even see a pack on them.

"What do you want to do?" I asked.

"Let's sit here. Maybe they'll just walk by."

I dropped down, propping myself up on an elbow, and stared into the darkness. Every now and then I would raise the goggles and see where they were.

"They're getting pretty close," I said.

"Yeah, I can hear them talking," Danny replied in a whisper.

We sat quietly as the pair drew near. Soon they were close enough that we could actually make out what they were saying.

". . . should have just given it up," a man's voice said.

"You didn't have to *shoot* him," a woman replied angrily.

"It's not like I had a choice! He should have just given it up."

"He had children!" she practically shouted.

"He wasn't dead. He was still alive when we left, and we can eat tonight."

Danny looked over at me, eyebrows raised. I knew he was thinking the same thing I was: whether or not we should do something. But without knowing exactly what had happened, it didn't seem worth interfering. The two continued to talk as they approached. The woman asked where they were going to sleep for the night.

"I don't know. Let's get some distance behind us."

As they were passing our little road, the woman asked, "What about here? Let's just go find a house and sleep there. Not like they'll come looking in all of the houses."

The two stopped and looked around. "I don't know. I'd rather get farther down the road," the man said nervously.

"But I'm tired! My feet hurt. We've been walking all day. It's not my fault you lost your damn mind."

"You need to keep moving," Danny said in a stern voice, surprising me. Hearing his voice, they both spun around, the man shoving a hand into his pocket. I jumped up, as did Danny. We both lit them up with the lights on our carbines.

"Just keep walking. We don't need your kind here," Danny said.

"Don't shoot, please don't shoot!" the woman cried.

"Sounds like you didn't have a problem with shooting a minute ago," Danny said.

I called out, "Take your hand out of your pocket real, real slow, mister."

Seeing he was outnumbered, he slowly withdrew his hand. "We're not looking for any trouble. We'll be on our way."

"What was worth killing a man over?" Danny asked.

The woman looked at the man, the fear on her face obvious. Neither of them answered so Danny shouted the question again, causing them both to jump and the woman to cry.

"Show him, just show him!" she pleaded with the man.

He slowly took a pack off his back and unzipped it. Reaching in, he withdrew a can and held it out.

"You killed a man over a can of corn?" I asked.

"We didn't mean to!" the woman cried.

"You killed a man with kids to take that?" Danny asked.

"I didn't want to. It just . . . sort of happened," the man muttered.

"Get on your knees!" Danny shouted. "Hands on your head!"

The woman jumped at the shout but quickly complied, crying all the while. The man hesitated. I was just as enraged as Danny and shouted at him, "On your knees or I'll put you in the ground!"

He slowly went to his knees and put his hands on his head. "Cover me," Danny said. "If he moves, shoot his ass."

As Danny started toward them I stepped forward, my carbine centered on his chest. The man's eyes followed Danny as he circled behind him. Once behind the man, Danny jammed the muzzle of his rifle in his back. "You blink and you're a dead man."

Reaching into the man's pocket, he pulled out a small silver revolver. He quickly patted the rest of his pockets and produced a small handful of bullets. Tucking the pistol in his belt, Danny backed around them and returned to where I was standing. He opened the cylinder of the pistol and inspected it, then extracted one fired case.

"We should just shoot your ass," Danny said.

"Please don't kill us!" the woman cried.

"I didn't mean to," the man replied, looking at the ground. "He should have just given it to me." His shoulders slumped. "Just do it if you're going to do it."

"Awful brave all of a sudden," Danny said.

"You're not even worth killing. You're the scum of the earth. Just get the hell out of here and *never* come back," I said.

"You can't send us out without a gun. We'll get killed," the man said.

"Maybe. Maybe you'll come across someone just like yourself. Maybe they'll kill you for something, or for nothing. I don't care," Danny added.

The man looked at the woman with him. Her hair was long but matted and in her face. "Think of my wife. How can

I protect her?" He paused. "There are worse things than death."

"You think about that while you walk. Think about some woman and kids you just left down the road with a dead man you just shot."

"Go, now," Danny said.

Apprehensively the woman rose to her feet. The man stood as well but made no indication he was going to leave.

"Mister, if you don't start walking I'm going to shoot you," Danny said.

The man shook his head. "This ain't right," he said, then he suddenly made a rush at us. Danny pulled the trigger an instant before I did, both bullets striking the man in the chest. The woman let out a bloodcurdling scream and rushed toward him.

She rolled him over and I could hear the gurgle of blood in the man's throat. She wrapped her hands around his face and wailed as he said something to her that I couldn't understand. Her head dropped onto his chest as she lost control of herself. At the same time, the sound of ATVs starting to gain speed drifted through the night. I could see the headlights of the two machines bouncing along the dirt road. Thad was surely on one of them.

The woman looked up, her eyes full of tears and snot dripping from both nostrils. "What am I going to do now?" she screamed, her body wracked with sobs.

I felt for her in a way. She'd just lost someone she obviously loved, but how could they kill someone over a damn can of corn, and then try to attempt to hurt us, even after we said they could go?

The two ATVs came flying up and skidded to a stop. Jeff and Thad were on them and both were off and looking around before the machines even stopped, it seemed.

"What happened?" Thad asked, looking at the woman.

Danny relayed the story to them. As he did, Jeff walked over and picked up the can lying on the pavement. "How can you kill someone over a can of corn?"

"Believe me, we've been thinking the same thing," I replied.

Thad looked down the dark road, and I could tell by the look on his face that he was beyond himself with the thought of such an injustice done to a family. "We should probably go down there and check on the family, see if we can give them shelter for the night," he finally said.

"You think it's safe?" Danny asked.

"No more or less than standing here, probably," I replied. "Besides, if some poor gal is sitting on the side of the road with a couple of kids and a dead man, we should try and help."

"What about her? What are we going to do with her?" Jeff asked, pointing at the woman lying in the road.

"I don't know," I said, looking at Danny.

"We can't just leave her out here," Danny said, glaring down at her pitiful form. "It's not like she did it."

I looked down at her again, really unsure of what do about her. In the end, though, she wasn't my problem. I didn't create the situation. I really couldn't care less what happened to her. "You need to move on. You can't stay here."

She didn't react, just sat there staring at her dead husband. Stepping up, I poked her shoulder with the muzzle of my rifle. "I said you need to go."

She looked up, a wet sneer on her face, but it was her eyes

that I noticed. What I saw is hard to describe: rage, hate, maybe terror. "You're disgusting! You just killed my husband and all you can say to me is that I have to leave? What's wrong with you? What kind of a person are you?" she shrieked at me.

I stared at her for a moment. "I don't know anymore. One thing I'm not, though, is the kind of man that would kill another in front of his children for a can of corn."

She looked back at the body of her husband. In a near whisper she said, "It was an accident. It shouldn't have happened."

"You're right about that. Now get moving before we find out if I'm the kind of guy who would shoot an unarmed woman." I replied in a monotone, though I certainly didn't mean it—I just wanted her to go.

She looked up at me, obviously unsure herself. Taking another look at her husband, she leaned over and kissed his forehead. Rising to her feet, she turned and started down the road toward Altoona. I watched her go until the night consumed her. It was so quiet. I looked up at the stars above, then back down the road. Thad's voice roused me back to the moment.

"Morg, let's go and see if we can find the man he killed," Thad said, looking down the road. "I can't bear the thought of a couple of kids sitting out there somewhere with their dead daddy."

Thad and I got on the ATVs and headed down the road, each taking a lane. The ATVs moved us along quickly and it wasn't long before we were at the Pittman Center. It was a cool place. The little cabin was one of the few remaining buildings from the Civilian Conservation Corps days. It sat under a scattered canopy of oak trees right across the road from Lake Dorr. As we edged closer, movement caught my eye. I swung into the lime-rock drive, the headlights illuminating the parking area. The white drive was littered with debris dropped from the trees overhead and the grassy area to the side of the cabin was a tangled mass of choking weeds and untamed grass. Lying at the edge of the mass, faceup and arms spread out as if crucified, was a body.

Beside this gruesome scene, a woman and her two small children were hunched over, all crying. They appeared to take no notice of our arrival. The woman was holding one of the man's hands as the two kids clung to her. Stopping the ATV, I stepped off and walked toward her, pausing about twenty feet away. I knelt down in an attempt to be on her level and not appear as a threat.

"Ma'am?" I said. She didn't look up but continued to cry.

"Ma'am, we're here to help you," I said as I moved a little closer and turned on my flashlight, shining it on the ground.

This time she looked up. Her face showed no fear, only anguish. "Help? You can't fix this. They killed my husband!" She began to sob again. "Over a can of corn," she said, pounding the ground with her fist.

"I'm really sorry for your loss, and I can't imagine what you're feeling, but you can't stay here. Can we take you and the kids someplace safe?"

She looked around into the darkness, then at the kids. "We were trying to find someplace safe. The fire drove us out of our neighborhood. I told him we needed to hide"—she started to sob again—"but he said we'd be okay."

"Let us help you out. We can take you away from this, get some food for the kids."

She gripped the kids tight to her. A sudden change came

over her. "Why? Why do you want to help us? Who are you anyway?"

"I'm Morgan"—I pointed back to Thad—"and that's Thad, and we want to help because that's what people should do in situations like this. Not everyone is a predator."

Again she looked at the kids but didn't answer. I stood up. "I'll be right back."

Thad had been keeping watch over us and the road. I walked back to him. "Hey, can you run back and get the truck, and maybe Mel or one of the other girls, and bring them back. We can't leave her and the kids here, but she needs to know that she can trust us."

Thad looked around. "You gonna be all right here?"

"For a little while, but just hurry the hell up. I don't need any more encounters with creeps from the street."

Thad nodded. "All right, I'll be back as fast as I can."

"Please do."

Thad jumped on the ATV and took off, this time running wide-open. I walked back to the woman and knelt down.

"We're bringing a truck. My wife, Mel, will be coming back with Thad as well." Mentioning Mel seemed to offer a little assurance to her.

"Mommy, I'm stirsty," the little boy said.

"Mom, why don't you and the kids come over to the cabin. Let's sit on the steps and I'll give them a drink of water."

She nodded with blank eyes, and I extended a hand to help her to her feet. She held the kids' hands as we walked over to the cabin. As we walked the little boy said, "My daddy's dead."

My heart broke. This little boy couldn't have been more than five, his sister probably three. At the steps of the cabin, I pulled out the canteen, spun the top open, and handed it to the little girl first. She took only a small sip from it and handed it to the boy, who gulped from it greedily, water spilling out and running down his chin and onto his Spider-Man shirt.

"You stay here. I'm going to check this place real quick," I said to their mother. She didn't reply as she watched the boy drink from the canteen, just nodded absently.

Shouldering my carbine, I flipped the weapon light on and stepped onto the porch. The door to the cabin was open and it was obvious people had been living here at various times. In the small store they had sold books and maps, topo maps of the forest. The books were scattered all over the place with pages torn out and strewn about—senseless destruction for no purpose other than the act itself. People amazed me, and suddenly I was hit with a thought: How long would it be before another book was printed? I quickly pushed that depressing thought aside and continued clearing the small cabin. Returning to the front room, I started going through the maps and books that littered the floor. I was surprised to find several of the maps still in usable condition. It appeared someone had lined the floor and slept on them but they were still in remarkably good shape. I thought it odd that they wouldn't see them as a valuable resource with more uses than just a glorified pillow.

Rolling up the maps I went back out to the porch. As I walked down the steps she handed me the canteen. "Thank you."

"Don't mention it. Have the kids had anything to eat today?"

She shook her head. "We were saving the corn: we were going to eat it tonight when those two people showed up. They asked if they could have some, and my husband told them he was sorry but it was for the kids. The man got mad and pulled a gun. He told Lee to give him the can, and Lee said no, and the next thing I knew the man shot him." She delivered the description in a monotone.

"I'm really sorry to hear about this. Where are you from?"

"We lived just outside of Palatka. When the fire started, we had to leave, and we've been walking ever since."

"What's your name?" I asked.

Without looking up she replied, "Kathy."

"Well, Kathy, just know you'll have a place to sleep tonight."

We sat there in silence, which was occasionally punctuated by the sound of sobs from Kathy. Soon the sounds of the old Suburban rumbling toward us were clear. It was music to my ears. Presently the truck came into view and Mel and Jess got out along with Thad.

"Glad to see you guys," I said, walking up to them.

"Any trouble?" Thad asked.

I shook my head. "No, let's just get them loaded up and get the hell out of here."

We walked over to Kathy and her kids. "Kathy, this is my wife, Mel, and this is our friend Jess."

Mel knelt down beside her. "Hi, Kathy, let's get you someplace safe for the night. We've got food for the kids too."

Kathy looked up at her but didn't reply. Jess knelt down as well. "It's going to be all right. You'll be safe."

As Mel and Jess got Kathy and the kids moving, Thad pulled me off to the side. "Let's get the body wrapped up so we can bury it." He had a roll of plastic under his arm.

I nodded and we went over to the body and laid out the plastic. As respectfully as we could, we rolled the body onto the plastic and wrapped it up. Thad opened the tailgate and we slid the body in. I told Thad to drive the truck and I'd take the ATV back. At the barricade, I pulled up beside the truck. Jeff and Danny were talking to Thad in hushed tones.

"Take them to my place. We've got the room," Danny said.

Thad stepped out. "You take them. I'll stay here with Jeff. It's our shift anyway."

I nodded and followed Danny as he drove the truck down to his place. Mel and Jess helped Kathy get the kids in the house, where Bobbie showed them to the downstairs bedroom. They were offered food, but Kathy politely declined, saying she was tired and just wanted to be with her kids. Jess said she would stay there, sleeping on the sofa just in case Kathy needed anything. As they were getting settled in, I told Danny in hushed tones that I would leave the truck there. We'd have to bury the body in the morning.

"Both of them," he said.

"Oh yeah, I guess so," I replied, thinking of the other one still lying in the road. "See you in the morning," I said as I took Mel's hand and headed for the door.

Mel and I crossed through the hole in the fence, walking quietly. She asked what had happened and I told her the story. She didn't say anything while I replayed the events at the barricade and our trip down to the welcome center.

"Over a can of corn?" she finally said in a near whisper.

I squeezed her hand. "Yeah, over a can of corn."

Chapter 8

I was up early the next morning to the heavy smell of smoke. It was always worse in the morning, the dew holding the smoke close to the ground. Going outside I could actually see the smoke now as it hung in the trees and moved in wisps through our neighborhood. We were going to have to call Sarge today and deal with the plan for fighting this fire. But first things first. I pulled on my shoes and headed over to Danny's place.

On the back porch, I found Jess frying eggs, with Kathy and her kids sitting at one of the tables.

"Hey, Jess," I said with a smile. She smiled back and went back to tending her eggs.

Kathy looked a lot better this morning. Looking up she offered a slight smile. "Good morning. Thank you for what you've done."

"Don't mention it, it's the least we could do," I replied. I gestured to the pan. "You guys getting some breakfast?"

Her face brightened a bit. "Yes, scrambled eggs. I can't remember the last time I had eggs."

"These two should like them, I would think."

She smiled at the kids. "Oh yes, they're going to be very happy."

"You guys get breakfast down and we'll sort out where you can stay later today."

Kathy looked surprised. "Oh, I don't want to stay. You're all very nice, but I want to get to my sister in Eustis. I tried to get Lee to go, but they didn't get along, but now . . ." She trailed off.

"I'm sure we can arrange that. We'll work it out," I replied.

While I was talking, Danny came out on the porch and sat down to put his boots on.

"You guys sleep good?" Danny asked Kathy.

"Oh yes, it was really nice to sleep in a bed again."

Jess fixed three plates and carried them over to the table, setting them out. The kids quickly went to eating. Kathy looked up. "Are you going to eat?"

"We will in a bit. We usually wait until everyone is here. We prepare all our meals here and eat together," Jess replied.

Kathy pulled the plate toward her. "That sounds like a wonderful tradition."

I nodded at her, then looked at Danny. "You ready to run to the camp?"

"Yeah, but we need to unload the truck." I nodded and looked over at Kathy. "Later today we will have a service for your husband if you want. It's the least we can do."

She looked up. "He's here?"

Danny and I both nodded. "We brought him with us last night."

She looked back down at her plate and picked at the eggs with a fork. After a moment, without looking up, she replied, "Thank you."

Danny and I unloaded the body, putting it in one of the sheds for the current moment. With that unsavory task completed, we headed out in the truck. Tyler, Brandy, and the kids were coming through the gate as we went out. I stopped for a moment to talk to them.

"Hey, Tyler, can you take a turn on the barricade in a bit?"

He nodded. "Sure thing. I'll get down there in a minute."

"Thanks, I'll see if I can get Fred and Aric to come down too."

"How's that woman this morning? Mel told me about it. It's just awful," Brandy said, shaking her head.

"She's all right, still processing it." I looked at the kids. "Having these two around will help, give her kids something to do until they head to Eustis."

"I'm sure they will," she replied with a smile.

"We'll see you guys later," I said as I pulled through the gate.

At the road to the house shared by the girls, Thad and Jeff and I turned off. As I pulled into the driveway, the door opened and Fred and Aric came out.

"Hey, guys," Danny said.

Fred yawned. "Hi."

"What are you guys up to?" I asked

"We're on the barricade this morning," Aric replied.

"Hop in, we'll give you a ride," Danny said.

After getting in, Fred asked, "What happened last night?"

Danny gave them the elevator version of what happened, and the looks on their faces said it all.

"You gotta be kidding me. They killed him over a can of corn?" Aric asked.

"Apparently life is cheap now," I replied.

We got out at the barricade to talk with Thad and Jeff. Jeff was lying on the top log of the barricade, like a cat sleeping on top of a TV. Thad was standing out in the road, looking north.

"It's getting worse," Thad said without looking over.

"We're going to go up to the camp and see if they can help us," I replied.

"I'll go with you."

I looked over at him. "Aren't you tired?"

"No, I'm good. Plus, this is more important," he replied as he turned and walked back toward the truck.

"All right, then. Tyler is coming down shortly to join you guys. We'll be back soon," I said.

"Good luck, Morgan," Fred said. "I really hope that with all of us working together, we can fight the fire."

As we drove down the road, we passed a number of people walking south. All of them looked woeful—just weary souls slogging down the road.

As we approached a group of several people a man jumped out in the road gesturing wildly, waving a rifle over his head. I swerved off the right shoulder, only to see the guy raise the rifle.

Danny screamed, "Gun!" and raised his carbine. He didn't hesitate and began firing—directly through my windshield. Glass splintered around the cab and the report was deafening, causing me to nearly lose control of the truck. The people on the road scattered, running for cover. I saw the man go down as I tried to regain control of the truck, swerving back onto the road. The truck fishtailed, and there was a sickening bump as we bounced over the man's body.

When I looked in the mirror, the body was still rolling in the road. Thad was looking back as well, then he looked at me in the mirror with horror in his eyes.

"I didn't mean to, man—that was an accident!" I shouted.

"Doesn't much matter now, I guess," he replied.

Danny was looking back as well. When he turned in his seat I looked at him, then at what was left of the windshield, then back at him. "Dude! The windshield! Really?"

He looked at me like I was nuts. "What the hell did you want me to do? You were swerving to the right, I couldn't get a shot. Would you rather he shot at us?"

"I know, I know why you did it." I shook my head. "But look at it."

"We're still here, though," Thad said.

I drove considerably faster now, not wanting to give anyone the opportunity to fire at us again. As we neared the camp, a string of trucks was pulling out. I stopped beside the lead Hummer, where Ted was behind the wheel.

"Hey, man," I said as I stopped.

Ted was looking at the windshield. "Are those coming in or going out?"

"Going out."

"Getting a little hairy, huh?"

"Yeah, the road is packed with people. Some of them needed a little persuasion to get out of the way."

"I see." Ted leaned back and shouted up into the turret, "You hear that, Mike?"

"Yeah, I won't have to shoot the windshield out, though," Mike called back.

"I would hope not. That'd be a hell of a trick from up there."

"Where's Sarge and Sheffield?" I asked.

"They're back at the CP. What's up?"

"We want to see if they'll help us with this fire," Thad replied.

"Go on in, you got any ideas?" Ted asked.

"Yeah, it might work," I said and pointed at Mike. "And he knows how to do it."

Ted started laughing. "You're relying on him to save your place?"

I nodded. "I think he can do it." Mike smiled and winked at me.

Slapping the cab of the truck, Mike shouted, "Told you I was a firefighter!"

Ted shook his head. "Yeah, well, I always figured you more for one to set fires, not put them out."

"I'm good at that too!" Mike shouted.

Ted shook his head. "See you guys later, we gotta get moving." We waved as he pulled away and headed into the camp. Once again, the place was buzzing with activity. All manner of stuff was being sorted and stacked. Pulling up to the CP, we jumped out and went in to find Sarge, Livingston, and Sheffield in the conference room. I rapped on the door frame. "Can we come in?"

"Sure, Morgan, come in, take a seat," Sarge replied. "You fellas look like you have something on your minds."

"We do, we need some help," Thad said.

"What do you need?" Sheffield asked.

"We need some of your people to join forces with us to help with the fire," I said.

Sheffield's head cocked to the side. "You've got a plan to stop it?"

"We've got an idea of a way to try and redirect it. There's no way we can put it out, but maybe we can push it from spreading south into more communities."

"What are you thinking?" Sarge asked.

"I was thinking of a back burn, to try and keep it from continuing south."

Sarge nodded. "That's one way, for sure. Where were you thinking of setting it?"

I walked up to a wall that had a large map of the area. "I was thinking of starting it on the north side of this gas line right-of-way here. Originally I was thinking of doing it here on 485, but I think this would work better," I said, putting my finger on the map.

Sarge got up and came over, looking at the line, which cut straight as an arrow across the map.

Sarge returned to his seat. "We're hoping the fire will stop at Highway 40. It might jump it, but we're hoping it won't."

"We should find out today," Livingston added.

That got our attention. "It's already down to 40?" Danny asked.

"It'll probably be there today."

"Damn," Thad said.

"How much longer until you guys are out of here?" I asked.

"We should make our last trip today, late this afternoon hopefully," Sheffield said.

"What about the civilians here?" Danny asked.

"The ones left are hell-bent on staying, won't listen to reason," Sarge said.

"This place will go up like gasoline," Thad said.

"We've told them, we've tried to convince them to leave," Livingston said.

"I addressed the camp yesterday, told them about the fire. Some people decided it wasn't worth the risk, but many of them think that because this place is surrounded by sand the fire can't get here. They think they'll be safe, so they're going to stick it out," Sheffield said.

"They don't seem to understand that the fire's going to come from the sky. Enough embers fall on those tents and this place is going up," Sarge added.

I shook my head. "Some people will never learn. But back to the question: Will you guys help us?" I asked.

Sheffield studied the map for a moment. "How about this," he said, pointing to a forestry road just north of the camp. "Let's start one here, on the north side of this road. It'll offer the folks here some protection if it works. If it doesn't work, we can use the same strategy on the line you indicated, to try and push it around your place."

"That makes sense. We can work on it up here and see how it reacts," Danny said.

"How are we going to light this thing?" Sheffield asked, then looked at Livingston. "We got enough fuel to do this?"

"We've got a bunch of drip torches and some fuel. It's a mixture of diesel and gas," I said.

"Where'd you get those?" Livingston asked.

"We found them," Thad said with a smile.

Sarge smiled broadly. "I bet you did."

"When do you want to do this?" Livingston asked.

"We should do it before it hits 40. If it was to jump, the two could just merge into one, adding even more fuel to the bigger fire," Sarge said.

"True. All right, we need to get organized for this. Sarge, you take command. How many people do you think you'll need?" Sheffield asked.

"Right now not too many. Mikey has experience with this sort of thing, so I need him. Jamie too—she's a firefighter as well. With Morgan's people and a few others we can probably handle this for now. If it was to jump the road up there, it'll be a different story, though," Sarge replied.

Sheffield nodded. "All right, take who you need." He looked at Livingston. "You keep track of what's going on with this, who's on the detail, and rounding up anything they need."

Livingston nodded. "Roger that. Mike is out on the convoy to the armory, and when he gets back we'll pull him." He looked at Sarge. "Why don't you guys go see where it is? Let's get some intel on what we're dealing with, in the meantime I'll put together a unit for you. When you get back we can go over the plan."

"We're going to try to get the last of this mess organized. I want to finish the move today, especially if this fire is encroaching," Sheffield said. "And I'm going to tell the civilians one more time that we recommend them moving. There's no way that anyone should try and wait this out."

"Roger that. And get those other boys ready. We're going to need to move on this as quickly as possible."

With that, we piled in my truck and headed north, crossing Highway 40. The smoke was now over us, being blown by upper atmosphere winds. As we got closer to the fire, the surface winds began to pick up. It was creating its own winds in order to feed itself. Before we got to Juniper Run we could see the flames leaping a hundred feet into the air. Stopping in the road, we got out and stared in awe at the spectacle before us.

Sarge craned his neck to look up at the flames. After a moment, he said, "You know, maybe we should just start the back fire back there at the highway. The road and easements on either side might offer some buffer."

"It might be better to try it way up here instead, since we're at least a mile north of 40. If it doesn't work it'll give us more time for a second try," Thad said.

"If we're going to do that, we need to do it damn quick. That thing will be down there in a couple of hours probably," Danny said.

"That's why I think we should start it down at the highway. We just don't have the time to get set up here"—Sarge pointed into the woods—"not to mention how hard it's going to be to try and do it in that mess. If we do it down at 40, we can just walk down the side of the road to set it."

I nodded. "That's a good point. If we went out there into the forest, we could find ourselves on the wrong side of a fire in a hurry with no way out."

"Let's get moving, then," Sarge said.

On the way back to the camp, we discussed the plan. We'd go back and get the drip torches and fuel while Sarge would meet with Livingston and lay out our plan. We'd ride the ATVs back and use them, riding along the side of the road with the torches dripping to start the fire. We'd start it on both sides of Highway 19, using the grassy easements to encourage it to burn to the north.

After dropping Sarge off, we hurried back to the neighborhood, only waving at the crew at the barricade as we passed. At Danny's, we got out and started to load the torches and their fuel, along with some of the other firefighting essentials. We had an assortment of tools that we thought would come in handy. Once we had everything loaded up, we went into Danny's for a fast bite to eat. All the ladies and kids were out back, the kids playing in the backyard. We quickly explained the situation, and I could see the fear in their eyes, though I tried to keep my tone as light as possible. I didn't want to scare the kids. We scarfed down some food—I didn't know when the next time we'd be eating would be—and then we were on our way again.

At the camp, Sarge was waiting at the turn-off with a couple of Hummers and some Guardsmen. As we approached, they pulled out into the road and led the way. We stopped in the middle of the intersection of Highways 40 and 19 to discuss the plan.

"I've never done this before, you know. I wish my dad were here. He's done a bunch of these for the state," I said to Danny as we walked up to the group.

Danny stopped and looked at me square in the eyes. "You got your daddy's spirit. We're gonna do this thing."

We walked over and joined the group. Sarge was looking north toward the towering thunderhead of smoke. Pointing, he looked back at those of us assembled. "Gentlemen"—he glanced at Jamie and smiled—"and you, Jamie: there is no way in hell we're going to stop that, but we may just be able to part it, as it were."

"He's right, there is no way we can stop this—we simply don't have the resources—but what we're going to attempt is to create a burned wedge of ground and allow the fire to burn around either side of it. Hopefully it will bypass us." Mike looked at me. "Morgan, can you get the torches and other gear?"

I nodded and Thad, Jeff, and Danny followed me to the truck. We quickly loaded the gear and with the help of a couple of the Guardsmen carried it all over to the group. Mike picked up one of the torches and started talking.

"Starting the fire is easy, keeping it where we want it is

another issue entirely." He motioned skyward. "This wind is going to make this very difficult. To start the fire, we'll ride down the side of the road on the two four-wheelers and drip the flame. Everyone else will be on the far side of the road." He reached into his pocket and produced a handful of OD green whistles on cords. "If anyone sees a spot fire start on the opposite side, blow your whistle. When you hear a whistle, everyone needs to get there and get that fire under control, then quickly get back to your position to watch for more. Understand this, there *will* be fires, they are going to start, and if we can't control them we'll be overrun by them. So we have to be on top of it as soon as possible. Everyone understand?" He was answered with solemn nods from all of us.

"Morgan, you and Danny get on them ATVs and get this thing going while we get everyone else positioned," Sarge said.

"I'll go east," I said to Danny. He nodded, grabbed a torch, climbed on his Polaris, and sped off to the west.

Riding slowly at the edge of the woods, the flame from the torch dribbled out onto the dry grass and palmettos. A quick glance backward revealed that the small flames were quickly growing. The small spots of fire were merging into a wall of flame as it burned into the woods. Far down the road to the west I could see the smoke starting to build from the fire Danny was starting. The smoke from our combined fires began rising into the sky, creating another layer of smoke, dwarfed by the much larger head of smoke high above it.

As I rode I could see Sarge and Mike organizing the rest of the crew. They were being positioned on the side of the road with shovels, axes, beaters, and Pulaskis. Everyone looked on edge. While the fire was growing, it was still manageable, and so far everything was going according to plan, but it could turn at any moment. With everyone in position, Sarge and Mike rode up and down the stretch of highway keeping a close eye on the fire.

Danny and I met at the intersection where the Suburban was parked. We traded the torches for a couple of shovels, just to be ready for any spot fires that may pop up. Sarge rolled up beside us. "So far, so good," he said.

"Looks that way. Hope it lasts," Danny replied.

"We're just getting started. As things build, it's going to get busy," Mike said.

As we were talking the first whistle sounded. Looking to the east I saw some of the Guardsmen running. "Looks like we just got busy," I said as I started the ATV and pulled away with Danny and Sarge following.

We all got to work putting out the fire with shovels and other tools. It wasn't a big fire and was quickly brought under control. "That wasn't so bad," Thad said as he wiped sweat from his forehead.

"Not bad. Good job, guys. Everyone back to their positions—this ain't over yet," Mike said.

"Sure thing, Captain Bring Down," Thad said with a smile as he started walking back down the road.

"Come on, let's get back down the road," I said with a smile.

Before we could get back on the machines, another whistle sounded, back toward the intersection this time. Just as with the previous one, several Guardsmen were making their way toward the fire. Danny and I skidded to a stop and hopped off. This fire was larger than the last, and spreading even more quickly. We were tackling it just like the first one, but it wasn't working out nearly as well.

Danny was beating the ground with a rake and looked up. "This is going to be a long day."

"No shit," I replied as I tied a bandanna around my face.

He looked at me. "Damn, that's a good idea."

Reaching into my pocket, I tossed one to him. "It is."

Mike waded into the mass of flailing shovels, axes, and beaters and started giving orders. "Morgan, Jeff, you guys get on this side, start raking the ground litter back. We need to create a break here." He pointed to two Guardsmen. "Get on the left side and start pulling the downed wood out. Pull it away before it catches."

We worked frantically, as hot ash and soot were falling all over us. Thad appeared with a rake, helping me and Danny as we worked on the break on the far side. Mike had a Pulaski and was hacking down some brush. "I hope it doesn't get any worse!" I shouted, throwing a shovelful of dirt into the fire.

"Shit, this ain't even bad yet," Mike called back.

Over the clanking of shovels and rakes, another whistle sounded, then another. Sarge was standing by the road and shouted to Mike he would go check on it, to stay with this one. He quickly returned to the Hummer and headed back east.

It took another several minutes for us to get the fire under control. It was hot, miserable work and we were just getting started.

"Come on, guys, let's get down there," Mike said as he came out onto the road. Danny and I got on the ATVs. Thad climbed on with me and Mike with Danny.

"No, I'm good, guys. I can walk," Jeff said with a wave.

"Looks that way," I replied with a smile.

We quickly made it to Sarge, and he waved Danny on. "You two go check the other one, I think we can handle this." Danny nodded and continued on down the road as Thad and I waded into the woods again.

It was more shoveling, raking, and beating to get this fire under control, then we heard another whistle and another and another. I looked at Sarge. "This is getting out of hand."

"Thanks for the stunning report, Captain Obvious," Sarge snapped back as he walked back out toward the road.

Sarge got in the Hummer and rode slowly down the road, checking all the locations where new fires were now being fought. There were a total of four spot fires now being fought. Sarge shook his head. *Shit,* he thought. Arriving at the fire where Mike and Danny were working with one Guardsman, he got out and waded into the smoke.

"Mikey, this shit's getting out of hand!" Sarge shouted.

Mike turned around and looked down the road, wiping ash and soot from his face with a dirty hand. "I know. We need more people. We can't do this with what we have."

Sarge nodded. "Get this under control. I'll round up some more help."

Sarge went out to the Hummer and grabbed the radio mic. "White Four Delta, White Four Delta."

"Go for White Four Delta."

"We're in a situation down here. We need more manpower. Things are getting out of hand."

"Roger that, Stump Knocker. I'll get some people headed your way."

"Roger that, you might want to impress upon those

thinking of staying there that they should leave. And send some water out too, we could use it," Sarge replied.

"Will do. White Four Delta out."

Sarge was standing in the road when we pulled up. "What's the word?" I asked.

"Shit's starting to get deep. Just called in reinforcements."

I looked at the fire that Mike and the guys were fighting. "I think we're going to need them."

"I just hope it's enough," Thad added.

"Me too," Sarge replied.

We fell in with a group of Guardsmen fighting another spot fire. The drill was always the same: try to pull fuel away from the downwind side of the fire, scraping the ground clean while cutting any trees or other standing brush that would allow the fire to climb higher. When the fire that the Guardsmen were fighting was sufficiently corralled, Thad and I walked out onto the road.

"This is starting to look dicey," Thad said.

Rubbing soot and dirt from my face, I said, "I don't know how much more of it I can take. I'm burned up."

"Yeah, this is some hot damn work," Thad agreed.

As we were talking a couple of large trucks pulled into view at the intersection. Sarge pointed at them. "Looks like the cavalry is here. Hop in, let's ride down there."

Livingston was at the intersection, looking the road up and down at the fires now raging on both sides. As Sarge pulled the Hummer to a stop, he came up to the window. "Jesus, Linus, this isn't good. This looks bad, real bad."

"That's why I called."

"Where do you want them?"

"Send one east and one west. They can get on the line

anyplace it's burning. Start getting them out—I'm going to go find Mike," Sarge said as he pulled away.

Driving down the road, Thad spotted Jamie with two Guardsmen trying to get a line around one of the larger spot fires. "Let us out here, we'll go help Jamie," Thad said.

Sarge stopped the Hummer and we jumped out, dragging our shovels with us. Sarge drove off and we headed for Jamie.

"Need some help?" Thad asked when we got to her.

Jamie stopped and wiped her forehead with the back of her gloved hand. "Sure, but I don't know how much help you're gonna be. I think we're in the middle of a losing battle."

"Sarge called in reinforcements. They just got here," I said as I started beating on the flames with a shovel.

The heat was getting intense, the smoke, ash, and soot choking us as we flailed against the flames. All of our faces were black with grime, muddy rivulets of sweat running down our faces.

"We need a chainsaw to drop this tree!" Jamie shouted.

"I'll go get one from the Suburban," I replied as I started to run for the truck.

Out on the road I got a better view of what was going on. Livingston did indeed bring the cavalry. I could see a couple dozen people, both Army BDUs and the uniforms of the refugees were intermingled along the line of the fire. One of the large trucks rolled slowly down the road. As I was pulling a chainsaw out of the Suburban, a voice called to me, "Hey, need water?"

I turned to see two women in the back of the truck. "Hell yeah!" I shouted.

One of them tossed a canteen to me. When I caught it I was momentarily stunned—it was ice-cold. I ran it across my forehead, savoring the chill, then quickly spun the top open and turned it up. The water was so cold it hurt when it hit the back of my throat, making my head ache. Swallowing the icy water, I looked at the woman. "Ice? Where'd you get ice?"

"We have a big ice machine at the camp, so we brought a bunch with us. That officer guy thought you guys would need it."

"Can I have a couple more canteens?"

She nodded, grabbed them, and handed them over. Taking the chainsaw with my free hand I ran back to the fire. As I came up I handed Thad a canteen. He looked at it for only a moment before turning it and drinking deeply. I handed another to Jamie and the last to one of the Guardsmen.

"Damn, you're a lifesaver," Jamie said as she unscrewed the bottle.

"My Lord, that's good," Thad said as he ran the cold bottle over his forehead.

Holding out the saw, I asked, "What do you want to cut?"

Still drinking from the canteen, Jamie pointed to a pine tree on the edge of the fire. "Which way do you want it?" I asked.

She jutted her thumb over her shoulder, indicating the road. I quickly started the saw and made my way through the smoking tangle. In a matter of moments the small tree was falling back away from the fire. One more task handled.

We worked for what seemed like forever. Gone now were the small spot fires, and there was now a continuous line of fire on the south side of the road. We were losing, and we were exhausted. That exhaustion reached dangerous levels when Jeff collapsed, simply overcome by heat and dehydration. He fell standing between Danny and Thad, and the two of them quickly pulled him away from the fire, out onto the road. Sarge must have seen them because the Hummer was quickly there. I patted Danny on the shoulder, pointing out to the road. He nodded and I ran out to check on Jeff.

Livingston and Sarge were tending to him when I got there. He was unconscious and Sarge was wiping his face with a wet rag. "This just isn't working. We need to get everyone the hell out of here before we lose someone," Livingston said.

Sarge looked at the line of flames on either side of the road and nodded. "Yeah, it's time to call it. We can't control this." Looking at me he said, "Get 'em off the line."

I nodded and ran back to the line, coming first to Thad. "Sarge said to get everyone off the line. We're pulling out, pass the word." He nodded and we both began spreading the word down the line.

It didn't take long for the word to spread and people were quickly spilling out onto the road where the trucks were waiting. Danny, Thad, and I went over to the Hummer, where Sarge and Mike were still tending to Jeff, who was now resting against a tire of the truck, sipping from a canteen.

"Let's get everyone loaded up and headed back to camp," Livingston said.

Sarge looked at me. "We tried, Morgan. I know you've got a plan B. Let's hope that one works."

As I looked back at the enormous fire, Mike came up beside me, looking utterly defeated.

"Mikey, what went wrong?" Sarge asked.

"Too much wind, too much real estate, not enough people or equipment. It was just too big a job, really."

"What are we going to do now?" Danny asked.

"Get the hell out of here to start with," Sarge replied as smoke swirled around the truck.

"No shit, Sherlock. But what are we going to do about this now? This is out of hand."

"I would suggest you go home and get your people ready to move."

"Shit," Thad replied.

"Yeah, I think we're all in the shit now," Sarge replied.

Jeff awoke, coughing and sputtering.

"Good to see you awake, buddy," I said. "Can you walk?"

He nodded. "Yeah, just help me get up."

"Let's move, people! We need to get the hell out of here before it gets any hotter," Livingston shouted.

"We're headed home. I'll call you on the radio later," I said as Danny and Thad helped Jeff up.

"Come by the camp first. Fill up your trucks," Livingston said. I was surprised by his generosity, but accepted it. If we were going to have to get on the move, it made sense for us to have a full tank.

We followed Sarge and Livingston into the camp, pulling up in front of the CP. Before I could ask Sarge about the fuel, Danny tapped my shoulder, jutting his chin in the direction of a man walking toward the bunker.

"Recognize him?" Danny asked.

I studied the man for a moment. He looked damn familiar. Before it came to me, Danny said, "Remember putting him in a set of stocks?"

"Oh *shit,* yeah, I do. What the hell is he doing here?"

"Remember Mark took him off and disappeared with him?"

"Yeah, I remember him now. What the hell is he doing

here? I knew those guys were sent by the damn federal goons," I said.

Sarge looked over to see who we were talking about. "What's his story?"

"We caught him in a raid one night on our place. We had him in a set of stocks for a while, actually," I said.

"Before that deputy Mark disappeared with him," Thad said through the cab.

Sarge spun around and rested on the side of the truck, sucking his teeth. "Well, that's interesting."

"What's he doing here?" Danny asked.

"He's the newly elected leader of these people," Sarge replied as he swept his arm over the camp. "And a damn stupid one, if he's telling people to stay here at this camp."

I looked back at the man as he went into the CP. "I'd keep an eye on him before you all go."

"Yeah, I'd watch your back if I were you," Danny agreed.

"That dude's going to be trouble," Danny muttered as we headed for the gate.

Chapter 9

Sarge walked into the command bunker and fell into a chair in Sheffield's office. Livingston took the one beside it. Sheffield looked at the two of them for a moment. "You two look like shit. I'm guessing it didn't go well."

"No, it didn't. We lost control of it, and it's now on the south side of the road," Livingston said.

"We tried our damndest, but it got away from us," Sarge added.

"So how long do we have before it's here?" Sheffield asked.

Livingston shrugged. "Hard to say, but not long. Not long at all."

"You need to tell these people again to leave. They can't stay here," Sarge said.

"We also need to get this move done as fast as possible. We need to get the hell out of here," Livingston added.

Sarge shook his head. "They're nuts—they've got to leave. If they stay here they'll die."

Sheffield took it all in. "All right, I'll speak with Neil again, but I don't think it will make a difference. As for the move, keep it rolling. Our orders tell us we have to be out of here ASAP. The fire only reinforces that fact. You two get cleaned up, and I'll get with Neil."

When Sheffield finished, there was a knock at the door,

and everyone looked up to see Neil standing there. "Got a minute, Captain?"

Sheffield waved him in. "Just the man I needed to see. Come in."

"That's good news," Neil added.

Sarge looked at the man. "You people still planning on staying here?"

He nodded. "Yes we do. Now that you've stopped the fire from coming this way, we don't have anything to worry about."

"We didn't stop it. It's already jumped the road and heading this way. I've said it once and I'll say it again: you folks would be better off leaving here. There's just nothing out here for you. With the fire now certainly on a course for the camp, it's a death wish to stay here."

"There isn't a tree for several hundred yards around the camp, there's no way the fire will touch it," Neil replied. "Plus, you're leaving us food and supplies. We'll be all right. Better than scavenging on the road."

"What we're leaving you won't last long. Neil, I urge you to look at this sensibly. You could have lives on your hands," Livingston added.

"I urge you to look at the mess you're leaving us in. Buncha *cowards* abandoning the people, I say. I've come here to negotiate terms. What weapons will you leave us?"

"You're some kind of special dumbass, aren't you?" Sarge spat back.

Neil glared back at him. "You are cowards. You're running with your tails between your legs, abandoning all these people." He looked back at Sheffield. "What about my weapons?"

"*Your* weapons? I thought they were for the good of the

group," Sheffield said flatly. "When we're finished moving, I'll give you the key to the armory."

Neil thought about that for a moment, nodding his head, then asked, "What about those buggies you guys ride around in? Are you leaving any of those?"

"No, they're going as well," Livingston said.

"We're going to need some way to get around, and you've got several of them. Leave us one or two."

"Neil, I told you we were taking all our equipment with us. We'll leave you some stuff, tents and that sort of thing, but everything else goes with us," Sheffield said.

"We're not leaving any buggies here to get all burned up," Sarge added.

"Those buggies are pretty important to some of the guys here. They're not going to be happy when I tell them you aren't going to leave one. They might get a little pissed off," he said with an edge in his voice.

Sheffield looked Neil directly in the eyes. "Just remember what I told you: I hold you responsible for their actions. You, nobody else."

"I'll do what I can, but these folks don't work for me."

"If any of these people here start getting the idea that they're going to try and take anything, or start any sort of trouble, just remember we have more than enough capability to stop anything you're thinking about," Sarge added.

Neil waved a hand. "No, no, I'm not saying we're planning anything. Just that some of these guys are wanting a vehicle—you know, to make it easier to get water and things like that."

"I understand. There's a lot of people out there that would like to have one of them, but we're not leaving them. You wouldn't have any fuel anyway," Sheffield replied.

Neil looked agitated and shifted in his seat. "What do you mean? There's fuel in those tanks out there."

"And we're taking it," Sarge said and pointed to the north. "I know you can't get it through your thick fuckin' skull, but there's a massive damn fire coming this way."

Neil was getting more agitated. "Now, this is bullshit—we're going to need fuel too. You can't just abandon us here with nothing."

Sheffield sat up in his chair. "First, we're not abandoning you. We told you to leave, and you want to stay. We're leaving you gear, but you're not getting whatever you want. It's our property and it goes with us."

Neil snorted. "Your property? It belonged to the Department of Homeland Security. Your guys took it when you 'liberated' this camp," he said.

"We're done here," Sheffield thundered. "We've got a lot to do and I can't have you pestering us for more. Just keep your people out of our way, and when we're done I'll give you the key to where your weapons are stored."

Neil sat there, not moving to leave. Sarge stood up. "That's your cue to kick rocks."

Neil glared at him but got up and headed for the door. As he went out he stopped and looked back. "I'll be around when you guys are ready to leave so I can get that key."

"We'll give it to you at the gate," Sarge said.

Annoyed, Neil asked, "You're going to make me walk all the way to the gate?"

"Yes, yes, we are," Sarge replied with a smile.

Sarge watched him go, then turned around to the other two men in the room. "He's going to be trouble. I've got a feeling leaving them here is going to create a pretty serious issue for the area. Morgan and them boys said they've run into him before," Sarge said.

Livingston looked over in surprise. "Where?"

"Said they caught him in a raid on their place one night. They actually built a set of stocks and put him up in them. Then some deputy sheriff took him off." Sarge cocked his head to the side. "You guys sure none of them federal boys decided to ditch their uniforms and fall into the crowd? That one's sure worried about getting his hands on some guns."

Livingston and Sheffield looked at each other, then Sheffield replied, "I can't say it didn't happen."

"We need to sniff around. I'd like to know if he's something more than what he's representing himself to be," Sheffield said.

"We have the database with all the refugees in it. I'll go through it and see when he came in here," Livingston said, standing up.

Sarge shook his head and leaned on his walking stick. "I'm getting too old for this shit."

The runs to the armory were getting hairier and hairier. There were numerous civilians on the roads, and all of them saw the convoy as salvation. When the trucks didn't stop or offer any sort of aid, they became irate. So far the convoy had been fortunate and hadn't had to use force on any of them, save a few warning shots fired. However, closer to the armory proved to be easier. The sheriff and his crowd weren't an issue: they made sure to have the road into town open as soon as they saw the convoy rolling toward them. And the civilians here kept their distance, staying across the street at a minimum.

Most of them loafed about in the shade watching the new activity, while others sauntered up or down the road.

Ian was standing at the gate to the armory when the trucks rounded the corner. Mike smiled at him and gave him the finger. Ian returned the salute.

Mike climbed out of the turret after Ted shut down the Hummer.

"How's tricks?" Ted asked.

"We're busy, that's for sure," Ian replied, then shouted to the driver of a truck, "Pull up to the maintenance shop!"

"Having any trouble with the natives?" Mike asked.

"They're keeping their distance. The only time we have direct contact with them is when we go to get water out of the lake. That's always interesting."

"The lake a popular place?" Ted asked.

"Yeah, during the day everyone's down there. The kids go swimming and the adults go fishing."

"They aren't worried about gators with the kids in the lake?" Mike asked.

Ian laughed. "Yeah, I asked them about that. They laughed at me, saying if I saw a gator to let them know. Apparently they've shot them out and don't see them anymore."

Ted nodded. "Makes sense. Hell, I'd be eating lizards, if I had to."

"Had to? Hell, I like 'em. Could go for one right now," Mike quipped.

Ian laughed. "Mikey likes it."

Ted shook his head. "He's like a dog: he'll eat anything."

"I resemble that remark." Mike laughed.

"Back to business, boys. Is this the last load?" Ian asked, looking at the cases of MREs and ammo stacked before him.

"One more, I think, and we're done,"Ted answered.

"Wow, really? When's it coming?"

"Soon—they want to finish this today."

"We have to. We tried to stop the fire with a back burn, but it jumped the road. It's bearing down on the camp now," Mike said.

"Yeah, Smokey the Bear here couldn't get the job done." As Ted spoke, the sheriff and a couple of his men rode by on ATVs. Ted nodded his head at them as they passed. "What about them?"

Ian gave them a dismissive wave. "They're a goofy bunch, really."

"What the hell's he doing around here? Enforcing the law?" Mike asked.

Ian shrugged. "Not much that I can see. They zip around here on the ATVs, stop and talk to people every now and then. Come to think of it I've never seen them do anything, good or bad."

"Are there any other barricades set anywhere?"Ted asked.

"I don't know. We've only done very local patrols. I'm waiting till we've got more bodies here before we venture too far away."

"There will be plenty soon enough,"Ted replied.

Ian paused for a moment, looking north at the anvil of smoke as it piled up in the sky. "Is that thing going to make it all the way down here? Is it possible?"

Mike gazed at it as well. "It very well could. The cedar fire near San Diego in oh-three burned over two hundred and eighty thousand acres, hundreds of homes, and killed more than a dozen people, so yeah, it could."

Ian swallowed hard. "Don't even want to think about that.

On that happy note, let me go check on these guys unloading the trucks."

"I want to take a ride,"Ted said."Go find Jamie and get her truck to go with us."

Mike nodded and wandered off into the buzz of activity to find her. He found her at the back of a truck, in a line of soldiers passing ammo along as it was unloaded from the truck. He waved at her. "Come on, we're going to take a ride."

She stepped out of the line, those on either side moving in a bit to make up for the loss. "Where we going?"

"Ted wants to take a ride through town. Go find the guys you rode up here with. We want enough security."

She nodded and disappeared. Mike went back to the truck that was already running when he got there.

Ted maneuvered the truck around to face the gate. As he was doing so, Jamie's Hummer pulled up behind them. Mike motioned to one of the guys on the ground, who opened the gate, standing by as they pulled through and closing it behind them.

There were a lot of people out on the dock that ran along the shore. A bunch of kids were down at the boat slips, jumping off into the water. Along the dock were several gazebos, all occupied by people, who were fishing. If not for the current conditions, it could've been a normal summer day.

As they came to Ferran Park, Ted whistled. There were more people grouped here than he had seen in a long time. The park appeared to have become the spot for traders to gather, and several people had their wares on display.

Ted stopped the truck beside the row of trees where most of the traders were set up.

"Keep an eye on things," he instructed. "I wanna take a walk around."

"Go for it," Mike replied as he swiveled around.

A few people were trading fish, laid out on the sidewalk. A frail-looking woman squatted over a row of small bluegill, slowly fanning the flies away from her merchandise in the midafternoon sun. Another merchant, an older man in overalls that looked two sizes too big, stood behind a folding table with several large catfish sitting on it. He was obviously worried about his inventory, taking the time to soak a towel and cover the fish, pulling it back for the occasional passerby to inspect the offering.

The group moved in toward the traders. While they were getting a lot of attention, none of it seemed hostile. Ted stopped in front of the table with the towel-covered fish. Smiling at the man, he said, "Howdy."

"Howdy back," the old man replied.

Ted lifted the corner of the towel, inspecting the fish. "What're you asking on these?"

"What'cha got to trade?"

"Well, I don't know. What're you you lookin' for?"

The old man smiled a gap-toothed grin. "Everthin'. Anyone can fish—fish is cheap."

Ted noted that, nodding his head. "Let me think about what I've got and maybe we can make a trade," he said as he walked off to visit with the others along the sidewalk.

The items being offered were varied: all manner of clothes and assorted shoes that had seen better days, various electric devices. At one table, a man was making knives. He worked in the open, a vise clamped to the table. He was filing a mower blade into the form of a knife. Others were in various stages of completion, awaiting handles, or completely done. One booth in particular had an interesting marketing technique. The trader standing behind a small table made of stacked milk crates and piece of plywood displayed a sign that read, ALL ITEMS WORK, TESTED WITH GENERATOR.

Ted stopped and read the sign, nodding at it as he said, "Does the sign help business any?"

The man smiled through a shaggy beard. "Not really, but it don't hurt none either."

"What are people asking for most often?" Ted asked.

The man chuckled. "Ain't it obvious?" he asked, pressing his shirt against his thin chest. "Food! They want food and medicine, toothpaste."

"What do you usually trade for?"

"It depends on what I have. If you can find something everyone else has overlooked and make it usable, I like to trade for that type of stuff."

"Like what?" Jamie asked.

The man pointed down the sidewalk. "Check out that guy down there, the one with the big sombrero on. You'll see what I'm talking about."

Ted nodded. "Thanks."

Before he could walk away the man asked another question. "Hey, are you guys here to help us?"

"We'll be around, but we aren't going to be handing out food and medicine, if that's what you're askin'."

"Then why are you here?"

Ted smiled at the man again. "We gotta be somewhere too." With that the group moved down the sidewalk.

A short walk down they came to the man in the big straw hat. He sat behind a blanket laid out on the side of the concrete walkway. As the group approached he looked up from under the rim of the hat and squinted, a half smile revealing a gold tooth. "Howdy."

"How's it going?" Ted asked, looking at the various jars and plastic containers arrayed in front of the man on the blanket.

"Living the dream, my man," he replied, getting a chuckle from the group.

Ted nodded his head. "Don't get much better than that. What'cha got in these jars?"

"Starch—you can use it to cut flour to make it go farther if you have any or you can dust yer fish with it and fry 'em, if you got oil. Do a lot of things with it."

Jamie knelt down and picked up a jar, inspecting it. "What is it?"

"It's made from cattail."

"Oh, from the roots," Ted said.

"Yeah, most folks don't know about it," the man replied.

"We've got a friend who's made it. Hell, we ate it."

"Cool, cool," the man replied and leaned out and picked up another jar with a dark yellow powder in it. "Ever seen this?"

Jamie took the jar and rolled it, looking at the powder inside. "Pollen?"

The man smiled and pointed at her. "We have a winner!"

"You go out and collect this stuff?" Ted asked.

"Yeah, you know, you gotta have something to trade that others either don't have or won't go get."

"Little industry, huh?" Jamie asked.

The trader smiled and looked at her. "Yeah, you can call it that." Then he raised the brim of his hat and whistled. "Damn, what the hell happened to your face, young lady?"

"You should see the other guy," Jamie replied, flexing.

The trader snorted, clearly impressed that someone so small could pack such a punch. Ted motioned to the others that it was time to go, and thanked the man for his time. At the trucks, they quickly mounted up and headed back toward the armory.

When the armory came into view the trucks were already forming up to head back to the camp. Ted pulled up to the front of the column and got out. He found Ian by the gate giving orders to some of the Guardsmen about the load just delivered.

"You guys are all ready to go?" Ian said when he finished.

Ian looked at Jamie with a pained look on his face. Pointing at his forehead he said, "You've got something on your face, not so much here"—he moved his finger back and forth across his forehead—"but here." He opened his hand, palm to his face, and moved it around.

"Screw you, Ian," Jamie spat.

Ted looked at Ian. "You guys keep messing with her and she's going to shoot your ass."

Ian looked at Jamie, and she adjusted her grip on the M4 and glared at him. Ian cocked his head to the side. "I'm jus' playin'."

"All right, we're out. Hopefully we'll be back some time this evening with everything done," Ted said.

"Cool, we'll be ready."

Ted and Jamie walked together back to the trucks. Jamie stared at the ground as they walked. Ted glanced over at her and asked, "You all right?"

She nodded. "Yeah, seeing those people at the park was kind of sad. We were out in the forest for so long, and then in the camp, we haven't really seen what's going on out here."

"Yeah, it's not pretty."

Ted stopped at his truck, Jamie paused and looked at him. "And there isn't shit we can do for them, is there?"

Ted took a deep breath and let it out slowly, thinking about the question. "No, not really. We're pretty much in the same position they are. We just have a little more organization and some supplies."

"What are we going to do? I mean, how long will the food we have last before we're like them?"

"I don't know, but we'll work it out. Don't worry, you're not going to be squatting over a pile of fish trying to fan the flies off them." He smiled, trying to reassure her.

"I'm know I'm not. I know how to hunt."

Ted slapped her on the shoulder. "Thatta girl."

Jamie smiled and turned to head for her truck.

"A country girl can survive!" Mike shouted from the turret.

Jamie pointed up to him and grinned. "You know it."

Ted stepped out and looked down the line of trucks, raising his arm over his head and swinging it in a circle. The sounds of diesel engines rumbled to life and blue smoke filled the air. Ted climbed in behind the wheel and called up to Mike, "You ready up there?"

"Yyyyeesssss!" Mike called back.

Ted smiled and shook his head as he put the truck in gear and pulled away. As the convoy rolled through, kids rushed to the side of the road to watch the big trucks go by. Even now under the circumstances, a few of them pumped their arms up and down to get the drivers to blow the horn. They of course did—seeing such innocence brought a smile to everyone's face.

The trip back to the camp was fast—it had to be, as they were quickly running out of time. Up in the turret the smoke was really getting to Mike, so he wrapped a shemagh around his face and pulled his goggles down over his eyes. The lightly woven cloth helped filter the smoke and the ever-increasing odor of garbage.

As usual Mike was up in the turret hamming it up for the kids. Jamie had the best view of Mike's antics. She shook her head, but she too couldn't help but smile. "Freakin' dumbass."

The Guardsman beside her in the front seat was laughing. "That guy is shot the fuck out."

"You have no idea."

"Who are those guys? I know what we've been told, but who are they?"

"They're just some spec ops guys. I guess they've been together for a long time."

"And that old guy, he's their boss?"

"He was at one time. I'm not sure how they got together or even what they're really up to."

"Well, I'm glad we've got them. They seem to know their shit. Which is more than I can say for most of the people around here."

Jamie scowled at him. "Hey, we're not that bad."

"Pfft, whatever. We're National Guard. I only signed up for the benefits. Remember, two weeks a year and all that shit?"

"Our primary mission is disaster relief." Jamie looked over at him. "I think this qualifies."

"Ha-ha-ha-ha, disaster? This is fucking Armageddon."

"Boxer, would you rather be here"—Jamie pointed out the windshield at a pathetic group standing beside the road—"or out there with them?"

He studied them for a moment, then replied, "Nope, I'm good. Go Guard!" He and Jamie both started to laugh.

Passing the barricade at Morgan's neighborhood, Ted waved at Jess and the two people with her. They waved back excitedly, Jess bouncing up and down. Mike, ever the ham, blew kisses at them as they passed. They were moving at a pretty good clip when a Hummer came into view going the opposite direction. Ted slowed as the truck approached.

Sarge pulled up beside him and stopped. "How was the trip, Teddy?"

"A milk run." Ted looked past Sarge. "Hi, Miss Kay, where you going?" Kay waved back as Sarge answered. Doc was in the turret above them manning a SAW.

"To get Morgan and that DHS boy you shot up."

"You mean the one who shot you?" Ted asked with a slight grin.

Sarge ignored the jab. "We want to see if they know anything about that old boy back at the camp."

"The one acting like the boss?"

"Mmhmm. I'm thinking he's up to something."

Ted pointed up the road. "That's looking pretty bad up there."

"Not going to matter to us much shortly anyway. We'll be out of here by nightfall or turned to cinders. But I don't want to leave a potential issue behind only to have to come back and deal with it later."

"We hope to be. Burning to death would be a bad way to go," Ted said.

Everyone laughed at the joke, but it was a nervous laugh. There was a truth to it, and it was a truth that no one wanted to face.

Chapter 10

"Did you set the fire, Daddy?" Little Bit asked as she wrapped her arms around my waist.

"We sure did," I answered, rubbing her head.

"Ew, you smell like smoke."

Mel and Bobbie were sitting in rocking chairs on the front porch.

"Oh my God, you guys look like hell," Bobbie said.

"Feel like it too," Danny replied.

"You guys are so dirty. What happened?" Mel asked.

"It was hard, Miss Mel," Thad replied.

Mel looked off in the direction of the fire. "Looks like it's still burning," she said.

"It is, a little more now that we started the other fire," Thad said.

"Did it work?" Bobbie asked.

"No, we lost control of it. It's on this side of 40 now," Danny replied.

"We tried. Sarge even called in more people. They sent civilians and more Guardsmen from the camp, but we just couldn't control it," I said.

Jeff sat down on the steps, still weary from the heat exhaustion. "It wasn't for lack of effort."

"What are we going to do?" Bobbie asked.

Danny slowly sat down beside Jeff, holding his head in his hands. "We need to get ready to leave."

"What? Is it coming here? Is it that fast?" Bobbie asked.

"We need to be ready in case. We're going to try again tomorrow with a last-ditch plan, but if that doesn't work, then yes, we're going to have to leave," I said.

Brandy and Mary walked out onto the porch, Brandy slowly looked us over. "How bad is it?"

"It's bad," Thad replied.

Her hands flying to her mouth, Brandy asked in a voice barely above a whisper, "What do we do now?"

Mary was staring off to the north at the billowing smoke. Emotionlessly, she replied, "Prepare to leave." With that she turned and went back in the house.

Thad let out a big sigh of exhaustion. "I know we're all tired, but we have to dig a couple of graves. I'll go get the tractor," Thad said.

"Good idea," I replied as we all filed into the house.

I looked over at Kathy. "How you feeling today?"

For the first time she smiled. "Better, thanks."

"In a little bit here we're going to bury your husband. Once they have the grave ready, I'll let you know."

She nodded but didn't reply. After we washed up, Jeff and I went out to the truck. Danny was at the shed with the door open. I motioned for Jeff to follow and we went over to him.

"Let's get him out," Danny said as we walked up.

Together we managed to get the body outside and laid out. It was still wrapped in plastic but with the heat was already starting to smell.

Jeff covered his face. "Holy shit. I don't mean to be rude, but what a stink."

"Yeah, we need to get this done quick," Danny said.

"Don't forget the other one, up by the barricade." I said.

"Yeah, we'll get that one with the tractor. I'd like to just leave him lying there, though," Danny said.

"Yeah, well, I don't want to have to smell it. He's not worth burying, but we have to."

Danny nodded. "Plus it would just beg for disease or something."

"Where are you guys going to bury them?" Jeff asked.

Danny pointed to a pasture across the road from his house. "I guess over there. No houses on that piece."

"Sounds good to me, just keep some distance between them. Just doesn't seem right to bury him beside the man that killed him," I said, looking at the body.

"True, we'll make sure to keep them far from each other," Danny replied.

As we talked, Thad pulled up with the tractor. He lowered the bucket and we rolled the body in.

"We got it," Danny said.

Jeff looked over. "You wanna hear something weird?"

"What's that?"

"I saw a bunch of deer earlier. A herd of them."

I looked up. "Did you shoot any of them?"

"No, I was kinda shocked by them. There were so many, it was really bizarre."

I pointed at the thunderhead of billowing smoke. "Fire's probably pushing them. We need to take advantage of that."

"Definitely. I should have had my shit together and knocked some down when I saw them."

"Don't worry, we'll get 'em. Let's finish with this. First things first," I said.

After we dug a hole, I wiped the sweat from my forehead and let out a big breath.

"You guys ready to get him in there?" I asked.

"You think we should cover him up or wait for Kathy to see him?" Danny asked.

Looking at the roll of plastic I said, "I think we should cover him up. She doesn't need her last memory of him to be worse than it already is. That smell will stick with you."

"True, let's get him in," Thad said.

Danny grabbed the feet while Thad grabbed the shoulders. Together they scooted the body into the sloped hole. Once it was in there, I climbed up on the tractor and started pushing dirt over it. With the hole covered, I graded the area out. It felt strange to run the tractor over the hole and feel it sink into the freshly disturbed earth, knowing there was a body under it that I was compressing.

Thad produced a small cross made from some scrap lumber and pushed it into the soft earth. We stood around for a few minutes not really knowing what to say, so we headed for the house.

"Let's go in and let Kathy know we're done. I want to get this over with. I hate doing this," Thad said.

We went up to the house. From the porch we walked around to the rear of the house. Thad went over to Kathy and knelt down beside her.

"Miss Kathy, we've finished the grave. Would you like to come out and pay your respects?"

She stared off across the pond, and after a moment she replied, "I think that would be good."

Thad looked at the little ones. "Would you like to take them?"

"They're so young, I don't think it will mean anything to them"—she paused for a moment—"but I would like to take them."

As a group we walked out across the yard and through the gate. The recently dug gray sand had a small cross atop of it, the sight of it standing out against the long green grass of the pasture. Kathy held her kids' hands as we approached, and I could hear her sharp intake of breath. We gathered behind them in silence.

These things are always difficult, and not knowing the person you just buried made it harder in some ways and easier in others. While the emotional effect of placing a stranger into the ground is considerably easier, the next part is, if not harder, then certainly more awkward. What could we say about a man we didn't know?

After standing in front of the grave for a moment of silence, Thad, always the kindest among us, spoke. "Miss Kathy, would you like to say a prayer?"

Without much hesitation she replied, "No, Lee wasn't a religious man. Thank you for the cross, though. It's a nice touch."

The little boy let go of his mother's hand and walked to the cross. Placing his small hand on top of it he looked back at his mother. "Is Daddy in here?"

It was striking, the wisdom of one so small. We thought we'd been careful around the kids not to say anything to upset them, not to let it be known what we were doing. But here this little boy knew in spite of our efforts. He looked back at the cross and tilted his head. "My daddy's in here." He leaned over and kissed the cross. "I love you, Daddy." Then he dropped to his knees and wrapped his arms around it, knocking it slightly askew.

It was a very emotional scene and there wasn't a dry eye among those assembled. Even Danny, an emotional stalwart, was wiping his eyes. The little boy returned to his mother, taking her hand once again. Kathy stood there for a moment then turned to face us. "I think that's enough."

We parted as she and her children walked through the group and followed them back to the house. There wasn't a lot of talk when we returned and gathered on the back porch again. An awkward silence fell over all. But it was the kids who were first to show that life goes on. Little Bit ran off the porch, yelling for the others to follow. In a flash there was a mass of small bodies rushing for the door. I couldn't help but smile, grateful that they still possessed some innocence.

Danny, Thad, and I walked out to the front porch to see a Hummer coming down the road, Doc bouncing around in the turret. Jeff walked up behind us and in a harsh whisper said, "That was saddest fucking thing I've ever seen."

Watching the Hummer roll down the road I replied, "Yeah, but they took it well."

"Still, that was messed up."

As the truck passed in front of the house I could see Doc manning the turret. When it turned through the gate I could see the old man behind the wheel and Miss Kay in the passenger seat.

"Evenin', fellas," Sarge said as he got out, followed by Doc. Miss Kay came around from her side and waved.

"What's this all about?" Thad asked with a smile.

"Hi, Miss Kay. Can't say I blame you for having a chaperone when you're out with this guy," I said with a smile.

Sarge cut his eyes around. "Watch it, smart-ass," he said, then glanced at Miss Kay.

Miss Kay smiled. "Oh, I don't need a chaperone. Linus is a gentleman." She glanced at him. "Besides, I can handle him."

A big grin spread across Thad's face. He was about to say something when a look from Sarge stifled the thought and the grin faded. Whatever he was about to say, he decided against it, probably for fear of the old man whacking him with his "walking stick."

"I was hoping you guys would come back down to the camp with Aric here. We want to see if he knows anything about that old boy you told me about the other day," Sarge said.

"Sure." I looked at Aric. "Did you know that deputy Mark who moved out to the camp?"

"Yeah, I remember him. He was a little weird, but the brass back at the camp seemed to like him. He disappeared, though, and we didn't know what happened to him."

"We do," I said.

Aric looked a little confused so I relayed the story of the day Mark was killed, how he was trying to force us into the camp and the assaults they made against us.

"We knew they were doing something like that. Plenty of people that came in had stories like that. But they didn't use us. I think they were using gangs or something."

"They were. They got dealt with too, around here at least," Jeff said.

"So who's this guy?" Aric asked.

"We caught him during one of the raids. We had him locked up, but Mark took him when he left," I said.

"They had a little group that was always together, but I didn't know much about them."

"This ole boy's name is Neil, know him?" Sarge asked.

"There was a Neil who worked out of the camp. He went with us once on one of our scavenging runs. Come to think of it they would send him out to work with local militias of sorts, so maybe those are the guys you were talking about raiding your place."

"Was he with the DHS?" Sarge asked.

"Oh yeah, but he didn't wear a uniform all the time. A lot of the time he was in civilian clothes or some odd combination of camo, to blend in with the guys he worked with."

"Let's go down and you take a look at him, make sure it's him," Sarge said.

"You still want us to come down too?" I asked.

"Yeah, we may let him see you guys, see how he acts."

"All right, let's go. We'll be out of that camp soon," Sarge said.

The kids came tearing around the house, each of them had a fistful of palmetto stems. When Little Bit saw Sarge she ran up to him and threw her arms around him. "Hi, Mister Sarge!"

"Hey, darlin', what'cha got there?"

She held out the stems. "We're going to make bows and arrows!"

"Oh, I remember you doing that down by the river. You sure can shoot 'em."

"I can." She looked at me. "Daddy taught me."

"Now, don't go shootin' each other's eyes out," Sarge said, a tenderness in his voice. "I'm gonna need you around, Little Bit, to be shootin' with me and the guys someday."

"You're funny, Mister Sarge," she said. "Okay, bye!" she shouted as the kids disappeared around the back of the house.

Kay smiled. "They are so sweet."

Sarge rubbed his chin. "You guys growing them in a closet or something?"

"What do you mean?" I asked.

Sarge pointed in the direction they'd run off in. "Them young 'uns. You've got even more now."

I laughed. "Oh no, we have another lady here. Those two small ones are hers. Her husband was killed the other night and she didn't have anyplace to go, so they're staying here for the meantime."

"Her husband was killed?" Kay asked.

"Yeah, over a can of corn," Thad said.

Shocked, Kay covered her mouth. "That's horrible."

I sighed. "There's some awful people out there," I said.

"God help us," she said quietly.

Livingston appeared in the door. "You ready?" he asked.

Sheffield nodded and Livingston stepped aside. Neil walked in, stopping in his tracks just inside the door. He was looking around the room, obviously unsure of what was going on. He slowly scanned our faces, going around the table. After a moment he asked the obvious question: "What's this about?"

Sarge motioned to an empty chair at the end of the table. "Have a seat."

"Why? What's this about?" he asked, clearly irritated.

Ted stepped up behind him, putting a hand on his shoulder. "Just sit down."

Neil looked back but slowly did as he was told. He sat uneasily in the chair, again looking around the table. Sheffield stared at the man intently for a moment then spoke. "When did you get here?"

Neil fidgeted for a moment. "I guess I've been here a couple of months."

"What have you been doing while you're here?" Sarge asked.

Neil sat up in his chair. "Same thing everyone else has been doing. You know, whatever we're told to."

"How do you know Mark?" I asked, even though this wasn't my show.

He looked at me, the recognition coming to him obvious. "I don't know what you're talking about."

Sarge looked at Kay. "Miss Kay, you ever see him in your mess hall?"

She wouldn't make eye contact with him, choosing to stare at the table instead. "I believe so, him and the deputy you mentioned." Neil glared at him.

"I'll back that up," Aric said. "I've seen him and Mark together several times. Not to mention the fact he went on at least one scavenging run with me, in uniform."

Neil could tell he was being cornered and didn't like where it was going, so he chose to continue his trip down the river of denial. "Look, I don't know who you're talking about—or *what* you're talking about for that matter."

Looking at Aric, he added, "I was told to go. I just did what I was told."

"Do you remember having your neck locked in a set of stocks?" Thad asked. "Remember that night you and some of your buddies raided our neighborhood? Do you remember that?"

Neil stared back not saying anything, then Danny said, "I do."

I quickly followed him. "Me too. So does my daughter who took a bullet in her leg. She damn sure remembers."

Neil's eyes darted around the room, and a slight grin cut Sarge's face. "Don't even think about it, son."

"All right, look, yeah, I was chosen to work with them, and we did things they didn't want their people doing. But it's not like I'm one of them. I just did what I had to do."

"You know, Neil, I think you're full of shit, personally," Sarge snorted. "I think leaving you here with any sort of weapon is a really bad idea. It's pretty clear you were on the DHS payroll and for some reason tried to hide out. Now, why'd you go and do that?"

"I agree," Sheffield said.

Neil's shifted in his seat. "Okay, yeah, I was an agent with them for a long time before all this started. I didn't say anything because I didn't agree with what they were doing. I just wanted to be free to live my life."

"Free to live your life, huh?" Sarge chided. "You sure didn't mind running around trying to take away other people's freedom. Now that the shoe's on the other foot you just want to be left alone."

Neil licked the sweat that was rapidly building on his upper lip. "I haven't given you guys any trouble. I've kept everyone in check just like you asked. All I asked for was some supplies and weapons to defend ourselves with."

"You aren't getting any weapons," Sheffield replied.

"Wait a minute! You can't leave us here with no way to defend ourselves!" Neil shouted.

I shifted in my seat. Sarge saw it and looked at me. "You got something to say, Morgan?"

I stared intently at the man for a moment. "I don't think you can leave him here at all. He's a threat to us, as he's already shown."

"I agree," Danny said.

"Me too," Thad added.

Neil stared at us, going over the meaning of what was just said. "Now, hold on a second," he said, waving his hands in front of him. "You can't be saying what it sounds like you're saying. You can't do this."

One of Sheffield's people poked his head in the door. "Captain, we can see flames over the northern tree line."

Everyone was quickly on their feet. "What? Already?" Sheffield asked.

"Yes, sir, it's getting close."

"We need to wrap this up," Sarge barked as he headed for the door.

Neil started to stand, and Sarge pushed him back into his seat and looked at Mike. "Keep him here."

Mike stepped around to the side of the man. "Don't worry, we got this turd." Neil started to protest, and Mike jabbed him with the muzzle of his rifle. "Shut up, shit bird." Neil looked at him. To his credit he recognized the grim determination on Mike's face and said nothing.

The rest of us ran outside, Sheffield and Livingston in the lead. We nearly crashed into them as they stopped in their tracks, staring at the flames leaping over the trees.

"We need to get the *hell* out of here," Livingston said. "Now!" he barked.

Sheffield looked around, dozens of people were staring at the flames. Sheffield began to shout, "You people see this? You see now why we said you need to leave?"

While Sheffield railed at the crowd, Danny turned to me. "This is going to burn straight toward us."

"I know. We're going to have to try to stop it again, somehow," I replied.

"I want to head home as soon as we can," Danny said.

"I'm with Danny. Let's go," Thad added.

Sheffield's shouting had an impact on a number of the people: they were suddenly motivated to get going.

Sarge laughed. "Look at 'em go."

"They better hurry," Sheffield replied. Looking at Livingston, he said, "Let's get the last convoy on the road ASAP."

Livingston was looking at the flames, growing larger as the fire approached. "Roger that, sir," he replied as he slowly backed away.

A moment later Ted came running out of the bunker and jumped into one of the side-by-sides and waved for us to follow. We piled into the truck and followed him as he drove back through the camp. He stopped in front of some large connex containers.

Getting out, I asked, "What's up?"

As he opened one of the bunkers he said, "We've got some stuff Sarge wants you to take with you," and disappeared through the door.

I got out and walked over to the open door. Thad followed me. Ted came out of the door carrying two SAWs. "I'll put these in your truck. Go in there and empty those racks—take everything."

"Are you serious?"

"Yeah, hurry up," Ted replied and trotted off toward the truck.

Thad and I went in the bunker. We were both stunned. There were racks and racks of firearms, everything imaginable. I looked at Thad, not knowing what to say. He shrugged and we both started grabbing weapons. Coming out, we passed Ted going back in with Danny.

"Dude, why are you guys giving us this stuff?" I asked.

"The old man doesn't want all the eggs in one basket, just in case. Just take it and store it for now. He also wants you guys to take his war wagons to your place, both of them. Thad, can you drive one and maybe Danny can drive the other? We're not leaving these guys any weapons. That guy's up to no good, and having him armed is a bad idea."

We worked for nearly fifteen minutes loading all the captured civilian weapons. We piled them into anything we could—empty ammo cans, boxes, crates, whatever we could find. Once it was all loaded we were standing near the buggies.

"What's in that?" Danny asked, pointing to a small trailer attached to the back of the smaller of the two buggies.

"Gas," Ted replied.

"Just what we need with a massive fire burning down everything around us."

Ted smiled. "Put it somewhere safe."

"Where are you guys going?" I asked.

"We're going to run down to the river and get the rest of our stuff, then we're going to the armory. After that I don't know."

"You better get my boat," Danny said.

Ted laughed. "That's the biggest reason we're going back. We'll bring it by."

"Well, thanks, man. We're outta here. We need to get home," I said.

Ted shook my hand. "You guys be careful. Oh yeah, there's also a portable radio and charger in there, you can reach us anytime on it."

"Thanks, man, you guys be careful," I said.

"You too, now go on and get the hell out of here," Ted replied.

Chapter 11

Sheffield thumbed through the file Livingston provided him. "He's nowhere in here. He's definitely not a refugee," Livingston said.

"I think we've established that pretty clearly now," Sarge replied.

"The real question is what was he up to and what do we do about him now," Sheffield said.

"I'm more curious about what he's been up to while he's been hiding out. There was that interrogator too, whatever his name was. If two of them slipped through, there could have been more. They'd managed to get a couple of the civilians to try and help with their little escape plan. Who knows how many more of them are on their side," Sarge said.

"He is awful worried about getting those guns," Livingston added.

Sheffield looked over the file. "Which they're not getting."

"Not now," Sarge quipped.

Livingston looked at him. "What do you mean?"

Sarge smiled. "Can't have what ain't here."

Sheffield dropped the file onto his desk. "What do you mean *ain't here*?"

Sarge shrugged. "Just that: they ain't here. All those captured weapons are gone."

"Where'd they go? How'd you get them out of here?" Livingston asked, concern edging his voice.

Sarge waved him off. "They're safe. They're in a safe place."

"That was a hell of a lot of guns. I sure hope they're with people we can trust," Sheffield replied.

Sarge didn't reply, just smiled back. After a moment of silence he said, "Let's go deal with this fella."

They left his office and made their way to the conference room, where Mike was still standing behind Neil, making sure he didn't try anything.

"The fire's heading straight for this camp. For the last time, we suggest you people leave here. This camp will burn to the ground," Sheffield said.

"No, it won't. There's a huge buffer of sand around this place, so it can't burn into here." Neil snorted.

"You are a special kind of dumb fuck, ain't ya?" Sarge said. Neil sneered back at him. "What do you think is going to happen to these tents when them embers start falling from the sky?"

"They're treated. They won't catch just from an ember," Neil shot back.

Sarge looked at Livingston. "This is a waste of time."

Sheffield nodded. "I agree."

"Let's go, then," Sarge said as he moved for the door.

Neil went to stand up, but Mike pushed him back into the chair. Sarge looked at the man. He was obviously pissed.

"Mike, secure him to that chair, I don't want any shit out of him while we're trying to get out of here."

"Wait a damn minute! You're not going to tie me up here! You've got to give me the key to the weapons!" Neil started to pull against Mike's hand and Mike drew his Taser.

Sarge looked at Mike. "Mikey, get him tied up." Then he looked at Neil. "You keep it up and he's going to light your fire."

"I've already told you you're not getting any weapons," Sheffield replied.

Mike pulled out several sets of flex cuffs and secured Neil's wrists to the armrests and legs to the center post of the chair. He pulled against the bindings.

Sarge looked down at the man. "We aren't giving you any weapons—we'd be stupid to do so. You're a menace. Morgan wanted to kill you, and he was probably right."

A venomous hate boiled out of the man. With wide eyes and flared nostrils he began to scream, "You can't do that! You can't leave us without weapons! You will regret this! You have no idea who you're fucking with!" Neil rocked against the bindings as spittle flew from his mouth.

Sarge laughed and looked at Sheffield. "Yep, special kind of stupid. We can't leave this guy here. There's no way."

"What do you want to do, take him with us?" Livingston asked.

"What? Hell no," Sarge replied and looked at Mike. "Put him to sleep. Forever."

Sheffield moved to protest, but Mike was quick. Wrapping his forearm around the man's neck and locking his hand in the crook of the opposite elbow, Mike placed the other hand on the back of Neil's head and applied pressure. Neil tried to struggle for an instant, then with a twisting motion and a violent pull up, Mike broke the man's neck and his body went limp.

"Jesus Christ!" Sheffield shouted. "What the hell is wrong with you guys?"

"What'd you want to do with him? Some people just need killing. There's just nothing you can do about that." Sarge pointed to the body tied to the chair. "He needed killing."

"Who are you to decide? What makes you God?" Sheffield shouted back, incensed.

"Captain, with all due respect, you need to get your head out of your fourth point of contact," Sarge fired back. Sheffield looked stunned as Sarge continued, "You need to get with the now. Things are different. We have to make decisions that suck, ones we wouldn't ordinarily make." Sarge pointed at the bound body. "He should already be dead. He sure as shit ain't no fucking civilian. He is a mad dog, and there's only one way to deal with a mad dog."

"People like you scare me. I hope there's not too many of your kind in the world," Sheffield spat back, then pointed at Mike. "And you're really fucked in the head."

Mike shot back, "Why? Our government, the same one that pays you, spent a lot of time and money teaching me to do that. Like Sarge said, some people just need killing. I don't like it, I don't look for the opportunity, but when the time comes I accept it as my job—nothing more, nothing less."

Sarge stood up to go. "We're done here. Permanently. We'll help you wrap up the evacuation of the camp, then we're going to get with Morgan. We need to try and save his place if we can."

Sheffield didn't reply. Staring at the body for a moment, he turned and walked away.

Outside, the camp was buzzing. Many of the civilians, seeing the fire was so close, had decided to abandon their plans and get out as quickly as possible. Livingston ordered some of the men to hand out any packs they could find to these refugees, and Kay was distributing what food she could.

"Where are we supposed to go?" a woman asked as Kay filled her empty pack with MREs.

Kay looked at her for a moment, ash collecting in her hair. "Home, go home."

The man looked north. "We can't."

"Then just get away from here," Kay replied.

"I don't know what we're going to do. I don't know where to go," the woman replied frantically.

"Head south. Eustis is down there. Hopefully the fire won't make it that far," Kay said, dropping another can into the bag.

"I know some people there, maybe we can stay with them . . ." the man said, trailing off. He looked in his bag, and then up at Kay expectantly, gesturing for her to continue.

"I'm sorry, but that's all I can give you. Be sure and get some water before you leave."

The man nodded slowly, sadly, as if defeated. Kay watched them go, and her heart hurt, thinking about all the people that would be on the road. Compared to them, she was fortunate, for now.

The last of the trucks were now in line. Sheffield and Livingston walked up and down the line as a constant snow of white ash and hot cinders fell around them, checking on the contents, making sure that everything they intended to remove from the camp was loaded.

"It looks like we've got it all," Livingston said.

"These guys are going to be tired. They must have worked all night," Sheffield replied.

"Yeah, they did a hell of a job, but leaving anything here would be a waste. This place is going to go up."

"I'm afraid you're right," Sheffield replied and looked again at the encroaching wall of flames. "Get a head count, get 'em loaded up, and let's get the hell out of here."

Livingston nodded and ran toward the head of the column, blowing a whistle. Trucks began to rumble to life, adding diesel exhaust to the already suffocating cloud in the air. The Guardsmen were throwing their personal gear onto the trucks and helping civilians and their family members aboard. Many of them had stayed to help with the demobilization, though the women and children had already been moved to the armory.

Sarge and his crew were helping to get a drum of fuel onto a truck, the last one. Hearing the whistle Jamie looked up. "Sounds like it's time to go. I've got to get to my ride. See you guys later," she said.

"Take care of yourself," Sarge said with a smile.

"I'll be fine. I'm worried about you guys, though. Where are you going?"

"We're going to try and help Morgan again, see if we can keep the fire off his place," Mike said.

"I wish I could help. You guys be careful," Jamie said.

"We will." Mike smiled, and Jamie moved in and hugged him. Mike returned the embrace and they held each other for a moment.

Jamie pulled back and wiped her eyes. "Damn ash."

She then hugged Ted. "Keep him out of trouble."

Ted smiled. "It's a full-time job."

She looked at Doc. "Thanks for everything you've done for me."

He smiled. "No worries." Then he gave her a hug.

Jamie looked at Sarge. "Take care of yourself, and these three," she whispered into his ear.

Sarge squeezed her tight. "We'll be fine. If you ever need anything, we'll be here."

Jamie smiled at them. "Time to go." With a wave she turned and jogged toward her waiting Hummer.

Ted disappeared, returning in a Hummer, "Time's a-burning, boys! We gotta get the hell out of here."

"When yer right, yer right, Teddy. Come on, boys. We're off like a prom dress," Sarge replied as he got in.

Mike climbed up into the turret, once again wrapping his face and pulling his goggles down. Pounding on the roof, he shouted, "What are you waiting for? Let's go!"

Ted put the truck into gear and they rode down the line of trucks heading for the gate, the several dozen civilians that were staying lining the road. Sarge watched them as they passed. *They have no idea what they're in for,* he thought, shaking his head.

"If you're gonna be stupid, you gotta be tough," he said.

Ted glanced over. "These must be some tough sumbitches here."

Ted stopped when they got to the gate. He looked north, where the fire raged on both sides of the road and flames leapt nearly a hundred feet into the sky.

"I don't think anyone's that tough," Doc nearly whispered.

After a moment Ted turned out onto the road and headed south.

Chapter 12

Back at the house, the focus was on getting the trailer put together. We were discussing what needed to be done. I was bent over a bin of PVC fittings looking for the right ones when Mel came out.

"Morgan, Kathy wants to leave. She wants to go to her sister's place in Eustis."

"We don't have time for that right now," I replied.

"Why don't you have them come out to the barricade and wait for the convoy that's heading into town? I'm sure the boys wouldn't mind giving her a lift," Thad suggested.

"Good idea. Tell her she can walk down there and wave them down. They're going into Eustis anyway," I said.

"And tell her to hurry. They'll be coming by any time," Danny added.

"Sure thing. And I'll give them a little care package for the road," Mel said with a smile.

Thad left to go get the truck and Danny helped me get the pumps out. Once the tanks were loaded we planned to plumb the pumps in. It wouldn't be much of a fire truck, but it was the best we could do. Thad quickly returned with the truck and we hooked up the trailer. Thad and Danny went to get the two tanks, and while they were gone I went through the

PVC fittings we had. As I was rummaging around in the bins Little Bit showed up with the other kids in tow.

"What'cha doing, Daddy?"

"Looking for some parts. What are you guys up to?" I asked. They looked like something from *Lord of the Flies*. Each of them was festooned with an assortment of crude bows and palmetto arrows. "You're a wild bunch, aren't you?"

"We're playing!"

"Be careful with those arrows."

"We will!" they yelled.

Mel came out with Kathy and she called her kids over. Little Bit asked where they were going, a look of curiosity on her face.

"They're going into town to stay with their aunt," Mel said.

Putting on a pouty face, Little Bit replied, "Aww, I don't want them to leave."

"Sorry, kiddo, but they need to go stay with their family."

"They have cousins there to play with," Kathy said.

"But I like to play with them."

"Maybe one day we'll come back and visit," Kathy said, kneeling down. "I know the kids would like that." Little Bit nodded and waved good-bye to her friends.

"Good luck, Kathy," I said as she stood up.

"Thank you. And thank you so much for everything you've done for us."

"No problem, it was the least we could do." I shook her hand. "Now if you don't mind, I'm going to get back to being an amateur firefighter."

The guys pulled up in the truck and we quickly got to work on the plumbing. Yet again Danny's habit of collecting all manner of hardware really paid off. We were able to reduce the large fitting on the valve down to fit the inch-and-a-half pipe that Danny had. Using a T fitting, the two tanks were tied together and one of the suction hoses was cut and attached to the pipe with clamps. This way we could take the pump off the trailer and set it on the ground to prime.

Once everything was ready, Thad drove the truck back to the pond behind Danny's house, where we used the pump to fill the two tanks. Danny tossed the small basket on the end of the suction pump into the water. I started the pump and used the manual prime pump to get the pump drawing water. As it started pumping it created a small vortex on the surface of the pond.

"Hope it doesn't suck up any of my fish," Danny said.

"It'd be some small fish if it did," Thad replied.

The small pump filled the two tanks with surprising speed. Once full, they took on a brownish hue from the tannin-filled water of the pond.

"That's about all we can do for now," Danny said.

"No, there's one more thing we can do," Thad said. "Meet me over in the field back there, on the other side of the pasture."

Danny and I headed around the house, where we ran into Taylor and Lee Ann in the front yard. "What are you guys doing?" Taylor asked.

"We're going over there to meet Thad to finish our makeshift fire truck project," I said, pointing at the field.

"Can we come?" Lee Ann asked.

"Yeah, come on," I said, throwing my arm around her shoulder.

Together we walked across the road and through the

pasture. At the back of the pasture we had to hop a fence. In the Before, this land belonged to the state, excluded from development and maintained as a preserve. From the pasture there was a grassy field a couple hundred yards wide before reaching a tree line. The grassy strip extended the full length of our little neighborhood.

"This is nice over here," Taylor said.

"Makes for a good buffer," I added.

After a few minutes, the sound of the tractor drifted on the breeze. Thad came into view on the western end of the field, bouncing along on the tractor. We started walking toward him, meeting him in the middle of the grassy strip. He'd mounted a disk on the tractor, an implement with a series of round blades on it in several rows, used to break up the ground. I knew immediately what he was thinking and it was a great idea.

"Let me guess—you're going to disk a break in the grass?" I asked.

"That's what I'm thinking. Cut a line just outside of the tree line and do another one out in the middle here, just in case it gets past the first one."

"Good idea, that'll keep it from burning across here. This grass is high and would catch easily," Danny said, nodding approvingly.

"Can we help?" Taylor asked.

Thad looked at her. "You want to drive the tractor?"

"Sure, if you show me how."

"You guys watch me for a while, then I'll show you how to drive this thing."

Thad drove toward the tree line and dropped the disk. The girls walked over to watch him as the blades cut and folded the sod over. It took a couple of passes to actually get to the dirt because of the length of the grass. Danny and I watched them for a minute, then he said, "We've got some time to kill now that Thad's handling this. What do you want to do?"

"Let's call the old man and see when he's coming, then fill in the girls on what's going on."

Danny and I went over to his house. Mel and Bobbie were sitting on the back porch with a large pot on the table. Lifting the lid, I looked in. It was full of beans soaking.

"Soaking the farts out of 'em?" I asked.

"Yeah, this many people around we figured it'd be a good idea," Bobbie said, stirring the pot.

"You get Kathy down there in time?" I asked Mel.

"Yeah, just in the nick of time. They were coming down the road as we pulled up. At first they didn't want to take her, but that girl Jamie put her and the kids in a Hummer she was driving."

"That's good. I hope she finds her sister."

"Does she even know if they are still there?" Danny asked.

Bobbie shook her head. "She just assumes they're there. She said, *Where else are they going to go?*"

"That's a hell of a gamble," I said.

"Hope she makes it," Danny added.

"We've got to make a call on the radio real quick," I said. With most of the solar setup now at Danny's place, we'd moved the radio to one of the upstairs bedrooms. The antenna was strung out to a large pine tree, giving us very good reception.

I sat down at the radio. "Stump Knocker, you out there?"

"Go for Stump Knocker."

"You guys headed this way?"

"Roger that, just wrapping up a couple of things and we'll be on the way."

"Was that the last convoy from the camp that passed a little while ago?"

"Affirmative, camp is empty of our people. You guys getting prepared for the worst?"

"We are, see you soon," I replied.

"Stump Knocker out."

"I wonder how many people stayed behind," Danny said.

I shook my head. "Who knows? It's foolish to stay there, though. Let's go talk to the girls . . . They're not going to like this," I replied.

"What's happening with the fire?" Mel asked as soon as we walked in.

"It jumped the road and is heading this way," I said.

"We just got settled. I don't want to have to leave," Mel said, her eyes welling with tears.

I grabbed Mel's hand. "I know, I don't either."

"But what are we going to do? It's burning this way, can it be stopped?" Bobbie asked.

"I don't think we can stop it, but we're going to try and turn it, steer it away from us. Sarge and the guys are coming. They're going to help us. In the meantime we need to get ready to bug out, just in case," I said.

Tears were now running down Mel's cheeks as she silently wept. "Why? Why all of this? Why's it got to be so hard?"

I sat down beside her and took her hand. "Hey, you know we're going to do the best we can. If we have to leave, then we'll just find another place. As long as we're all together, we'll be all right," I said.

She looked up. "But are we always going to be running? Running from something—people, fire, what's next?"

"Babe, whatever comes, whatever is next, we'll face it together."

"All of us," Danny added.

Mel looked up at him, then at Bobbie. She nodded and wiped her face. "We've got work to do. Let's start getting things ready to go." Mel looked back at me. "Just in case."

I smiled and hugged her, kissed her forehead, and said, "Just in case."

The dogs started barking and the kids came stampeding around the house as well. Danny stood up. "Someone's here."

"Must be Sarge and the guys," I said as we all walked around the porch.

Sure enough it was a Hummer pulling through the gate, Danny's boat attached to the rear. Mike was in his usual perch, waving and blowing kisses to the girls like a parade queen.

"Hey, fellers," Sarge called out with a wave.

"Hey, guys," I replied. "How's the camp?"

"I guess they completed what they set out to do. We left to go get our crap from the river packed up."

"Cool, you guys just bringing the boat or are you staying?"

"I reckon we'll stay here. Livingston and Sheffield made it clear that our services aren't needed anymore."

"Yeah, apparently they figured out the old man's an ass," Mike said.

"Really, they don't want you guys around?" Thad asked.

"Ah, they'll get over it. I don't want to live at that damn

armory anyway. You got a place around here we can use if this fire doesn't burn us alive?" Sarge said.

I looked at Danny. "What do you think?"

He thought for a minute. "How about that one you guys found all the food in?"

"That'd be a good one," I said, then looked at Sarge. "You'll like this place, it's pretty cool."

"Good, where is it?"

"I'll ride a four-wheeler over, just follow me."

Sarge nodded and got back in the truck. "Danny, where you want this boat?"

Pointing at an open spot in the pole barn he said, "Back it in over there." Sarge nodded and started maneuvering the trailer around. Ted was behind him guiding it in. He got it in place on the first try and Ted quickly unhooked it from the truck, then they all got back in the Hummer.

Jumping on one of the ATVs, I rode through the cut in the fence to get my picks. Getting them out of the house I rode out through the gate and the Hummer followed me.

"Looks like a nice place," Ted said.

"It is, real nice house," I replied.

"What's up with the windows?" Mike asked.

"That's one of the cool things here—they have some sort of security film on them."

"Why aren't you guys staying here?" Sarge asked.

"We only got into it recently, after we had already settled in."

Sarge held out his hand. "Key?"

I pulled the picks from my back pocket. "Little harder than that."

"You gotta pick the lock?" Ted asked. I nodded and he held out his hand.

"You pick locks?" I asked.

"What do you think?"

And, damn, did he. Ted was in the door in under two minutes. We opened the garage door and some of the windows in the house to air it out. Then we gathered in the garage.

"Will this work?" I asked.

"Yeah, this is great," Mike said.

"I think we can make it do," Sarge said with a smile.

"So what are you guys going to do for now?" I asked.

"Before we unload anything, we need to think about this fire. Be a waste of time to unload just have to pack it up again," Sarge said.

"Supper's around five thirty—let's hash it out then. I don't think we've got much time beyond that," I said.

"Good deal, we'll be there."

When I got back the guys were unloading all of the guns from the camp. There was nearly every kind of gun imaginable: shotguns of all varieties, bolt-action rifles, semiautos, a slew of pistols, and a bunch of AR and AK variants. A nice double-barrel caught Thad's eye.

Holding the smoke pole up, he looked at it. "That's nice. I like that."

"Take it," Danny said.

"Yeah, take it if you want it," I added.

"You sure?" Thad asked.

Danny pointed at the pile of guns in the back of the truck waiting to be unloaded. "Yeah, Sarge made it clear that they're ours for the keeping."

Thad smiled. "All right, good deal."

"How are the girls doing on that tractor?" I asked Thad.

"Good, they're naturals."

Just as I thought, the guns filled the closet in the downstairs bedroom, so much so that we actually had to pile the ammo up outside of it. Mel and Bobbie watched us as we made trip after trip through the house with guns and never said a word. Once the guns were all in the closet, they came into the room.

"Do we even want to know where all that came from?" Mel asked.

"We got them from the armory. Sarge gave them to us," I replied.

Bobbie walked up and looked in the closet. "That is a lot of guns, even for you guys."

I had to chuckle about that one. While neither of us had that many to begin with, everyone acted like we were forming a militia. None of us thought we had that many, but this—this was a lot of guns.

"What in the world are you going to do with that many guns?" Mel asked.

"Nothing for now, but you never know," I replied.

"Yeah, in this world, they're worth more than money," Danny added.

"Damn right they are. We could probably get anything we wanted trading these off," Thad said.

"What are you going to do if we have to leave? You just loaded them in here, why not leave them in the truck?" Bobbie asked.

"We're hoping we don't need to leave. Besides, I'd rather not drive a truckload of guns and ammo into an inferno," I replied.

"We've already been getting things ready to go," Bobbie said, pointing to a pile of bags and assorted boxes.

"I've done the same at our house," Mel added.

Looking at the stack of stuff by the door, I said, "Wow, didn't even notice. You guys have been busy, then." Looking back, I added, "But I hope it's all for nothing. I'm really hoping you wasted your time."

Neither of the women looked convinced, but they didn't say anything else about it. After everything we'd done, I was worn out. In the living room I fell onto the sofa.

Thad smiled. "That's a good idea, think I'll go home and do the same."

"Cool, man, see you later," I said. I passed out within minutes, only waking up when Lee Ann and Taylor came busting in. "It's *so* hot out. We need a drink," Taylor said.

"How'd it go?" I asked, stretching and rubbing my eyes.

"Good. We did it like Thad showed us. It wasn't too bad," Lee Ann replied.

"Good deal, about time you girls started pulling your weight around here," I said with a smile.

"Hey! We do a lot," Taylor said from the kitchen.

"I'm just teasing."

"Better be," Lee Ann said with a smile.

It was getting close to dinnertime, and people started showing up. First was Brandy and Tyler with all the kids in tow.

"Hi, Mom!" Little Bit said, coming in.

Mel looked at her. "Have you had a bath?"

"I washed them all up. They were filthy," Brandy said with a smile. "Too much time playing in the mud."

"Thanks, I'm sure they needed it."

Thad soon arrived with Jess, Fred, Aric, and Jeff. The house was filling up quickly. Once Sarge and Mike arrived, the house sounded like a busy restaurant, all pots and pans clanging and chatter and laughter. With so many people it took nearly every dish in the house to feed everyone.

Forming a line, everyone made a pass by the kitchen bar, where Mel and Bobbie dished out dinner, handing out plates and bowls as each person passed by.

I sat at a table with Sarge, Mike, and Danny. As the sun started to go down the smoke was hanging closer to the ground, and the acrid smell permeated everything, actually affecting the taste of the meal.

"So what's your plan? Back at the camp, you had another idea for a place to try and turn this thing," Sarge said.

"I was thinking as I drove along the road to Alexander Springs, but I've been looking at the map and think I've found a better place," I said.

"Get on with it, then."

"Hang on." I went and retrieved the maps I'd taken from the welcome center and unrolled it on the table. "Right here is a natural gas right-of-way. I think it would be a better spot," I said, running my finger across the map, then pointing to a dark green area. "With Lake Dorr right here and this swamp here, they will be natural buffers to the fire. They'll form a pocket."

"That swamp will likely slow the fire some," Mike said.

I nodded. "That's what I was thinking. Not enough ground litter to fuel it as fast."

Mike ran his finger along the dotted line that indicated the pipeline. "Start the fire on this side. There isn't a lot to burn on this side of the lake. It could burn around the other side, but then there's this swamp to the east."

Sarge studied the map for a moment. "I think it's our best bet. We'll have to see what happens on the west of the highway, though. That could be a problem. It could burn all the way down through here."

Grabbing another map, I said, "I thought of that too—look here." I ran my finger along a road and another hashed line. It cut a straight line east to west on the western side of Highway 19. "This is a forest road with a power line running down it."

"That's a really wide-open stretch of sand there, fire'd have a hard time crossing that," Danny said.

"How wide is it?" Mike asked.

"Couple hundred yards and it's mostly sand, only a little brush," Danny replied.

Sarge shook his head. "First thing in the morning we need to go check this out. If Mikey thinks it will work, we'll give it a try, but everyone needs to be ready to go just in case."

Tyler and Brandy watched and listened as we talked. "You think it will work?" Tyler asked.

"It's our only play—it's that or run. Even if it does jump this line, we'll still have time to get out of the way," Sarge replied.

"Where will we go?" Brandy asked.

"We need a rally point, somewhere safe everyone can get to quickly. Once we see where the fire's headed we can decide where to go from there," Mike said.

"How about the sod farm? It's a couple hundred acres of open grass land, no brush of any kind," Danny asked.

"That would work. Where is it?" Mike asked.

"Just across the road there. We could walk to it," I replied.

"All right, sod farm it is. If it jumps the line we'll call on the radio and let everyone here know, and we'll meet them there," Sarge said.

"Someone's going to have to man the radio, then," Tyler added.

Sarge nodded. "All day, keep someone in front of it. Let's finish supper and get some rest. I think we're going to need it tomorrow."

While we were eating, Sarge's radio crackled. Ted's voice came through.

"What's up, Teddy?"

"There's a Dylan here looking for Morgan."

"Tell him to let him through. I'll ride down there and see what's up," I said, getting up from the table.

"I'll go with you," Thad said, taking his plate into the kitchen and setting it in the sink.

"Where are you going?" Mel asked. "I mean, really, Morg? We haven't seen you all day."

"Duty calls. Someone's at the barricade," I said.

"Don't go running off anywhere . . . It's dark."

I smiled and kissed her. "I'm not. Just going to go see what he wants."

Thad and I went out and used two ATVs to run down to the end of the road. Dylan was talking with Ted and Doc when we pulled up.

"What's up, Dylan?" I asked as I stepped off the ATV.

"Hey, Morgan, I hate to bother you folks. I followed the dogs back."

I waved off his apology. "Don't worry about it, man. What's up?"

"Have you guys seen anyone around lately? Anyone come by here?"

"A couple people. We had a group stop by a few days ago, with an old man who acted like their leader. They had a big old truck with a bunch of kids on the back of it."

"Yeah, the old guy, that's probably him."

"He come around to your place?" Thad asked.

"Yeah, him and two younger men. The younger guys are the ones that's really bothering me. They keep making dirty comments about Gena and it's starting to piss me off. If it was just him that'd be one thing, but there's always two or three of them when they come."

"Why are they coming over? I mean, why do they keep coming back?" I asked.

"You know Gena's a sweet soul. She gave them some food the first time they showed up. They had some of the kids with them and she felt sorry for them. Now they come nearly every day wanting more and more. I wouldn't bother you but I'm afraid things are about to get dangerous. They've made it pretty clear they need *more women,* as they put it."

Looking at Ted, I said, "I think we can help. Don't you think so? Let's call Sarge up here."

Ted nodded and called Sarge on the radio. It wasn't long before the Hummer pulled up with Sarge and Mike.

I introduced the other guys to Dylan and they all shook hands. "What can we do for you?" Sarge asked.

I relayed Dylan's story to him, adding in the confrontation we had with the same people. When I finished the details, he stroked his chin. "Sounds like a bunch of troublemakers. The types we don't need around here. I think we can help you."

"I sure would appreciate it. How can I let you know when they show up?"

"Oh, you won't have to do that, we'll just be there," Sarge replied.

"Yeah, we'll just post up over there," Ted replied, then looked at me. "You've got enough people here to keep an eye on your place, don't you?"

"Yeah, we can cover things here."

Dylan was looking at the men and the Hummer, eyes narrowed. Finally he had to ask, "Who are you guys?"

"We're just some friends of these guys," Sarge replied.

Dylan looked at the Hummer. "Damn. Sure wish I had friends like you guys."

Sarge smiled. "You do now."

"What kind of guns do you have?" Ted asked.

Dylan pointed to the revolver on his hip. "I've got this and a shotgun."

"Oh shit, that's all?" I asked.

"Yeah, just never really was into guns before. Wish I had been now."

"I'll be right back," I said as I hopped back on the ATV and headed for the house.

Danny met me on the porch. "What's up?"

"Remember that group that came up in here the other night?" Danny nodded. "They're giving Dylan and Gena some trouble."

"I figured we'd see them again," Danny said.

"Yeah, and Dylan doesn't have much in the way of guns either. He's afraid they've got the idea in their heads to try something with Gena. Let's go get them some hardware," I said, going into the house.

We stood in front of the closet, looking in. "What should we give him?" Danny asked.

"I guess a rifle or two and a couple of handguns."

"Let's give them two of the same," Danny said. Reaching into the closet, he picked up two AKs. He sorted through the pistols and came up with a couple of Smith and Wesson M&Ps in 9mm.

While he was getting the guns out I went through the piles of ammo and mags, getting a couple for the pistols—two each—and a half dozen AK mags. We put the ammo and mags in a pillowcase and headed back out.

"I'll come with you," he said as we passed through the living room.

"What's going on?" Mel asked.

"Just giving some guns to someone who needs them."

"Don't get into anything tonight," she half pleaded.

I turned around. "I'm not going anywhere," I said and smiled.

"You better not."

Danny and I hurried back down to the barricade. I handed the pillowcase to Dylan. "Here, take this with you."

Dylan looked in the bag, then at me. "What's this?"

"You need more firepower. Take these too," Danny said, holding up the rifles.

"You know how to use those?" Sarge asked.

Dylan took one of the rifles. "Yeah, it's been a long time, but I remember."

"Good, hop into the truck and we'll give you a ride to your place," Sarge said.

"You want me to go?" Ted asked.

Sarge shook his head. "Nah, me and Mikey will go. You guys need to get some food in you."

"Ted, you guys go back. Me and Danny will stay here," I said.

"Are you guys going to stay at our place?" Dylan asked.

"We sure are. You and your missus can get some sleep tonight. We'll keep an eye on things for you," Sarge replied.

"I appreciate that, but our place is small—"

Sarge cut him off. "We're not going to be inside. We'll stay in the truck. You don't have to worry about us." The old man had a glint in his eye.

"I don't know what to say—thank you, though. I haven't had a good night's sleep in days," Dylan replied.

"Well, let's get going, then," Sarge said, clapping his hands. "You guys can catch some *Zs* and we'll catch some predators."

Sarge gave us a wave as he maneuvered through the barricade.

"You guys run down to the house and get something to eat. Tell Bobbie and Mel we're going to stay down here and get someone set up to relieve us later," Danny said.

"Will do. I'm hungry," Doc said.

Ted got on the ATV, telling Doc to get on the back. When Doc got on, Ted turned his head. "Hold on tight, darlin'."

"Just drive. I'm not going to hug you no matter how bad you want it," Doc replied, making Ted laugh.

Once everyone was gone, it was eerily quiet. The smoke was getting worse, burning my eyes and throat. I pulled a bandanna out of my vest, then a canteen. After pouring some water on the bandanna, I wrapped it around my face, looking for some relief.

"You got another one of those?" Danny asked. I nodded and pulled out the spare I had in my vest.

"Thanks, man. Anything to help right now," he said.

"Man, I wish that would've worked. I wish we stopped up there on 40," Danny said.

"Me too, as if there isn't enough shit to deal with. Like what Mel was saying earlier: What's next, ya know?"

"I know all too well, brother, it's just one thing after another. I'd give anything to go back to how it was before. We used to bitch about working and all the other bullshit that went along with a normal life," Danny replied.

"No shit, I'd go to work today nailing shingles if things would just go back to normal, and you know how much I hate roofing," I said with a chuckle.

"Not as much as plumbing." Danny laughed.

"Sanitary, just drains."

"Well, if tomorrow doesn't do it, we're in for a hard time. Where do you want to go? I imagine the cabins will be gone, so they won't be an option."

I shook my head. "I have no idea. We're going to be like everyone else, I guess. On the road."

"At least we've got the trucks," Danny replied.

"If we can keep them. On the road everyone's going to want them, and we'll have no security at all."

"All the more reason to make sure we don't have to leave. We have to get it done tomorrow. There' s no other choice."

We sat there for some time in the quiet as flakes of ash fell around us. I looked up into the murky sky. "You think it'll ever get easier?"

"Easier? I thought this was easy." Danny laughed.

"Yeah, it's easy. Between wildfires, raiders and murders, and trying not to starve to death, I can't imagine it possibly being any easier."

"All we can do is what we can do," Danny replied.

"But there's so much to do."

It seemed as if the haze hastened the setting of the sun, the looming dusk giving everything an otherworldly look. We went across the street, taking up a place on the fence. Out there, on the edge of the pasture, we could take advantage of what breeze there may be and get a little relief from the mosquitos.

We sat in the eerie quiet in silence. Not even crickets were playing their evening arias. To the north the sky was angry and ominous in both attitude and appearance, as if the very earth itself was seeking its vengeance for some injury. And maybe it was: here at last, man was knocked down a peg or two. Without the benefit of all his technology, man was reduced to clawing at the earth for his own survival, nearly on par with most of the beasts of the wild.

Danny was pulling up the seed stalks of St. Augustine and biting off the soft sweet tips, then throwing the stalks like arrows.

"You know," he said, nibbling on a stalk, "we have very little chance of stopping that thing."

"Yeah, but what are we supposed to do? All we can do is try."

Danny stretched his arms out and put his hands behind his head. "And try we will."

Chapter 13

As the convoy approached Morgan's neighborhood, Jamie could see someone waving. None of the drivers of the other trucks paid any attention as they'd been instructed not to stop for civilians, but to Jamie this was different—she knew these people. She pulled out of the line and stopped as Jeff jogged over. "Hey, Jamie."

"Hey, Jeff, what's up?"

He pointed to a woman with two kids standing behind him. "Can you give them a ride into town? She wants to go stay with her sister."

"Who is she?"

Jeff leaned in a little closer. In a low voice, he replied, "Her husband was killed down the road here, Morgan and Danny got the guy who did it, and we buried both of them. She's just kind of stuck here."

It wasn't a hard decision for her. "Yeah, tell her to get in."

The Guardsman sitting in the passenger seat leaned over. "Hey, we're not supposed to give anyone a ride."

Jamie shot him a disgusted look. "What the hell could it possibly hurt? It's just a ride."

He was clearly annoyed by her answer, but he didn't say anything more. Jeff waved Kathy and the kids over, helping them get into the truck. The two little ones shared one of the rear seats. To them it was a grand adventure to ride in the big army truck.

"Thanks, Jamie," Jeff said, waving good-bye to Kathy.

Jamie pulled off at the rear of the convoy, the last truck in line. As they rode along, Kathy didn't say anything and Jamie didn't press her. From what Jeff said she'd had a rough time lately and there was no sense in making her relive it.

As they approached the barricade on the edge of town, Jamie asked where her sister lived. Kathy directed her past the armory, getting some curious looks from some of the other Guardsmen as they continued on. Kathy eventually told her to stop in front of a small house. She quickly got out and walked up to the house and rapped on the door. After a moment it opened a crack, then swung wide-open as a woman rushed out and they embraced in a hug. The two women, still holding each other, walked out to the street. Kathy opened the door and the kids hopped out, both hugging their aunt.

Kathy stepped around to the driver's door. "Thank you for bringing me here. I can't thank you enough."

Jamie smiled, warmed by the interaction. "No problem. Hope you and the kids are safe here."

"Oh, we will be. Thank you again."

Jamie gave her a smile and waved as she pulled away. The ride back to the armory was short, and in no time she was parking the Hummer with the others in the lot. As night began to fall, all the vehicles were crowded into the small fenced yard. It was alive with rumbling engines as the drivers attempted to jockey them into position. People moved through the clouds of exhaust in a dangerous unscripted choreography. Jamie sat on a large metal box, an open canteen in her hands. Seeing Ian walking through the yard she waved him over.

"Hey, Jamie."

"Hey, got a question for you."

"Sure, what's up?"

Jamie looked around for a moment, then asked, "Do you want to stay here?"

"Or go where?" Ian asked with half a laugh.

"Sarge and those guys are staying over in that neighborhood where Morgan lives. We could go there."

"That place is probably going to burn down. Why aren't they coming here?"

"You really think it's going to burn? Damn, I was thinking it would be better."

Ian removed his cover and scratched at his head. "You don't want to stay here?"

"Not really. We're going to be packed in here like sardines, way too many musty balls for me."

Ian started to laugh. "Musty?"

"Yeah, you dumbasses stink," Jamie replied with a smile. "I was going to see if Perez wanted to go too."

"I guess we could." Ian looked around. "There isn't going to be much going on around here." He looked at her seriously for a moment. "You're not worried about being AWOL?"

"AWOL? Hell no, there's no DOD anymore." Thinking quickly she added, "Besides, we could just say we're attached to Sarge and his guys. He's got actual contact up the command chain. Long as we're with him, we're not absent."

"You got a point there."

"Think about it. Just don't say anything to anyone. I'll talk to Perez," Jamie said.

"We have to wait and see what happens with the fire. If that works out, I'm good with it," Ian replied.

Jamie found Perez by accident. Walking through the parked trucks, she smelled smoke of a different variety and pulled the canvas flap back on one of the trucks. Perez was sitting there smoking a cigarette, which he quickly tried to hide.

"Where the hell did you get a cigarette?" She asked.

"You scared the shit out of me." Perez smiled. "I got my ways," he said, taking a long drag on the smoke.

Jamie climbed up in the truck with him. "Give me one of those."

Perez squinted at her and reluctantly pulled a pack from his blouse pocket, shaking one out. "Didn't know you smoked."

"I don't, but I could use one right now." Jamie stared at him for a second. "Light?"

Perez produced a lighter and Jamie leaned in and lit her cigarette, taking a long drag. "Oh, that's good." She looked at it. "Where did you find these?"

"We found a shit ton of them at the camp when we were going through stuff."

"You get your share?"

Perez smiled. "Plenty."

"I wanted to ask you something."

Perez looked over and Jamie went into her offer. Perez listened intently without interrupting her, staring at the floor. When she finished, she asked, "What do you think?"

"You don't want to stay here?"

"No, do you really want to stay here? What do you think we'll be doing, packed in here like we are? It's going to suck."

"Yeah, I was already thinking of camping out here. That damn hall is going to get rank quick."

"I know. Over there we can stay in a house, away from all these people who think we're here to save them when we don't have shit for them. Soon as they figure out we're not giving them anything, they're not going to be so nice anymore. I'd rather be out in the woods."

"What'd Ian say?"

"He was up for it."

Perez sighed. "What the hell, I'm in too."

"We'll have to wait and see what happens with the fire. There is a chance their place could burn. Once that's over we'll see. I'm going to go look for Ian."

Perez pulled the pack from his pocket, shaking out another. "You do that. I'll be right here."

As Jamie walked through the yard, members of the unit were setting up their spots for the night. Small tents and combat shelters were being put up on any available ground. Jamie worked her way through the chaos looking for Ian. Occasionally she would ask where Ian was, but it quickly became obvious no one knew. After searching the yard she went into the hall where others were laying out sleep mats and bags. In the admin section of the building she heard Ian's voice coming down the hall. Not wanting to interrupt, she paused at the end of the hall and leaned against the wall.

After a short time, Ian appeared in the hallway. As he walked up, Jamie asked, "What was that about?"

"I told them we were going to leave if the fire doesn't burn the place to the ground," Ian replied matter-of-factly.

"What? Why would you do that?"

He looked at her like she was nuts. "Because it was the right thing to do. What was your plan, steal a Hummer and drive away?"

Jamie shrugged. "It was a thought."

"Yeah, a bad one. Right now it's just wait and see."

Stunned, Jamie stepped in front of him. "Really? They didn't care?"

"They cared but understood. There's already too many people here and getting rid of a couple of us will ease the burden a bit."

"I can't believe they let it go so easy."

"Well, I told them having us out there would serve as a remote post. With us and Sarge and his guys it's a decent squad," Ian replied.

"I thought they didn't want them around anymore."

"No more than the regular army generally wants SF types around. You know, those guys generally don't play by the rules and can be a bit of a pain in the ass. But they know they'll need their help at some point."

"This worked out better than I thought it would."

"Yeah, and we don't burn any bridges here. We'll probably need their help someday too."

"That's good—better. I sure hope they get through it," Jamie said.

"Let's just hope it goes well."

"Cool, I'll go tell Perez. He's set up camp in the back of an empty truck. I'm going to stay there too."

Jamie went to the Hummer and grabbed her pack. Perez had his gear in the back of the truck and she decided she was going to stay there with him—out of sight, out of mind. When she climbed in, Perez was stretched out in his sleeping bag.

"Well?" Perez asked, looking up.

"It's a go. They're actually going along with it. Ian sold the captain on the idea of having us as a squad out there."

Perez lay back. "Good."

"I'm staying here tonight."

"Whatever blows yer skirt up."

"Nice, Perez, real nice," Jamie said as she unrolled her bag.

Dylan was worried about leaving Gena home alone, but he didn't know what else to do after being faced with day after day of intimidation from these troublemakers. He was relieved when the house came into view as they bounced down the dirt road. Sarge swung the truck in a loop, stopping with it facing back the way they'd come. Dylan quickly hopped out and walked to the house.

At the door he knocked. "Gena, it's me." A muffled voice replied and the door opened. "Is everything all right?" he asked.

"I'm just happy you're back." Gena looked past him at the Hummer. "Who's that?"

"They're friends of Morgan's. They're going to stay here and help us. I'll introduce you to them."

Looking at the Hummer, she asked, "Are they in the army or something?"

"I don't know, but they sure look like it."

Mike and Sarge were leaning on the hood of the Hummer. Seeing Dylan and his wife approach, they stood up.

"Ma'am," Sarge said with a nod.

"Sarge, Mike, this is my wife, Gena," Dylan said.

"Hi, Gena, nice to meet you," Mike said.

Sarge smiled. "Call me Linus."

"I can't thank you guys enough for coming here. I had no idea we'd get this kind of help. I'm really getting worried—the way they look at me, the crude comments they make . . ." She shuddered visibly.

"We'll do what we can for you. We should be able to convince them to leave you alone," Sarge replied.

"That sure would be nice. At first I didn't mind helping them, but now they come back every day wanting more."

"Kinda like a stray dog. Once you feed it, it'll keep coming back."

"She has a soft spot for dogs too," Dylan added.

"Well, the big dogs are here now," Mike said.

"It's been hard. They come at night, every night. And they've been threatening. Every day they want more, always more. Been hard to sleep," Dylan said.

"You folks can get some sleep tonight. We'll keep an eye on things," Sarge said.

"Would you guys like some coffee?" Gena asked.

Sarge perked right up—just hearing the word had a stimulating effect. "Coffee? You got coffee?"

"Well, it's not all coffee. I grow chicory in the greenhouse and I cut my real coffee with it. It's still pretty good," Gena replied.

"Like Café Du Monde in New Orleans?" Sarge replied.

Gena smiled. "That's where I got the idea. We spent a week down there a few years ago and really enjoyed it."

"Yeah, I had them little pastries every day we were there," Dylan said with a smile.

"Be glad you're not there now. I can only imagine what that place looks like," Mike added.

"Can you imagine? Every day would be like the aftermath of Katrina," Dylan replied, shaking his head.

"How do those poor people live? Not just there but in any big city?" Gena asked.

"Wouldn't be easy. Nothing to hunt and not too many

places for a garden, not to mention once you planted a garden you'd have to guard it twenty-four hours a day," Sarge said.

"There's plenty to hunt: pigeons, squirrels, all manner of cats and dogs. Delicious," Mike said.

Sarge shook his head. "You'll have to forgive him—he was kicked in the head as a child."

Laughing, Gena said, "You boys are silly."

"Miss Gena, if you wouldn't mind bringing out some of that coffee, you folks can go on and get some rest," Sarge said.

"Sure thing. I'll put a fresh pot on," Gena replied and headed back for the house.

"Thanks for coming over here. I know this is going to get worse. They started saying things about Gena, nasty things. She's got MS and isn't well, and the things they were saying . . ." Dylan trailed off.

"Don't worry, Dylan. We don't take to people that try and bully others or people that hurt women. The two together is at the top of my shit list," Sarge replied.

Dylan looked up. "Well, tonight, in all probability, you'll see some shit. These people are horrible, and I think they're doing some terrible things to the kids they've got."

"We'll have to see about that too, then," Sarge replied with a stern face.

"I'll go help Gena with that coffee," Dylan said and went to the house.

"What do you think? Just sit here and wait or do you want to move off where they won't see us?" Mike asked.

"I was thinking of sitting here and letting them come up. The truck might scare 'em off. Plus I want to see what they got to say when they get here. After they bring the coffee out, move the truck around back. Let's see how this plays out."

"Roger that, boss."

Dylan came out carrying a thermos and two coffee cups. He set them on the hood of the truck. "Here you guys go."

"Thanks," Mike said as he picked up a cup, looking into it. "Hey, can you drink coffee out of something this clean?" he asked, looking at Sarge.

"I can drink all this coffee from a clean cup." Sarge smiled back, pouring himself a cup.

Mike looked at Dylan. "You should see the cups he uses—our medic wouldn't even use them."

Laughing, Dylan replied, "Nothing like a seasoned cup, is there?"

"You got that right. Now, Dylan, we got you covered tonight. Go get some rest," Sarge said and watched Dylan walk to the house. After he was inside, Sarge looked at Mike. "Give 'em a few minutes and move the truck."

Mike leaned against the hood and poured himself a cup. He took a sip, smacking his lips. "Well, that's different."

"Suck it up. Best coffee I've had in a long time."

"It's the only coffee you've had in a long time."

"Exactly," Sarge replied, draining his cup and refilling it.

"Move your shit. I'm gonna move this thing," Mike said.

Sarge grabbed the thermos and Mike pulled the truck around behind the greenhouse. Sarge met him on his way back. "Let's set up under these juniper trees," he said, pointing to a row of trees along the fence. Moving under the trees, they took a seat in the soft litter of fallen needles.

"Get comfy, sweetheart," Sarge said as he broke off a couple of small limbs from the trunk of the tree.

Mike sat quietly, using his NVGs to keep an eye out. Having gone so long without any caffeine, the chicory coffee was producing a hell of a buzz, so staying awake wasn't going to be an issue for him. Feeling as energized as he was, Mike was surprised to hear a small snore come out of the old man after about an hour of observation. He looked over to see Sarge's chin on his chest. He kicked his boot, waking him up. Ordinarily he would have given him hell for falling asleep, but they had to be quiet. Mike was then hit with a realization: his mentor was getting older. He had a lot of respect for Sarge, having spent years under his tutelage, but the undeniable fact was that he was moving into his twilight years. With age, things changed whether you wanted them to or not. Mike could see Sarge's silhouette in the darkness, stretching. Smiling to himself, Mike decided to let it go. If the old man needed a nap, he could have one.

It was about midnight when the visitors showed up. Sarge saw them first, tapping Mike's leg to indicate that he had them in his sights. Through the NVGs, they watched them approach, walking up the dirt road as though they didn't have a care in the world. There were three of them, all carrying some sort of long gun.

As they approached, Sarge whispered to Mike, "Wait for them to get to the door. Let's hear what they've got to say."

"How do you want to take them down?"

"You still got that Taser?"

"Yeah," Mike replied.

"We'll just knock two of them in the head, give that third one a jolt if need be."

Mike nodded. As the visitors came closer to the house they could hear their conversation.

"They better have more today. I told them last time what they gave us wasn't enough," one of them said.

"Why don't we just move in here? It's better than that shitty-ass trailer we're in."

"Soon enough. The more we get out of them now, the better for us. If we move in on them too soon, they'll just try and shut down. Right now they're growing a lot of vegetables. When that's all ready to harvest we'll take it. Let them do the work for us," an older man replied.

"We could just take 'em and make 'em do the work. It's worked before."

"Yeah, I got a job for that little bitch," one of the men said with a laugh.

"You ain't the only one. I want some new pussy too."

"If your pecker was an inch longer, you'd get some new pussy with what we got now," the old man responded, causing the other man to laugh. Sarge's blood boiled at the callous way they were talking about Gena. Mike could see his clenched jaw in the darkness.

Two of the men hung back as the older man approached the house and pounded on the door. After a moment he pounded again. "Don't make me wait too long!" he shouted.

Shortly a dim yellow light flickered in the windows. Dylan stood in the doorway and looked out, looking around. The old man looked around too. "What'cha looking for? I'm right here."

"Nothing, just looking around."

"Where's my groceries?"

Irked, Dylan replied, "Let me go get 'em."

"Send that sexy little piece of ass out with them!" one of the other two men called, getting a belly laugh from his partner.

Dylan glared at the man. The old man urged him on.

"What? You gonna do somethin' about it? Don't get stupid, just go get what's ours and we'll be on our way."

Dylan quickly returned with a plastic shopping bag, handing it to the old man. He took the bag and hefted it. "What's this shit? This ain't enough for us."

"Look, we gotta eat too. We can't provide all your food."

As they were talking, Sarge motioned to Mike and they slowly and quietly started to move out of their hide. They deftly made their way toward the open gate as the old man continued.

"I told you last time we needed more, and this isn't even as much as we got then. You're going in the wrong direction. Get back in there and find us something else."

"It's all we have until some of the other plants in the garden are ready. I'm not going to starve so you can eat. I grow this food. Be glad you're getting anything," Dylan spat back.

"What'd you say?" one of the other men barked as he walked toward the house. "You got a smart mouth on you. Now get your ass back in there and get us the rest of it!"

The third man was obviously hyped up, bouncing on the balls of his feet. Sarge motioned to Mike that he would take this one, and for him to move quickly on the other two. Mike nodded as they closed the last couple of yards. In a swift motion, Sarge planted the butt of his carbine into the base of the man's skull as Mike moved quickly for the other two. The sound of the first one falling caused the second man to begin to turn. Mike caught him just above his ear with the butt of his rifle, toppling the man.

The older man was startled by the sudden violence and tried to bring his rifle up, but Mike swung the butt of the carbine back, hitting him in the teeth. Staggering, the old man dropped his rifle and reached for his face. Taking a moment, Mike searched the two men for additional weapons, pushing the old man down to the ground. He removed their rifles and tossed them into the yard. When he finished, Dylan and Gena came out the door, each carrying an AK.

"Dylan, keep an eye on them two. Mike, go pull the truck around here and put some light on our subjects." Mike nodded and trotted off to get the Hummer.

Dylan was imbued with rage. Kicking one of the men, he shouted at him, "You sons-a-bitches! Who do you think you are?"

The old man was lying in the grass, moaning. From the way he sounded, his mouth suffered some serious injury. "Whaf the hell's goin' on?" he mumbled.

Mike pulled up in the Hummer. Flipping on the high beams, the yard was flooded with light. The old man shielded his face from the light as he looked back over his shoulder. The first man, the one Sarge took down initially, was also coming around, sitting up in the grass and holding his head.

"What the hell's going on?" he asked as he rubbed the back of his head.

Sarge stood in front of the old man. "Get out there with your partner," Sarge said, pointing with the muzzle of his carbine. When the old man didn't respond, Sarge kicked his thigh. "Get your ass moving! Get out there." The old man raised a hand in submission and began crawling across the yard.

"You too," Mike said to the other man, giving him a motivating kick to the ass.

"You boys are in the wrong business. It's time someone showed you the error of your ways," Sarge said.

"Who the hell are you?" the man struck in the back of the head asked.

"A life lesson incarnate," Sarge replied. "You've been taking advantage of these good folks here, and that's done now."

"We gotta eat too," the old man said, spitting blood into the grass.

"True, you do. But you can't take it from someone else. You need to find your own way."

The old man was holding his jaw. Looking up, he said, "You can take, you have to take."

Sarge grunted. "You can, huh? You just go around taking what you want?"

The old man looked up at Sarge, grinning. "We take what there is to be taken. Survival of the fittest."

"You bastards are done taking from me," Dylan said, then spat at him.

"The question now is, what are we to do with you?" Sarge said.

"We got your message. We won't be back," the old man said.

"Like hell," one of the others muttered. The old man looked at him and shook his head slightly.

"And there's the problem with shit like you: instead of seeing the error of your ways, you're just going to want to get even. That only leaves us with one option," Sarge said.

The old man squinted into the light. "Oh yeah, what's that?"

"To put you somewhere so you can't bother anyone else."

"The fucking dirt," Mike said sternly.

The reality of the situation suddenly struck them. "What? Are you crazy? We haven't hurt anyone!" one of the younger men bellowed.

Sarge snorted. "I find that hard to believe. You may not have hurt these folks, but I'm pretty sure you have hurt people in the past and, left unchecked, you will in the future."

"We only do what we have to! It's a hard life now."

"We've got a bunch of kids we're taking care of. They need to eat," the old man said.

"Where'd the kids come from?" Sarge asked.

"Here and there. We find 'em and take 'em in. We're doing the world a service, taking them young 'uns in."

"How many of their parents did you kill?" Sarge asked. The old man made eye contact with the other two, but none of them replied. "Where's the rest of your group?"

With a snicker, the old man replied, "You really don't expect me to answer that."

"I didn't ask it to hear myself talk. Where are they?"

"We ain't telling you shit," one of the younger men barked.

Sarge waved Dylan over and whispered into his ear. Dylan nodded and disappeared back in the house. The three on the ground watched him go, unsure of what was happening. When Dylan reappeared, he was carrying a hammer.

"What the hell you going to do with that?" one of the young men asked.

Sarge took the four-pound mini-sledge from Dylan and held it up. "It's called negative reinforcement."

"What?"

The old man looked over at his partner. "It means he's going to bash you with it, jackass."

"Whether or not you get hit with it is totally up to you. Now, where's the rest of your group?" Sarge asked.

"We can't tell you that. You wouldn't tell us if the shoe was on the other foot," the old man replied.

"I admire your tenacity, but you know we can't just let you go," Sarge said, letting out a long breath.

"I give you my word we won't come back. We'll be on our way," the old man said.

Sarge knelt down in front of the man. "You know, I would really like to believe you, I really would. But would you believe me if, as you said, the shoe was on the other foot?"

The old man looked at the grass and slowly shook his head. "No, I wouldn't."

"Where's that leave us, then?"

"I reckon that's up to you."

"Just let us go. We won't bother them again," one of the other men said.

"Maybe not, but you'll find someone else to steal from, to intimidate," Mike said.

Sarge pointed to the old man. "What's your name?"

"Name's Claude." Pointing to the younger men, he said, "That's Billy an' that's David."

"All right, Claude. You three, get on your feet," Sarge barked.

As they stood, the old man asked, "Where are we going?"

"Out there to that truck. Go on, grab that push bar there," Sarge said, pointing to the tubular push bar on the front of the Hummer.

Wearily the three men moved out to the truck. Sarge told Mike to get some of the heavy zip ties from the back of the truck. Using these they tied the men's hands to the bar.

"What are you doing?" one of the younger men cried.

"The way I see it we only have two choices here: either I kill you, which honestly is my first choice because that way

I know you won't be back, or I fix you so you can't hurt anyone," Sarge said.

The old man gripped the bar. "And how are you going to do that?"

Sarge set the hammer on the hood of the truck, resting on its head with the handle upright. The old man closed his eyes tight. "Get on with it."

"You can't do this!" David shouted and tried to pull against the tie wrap, but it was useless—there was no way he was getting his hand out.

Sarge gripped the hammer. "It's this or a hole in the ground."

"Why the hell are you doing this?" Billy cried.

"If you can't hold a weapon, you aren't a threat, are you? You know, in the Middle East they cut your hands off for stealing. I'm not going to cut your hand off," Sarge replied.

"Just smash it," Claude muttered.

"We weren't stealing. They gave us the stuff," Billy pleaded.

"Like we had a choice! You three showed up here with guns after we did freely give you some food. You came back with guns and told us to give you more and more. Every day it's more," Dylan said, then stepped around them so he could see their faces. Pointing into the face of one of the younger men, he added, "And I heard what you said about my wife too."

"And I heard what you said earlier," Mike said. "Disgusting."

Billy looked at him. "It was just talk. Please don't do this!"

"Not used to being the ones begging, are you?" Dylan asked.

Sarge took the hammer from the hood and gripped

Claude's wrist. "Remember, you brought this on yourself." Claude closed his eyes and grit his teeth. Sarge raised the hammer and brought it down on the knuckles of his right hand, resulting in a sickening thud and crunch. Claude's knees buckled as he let out a scream of pain. Raising the hammer again, Sarge delivered the left hand a similar blow. Again, Claude emitted a howl of pain as his knees gave completely and he slumped against the front of the truck moaning.

The other two men began to violently struggle against their bonds, screaming profanities they fought to get loose. Mike drew the Taser. Removing the cartridge from it, he placed it against David's neck and hit the trigger. David went rigid as a result of the voltage coursing through him. Sarge used the opportunity to deliver the first blow. Through the incapacitation he still managed to scream, a bloodcurdling screech that rose in pitch. After five seconds, the Taser timed out, and before he could recover Sarge brought the hammer down on his other hand. This time the scream was more forceful, filled with agony. Billy, having seen what awaited him, was blubbering. He'd wet himself and begged for relief from what surely awaited him.

Gena stood on the porch, her hands covering her face. The mechanical approach the old soldier displayed was horrifying. He was maiming men with no more thought, it appeared, than one would have about swatting a fly. The smoke now hanging low to the ground only added to the surreal scene, like something from a horror movie. Not able to take any more, she went in the house and shut the door.

Once Mike placed the Taser to Billy's neck, he started to shout but was cut off by the application of voltage. Sarge quickly grabbed his right wrist and delivered the two blows swiftly and efficiently. Just as the first two had, Billy let out wails of pain, slumping to the ground. Sarge stepped back and looked at the three men. The blows had been savage. Blood ran down their arms and dripped from their limp fingers. Bones were obviously broken, as well any number of blood vessels.

"Cut 'em loose, Mike," Sarge said, setting the bloody hammer on the hood of the truck.

Mike used a pair of EMT shears to cut the ties. It took some maneuvering to get them into position, causing even more pain for those involved. Once cut loose, Mike and Sarge stood the men up, leaning them against the truck.

"You boys can be on your way now. Be glad you're leaving with your lives," Sarge said.

With gritted teeth, Claude looked at his hands. "You've killed us. It'll just take longer."

"That's up to you an' your group, ain't it? Next time you might come up against a group that will kill you. Taking from others isn't going to get you far."

"Come on, boys," the old man croaked. The three started to stagger off, holding their injured hands out in front of them like a surgeon after scrubbing up.

Sarge, Mike, and Dylan watched them disappear into the darkness. Once they were gone, Dylan said, "You think they'll die from that?"

"Could, but probably not. They got other people with their group that can take care of them. Speaking of which . . . Mikey, follow them and see where they go," Sarge said.

Mike lowered NVGs down over his eyes and started following them, disappearing into the murk. Sarge and Dylan stood in awkward silence for a moment, then Sarge asked, "You all right?"

Dylan nodded. "Yeah, just not what I expected."

"What'd you expect? You wanted to kill them?"

Dylan shook his head. "No, I don't really know what I expected. It just seemed brutal."

"It's a brutal world. This is how things are now. The rules are what you make them. They had their own rules, coming here and taking from you. We just made new rules."

"Don't get me wrong, I appreciate it, but it was just that seeing it . . . made it different."

"Always is."

Dylan pointed off in the direction Mike went. "What's he going to do?"

"I want to know where they're staying so we can keep an eye on them. If they don't move out soon, we'll move them out."

"They aren't a threat anymore. They can't hurt anyone now."

"We don't know that. How many more are back there? Do you know?"

Dylan shook his head. "Guess I don't."

"I think you should go check on Gena. I'll be out here for the rest of the night. Mike will be back soon."

Sarge retrieved his thermos and returned to the truck. After pouring himself a cup, he rested on the hood, sipping the coffee and staring into the darkness.

Mike stayed far enough behind the three men that they wouldn't see him should they venture a look. It really wasn't a worry, though, as they were too consumed with their injuries. Their hands were useless to them—they couldn't so much as unzip their flies to take a piss. The three staggered along, heading on the paved road toward Altoona. From time to time Mike could hear the men say something: sometimes words, sometimes cries of pain. Their lamentations had no effect on Mike—he felt nothing for their plight. If they hadn't been out with nefarious intentions, they wouldn't be in their current situation.

Eventually the men turned onto a small dirt drive. Mike made a quick dash so as to keep them in view. They were approaching a small trailer, dim yellow light filling the windows. As they walked down the drive, Mike saw their watch before they did. He was sitting on a bucket beside a small shed. Hearing people approach, he quickly ran up to the men, then shouted at the house. The door opened and others came out. Mike used the commotion to get closer to the house, staying inside the brush to conceal himself. As he crept closer, he was able to hear them talk. The three were retelling the story—their version, anyway. The other members of the group were understandably upset at the injuries, and talk of vengeance filled the air. Three of them said they would head back to the house and get those bastards. Mike quietly chuckled to himself—they'd never see the house or Mike before he shot them.

It was the old man who stopped them from this plan. "No one's going anywhere."

"What do you mean? We can't let them get away with this!" another replied.

In the glow of the NVGs, Mike saw the man raise his hands. "These aren't the kind of men to trifle with. We've done what we need to do to survive, and we are the ones who usually put people in their places. Tonight we came against hard men. We didn't even know they were there till it was too late. That older man had no emotion in his eyes. I don't know how many of them there are, but they're dangerous. Going back would only result in people dying." The group remained silent as their sage spoke.

"What are we supposed to do, then?"

"Leave—leave as soon as we can," the old man said, looking back down the dark drive. "For all we know they're out there now."

"I say bullshit. We can't let these people scare us off," another group member said.

The old man held his hands up. "Do you see this?" he shouted. "We could be dead!" He looked around. "We've met our match. It's time to move on."

"Smart move," Mike whispered to himself.

The group went into the trailer, and Mike waited for a while to see if they would stay inside or not. He hoped they would—he didn't feel like dealing with them. He was tired and wanted some sleep. After another hour, when no one appeared, he made his way back to the house. Sarge was leaning on the hood of the Hummer.

"They're not coming back," Mike said as he walked up.

"Good, where are they?"

"Just down the road a ways in a trailer. There's probably eight of them."

"I figured they'd try for some payback."

"Oh, they wanted to, but the old man had a sudden burst of common sense. Told 'em if they did they would more than likely die. He said they'd met their match."

"Good. Doesn't seem like they're going to try anything," Sarge said.

Mike laughed. "Nope, they're probably scared shitless. What do you want to do?"

"Let's call it a night."

Chapter 14

After finishing the watch, I sat on the porch for a while, thinking over our plan. The smoke drove me inside faster than I thought, not that it was much of a relief inside. As the weather was warming we were keeping the windows open, but the smell of smoke was inescapable. My head was swirling with thoughts of the next day, but I knew that having a good night's rest could only benefit me, so I tried to shut off my brain. I quietly got into bed next to Mel, pulling the sheet over my head for a little relief. One of the girls coughed, and it broke my heart. I drifted off to sleep fitfully.

Pounding on the door jerked me from my slumber. Grabbing my pistol I quickly went to the door. "Who is it!" I shouted.

"It's me," Sarge's voice boomed back. "Open the damn door!"

"Who is it?" Mel asked, coming into the living room with a pistol.

"It's the old man."

"What the hell, man? It sounded like the police were here," I said, opening the door.

"Your ass shoulda been outta bed a damn hour ago. Come on, we got problems."

"What is it?"

Sarge pointed off to the north. "That big-ass fire! Or haven't you noticed?"

"Yeah, yeah, let me get dressed and I'll be out."

Sarge tipped his hat and smiled. "Mornin', Mel."

"Hi. You startled us."

"I'm sorry about that. Certainly didn't mean to. We've just got to do something quick about this fire."

Mel looked out the door. "How close is it?" Then she saw the smoke billowing over the tree line across the street. "Oh no!" she practically shouted.

I hadn't noticed the smoke when I first came to the door, but now I didn't understand how I could have missed it. "Oh shit," I muttered.

"Yeah, oh shit," Sarge replied. "Get a wiggle on it, Morg."

I got my boots on as fast as I could and told Mel to get the girls up and bring them over to Danny's. The old man's stride this morning showed purpose. At Danny's all the other guys were there, an impressive group gathered on the porch.

"I finally got his ass outta bed!" Sarge barked as we approached.

"'Bout time, Princess," Thad said with a smile.

"What the hell is this? Some kind of union meeting?" I asked.

"Yeah, we're organizing for better food and conditions," Mike quipped.

I laughed. "Good luck with that shit."

"All right, let's get down to business," Sarge said. Pointing with his stick, he continued, "That damn fire is just up the road, and we need to get our shit together before it gets here."

"Where is it?" I asked.

"It's burning up to 445 now," Danny said.

"Damn, it moved fast."

"Yes, it did, now we have to figure out what we're going to do about it," Sarge said.

"We cut some breaks in that field over there," Thad said, nodding his head in the direction of the pasture.

"We've got those tanks on that trailer, but that's only good for spot fires. We have to hope that the field that wraps around here holds the fire off," Danny said.

"There's no way we can cut a fire line out there in the woods. We just don't have the equipment," I said.

Sarge looked at Tyler. "Your place is over there across the street, isn't it?"

Tyler pointed toward his house. "Yeah, right over there."

"I think we should move you guys out of there, over to this side of the street. That dirt road will be our last line of defense. There isn't that much fuel here, so we may be able to hold it out there in that pasture," Sarge said.

"I think we should go take a look at it," Thad said.

Sarge nodded. "I agree, let's do that."

Sarge, Danny, Thad, and I hopped into Sarge's Hummer. The old man must have wanted to be a NASCAR driver at some point, because he only knew two speeds: stopped and wide-open. We were soon turning onto Highway 445, where we came face-to-face with the fire. As we rolled down the road we could feel the heat, like standing near a blast furnace.

The sight of the destruction was shocking. Half of Shockley Heights had burned, and everything on the north side of the road was on fire. We saw some people running around in the hail of ash and cinders falling from the sky.

"I think we've seen enough," Sarge said. "This thing is going to jump the highway for sure."

Sarge wheeled the truck around and we returned the way we came, noting a couple of small spot fires already burning on the south side. Back out on 19, I directed Sarge to pull into the campground on Lake Dorr. We drove through the camp to the boat ramp.

"See how things narrow down in here? We've got the road on one side and the lake on the other." I pointed back to the north. "There's a big bay head over there. The fire will have a hard time burning through that."

"You think this could push it around us?" Thad asked.

"It's already burning on that side of the road," Danny said, nodding to the west side of the highway.

"Once it's past the camp, it'll have to cross a wide power line easement, not to mention a lot of brush over there has been cut. There isn't much in the way of fuel," I said.

"So you don't think it will burn all the way down here?" Sarge asked.

"I think it's a good possibility. Plus there's another easement south of us, on this side of the road, that will act as another break."

"Let's go check that out," Sarge said.

"Let me drive," I said.

I headed back in the direction of the house, turning off the road at a small clearing. "This is a gas easement. It runs at an angle behind our place, and makes a wedge between here and the road. I think the fire could burn down into here and stop."

"Is this the easement you were talking about, Morgan?" Sarge asked.

"Yeah, this is it. It's wide enough to make a difference," I replied.

As we bounced down the dirt track, Sarge asked, "Where's your place from here?"

Danny pointed back over his shoulder. "Over there about a mile. This may give us what we need to keep it away."

"A mile ain't much." Sarge rubbed his chin. "But I think you're right: we should bring that water trailer and make our stand here. This wide track should really help keep it back, and we can knock down anything that pops up," Sarge said.

We all agreed and headed back for the house. The smoke was so bad outside now that the kids were inside.

"All right, we've figured out where we're going to try and stop this fire, or at least turn it away from us," Sarge said.

"Where?" Jeff asked.

"There's a gas line easement just up the road here. It's a wide sandy patch, perfect place," I said.

"What do we need to do?" Bobbie asked.

"We need to leave some folks here and everyone else needs to go. All hands on deck," Sarge said.

Once everyone was gathered, we went into the plan, explaining we were going to try and stop the fire at the gas easement. I laid out one of the maps and showed them where I was talking about, running a finger along the dashed line. Mel asked where it was in relation to our house, and I dragged my finger along the map a short distance. "Here."

"How far is that?" Mel asked.

"A mile or so," Danny replied.

"That's so close," Brandy said.

We went on to explain what we were going to do and how everyone needed to be ready to leave in case of an emergency. This particular point caused a lot of concern. Sarge took a moment to calmly explain the reason for it, the absolute importance of it. It was decided that Danny, Thad, Jeff, Jess, and I would go with Sarge and Mike to try and hold the fire, and everyone else would stay behind to keep security and be ready to leave should it come to it. Once everyone was clear on what was about to take place, we started getting things ready.

In short order, everyone was assembled. We'd have my truck—the small red one with the water trailer—Sarge's Hummer, and two ATVs with us. Danny led the way, with everyone following him off the road onto the easement. Thad drove the small red truck down the dirt road a ways so it could quickly move either direction. While he and Danny were priming the Striker pump, I handed out the gear we had: shovels, axes, Pulaskis, and beaters.

The smoke was so thick in the woods that visibility was cut to only a few yards. The hot white cloud seemed to cling to the ground, rolling outward. All we could really do was wait.

"Notice how the smoke is so close to the ground?" Thad asked.

Sarge looked up into the gray soup hanging over our heads. "Yeah, must be high pressure. Maybe a storm's coming."

"Somehow I don't think we're that lucky," I said.

"Hell, if it started raining right now, anything short of the storm ole Noah witnessed would be like pissing into a volcano," Sarge replied.

"I've done that before," Mike said quickly.

"Done what?" Jess asked.

"Pissed in a volcano. I did that once," Mike replied.

Just as I was about to make a smart-ass comment back to Mike, a crashing sound came from the woods followed by a large cloud of ash and embers that soared into the air. The temperature suddenly started to rise as well, heralding the approaching flames.

"Let's spread out along the road! Call out if you see any fires start on the south side of this line!" Sarge shouted.

Everyone started moving rapidly. Jeff rode back down toward the end of the road on the ATV. He had one of the beaters with him, its base resting on the footrest and its flapper end sticking up in the air. The black flapper waved back and forth as he sped away. He looked like some sort of surreal standard bearer rushing into battle. "Morgan, what is that?" Jess asked, pointing to a couple sections of pipe coming out of the ground.

"That's part of a gas line that runs through here."

She walked a couple of steps, then asked, "You mean like natural gas?"

"Yeah."

"Should we be here, then? I mean, is it going to blow up?" she asked, fear in her eyes.

I laughed to myself. The possibility of a gas line had never occurred to me. But there wasn't time to worry about it now.

"I don't think so. I doubt there's any gas in it—that should have run out a long time ago," I replied.

"You don't *think* so?"

"Best I can offer you: it should be out of gas by now. Besides, the fire isn't going to burn across here. That's why we're here," I said. I didn't bother telling them that the empty line was far more dangerous than a full one.

As the inferno approached, things changed: the wind picked up, being drawn toward the flames. Then there was the sound, a hellish, constant roar.

"Let's move back toward the trees here," I yelled, pointing to the opposite side of the easement.

As we moved I looked down the clearing. I could see Danny and Thad to the east with the truck and trailer. To the west, the Hummer with Sarge and Mike. It looked like the set of some really bad spaghetti western, with everyone in bandannas and all the smoke. Once we could hear the blaze, it wasn't long before we could start to see the flicker of orange back in the trees on the other side of the easement.

"Let's go. That's what we're here to stop!" I shouted as I ran toward the small fire. Everyone followed and, using the beaters and shovels, we quickly put the small spot fire out. "Keep your eyes open. That's exactly what we're looking for."

Out of the corner of my eye, I saw the truck suddenly move toward the far side of the cleared strip. Then I saw the smoke in the direction they were headed, so I started to jog toward them. I could see Danny on the trailer holding on to the water tank as they bounced along. The truck pulled parallel to the tree line. Danny jumped off before the truck stopped. He pulled the pump off, setting it on the ground, and quickly started it. By then Thad was dragging a hose out into the woods.

When I got to them they had two hoses going on a small but aggressive fire in a thick stand of pine trees. Using my shovel, I raked the debris back around the edge of the fire, containing that side. With two hoses going, it didn't take long to knock the fire down to a soggy, smoking mess. It struck me that this all happened without a word being spoken. We were dragging the hoses back out when Jeff roared up on the ATV.

"Fire down here!" he shouted, pointing east.

We quickly piled the hose and pump on the trailer. Thad

ran back to the truck while Danny and I clung to the tanks. When we jumped off, it was clear that this fire was much bigger than the one we'd just dealt with. Danny was setting the pump down when I grabbed a hose and took off running into the woods—that is, until the hose stopped, the nozzle jerked from my hands.

Turning around, I could see Danny trying to untangle the line. He started waving at me and I picked the nozzle back up and continued on. Getting close enough to the flames to be able to hit it with water I felt the pressure rushing through the hose and opened it up. A blast of air was followed immediately by the gush of water. It wasn't long before Thad added another hose to the fight. Danny and Jeff were working the edge of the fire with shovel and beater, slowing the spread.

For the next few hours we repeated the process again and again. Some of the spot fires were close to the clearing, some were farther out into the woods, requiring Thad to drive the truck out into the bush to get the hoses close enough to bring them to bear.

"We need to refill these tanks. They're nearly empty," Danny said, panic edging into his voice.

"Shit, shit, shit. Let's run over to the lake," I said.

Jeff pulled up on the ATV, his face black with soot. "Done? I've been out there in the woods putting out the little fires while you assholes played in the water."

"How's it look down there right now?" I asked.

Jeff looked back down the sandy swath. "It seems to be slowing down now."

"Follow us over to the lake, then."

"Hell yeah, I could use a dip!" he said.

The public boat ramp was only a couple hundred yards

down the road, and we were there in no time. Thad backed the trailer down the ramp to get the pump close to the water. To fill the tanks we had to disconnect the pump from the tanks, connect the suction hose, and drop it in the lake. This is where the priming pump came in handy: being able to use the small hand pump connected to it to quickly prime the pump.

As we were getting the pump set up there was a stampede of bodies down the ramp and into the water. Jeff ran down the ramp yelling like a wild man and dove into the water with a whoop. He still had his boots on, engineer-style motorcycle boots. When he stood up, the slick bottoms found no purchase on the algae-covered ramp, his feet immediately went out from under him, and he was back underwater in no time. Everyone was laughing when he came up.

"Don't know what you call that dive, but I'll give it a three," I said through my laughter.

"I'll go five for creativity," Thad added.

Jeff was wiping water out of his eyes when his feet started to slide again. After several acrobatic bouts, he managed to get his balance enough to get out of the water and take his boots off, pouring the water out of them.

"All right, tanks are full, we need to get back to it!" Sarge shouted.

Danny cut off the pump to a chorus of jeers, and very reluctantly everyone started out of the water. Jess made quite the show as she came out—I don't think she realized that she was looking the part of a wet T-shirt contestant. Jeff ogled her as she walked past him, and Mike caught the action too, though he was slightly more discreet about it.

"Hey, Jess," he said, and pointed down to his chest.

Jess looked down and turned bright red but then recovered. "You boys act like you've never seen them before."

"Oh, we've seen them, just not those," Mike said with a grin.

"Like Ron White said, once you've seen one you want to see the rest." Jeff cackled.

"Now that the show's over, can we get back to work?" Sarge asked, drawing some snickers from a few of us.

"Yeah, let's go. Nothing to see here," I said as Jess moved toward the Suburban.

We were back in the ash, soot, and smoke all too quickly. While we were gone a couple more spot fires had started. One was nearly an acre in size and took everyone's effort to knock it back. Every time we took one on, it was done in the same manner. On the downwind side we'd start raking back the litter from the forest floor while attacking with the hoses and working the edges with the beaters and shovels. The method was very effective and we were able to quickly gain control over all the small fires that appeared. After attacking one of these we were taking a break in the middle of the easement. Sarge was looking back toward the main fire. "Looks like it's starting to burn itself out," he yelled.

I looked across the open patch. Black soldering stumps and snags jutted out of the ground, some with small flames flickering out of them. "It does."

I told Jeff to take a break and jumped on the four-wheeler and rode down the easement looking for any additional fires. The only thing I found was the smoking remains of the fires we'd already dealt with, thankfully. Riding back I stayed on the north side of the easement, where the fire had originally approached from. The smoke was still heavy, heavier maybe than it was at the height of the fire. With the main blaze now burning itself out, it was no longer creating the updraft, drawing air in at ground level and pumping it along with smoke, ash, and embers out the top.

As we headed back toward the trucks, I caught a bright flash. *That wasn't* . . . I thought to myself. Another flash came, then a large wet drop landed on my forehead. Another landed on my shoulder, then another, then another. I whooped and spread my arms out wide as the large drops began to come down hard and heavy. The thunder rolled on for a long time, a crescendo signaling the end of our fight.

Pulling back up to the group, I shut off the ATV and held my hands up. "Look at it!" Everyone stood in the rain, soaking it up as it quickly built in intensity to monsoon proportions. Sarge was leaning on the hood of the Hummer smiling. "Think this will do it?" I asked.

Sarge squinted up into the sky. "I don't think it's going to rain for forty days and forty nights, but I think it will certainly do it."

"I'll take it. I don't care how long it lasts," Thad said.

"I can't believe it! I can't believe it!" Danny shouted, looking into the sky.

Mike held his hands out as the rain puddled into them. He shook his head. "Better late than never."

I looked up. "We're glad to see the rain now, but remember, hurricane season is right around the corner."

"Shut up and enjoy it, Morgan," Mike shot back. I couldn't help but smile.

The rain beat down what remained of the fire to the point

that there wasn't a flame to be seen. We'd been saved. It was a small miracle. Finally, something had gone our way.

"Saddle up, boys. Let's make like a donkey's dick and hit the road," Sarge said. He always did have a way with words.

Pulling up to the gate, we saw Doc and Tyler standing in the rain. Doc held his hands out. "Divine intervention?"

"I'll take it, no matter what it is," I said.

"Can you believe this rain? I can't remember the last time I saw rain like this," Tyler said.

"Just in the nickel dime," Mike said with a smile.

"I'm guessing this took care of it?" Doc asked.

"Yeah, it did. And tomorrow we're going to celebrate," Thad said.

"What're you planning?" Doc asked.

"We're going to roast a hog tomorrow."

That was met with a chorus of cheers.

Doc smiled. "Oh yeah, that's what I'm talking about."

"Really? A pig roast?" Tyler asked.

"Hell yeah! It's about time," Danny said.

Doc looked at Tyler. "And ole Thad here sure knows his way around a pig."

Thad smiled. "I can make one fit to eat."

I laughed. "That's an understatement. Are you guys good here for now?"

Doc nodded. "Yeah, we're good. I know you guys are probably tired."

"I'm beat," Thad said.

"Yeah, I've got a whole new respect for those guys who fight these wildfires," Danny added.

"You guys head on home and get some rest," Doc said, waving us off.

"Thanks, man," I said as Thad started to pull off.

Thad pulled the little red truck into my yard and I hopped out. I, for one, needed to change my clothes and relax for a bit.

"Catch up with you guys later," I said as I headed for the house.

I found Mel inside lying on the couch, Little Bit beside her. "The rain! Is it helping?" Mel asked.

"We don't need to worry about the fire anymore. Now, if you don't mind, I'm going to change out of these filthy clothes and take a siesta," I replied.

After showering, I fell onto the bed, asleep in no time. Mel came in and woke me what seemed like a minute later. Sitting up, I felt groggy. However long I'd slept, it was either too long or not long enough.

Rubbing my face, I asked, "What's up?"

"Danny's here."

I looked around. "What time is it?"

"Almost ten in the morning."

"What? I slept all night?"

"Like you were dead."

"I feel like I am. When did it stop raining?"

"Sometime late last night."

Getting up, I dressed and walked out to the living room.

"What's up, man?" I asked.

"Come over to the house real quick."

Still not entirely awake, I slipped on my Crocs and hung my pistol on my belt. As Danny and I walked toward his house I asked, "What's up?"

"You gotta see this," Danny said.

That piqued my interest. "What is it?"

As we passed through the fence between the houses, he pointed. "That."

Tyler was there, skinning a deer. Two others were hanging beside it, waiting their turn for the knife.

"Holy shit!" I shouted.

Tyler looked up. "Hey, Morgan, check it out—got three of them."

"I can see that! When did you do this?"

"This morning, early."

As we were talking, Thad walked up. "Someone's been busy," he said.

"Yeah, ole Tyler here bagged 'em," Danny said.

"Well, let's get to work, then," Thad said as he drew his knife.

"You still want to do that hog too?" I asked.

"I'd like to. I'll do it a little different now, though, considering we have these deer. We can render all the fat down. It'll really help with this lean meat," Thad said.

"We can freeze some of it, but the freezer's not big enough for all of this," Danny said.

"Don't worry, we can smoke most of it," Thad said.

"Dry some too. We have salt and vinegar still. I'll make biltong," I said.

"Sounds good to me," Thad said.

The smell of fresh hanging meat got the attention of the dogs. Their eyes tracked every movement and didn't miss a thing. Tyler had the hide off the first deer and was ready to open it up. He hadn't field dressed them as the organs were valuable. Simply dumping them in the dirt was an unthinkable waste.

We pulled out a large tub and set it under the suspended animal. Once opened up, most of the entrails fell out on their own. The heart and liver were removed and set to the side. When the offal landed in the tub, the dogs sat up. The lungs had to be cut out and dropped into the tub. I took them and cut them into three pieces, tossing them to the dogs, who eagerly set upon the fresh meat.

Thad and Danny were already working on the second deer. Its hide was quickly off, the tub was slid under it, and the process repeated. The dogs would certainly eat well today.

"I want to keep the brains," Danny said.

"Wanna tan some hides?" Thad asked.

"Yeah, I'll freeze the brains until the hides are ready."

"Cool, I've always wanted to do that," Tyler said.

The skinned animals were cut up, the back straps, tenderloins, and front and rear quarters removed. We even cut the ribs off, leaving nothing more than a spine and head. Danny used a hacksaw to open up the skull, and the brains were removed. He cut the spines into pieces and tossed them to the dogs, much to their delight. I was skinning the third as the first two were finished. Tyler was helping me, and just as the first two, it didn't take long to have it reduced to pieces.

Danny had a nice grinder and all the accessories to go with it. We'd hidden it in the garage down the road when we'd left. We piled the meat into the gray tubs and took it into the house, where we'd bone and grind it. Danny set a large poly cutting board out on the counter and immediately got to work. While he, Thad, and Tyler were cutting up the meat, removing the hams to use as roasts and cubing everything else, I laid the back straps out. Using a fillet knife I carefully cut the wide sinew from them, ensuring no meat was left on it. Once all three were removed I took them back out to the shop.

Finding a piece of plywood I stretched them out, tacking them in place with small nails. With all three stretched out I left it on the work bench to dry. While we didn't really need it, I wasn't about to waste it—there were simply too many uses for the stuff. With that done I went back inside. Bobbie was in the kitchen watching the work and making sure no one made too much of a mess in her kitchen.

"Danny, you got any extra screen?" I asked as I worked on a hindquarter.

"A little, what do you want to do?"

"I want to make a screen box of sorts, to dry the meat in. We really want to keep flies off it as it dries."

"I'm sure we can manage that. Let's get this all cut up and we'll check it out."

"Are you just going to hang it up and let it dry, not other treatment?" Tyler asked.

"Pretty much. What I'll do is sprinkle some vinegar on the meat and leave it in the fridge overnight. Then I'll salt it and then we'll hang it up to dry. It'll take a couple of weeks to dry to the point we can store it," I replied.

Tyler looked at me, obviously skeptical. "And that's safe to eat? You don't smoke it or anything?"

"Don't need to, man. I used to make it in the kitchen, hanging it up between two cabinets. Back then I'd put some cumin on it for flavor. It turns out just like jerky."

"I bet Mel loved that, bunch of meat hanging from the ceiling in her kitchen," Thad said with a smile.

"Yeah, first time she saw it she was like *What the hell is that!*" Everyone laughed at my impression of a pissed-off Mel.

"Brandy would probably strangle me in my sleep with it if I'd have tried,"Tyler said, tossing a handful of cubes into a tub.

Bobbie looked into one of the bins. "What's that?"

Danny looked over. "Brains."

"What are you going to do with those?"

"Freeze them for now."

"Not in my freezer!" Bobbie shouted.

"You know of another working one anywhere?" Danny said.

"Well, you better put them in something. I don't want to see them."

As we worked, other people started to drift in. First was Jess, Fred, and Aric.

"Oh wow, is that the pig?" Jess asked, looking at all the meat.

"No, Tyler shot three deer," Danny replied.

"It was easy too. They were moving away from the fire and ran out right in front of me,"Tyler said.

"Looks good! Are we having them for dinner?" Fred asked.

"Let's cook these back straps and tenderloins tonight," Danny said.

"Why don't we just dust them in kudzu flour and fry them up?" I asked.

"That'd work, let's do it," Danny said.

"As soon as you guys get out of here we can get started on it," Bobbie said.

"Now that most everyone is here, we can now officially say the fire is out, we don't have to leave," I said.

There was a round of claps and catcalls. It was a great moment, the threat over, the relief of the stress and the sudden abundance. After everything that'd happened recently, it was incredible for things to be making a turn for the better. I just hoped it would last. The house filled with talk—of the piles of meat on hand, of the fire's defeat, and of the rain. I sat back and took it all in. It was wonderful.

A rumble in the yard, announced by the dogs barking, let us know Sarge had arrived. I walked out on the front porch and waved as he and the guys got out. As they came up on the porch, Sarge patted me on the shoulder. "You get some rest, Morgan?"

I nodded. "I did, you?"

Sarge stretched. "Yeah, took a little nap. Feel better now."

"You guys are just in time. Come on in," I said as I turned and headed back into the house.

"Damn, look at all that meat," Mike said, clapping his hands together.

"So stay out of the damn way. I'm hungry," Sarge barked.

"Then you guys need to clear out so we can start dinner. Jess, Fred, Mary, can you help?" Bobbie said.

They quickly jumped at the request. "You know it. What do you need us to do?" Fred asked.

"I've got this. Why don't you guys go chill out so I can cook," Danny said.

"All right, Chef," Bobbie said, giving him a little salute. "I knew I married this man for a reason."

Sarge tapped me on the shoulder. "Morgan, why don't you and me give them boys at the barricade a break."

"Sure thing." We made our way over to the Hummer and hopped in. Doc and Aric were leaning on the barricade watching the sun drift toward the horizon. Hearing us coming they turned around and leaned back.

"'Bout time you got here," Doc said with a smile.

Sarge snorted. "Yer lucky I came at all. You boys seen anything?"

"Nah, there were a bunch of deer moving before, but they're gone now."

"There was all kinds of wildlife earlier. It was amazing," Aric said.

"That fire was pushing them," Sarge replied.

Doc looked at the old man like he was crazy. "Ya think?"

Sarge smiled and walked toward the pile of logs. As he did he flicked the back of his hand into Doc's crotch, finding the sweet spot, apparently. Doc folded up and went to his knees with a moan. Sarge smiled and looked at Aric, who was wide-eyed. When the old man's eyes fell on him, he naturally covered his jewels with his hands. It cracked me up and I started to laugh my ass off. Sarge saw it and laughed as well. Doc, however, didn't see the humor.

"Dammit, that hurts," Doc said as he straightened up.

"Sorry about that, Ronnie, I slipped," Sarge said with a toothy grin.

"I bet you did. Just for that I'm taking the truck. Your old ass can walk," Doc replied as he headed for the Hummer.

"Thanks for being down here, guys," I said.

Tyler and Doc waved. "No problem, Morgan," Doc said.

"You might want to hurry up. They're cooking some venison," Sarge said.

"No shit. Man, that's going to be good," Tyler said.

"Yeah, I'll be thinking of you while I eat it," Doc said, giving Sarge the finger.

I started to laugh again when Sarge headed for the truck. Doc hurried to start it, backing up as soon as the engine caught, an obvious look of relief on his face as he did. Sarge laughed and waved, then returned to the barricade. The sun was now kissing the horizon, a very dull orange orb balanced on the hay field across the road. With all the smoke still in the air it darkened the sun so much it looked like a giant pumpkin.

"How's the hip?" I asked.

Sarge kicked his leg out. "Almost back to normal."

Nodding, I replied, "Good, we were worried about you."

"Shoot, don't need to worry about me. Take more than that little snot nose to kill me."

I smiled. If he were half as tough as he thought he was, he'd be twice what he really is.

"Yeah, well, take it easy. We kind of like having you around."

With the sun almost gone I looked down the road toward Altoona and a pair of white eyes stared back at me. "Hey," I said, slapping Sarge's arm, pointing up the road.

"Looks like we got visitors," he said.

"Wonder who's got the stones to be on the road in the dark," I said.

"We're about to see."

As the lights got closer it became obvious there were two vehicles. I mentioned it to Sarge.

"Nothing to worry about: they're Hummers."

"How can you tell?" I asked.

"You don't think I've seen enough of them things to recognize it? Hell, I can *smell* the bastards."

In a few minutes he was proven right as the two Hummers coasted up to the barricade. I was surprised to see Captain Sheffield and Livingston in the lead truck.

"Wonder what they want?" Sarge said in a sigh.

The second Hummer pulled up beside it. Ian was behind

the wheel with Jamie up front. Sheffield and Livingston got out and walked up to Sarge.

"What brings you fellers down here tonight?" Sarge asked.

"We need to talk," Sheffield replied.

Sarge smiled. "I'm all ears."

"Came across some of your handiwork," Livingston said.

Sarge cocked his head to the side. "What work was that?"

"Three sets of busted hands," Sheffield replied.

"Oh, them boys. Guessing they came to town?"

"Indeed they did, and when they described what happened to them I knew who it was."

"I am kind of memorable," Sarge replied, pausing to smile. "But did they tell you what led to it?"

"Surprisingly they did," Livingston said.

"Then what's the problem?"

"Let's just get to what we're here for," Sheffield said. "I want to position a few of our people here, use this as an outpost of sorts."

Sarge looked over at Jamie and Ian. "You mean these two?"

"Three," Perez said from the turret.

"Yes, these three and the four of you would be a decent squad to have out here."

"Oh, we got more than a squad here," Sarge replied.

"Damn straight," I added.

"That's up to you guys. You just have to keep yourselves in check. This isn't the Wild West."

Sarge looked around. "If this isn't, what is?"

The comment annoyed Sheffield. "You know what I mean."

"I do, but do you get my point? I don't know what you want done or how you want to do it, but if I'm going to be dealing with this shit I'll do it my way. Those three could have killed. They were wrong, but they didn't deserve to die—yet. So I dealt with them. They'll recover."

"That's the problem: you're the army, not the local civilian authority, and we need to fix that," Sheffield said, then reached into his blouse pocket and extended a closed fist to me. I stared back at him. "Put your hand out."

I stuck my hand out and he dropped a gold badge into my palm. The word SHERIFF was stamped on it. I looked up at him. "What the hell is this?"

"Times have changed. We've met with the county sheriff. The county is simply too big and he has his hands full with Tavares and Leesburg. There's a sheriff for Eustis, and I was thinking about who would be a good fit for sheriff of the north end of Lake County. And that would be you, Morgan."

Sarge erupted in laughter and I stared at him, seemingly unable to speak.

"I don't want to be the fucking sheriff, I've got my hands full here! I'm sure you'll find someone who wants the job." I held the badge back out.

"That's exactly why you're getting it. You and your people have your shit together out here. I've heard you talking when you were down visiting the camp. You're smart. You think about problems and you come up with creative solutions. You have no idea the condition most are in. You have vehicles, you know the area, and so now you're the sheriff," Livingston said.

Livingston pointed at Sarge. "And you"—he pointed at me—"work for him."

"Oh, give me a break. He isn't going to listen to me, not that I'd want him to. Why don't you make him sheriff?" I said.

Sarge started waving his hands in front of him. "No, no, no,

I'll listen to the high sheriff. I don't want to be no sheriff," he replied, laughing.

Looking at Sarge, I replied, "Fuck you." It only made him laugh harder, snot coming out of his nose and tears running down his face.

"Linus, I need you to get in touch with your higher-ups. We need some help. Can you do that? I'm in contact with the people at MacDill, but I know you've got other contacts," Sheffield said.

Sarge was getting himself under control, he nodded. "I can do that. Can't promise anything, though."

"Looks like the fire's died down," Livingston said, looking north.

"We stopped it on this side. I think it's done over here," I replied.

"See, that's why you're the sheriff," Livingston said with a smile. I gave him the finger as a means of reply, which caused him to chuckle.

"Have you guys checked on the camp?" Sheffield asked.

"No, we were beat when we wrapped it up," I replied.

"I think you should go check on them."

"Me? You go check on 'em," I shot back.

Sheffield smiled. "You're the sheriff." I glanced over at Ian and Jamie. She had her hands over her mouth, obviously trying to hide her laughter. Ian, however, didn't even attempt to hide his enjoyment of what was going on.

I shook my head. "This is bullshit. We don't have very much fuel left, anyway. There isn't much we're going to be able to do."

"We'll get you fuel."

I was being cut off at every turn. It was starting to look like I was stuck with this crap.

"So what am I responsible for?" I asked.

"From Highway 42 north to Highway 40," Sheffield said.

"Holy shit, that's a huge area! How in the hell am I supposed to do anything in an area that size?"

"You'll need deputies," Livingston said, reaching into his cargo pocket. He produced a small cloth bag and tossed it to me. It clanged when I caught it. In the bag were a dozen or so silver stars with LAKE COUNTY SHERIFF DEPUTY stamped on them. "I think you already know some candidates."

I bounced the bag in my palm, the stars clinking together. "Look, if I have to do this I'm doing it my way"—I pointed at Sarge—"and if you don't like his way you're damn sure not going to like my way."

Sheffield crossed his arms over his chest. "Morgan, you are now the face of law enforcement in this part of the county. We don't have judges and juries, and there is no jail you can lock someone up in. With that said, though, you've got to be prudent." Sheffield looked at Sarge. "You can't kill everyone for everything."

I shook my head. I damn sure didn't want to do this. There was more than enough for me to worry about here. My family came first, my friends second, and nothing was going to change that. But, with all that said, it would give me the ability to affect change where it needed to happen.

"All right, but I need some support," I finally said.

Sheffield nodded. "We're going to move a few more people down here. I'm pretty sure you have the room."

"Who are you sending?"

Sheffield nodded at Jamie and Ian. "Those two, plus Perez."

Sarge snorted. "You ain't got anything that's housebroke?"

Jamie's head perked up. "Hey!"

Sarge smiled. "Not you, Jamie, that damn seagoin' bellhop over there."

Ian smiled and blew a kiss at Sarge.

"I think these three will be more than enough help for you," Livingston replied.

"Have you boys eaten yet?" Sarge asked.

"Yeah, I was going to invite you bastards to dinner, but now . . ." I trailed off.

"We're all right, Linus," Sheffield said.

"Fresh venison," Sarge teased.

Livingston looked at Sheffield. "Come on now, let's not be inhospitable. They invited us, after all."

Sheffield smiled. "Well, since you put it that way."

He turned back to the Hummers. There were two additional Guardsmen there. "You guys keep an eye on this here. We'll be back." The two men nodded.

"I'll make sure you boys get a plate too. We got plenty of meat down there," Sarge said to the two men as they took up positions behind the barricade.

Both of them smiled broadly. "Hey, thanks," one of them said.

"Come on, let's go get something to eat," I said as I walked toward Ian and Jamie.

Jamie was grinning from ear to ear. "Hi, Sheriff," she said as she started to laugh.

I gave her the finger as I passed, cracking Ian up in the process. Sarge opened the door to get into the Hummer and was surprised to see Miss Kay sitting in the back.

"Well, hi, Kay, didn't know you were there," Sarge said.

"Y'all didn't need me for anything, so I just stayed out of the way," Kay replied.

"What are you doing down here?" I asked.

Timidly she replied, "Well, I was kind of hoping I could stay here. It's just so crowded at the armory, and they don't need an old woman in their way."

Sarge scoffed. "You ain't old!"

"Of course you can stay here, Kay. I know some folks who will be happy to see you," I replied.

She smiled. "Thank you, Morgan."

Sheffield and Livingston followed us down to Danny's house. The house was already crowded with people, and we were adding eight more to it.

"We got enough to feed this crew too?" I asked as we came up on the porch.

"We got plenty," Thad said as he got up.

When Jess and Fred saw Kay they rushed over to her. "Kay! It's so good to see you. What are you doing down here?"

"Moving in," Sarge replied with a smile.

"Really? You're going to stay here now?" Fred asked.

"If that's all right with everyone," Kay replied. "I can cook, and I can clean."

"Cook and clean? You sound like my kind of woman!" Bobbie said.

"Of course it's okay for you to stay here—you're more than welcome," Mel replied, with a smile. "We've all heard so much about you."

After the events of the past few days, it was nice to sit down together. As Thad cooked up the venison, I sat in the kitchen, thinking about my new position. I really didn't want any more responsibility, more challenges. All I wanted was a routine, some semblance of normalcy.

Thad was busy at the stove, and I took a seat at the bar. "Hey, let's roast the pig tomorrow instead. I was thinking of going down to the lake, having a picnic of sorts. A celebration."

Thad smiled. "I think that's a fine idea. Here, this is for you," he said, handing me a plate.

"Thanks," I replied with a smile.

After dinner Sheffield and Livingston got up. "Thanks for the great grub, guys. Really appreciate it," Sheffield said.

"No worries. Let me get a plate for your guys," Thad said.

"Thanks," Livingston said with a smile.

"Who's supposed to be on duty tonight?" I asked.

"We are," Thad said as he finished the last plate.

"You want a ride down there?" Livingston asked.

"No, we'll ride down on the four-wheelers," I replied.

"Here's the plates for your guys," Thad said.

"Ian, you and Jamie stay here tonight. You too, Miss Kay. We'll work things out tomorrow with where you're living," Bobbie said.

Mel asked me to walk her and the girls home before I went down to the barricade. I told Thad I'd be back shortly and helped Mel round up the girls. Little Bit was sitting with Sarge, talking his ear off.

"Come on, Little Bit, time to go," I called.

She jumped up and hugged Sarge. "Bye bye, Mister Sarge, see you later."

He tousled her hair. "Good night, sweetie."

We walked home, Mel and I holding hands. Taylor and Lee Ann were swinging Ashley by her hands, much to her delight.

They set her down and Taylor looked at me. "Dad, is the fire really out?"

"It is, kiddo. I don't think we'll have to worry about that anymore."

"So we don't have to leave?" Little Bit asked.

"Nope, we're staying right here."

"Thank God, I really didn't want to have to leave," Lee Ann said.

"So are things going back to normal?" Taylor asked.

I thought about that for a moment. "Well, in a way." I squeezed Mel's hand. "I have something I need to talk to you about later."

She looked at me, concerned. "What is it? What's wrong?"

I smiled. "Nothing's wrong, baby, just something that's come up, not a bad thing."

"What is it?"

I smiled. "I'll tell you later."

We got the girls home and into bed. I gave Mel a kiss and told her I'd be back later. "I still want to know what's up."

"Tomorrow."

Thad and I rode the ATVs down to the barricade. Sheffield and his people were still there.

"We waited for you," Livingston said.

"Thanks, appreciate that," I replied.

"Remember what I said, Morgan: you've got to be prudent," Sheffield said.

"I know, I know," I said with a dismissive wave. Thad gave me a raised-eyebrow look.

"We'll see you later," Sheffield said.

Once they were headed down the road, Thad looked at me. "What was that about?"

I reached into my pocket and pulled out the gold star, holding it in my palm. He looked at with eyes the size of saucers.

"They want me to be a sheriff."

Thad stared at the badge for a minute. "Sheriff of what?"

"North Lake County, they say."

"What's that even mean?"

"I guess it means we're going to be responsible for dealing with shit around here," I replied.

Thad looked at me with raised eyebrows. *"We're?"*

"Oh yeah"—I pulled a bag out of the cargo pocket of my pants—"here," I said, handing him a star. "Deputy."

He took it and turned it over in his hand. "You really wanna do this?"

"No, but I guess someone has to, and I'd rather it be us than someone else."

"Got a point there. If you're in, I'm in."

"Thanks, Thad. Thanks a lot," I replied with a smile.

We didn't talk much for the rest of the night. I passed the time thinking about what lay ahead, hoping that maybe for a while—just a little while—things would calm down. We were relieved by Jeff and Danny sometime around midnight. I went home and quietly climbed into bed, trying not to wake Mel in the process. I drifted off to sleep in no time.

In the morning I got up early, leaving to go to Thad's before Mel and the girls were even awake. There was a lot of work to do to prepare for our pig roast. When I got to Thad's, he was setting up a large tub on a fire.

"Morning, Thad," I hollered. "You got a hog picked out?"

"I figured one would pick itself out," he said, leaning over the side of the pen. The pigs immediately took notice. Thad held his pistol in one hand and with the other he reached out. One of the hogs made a lunge, and Thad dropped it with a shot to the head.

After gutting the hog, we scalded it in the tub and scraped the skin and hair from the hide, the first step in preparing a whole hog.

"Help me load it in the truck, then you can go get everyone together," Thad said.

He already had the big smoker hooked to the red truck. We dumped the water out of the tub and loaded the hog into it, setting it in the truck bed.

"Who's going to the park with you?" I asked.

"All of 'em. They all want to go, at least they did yesterday when I talked to Fred, Aric, and Jess."

"Good, you guys be safe. We'll be up later."

I left for home, finding Mel still asleep when I got there. Since it was quiet in the house, I sat on the couch and closed my eyes. I was jarred awake when Little Bit jumped on me. "Good morning, Daddy!"

"Hey, kiddo, you sleep good?"

"I did! I wasn't scared of the fire anymore."

"Good, know what we're going to do today?"

A smile spread across her face. "What?"

"We're going to the lake for a cookout."

"Really? We are?!" She jumped up and down, clapping her hands.

"In a little while. Let's go see if Danny is awake," I said as I stood up.

"Okay," she replied, grabbing my hand.

We walked over to Danny's in the cool morning. It was still overcast and the ground was damp, a nice change in weather.

We found Danny and Bobbie sitting on the porch enjoying the morning as well. Little Bit ran up the stairs and sat on Danny's lap. I dropped onto a step. We talked a little about the plan for the day, but mainly we enjoyed the morning, soaking it in.

With the fire out we took the chance to relax and enjoy some downtime. In the afternoon, we organized who would stay at the barricade. I was surprised when Ian and Jamie volunteered for the whole day. "You guys could use a break," Ian said.

"Thanks, thanks a lot. We'll get you guys down there at some point," I said.

We headed down to the park in the afternoon. Everyone was excited to go—Little Bit was bouncing up and down the whole ride there. When we rolled up, Thad had the big smoker set up near the old swimming area of the park. Fred and Aric were sitting at the water's edge, and Jess and Mary were sitting at a picnic table.

"Holy crap, that smells good!" Jeff shouted, reaching for the smoker's lid.

Thad smacked his hand. "It needs another two hours."

"Well, since we have some time to kill, let's get everyone together real quick," I said. Everyone gathered, some with looks of concern on their faces.

"What's this all about?" Danny asked.

Mel crossed her arms. "Yeah, what *is* this about?"

"First, we've been under a lot of stress with the fire, but we beat it."

"With a little help from the rain," Jeff said.

"A lot of help," Mike added.

"Yeah, a lot of help, but we really came together and put

on a good show. Thanks for all the effort, guys." Fred and Jess whooped and hollered, echoing my thanks.

"Anything else?" Mel asked.

"Actually, yes"—I pulled the star out again and held it up—"it would appear that the army wants me to be a sheriff. We're going to be responsible for the north end of the county." I looked at Sarge, and he gave me a wink and a small nod.

"What do you mean?" Mel asked.

"Just that. Someone needs to step up, and if there's going to be someone around here enforcing their vision of the law, I'd like it to be ours," I replied.

"What do you mean, *ours*?" Danny asked.

I pulled the bag out once again and removed a badge from it, tossing it to Danny. "This is what I mean."

I continued passing out badges, and when I got to Jess I paused for a moment. "You up for it?"

"Really? You want to give me one?"

I looked around. "We're all part of this. It's going to take all of us."

Sarge stood up. "It is." Everyone looked over at him. "What you guys are going to be doing is important, and we'll be here to support you"—Sarge nodded toward Mike, Doc, and Ted—"plus a few others who are coming over to help out. But that's not what today is about. Let's enjoy this nice day."

"And eat—don't forget the eating part," Mike said.

"Amen!" Jeff shouted.

"You chowhounds will get your feed on. Cool your jets," Sarge added.

"The pig will be ready in a bit," Thad said.

Mel came up beside me. "I want to talk about this."

"We will, I promise."

Sarge came over. "Miss Mel, can I borrow him for a minute?"

She nodded. "Sure."

"We've got to take a ride. We'll be back before the food's ready."

"Where are you going?" Mel asked.

Sarge grabbed my shoulder. "The sheriff here needs to go take a look at the camp."

"Now?" Mel asked.

"We'll be back shortly. It won't take long," I replied, then gave her a kiss.

"Mike, Teddy, let's go. You too, Doc, we may need your services," Sarge said.

We drove through a scorched landscape. Blackened trunks and palmettos lined the road on either side. It was utter devastation. The sandbagged emplacements at the gate were nothing more than a pile of melted plastic and slumping sand. Pulling up to the camp proper, we took in the scene.

Ted stopped the truck on a small rise, looking out across the camp. Where tents once stood, there remained only their scorched remnants. We could see a couple wretched souls picking through what remained behind.

"Look at this place. It's gone, totally gone," Ted said.

"There isn't shit left," Mike called down from the turret.

"Take us through it, Teddy," Sarge said with a nod.

We rolled down into what remained, getting a closer look at the few people pawing through the scorched leavings from the fire. A man picking through a pile of ashes straightened when he saw the Hummer. Ted slowed as he pulled up. "Anyone hurt around here?" Sarge asked.

He looked around. "I don't know, most people ran off."

"What are you doing?"

The man looked down and shrugged, clearly dazed. "Looking for something, anything. I should have left. I shouldn't have stayed here."

"We tried to tell you," Sarge said, and then waved Ted on.

We rode through the rest of the camp. The only things that remained were the connex buildings. Everything else was burned. Soot and ash was the only sign the camp had ever been there.

"It's amazing to see it all burned," I said.

"I imagine the buzzards are going to be eating good for the next few days. I'm betting there's a lot of bodies out there," Doc said.

"I was just going to say something about the smell. It's not like the usual smell . . . I can't quite describe it," I said.

"Smells like combat, burned gear, equipment, bodies," Ted replied.

We drove back to the park in silence. I didn't know what should be done—hell, what could be done, for that matter. But for now it didn't really matter. All that mattered was a whole hog sitting on a smoker, and the people who I was going to enjoy it with.

We got back just as Thad was starting to pull the pig apart. We all dug in, and I have to say, it was one of the best meals I had ever eaten. The fact that I was sharing it with these great people—people who had overcome such hardship right alongside me, without complaint, and without ever losing their sense of humor—made it even more memorable. I really did feel grateful for where I was, all things considered.

The rest of the day was spent with my family and friends, eating sweet, tender pork and lounging by the lake. Little Bit and her sisters played in the water. The sun had burned off most of the cloud cover, but it hadn't gotten too hot. Mel and I sat with our feet in the water, watching the girls play. Looking back over my shoulder, I saw Jess and Mike sitting together, close together, at one of the tables. With full bellies, Doc and Ted were both sprawled out on a picnic table snoozing. I smiled again. Such a stark difference from where we were just a few days ago. A squeal of laughter brought my attention back to my girls. They were wrapped up in a knot, Lee Ann and Little Bit trying to push Taylor over. Life was good.

"I'm going back for seconds," I said as I stood up.

Mel looked up. "Don't you mean thirds or fourths?"

I smiled at her. "Who's counting?"

After eating, I stripped off my shirt and jumped in the lake with Little Bit. It didn't take long for everyone to follow suit. With full bellies we got into a rousing game of chicken. With Little Bit on my shoulders, Jess on Thad's, and Lee Ann on Taylor's, we splashed back and forth to the cheers of everyone on the bank. Tyler had Jace and Edie, one on either shoulder. Mike and Ted waded into the fray, and it quickly devolved into a splash fest, with children and adults alike laughing. Sarge lay sprawled on the bank with his boots off and his pants rolled up. Waist deep in the water I waved at Mel, and she smiled and waved back. For now, if only for a moment, I had my normal.

THE SURVIVALIST SERIES
From A. American

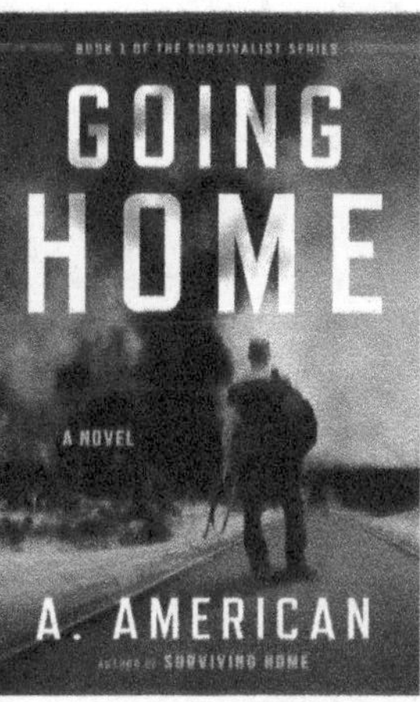

978-0-14-218127-0

978-0-14-218128-7

978-0-14-218129-4

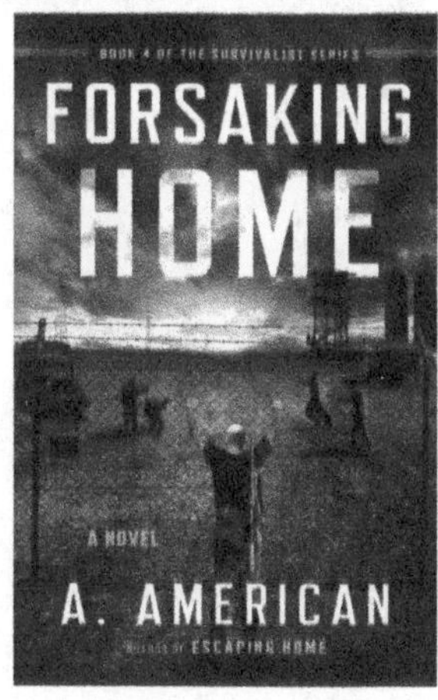

978-0-14-218130-0

978-0-14-751532-2

PLUME
An imprint of Penguin Random House LLC
www.penguin.com

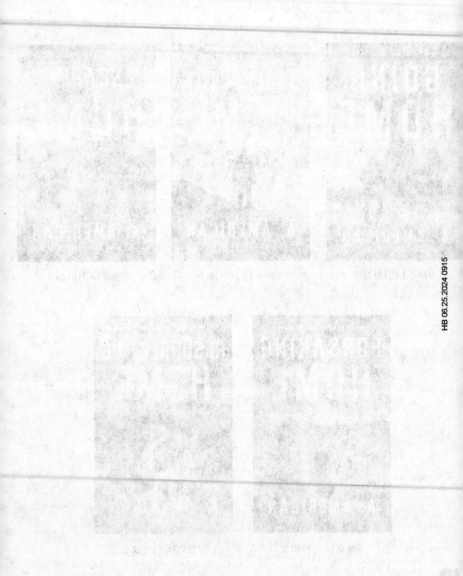